Kenneth Martin's first novel *A*  sixteen, became one of the fir Martin worked in London as a the United States in 1970. He i as a psychotherapy intern with families during especially dedicated to working with children as well as clients infected with HIV disease. His controversial dark thriller, *Billy's Brother*, about corruption in the American Aids industry, was published in 1989.

The Tin Islands

Kenneth Martin

Millivres Books International
Brighton

Published in 1996 by Millivres Books (Publishers)
33 Bristol Gardens, Brighton BN2 5JR, East Sussex, England

The Tin Islands
Copyright (C) Kenneth Martin, 1996
The moral rights of the author have been asserted

A CIP catalogue record for this book is available from the British Library

ISBN 1 873741 27 8

Typeset by Hailsham Typesetting Services, 4-5 Wentworth House,
George Street, Hailsham, East Sussex BN27 1AD

Printed and bound by Biddles Ltd., Walnut Tree House, Woodbridge
Park, Guildford, Surrey GU1 1DA

Distributed in the United Kingdom and Western Europe by Turnaround
Distribution Co-Op Ltd., 27 Horsell Road, London N5 1XL

Distributed in the United States of America by InBook, 140 Commerce
Street, East Haven, Connecticut 06512, USA

Distributed in Australia by Stilone Pty Ltd, PO Box 155, Broadway, NSW
2007, Australia.

In San Francisco thirty years later, as I eased a plastic glass with an inch of champagne in it against the lips of my lover who was dying, I remembered glasses glinting in the rich light at my first party in London when I was eighteen, a notorious face in a room full of celebrated men. It was a strange collision of people and times: different decades brushing against each other on a fault line, a pluck at my sleeve from hands that could not be there. I'd let the men at that party die long ago when I decided in my ignorance that there was nothing more for me to know about them.

LONDON 1960 - 1970

ONE

The agents' offices were at the tops of narrow corkscrew staircases in warehouse alleys off the Charing Cross Road that you'd never normally enter. I waited, a hormonal stew of romantic ambition and stubborn energy and agonising shyness, with other aspiring actors in a Tuesday afternoon meat rack. I was wearing a skimpy grey suit from Austin Reed in Belfast; the others wore clothes that were shabbier but infinitely more attractive to me: suede jackets, striped silk shirts, tight-fitting trousers. My only professional acting experience was playing highly strung children in radio plays on the Northern Ireland BBC before my voice broke. That afternoon I was heard to say in my blunt ingratiating Ulster accent "There's room here," as I moved over on a window seat to let a distracted chain-smoking girl sit down.

In a moment I became the focus of all the attention that counted in that room. Office activity stopped. Someone, not the receptionist, stared at me over her shoulder as she crossed to a closed door. I heard the thought directed at me, though surely it was my wishful thinking: "Don't go away till I get back." Left certain a momentous event was about to occur, but unable to identify what it might be, I waited. After a handful of slow seconds the woman returned, beckoned, and led me beyond the door to meet Beryl, the agent. It felt ordained. She asked me three or four questions, sounding barely interested, then phoned a casting director and arranged an appointment for me at Lime Grove the next morning.

"You do realise you'd be playing a queer?" the director asked at the end of that long day, an apparent bored afterthought after hours of my reading from the script and answering questions about myself and waiting while they decided what they wanted me to do next.

I'd been wondering if the director himself was queer, but I learned it was impossible to tell who was and who wasn't amongst the men who worked in television and wore

incredibly expensive shirts of bright solid colours. They all
looked queer to me. More wishful thinking.

"An actor should be able to play anybody," I said,
having already learned to utter decent-sounding platitudes
that systematically buried my truth.

"Don't tell them I told you, but you got the part," a
uniformed male attendant whispered as he escorted me
outside.

"Thank you very much," I said calmly, saturated with
excitement, close to exhaustion. The attendant was short
and past middle age and apparently cheerful about his
station in life. Or that was what I remembered when I was
middle-aged, after the frozen past finally cracked,
bombarding me with random splinters of memory, and
inexplicably it occurred to me to wonder who that man
was and what he'd really thought of the flushed ignorant
ambitious child who seemed marked for good fortune.

✳ ✳ ✳ ✳ ✳

A celebrated Catholic poet from the south of Ireland who'd
lived near Belfast during his last years had secretly written
a play with a homosexual subtext. After his executor's
attempts to deny that there was such a play caused a minor
literary commotion, the BBC was able to secure the
television rights.

A retired colonel was inspired to write to *The Times*:
"Those of us whose duties led us to far lands are only too
aware that such perversions exist. One cannot help but
wonder what public good is served by broadcasting them
on the BBC. May not some more gullible members of our
society construe such a broadcast as placing the seal of
approval on perversion? If so, the governors will have
much to answer for."

Six years earlier, their duty to report Lord Montague's
trial had allowed the British press to publish accounts of
alleged homosexual seduction in unprecedented salacious
detail. Now a few reformers were urging that homosexuality be treated as an unfortunate condition, rather

than a criminal activity that led certain policemen to spend much of their time trying to entrap offenders in public lavatories. *Tea and Sympathy* and *Cat on a Hot Tin Roof* had been performed in a West End theatre that had to go through the charade of turning itself into a private club because the Lord Chamberlain would not license public performances of dramas about homosexuality.

The BBC, at once stuffy and daring, argued that the Irish poet's prominence and the play's artistic merit demanded that it be broadcast. But their press releases ignored the homosexual content of *The Tin Islands*. The plot was described as a battle over an estate.

An upper-class Englishman comes to an Ulster country house to settle the details of his late brother's will; his differences with his Irish sister-in-law over the interpretation of the will mask a barely articulated struggle for the soul of the eighteen-year-old nephew who lives with his mother. The plot of *The Tin Islands* could be analysed as a symbolic account of the struggle for the future of Northern Ireland between the English landlords and the indigenous Catholics. What gave the rather abstract drama its only heat was the terrible unspoken attraction between a lonely eighteen-year-old and the fortyish widower who may lure him to London, capital of the tin islands, the lands whose natural resources, now depleted, once attracted invaders from all the seafaring tribes of Northern Europe. The plot detailed the heroine's gradual acknowledgment of an attraction she still almost believed was her own jealous imagining, and her struggle to save her son.

✳ ✳ ✳ ✳ ✳

I'd bought *An Actor Prepares* at Foyles my second day in London, but rehearsals turned out to be too matter-of-fact to allow me to make a fool of myself. I'd marked my script with questions about super-objectives and through lines and suggestions for lengthy bits of redundant realistic business, and rather hoped for heated battles with my director. Instead our performances were built from a series of small suggestions, not impassioned discussions or confrontations.

"Keep it clean, Daniel," Cliff, the director, told me a little testily the third day of rehearsals. "Just do what the lines tell you you're doing. Don't keep playing the emotions."

I wanted to be a flamboyant star, but I also wanted to fit in. I did what I was told.

The other actors were brittle, a little shopworn, but optimistic, astute and seemingly democratic, though the drama might have encouraged class divisions on the set. Like most plays, *The Tin Islands* assumed that only upper-class characters had important emotions. The servants were played by Catholic Irish character actors, of which there was a large supply: the feverish myths of their country and religion fostered imagination, which was distrusted in Protestant Ulster. To me, the expatriate Catholic actors all seemed bogus. They dressed and moved like the English until they opened their mouths, and then their accents sounded too creamy to me because I'd never met an educated Catholic. I, who had the only genuine Ulster accent in the studio, was ashamed of my provincial sound and started work on smoothing it away. Cliff was unhappy. I'd been hired because my confusion mirrored my character's confusion, my aspirations and emotions similarly inarticulate, half-blocked. Now I was beginning to sound like an actor.

"You must teach me your accent," Sara, the young English actress who played my Irish mother, told me expansively the moment she met me. She'd scored in two ingenue roles in Shaftesbury Avenue comedies, but played only highbrow roles on television because her eccentric features were not suited to romantic leads in popular plays. I took her at her word, but waited in vain to be asked to instruct her. She spent her free time on the set writing letters to her sons in public school, and in rehearsals soon gave up the pretence of wanting to play the role with an Irish accent. Her character had, after all, lived in England for a time.

8

The male lead was Michael Baker, a handsome dark-haired English actor who'd starred in pedestrian Pinewood crime stories and thin comedies. *The Tin Islands* was his opportunity to stretch his talent. He remained eager, amiable, and rather stiff.

At the first reading I was much taken with his dark moustache and manly bearing. As an assistant read the closing camera directions Baker turned to me with the air of a kindly young uncle: "I'll wager you never thought you'd get your big chance playing a poof."

I blushed and fell in love with him.

As rehearsals progressed Cliff couldn't understand why I kept slipping into a phoney English accent in my scenes with Baker. It was my involuntary way of demonstrating my lust for the actor. He told jokes about buggery to relieve his discomfort at playing a queer, at the same time treating me like a kid brother he gruffly adored.

The red-haired freckled actress who played the house-keeper suddenly murmured to me one day: "The heart has its mysteries." Once I realised what she was talking about, I blushed furiously. I had no idea I was so transparent.

Baker had few insights to offer on the art of acting. Instead he showed me photos of his wife and daughters. I hung around after rehearsals hoping he'd offer me a lift, but he always disappeared at the first opportunity. Late at night I sat up in bed drinking Chianti and queasily smoking Gauloises, on emotional overload from the wonderful life of rehearsals: the concentration, the stretch, the belonging to a team that treated me as an equal. But I mostly dreamed about a ride home with Michael Baker.

I imagined comfortable masculine silence, then Baker's sudden decision to pull over, my supposing we'd stopped to look at the view, Baker laying a hand on my arm as I moved to get out. The puzzled pause. The dawning hope. The awful honesty as our eyes finally met. The awkward stop-and-go as we moved towards each other and embraced. The kiss – I could feel every hair of Baker's moustache, the wonderful strength and smell of his arms and chest. My fantasy always stopped there, because I still didn't know what queers did together, apart from falling in love.

The BBC publicity department, nervous about how the young star of a controversial play might be exploited, arranged for my interviews to take place at the studios with a PR man present. The men and women of the popular press seemed to be as nervous as I was. They had to work hard to come up with a few routine questions, deeply uneasy talking about a play on a taboo subject. Five of the eight interviews made it to print, and all five sidestepped the play's subject matter – 'homosexuality' was never mentioned. They concentrated instead on the personality of the young discovery in the 'powerful,' 'controversial,' 'almost-banned' play.

Q: "How are you different from the character you play?"

A: "I'm Protestant and he's Catholic." *The English interviewers, searching for some ciphered way of reassuring their readers that I was normal, hoped I'd tell them I had a girlfriend. They couldn't understand why a young Ulsterman would be so preoccupied with the difference in religion. It was another five years before Northern Ireland began to be explained to the English, when the uneasy truce finally broke and Ulster turned into a war zone.*

"And my character stays in Northern Ireland, but I came to London. But maybe I shouldn't give away the ending."

Q: "Did your parents give you the money to come to London?"

A: "No, I worked in a shop in Belfast after I left school until I'd saved up £80. But my parents didn't charge me for my keep while I was working, so I was able to save up faster."

Q: "Did you have any relatives or connections in London to help you get started?"

A: "When I got here I stayed in Cricklewood with a family a neighbour of ours met at a holiday camp. Now I have my own flat in Swiss Cottage."

Q: "£80 can't have gone far. What did you live on?"

A: "I washed dishes nights and weekends at the Seville Hotel in Holborn." *When I got the part I had no one in London to tell except the Southern Irish kitchen staff and waiters I* worked with. *I blushed to utter what sounded like shameless lies: bragging about a role in a television play while my arms itched from the dishwater! But they believed me. Like me they'd grown up on exiles' songs about cities where you dug for gold in the street. Becoming a big actor seemed no more extravagantly unlikely than their own dreams of sudden windfalls or marrying somebody rich.*

"I had to work nights so that I could make the rounds of the agents' offices and the studios." *I showed up at the stage door of the Old Vic – "I'd even be a spear carrier" I blurted to the doorkeeper, and couldn't understand why the man laughed at me. I was directed to RADA and the Central School and discovered that even if I got a scholarship I'd be expected to live on half what I earned washing dishes. I took long train rides to film studios in the suburbs, expecting Warner Brothers but finding no signs of life around the closed buildings like aircraft hangars. The British studios had become neglected service facilities that rented to independent film producers.*

Q: "How do your parents feel about you appearing in such a controversial play?"

A: "My parents want the very best for me, and they know this is a wonderful opportunity." *My family was out of its depth trying to handle my outrageous ambitions. "If you stayed here," my Aunt Peggy told me when I announced I was leaving for London, "you could have everything you want with the money you saved, your own radio, an electric razor." The second or third time an interviewer asked the question, I began to romance:* "It's only since I left home that I've begun to realise how much my family really cares about me. When I ring them up, we can talk far better now that I'm living away from home."

"What an adult answer," murmured the woman from the *Daily Mail*.

Q (darkly): "How do you feel about appearing in such a play?"

A: "It's a wonderful play by a wonderful poet. Getting this part is like being given a marvellous present at the start of my career. I think I'm the luckiest young man alive."

Q: "Your ambitions?"

A: "I want to do stage plays and TV plays and films and radio too, because a lot of classics get done on the radio that don't get done anywhere else. I'd like to work with Cliff again, and all the other directors who have as much to teach me as Cliff, and with Michael and Sara and all the other actors in this play who teach me so much just by letting me work with them. But I don't want to know just about acting, because I've heard it can be such a closed world. I want to know all about the outside world. So if you asked me what was my single greatest ambition, I'd say I wanted to read philosophy, politics and economics at Oxford." *I wanted to except myself from the widespread suspicion that all actors are stupid, though my Senior exam marks barely qualified me for teacher training college.*

✿✿✿✿✿

TV plays were still essentially stage plays opened up to five or six sets – filmed inserts cost so much that they were discouraged except for establishing shots. The broadcast was live.

Prodigal ambition came easily to me, but I started to feel emptier and emptier as the night of the transmission approached. It helped that *The Tin Islands* rehearsals were like the radio plays I'd done, a scheduled progression that might have been designed to ward off stage fright: readings led to blocking sessions that turned into camera rehearsals that became gradually more complex, with the acting taken care of in the midst of the technical rehearsals.

The last camera rehearsal was early on the day of the broadcast. I was nagged by an unspoken impatient dissatisfaction Cliff seemed to have with my performance, but the director's last reminder only left me more perplexed: "Don't lose who you are." The BBC provided a light meal so that no one had an excuse to leave the studio. What had appeared on the schedule as a frightening gap of three or four hours before transmission, long enough to let nerves get the better of me, was spent in costume and makeup and last minute clarifications.

"You have a greasy skin," the makeup woman remarked comfortably, assessing the condition of my nose.

I made a face as if I was about to throw up.

"Nervous? It'll be all right, you'll see."

But suppose I was the exception to such generic wisdom? My stomach felt leaden and empty at the same time, and I was physically weary – it was nearly nine o'clock. And yet I felt as if I was about to come to life. I couldn't miss such chances. I had to prove myself.

For my first scene I stepped from darkness into the cocoon of light to be introduced to Michael Baker, whose dark eyes glittered in a crust of flesh-coloured makeup that resembled no flesh I'd ever seen. Remember, don't play the love; play the pride and fear fighting your attraction to him.

Almost at once I recognised that we were all blessed: to be the focus of such attention, to move in such an intensity of emotion. My confidence soared in the warm crackling air, I was certain I felt waves of response from the vibrant ocean of people watching.

We were getting it right. Baker's discomfort with his character's feelings seemed appropriate to a man forever thwarted from articulating his inner life. Sara at last seemed to feel the extent of her exclusion from the men's emotions; her plainness became poignant. And my passionate message rang loud and clear through the callow movements and monosyllables that were all the playwright and director had allowed me.

The play ended, daringly, in the eighteen-year-old's bedroom, although nothing overtly homosexual was said or done. After the final confrontation between the Englishman and his sister-in-law, when she threatens, her eyes and tone suggestive, outraged, that 'reputation' should be enough to make him think again about taking the boy to England, he comes into my bedroom to take his leave. We shake hands, staring grimly, heartbreakingly, into each other's eyes, and the camera watches over my shoulder as the Englishman turns to leave, pausing in the doorway, his back to the viewer. Will he turn into the room again, to me? He disappears from view.

"It's not so final," I objected in rehearsal, voicing my own wishful thinking. "My character could follow him to England."

I waited on the edge of the bed, eager, almost calm. It was nearly over, I'd managed to do it, but an empty letdown loomed, because nothing else in my life matched this intensity.

The climactic argument ended a few feet away beyond a piece of painted balsa wood, a hovering camera already awaiting its cue behind me.

The Englishman/Baker entered the nephew's/my room for the wordless good-bye. Baker gazed down at me, pausing before he held out his hand, his cheeks slightly puffy, as if he were testing a boiled sweet to make sure he liked it. His hand in mine was big and thrillingly moist, though as usual he didn't hold the final look for as long as I'd have liked him to. I felt the actor's body preparing to move away.

Then, directed from outside myself, I moved my head as if I had a secret to whisper in Baker's ear, and pulled the actor's right hand towards me. Baker, not knowing what was happening, had to follow my movements, to stay in character until he knew what I was doing. I quickly reached up and placed my left hand on the back of Baker's head and pulled his face the few inches down to me and kissed him on the lips. I felt the brush of every hair of Baker's moustache, the full moist suddenly trembling mouth, the smell of tobacco on his breath.

From the dense black cable-laden silence around us I heard an Irish-sounding gasp. I thought of pushing my tongue against Baker's teeth, and Baker read my mind. His mouth hardened and jerked back and he pushed me away. But he didn't completely let go. He clutched my shoulder with a shaking hand while he floundered for what his character would do. He swallowed hard, almost coughed, then forced himself to look into my eyes for two or three seconds with something that might pass for affection before he turned on his heel and went through the doorway,

14

forgetting too late that he was supposed to pause. He stopped in mid-stride for a split second, decided that he no longer cared, and stalked off.

*****

No one would speak to me. I waited alone at the table where drinks had been set up. A character actress stealthily appeared, took one look around, then bolted, her eyes scuttling off mine before I could connect. I went on waiting, unable to believe I had enough power to upset so many people, helping myself to drink, drinking faster and faster, because I could think of nothing else to do.

Cliff appeared on the opposite side of the floor and I headed towards him, courageous on gin. The studio manager Cliff was talking to saw me coming and excused himself. Cliff saw why and he too started to move away, studiously not looking in my direction.

"Cliff!" I cried, mimicking the warm expansive manner I'd learned from the other actors.

Cliff kept going, then changed his mind. He paused, his head still turned away.

"How was I?" I asked the back of his head, my courage fading. "I wanted –" I lost all conviction when he turned to me.

Cliff's face was soft, his eyes small and wet. His stricken expression made me feel guilty. But it altered immediately. He glared at me, his nostrils flaring, then turned on his heel.

I persuaded myself that I was innocent. "It felt right for the character," I told the makeup woman, an excuse, a reason, I was to use in other situations. For once she had no comfortable response on tap.

The popular dailies that I bought next morning, hoping for headlines, didn't even review the play. I missed the respectful notices in the *Times* and *Guardian* because I didn't realise the serious papers reviewed TV. The only notice I saw was George Malcolm Thompson's in the *Evening Standard*, which called the play mild and conventional. The

15

critic had obviously talked to someone at the BBC after the transmittal: "The only shocking scene may tell us more about the young actor playing the part than about the playwright's intentions."

Beryl didn't return my calls. I moved my chair closer to the door of my room and all day long dashed out every time the communal phone rang downstairs. But no one phoned me. In my isolation it was easy for me to misconstrue what was happening. I thought I wasn't making news. But people talked about the notorious young man, not to him. It took me years to understand how deeply I'd outraged both normals and queers, and why.

✳ ✳ ✳ ✳ ✳

London was haunted by shamefaced ghosts: the young men and women who'd had only a moment in the limelight and never lived up to it. Did they wish they'd remained nonentities, instead of being allowed to taste glory before they were forever denied more of it? I had no reason to believe I'd ever work again, and could look forward to only three or four months of freedom before I rejoined the city's unskilled labour pool.

I soon learned that I had social as well as professional limitations. To celebrate my getting the part in *The Tin Islands*, Beryl had taken me to lunch at Rules. She listened to my absurd ambitions with a shrewd amused look that made no predictions and promised nothing. Two weeks after *The Tin Islands* broadcast I received an invitation from Tom Finlay, an editor on a political weekly who'd stopped briefly at our table and whom I vaguely remembered as middle-aged and paunchy.

On the Wednesday on which he was At Home from 6:30 to 8:00, I discovered in a taxi from Sloane Square tube station that I was shaking with nerves far worse than on the night of the broadcast. I knew how to work and how to give interviews. I didn't know how to act the equal of successful older Londoners I believed were my social superiors. I climbed the red-carpeted stairs to Finlay's flat on ambition alone. Like a fool I'd put on brand new shoes. Slippery soles and the roaring in my ears warned me that I was about to lose my purchase on the world around me.

A man only slightly older than I opened the door and did not respond to my abjectly ingratiating smile.

"You're –?" he challenged.

My heart sank as I registered a daunting level of confident noise from a room halfway down the hall behind him, but even through a fog of nerves I guessed that the man recognised me for exactly who I was. With his white pinched face and pink-rimmed eyes above a starched collar and three-piece suit, he looked like one of Dickens' undernourished clerks.

I pushed past his provoking manner to stop myself fainting. "I'm Daniel Henry," I said brightly.

He allowed me a look that was mildly quizzically friendly, indicated the doorway the noise was coming from, and left me to it.

Thirty men were crowded into the moderate-sized room, but I still found myself trapped in a circle of empty space. To act in a warm island of light and air was to be magically protected from the audience; to stand alone at a private party was like attending my execution. No point in looking at faces – I couldn't possibly know anyone. Stranded, I forced myself to stare expectantly at the wall behind the crowd, starting to smile as if I thought I recognised my best friend in the world. Out of the corner of an eye I saw Tom Finlay detach himself from a group and approach me, his stout body moving so gracefully that he seemed almost to float. Humiliated by my neediness, I pretended not to see him until the last moment, continuing to react to my imaginary friend.

"How good of you to come," Tom said huskily, apparently not noticing he'd invited a disastrously shy boy to his party.

"I'm Daniel Henry," I said unnecessarily, trying to mimic the same expansive confidence every actor I'd ever met could summon in even the most unpromising circumstances.

Tom gave a broken little chuckle. "Everybody knows

who you are," he said.

But how could I believe him? The two men he introduced me to displayed not a moment's interest in me before they went on with their conversation. I was alone again, and felt my knees start to give way. I gulped desperately at my drink all the time pretending to hang raptly on the conversation that excluded me.

"Really!" I exclaimed, trying anything to belong.

I'd almost exhausted my repertoire of things to do. I pulled out my pack of Gauloises and thrust it towards the two men. In the part of Belfast I came from, you always offered your cigarettes to the company. One ignored me, the other shook his head irritably. The crowd had become so threatening I couldn't raise my head to search for an escape. I balanced the box of Swans against my glass to strike a match, wondering what I'd do after the cigarette was lit.

A lighter intervened. I looked up. The best- looking man in the room stood beside me, his shirt taut across his chest, his skin glowing, his hair wet and smelling alive. The other guests, their skin sallow, their torsos concave, seemed to depend on barbers and tailors for their looks, as if they'd forgotten they'd ever have to take off their clothes.

"I'm Gordon Bennett." He moved between me and the couple I'd been trying to belong to, his attentive eyes forcing me to focus on him, calming some of the chaos in my head.

"How do you come to know Tom?" he asked, his gaze so intent that my answer seemed to matter greatly.

"My agent introduced us at Rules. I'm an actor."

Such modesty might have seemed charming to anyone who recognised me, but Gordon did not acknowledge it. Perhaps he, and others, had decided a lack of attention wasn't my problem. "I'm in the army," he said, as if he took me seriously enough to want to explain himself to me.

In my experience the army was a last resort for the unskilled working class. Gordon was clearly not working class. "What rank are you?" I asked, blunt and shy together.

"I'm a captain," Gordon said. He chose not to elaborate,

less eager than the rest of the crowd to chatter. ("I like queers," a queer announced next to me, "but they have too much power. In the theatre, in publishing, even in politics." I was glad to hear that queers had power in the theatre, though I wondered how you could have too much of it.)

"I qualify for National Service if I stay in England for two years," I said. "I hope they abolish it before then."

"Just don't remind them you're here," Gordon said. "They'll probably assume that if you're Irish you must be from the south."

When I had time to think about it, when it was too late, I would be certain there was fire between us. Gordon's strength spoke to my nervous passion. But I was too proud to give him my full attention because I was ashamed of being the party's blushing orphan. I half turned away to watch the room, to pretend I had other irons in the fire, to plan who I would turn to if he abandoned me.

My nerves had calmed enough for me to recognise that my dreams were coming true. I'd known that men who wanted what I wanted must congregate in London. That was why I'd come here, an imperative I'd never confessed to anyone, though it was even more urgent than wanting to be an actor. I knew how ill-equipped I was to deal with company like this, and could only plan to somehow survive until I got better. For the moment it was enough to register that the world I wanted to belong to existed in this room: men who'd made a society with other men, who could afford new suits and presumably knew about politics and the arts, though the talk I overheard was strictly personal: "Oh he's a sweetie, but it would be libelling his wife to say she could possibly be pregnant again."

I liked Gordon because he didn't talk like that. "Do you live in an army barracks?" I asked.

"I have a flat in Westminster," Gordon said.

I waited. I certainly wouldn't invite anyone to my two furnished rooms in Swiss Cottage, not someone who lived in a Westminster flat, probably with rich curtains and rugs and expensive family furniture. I dared to steal another direct glance: I saw what I wanted in Gordon's glowing

19

face and saw him begin to open his mouth to ask me to leave with him.

But he didn't do it. It wasn't because a tall weighty figure had lumbered up to us; that happened a moment after Gordon changed his mind. None of the possible reasons occurred to me: not that Gordon might have a boyfriend or that I was jail bait (if these reasons had occurred to me, I would have regarded them as insufficient), or that Gordon couldn't afford to pay for dinner and had nothing in the house, or that he was scared of being seen with me in public, or that he was attracted not to boys but to other men like himself, or that I, fresh to London, seemed more interested in the crowd than in him, or that I was too green and therefore too much trouble. I thought only that I wasn't wanted, wasn't worthy.

"Have you met?" Gordon asked. "Patrick, this is Daniel Henry. Daniel, Lord Kinross. Would you like another drink?"

He pulled my glass from me and slipped away, something kind and proprietorial in the way he handed me over.

The potential for social catastrophe in shy Daniel meeting an English lord seemed great, but I'd sensed that I possessed something older men might want. I found them far less alarming than my contemporaries, who could be cutting and competitive. Kinross, with great flyaway eyebrows and a drinker's complexion and an eater's waist, looked down at me from full grand aristocratic height, but he did not risk being uncongenial. He was perhaps too vulnerable in his private life. Only his drawl was lofty as he quizzed me expertly.

Gordon pushed a fresh glass into my hand, and was leaving the room before I turned to thank him. By then I'd accepted a dinner invitation for next Tuesday and was pocketing Kinross's card. Such attention, and the warmth from the scotch, stopped me panicking as Kinross moved on. I backed against the wall and found myself standing next to Cliff, my director on *The Tin Islands*. He was already turning away.

"Cliff!" I cried complainingly.

The director hesitated for a split second, then shone an

enthusiastic public smile at me. "How are you?" he inquired icily and then, as I opened my mouth to reply, turned his back.

It was hard to understand how someone you ran into at a queer Chelsea party could still be upset because you'd kissed another actor on TV.

"This *is* a queer party, isn't it?" I asked the man to my left, another heavyset middle-aged man with the blotched skin of a drinker.

He gave an astounded rough laugh. "I rather think it is. What caused you to doubt it?"

"They told me Cliff had a wife and children," I said.

The man scrutinised me, then visibly scornfully decided I was not quite young enough to be so green. "What an extraordinarily naive remark," he snorted. "My dear boy, I'm married too. So are a quarter of the men in the room. Kinross used to be married."

It was not lost on me that people had been watching me with Kinross. Or that there was an aggressive sexual component to this man's cruelty.

"Cliff directed me in a play," I said, choosing to be conciliatory. "I thought I knew all about him. What do *you* do?"

"I'm a Member of Parliament." He separated the middle vowels of "Parliament" with a creamy insolence while he eyed me with a mixture of hostility and opportunism, giving nothing.

"Labour or Conservative?" I asked.

The MP gave me a thick haughty look, nosing out an insult. "Tory."

Then I forgot him as a celebrated face entered the room and paused just inside the doorway. It was an entrance, by Terence Rattigan the playwright, that took nerve because it demanded recognition and a response. So starstruck that I forgot my shyness, and made astute by ambition, I guessed that Rattigan was not comfortable making the entrance but felt his position required it of him. Perhaps Tom Finlay shared my ambitions for me, because he moved quickly to introduce us.

21

"Daniel, Terence Rattigan. Terry, Daniel *The Tin Islands* Henry."

We shook hands in the middle of Rattigan fitting a cigarette into a black holder and surveying the room. He was a handsome man grown beefy, his eyes receding behind pouchy eyelids, his hair greased down with an expensive equivalent of Brylcreem.

I blurted away to keep the shyness at bay. "I hope I won't always be known for just that play."

"Are you in another play?" Rattigan asked genially, eyeing the crowd.

"I'm resting," I said, so proud of using a professional word that it took the sting from reality. I had no prospects. Would Rattigan offer me a part? Would Rattigan offer me his bed? Rattigan moved into the crowd.

A more deferential guest joined me, a man in his thirties whose hair was thinning, whose chin seemed buried in his collar. What you remembered was a wet mouth and two beaming, perhaps profoundly disappointed eyes. "Did you like Jane's piece? I work on the *Mail*."

"Yes, *very* much. Thank you," I said. The article had been disjointed and vaguely critical; the feature writer wasn't sure how to handle me or the play. But I'd already decided, and never changed my mind when I had more grounds on which to base an opinion, that it didn't matter what the papers said about you – "Paper refuses nothin'," they said in Ulster – as long as you got the publicity.

"I expect you've already seen Ross?" Hugh, the *Daily Mail* man, asked.

"I'd like to see it again," I said, sniffing another invitation. "I wasn't sure what I thought about it."

Every avid reader of reviews and columns knew that well-made Shaftesbury Avenue plays were out of fashion. The subjects that propelled Rattigan's plots – waywardness of character that brought dire social consequences – were judged to be irrelevant in the age of the angry young men.

"I thought the critics were unfair," Hugh said. "It's quite interesting. I could get us a couple of comps."

"I'd love to," I said. "Is it true that all Rattigan's heroines

22

are based on himself?"

"Doesn't everyone always say that about queer artists?" Hugh protested mildly.

The well-behaved room was already breaking up. I'd registered scraps of behaviour that hinted at how these men would behave, and sensed they wouldn't stay too long, or talk too loudly or draw attention. Their love, their lust, were against the law – they tried to compensate with immaculate manners.

I walked on air down the stairs I'd climbed in terror. The lamplit Chelsea street under the starless pulsating London sky was the kind where rich dramas of politics and love would serve as a suitable backdrop for my own drama.

In Hugh's Great Ormond Street flat, three streets from the hotel where I'd washed dishes, I romanced drunkenly about my glamorous driven life. "I only go to parties where I know I'll meet people who can help me. Acting is the only thing that matters to me. I don't like to waste my time when I could be studying technique or reading Shakespeare."

I couldn't tell, and didn't really care, if Hugh was so besotted with me that he believed the wild lies. Late at night, he gently suggested that it would be more convenient for me to spend the night.

"I have an early morning meeting with my agent," I lied. Hugh was no match for my dreams.

Next morning, still dazzled, I told my landlady, an Austrian refugee who wore a leather apron to do the housework, about the party.

"There will be other parties, Mr. Henry," Mrs. Froelich predicted shrewdly.

I was so young that the promise came as a revelation.

✳ ✳ ✳ ✳ ✳

"They're talking about me," I mouthed, halting the *orange pressé* halfway to my lips in case movement drowned any further sound of my name. I stole a cool but appreciative glance at the next table in the dark restaurant while Tom Finlay scrutinised it more openly. But the two middle-aged normal couples seemed unaware that they were sitting next to a controversial rising star with the world at his feet, and were overheard to be talking only about the food on their plates.

"No," Tom said, almost as disappointed as I, who had to make myself stop listening for the sound of my name.

"I'm the most famous person in the room," I announced as a consolation price.

Tom balked, torn between his profoundly conservative values (there were civil servants and military men and political journalists in the restaurant whose doings mattered) and giving in to the pop fan values on which his sexual cravings and undeveloped emotions thrived.

He resorted to evasive praise: "I do so admire actors."

I basked in the praise, but was unprepared for Tom's reasons.

"Actors do what you feel you were born to do. Yet you have no security, while the rest of us have pensions and paid holidays and bonuses."

"Unless I get a long run in a play," I objected.

"But you never know if there will ever be another play," Tom cried cheerfully. "I know very successful actors who've been on the dole for most of their professional lives."

I blushed: no one in my family had ever quite resorted to the Labour Exchange, though it was only twelve doors from where we lived.

"I have enough money to live on for three months," I said defensively.

I didn't say that I believed against all odds that my career would be extraordinary, that the actors on the dole didn't have my talent or luck. Or that I preferred even the prospect of the dole to working in an office.

Christopher, the dark-eyed manager of the *Popote*, crunched a few more specks of pepper over the *steak au poivre*.

"Do you like my jacket?" he inquired. "I picked it up for five pounds and my ex relined it."

I wondered if his fidgety glittering eyes were a sign that he was on drugs, and thought that to have an ex must be the most sophisticated thing in the world.

"Does Peter Wildeblood come to restaurants like this?" I asked.

"I should imagine so," Tom said.

Hero worship made me oblivious to his tone. "It must have been so hard for him to show his face in public after he came out of prison," I said.

"He has only himself to blame if he insists on rubbing our noses in his homosexuality," Tom said crisply. "I sometimes think we'd have been better off if he'd let sleeping dogs lie."

"His books will help get the law changed," I said hotly, "so that the police won't be able to interfere in our private lives."

Tom merely smiled: the young were allowed to be passionately convinced.

"How was your dinner with Kinross?" he inquired with a shy sideways look.

I took the question literally. "He made a stew in one pot," I said, rather contemptuous as I cut into steak.

"*Pot au feu*," Tom supplied. "It can be rather good."

"Yes. And salad."

"Did he –" Tom gave a quirky growl to soften his impertinence. "Did he make a pass at you?"

"No. Not really."

The evening at Kinross's house in Warwick Avenue was difficult for me to describe, since I hadn't been sure what was happening. And I was still plagued by what I'd done at the end.

Kinross served the meal with military masculine brusqueness as if we were making the best of having to dine in an expensive tent in the desert. Afterwards we sat with brandies in dim pools of light on opposite sides of the cluttered study. The drink made it easy for both of us to sink into silence, in my case to dream romantic dreams of other rooms, though I was close to expecting that I'd end up in his lordship's bed.

"All I really know about is acting," I blurted apologetically into a lengthy rather drunken silence.

It was a remark that would not have withstood analysis,

25

but Kinross seemed to take it seriously.

"That's all you need to know about," he said.

So perhaps he wasn't judging me, perhaps he admired me for exactly who I was. The telephone rang once that evening, at ten o'clock or later. It was good to know I wasn't the only famous person who didn't get a lot of phone calls. Kinross excused himself to answer it, and I had a chance to examine his retreating behind. I decided that curiosity and laziness weren't good enough reasons to let a fat old man seduce me.

I sprang up and hunted through the drawers of the writing desk where I'd seen Kinross go for the flat Turkish cigarettes he smoked. By the time he returned I'd pocketed a box of cigarettes and a cigar.

I thought of asking Tom why I'd stolen. I felt almost as if I was expected to steal from Kinross. But I decided some things shouldn't be made public.

"My flat was robbed again," Tom said suddenly.

I stared, my face reddening. Could Tom read my mind? "What did they take?" I asked to cover my guilty look.

"Oh, just the money in my wallet. I suppose they were afraid everything else was traceable."

"Had you left your wallet in the living room when you went to bed?"

"No, it was in my pocket."

"You mean they attacked you in your flat?"

"They didn't hurt me," Tom said. "They came into the living room while I was reading and tied me to a chair and emptied my pockets. Two rockers from the wrong end of the King's Road. One of them looked like Cliff Richard. They jerked me off before they left."

"Why did they do that?" I asked suspiciously.

"Oh, I suppose they thought I wouldn't go to the police. 'You like that, don't you, guvnor?' one of them said."

"*Did* you go to the police?"

"Of course." Tom slapped the table gently. "That's the second time this year I've had to change my front door lock. I give talks to the local youth club. What amazes me –" (his voice had a wounded husky crack in it) "– is how can they expect to get on if they keep robbing the people who try to help them?"

Despite my inclination to believe everything sophisticated Londoners told me, I thought I'd rarely heard a story that seemed so full of holes.

I waited till we were leaving the restaurant to ask, as an apparent afterthought: "Does Gordon Bennett have a boyfriend?"

"I've no idea," Tom said, sounding as if he disapproved of the question.

Kinross hadn't known either. I had a hard time understanding how men who went to each other's parties knew so little about each other.

✳ ✳ ✳ ✳ ✳

I was dislocated, moving dazed between so many extremes that I could handle them only by pretending I had nothing to worry about. The rising young actor from Ireland lived in a house with old European Jews whose options seemed to consist of choosing how to interpret their memories. There was a public Daniel Henry who seemed to be fading from public memory far faster than the ink that created him, resurfacing only when I went out for the rare dinner with Tom or seat in the stalls with Hugh.

The private Daniel Henry spent most of his days alone. If I went to the theatre it was usually by myself in a seat in the upper circle after I'd eaten my tea. Dinner, they called it in the social circles to which I'd been introduced, or supper if it was a relatively modest meal in a restaurant to which you took your own bottle of wine.

The day I moved into my rooms in Swiss Cottage I tried to fry sausages and ended up with a smoke-filled kitchen and three burnt encrusted skins oozing raw grey filling. From then on I ate egg and sausage at the greasy spoon next to Swiss Cottage tube station, or Spam fritters, chips, peas and fruit pie at a stand-up grill open to the pavement in Leicester Square, after a matinee or before an evening performance.

27

Upper circle seats were the cheapest from which you could still see and hear most of what went on on the stage. My snobbery and shyness competed with the sense that I was doing something democratic and absolutely right for a young actor. It horrified me to think of being caught alone in these reduced circumstances by someone I'd met at Tom's party, but I had a story ready: my agent had given me a single ticket at the last minute. During the weeks that I saw every play in London I ran into only one person I knew, the reporter who'd interviewed me for the *Mail*. I found her sipping orange squash in the interval; she was alone like me.

"I'm reading some Irish poetry on the radio," I said before she asked me what work I had lined up, and I blushed at the lie. "I may be doing a film."

"Good," she chirped, and we turned away briskly, at the moment of no use to each other.

London, the inexhaustible city where power and consequence thickened the air and travelled abroad as confidently as the waters of the Thames, shrank to a few theatre streets where plays that purported to mirror the world seemed lacking to me even when I chose to praise them. I was the avid reader of *Encore* who laughed scornfully in the right places to demonstrate that I shared the views of the leftist critical elite. I groaned aloud at plays that contained feeble pretexts for elderly actresses to proclaim "When I was a gel –", submitting more willingly to the boredom engendered by some of the worthy new working-class dramas. I was the self-absorbed actor who searched every play for a part I could have shone in, and scrutinised every performance for lapses I could have improved on. Because I'd kept my Ulster common sense I recognised lazy acting when I saw it, and hoped that when I got a chance to be brilliant it would be amongst other actors who also shone, so that I wouldn't be tempted to preen. (Nothing on the London stage addressed the political and religious life of Ulster. Those plays arrived twenty years later, which led me to conclude that theatre, like the journalists, was usually a generation behind.) I was the hungry young queer who became infatuated with the looks of a leading man or young supporting actor, or inflamed by their trousers, who seized on every relationship or reference that might be a coded message about men loving each other.

Beryl was still not returning my calls. I tormented myself thinking it was childish to feel such anger and frustration. I wrote to her asking for a meeting to discuss the direction of my career. A week later I still hadn't heard from her, and I gave her another week before I started making the rounds of other agents. I had to believe my luck would hold if I worked at my exercises and studied the books on technique I borrowed from the library. Three or four afternoons a week I walked on Hampstead Heath. An actor must be fit.

One day in Holborn Circus I ran into one of the waiters I'd worked with, Declan, who stopped me to talk, impressed but bold.

"You should come by the hotel and we'll have a pint after work," he urged, holding my gaze with his black eyes.

"I will," I promised stoutly. But I never would. Even the promise of another man's reckless body, which I'd never experienced, couldn't crack my shell of class-conscious ambition. While I waited for a more suitable partner I wandered the streets, wallowing in buildings and scenery and autumn weather turning into winter. Only an actor's need to be precise, to observe and analyse discrete detailed moments, stopped me being grossly sentimental.

My future changed in an instant, turning on events that seemed beyond my control. Beryl called one morning at the beginning of November, the first time she'd talked to me since the transmission of *The Tin Islands*.

"It seems you haven't totally blotted your copybook," she said. "They want you for the film of *Boxing Day Hill*."

"What?" I realised that I was jumping up and down, though still not believing my ears.

"They want to meet you," the dry voice continued, "but I think the part is yours if you want it."

"Of course I want it! But who am I playing?"

29

I tried to visualise the cast of the play I'd seen three weeks earlier.

"Norrie," Beryl said.

"But he's a Scot," I protested. "I'll have to go to a dialogue coach."

"Don't do that until you talk to them. I think they're quite happy with the accent you have."

"Thank you, thank you, thank you," I cried, managing to make her laugh, softening the hostility she must have felt in me.

She sounded bemused, as if her professional judgment had been proven wrong and she wasn't sure what to think about that. "Filming starts in January. Oh, and one of my clients would like to meet you."

Michael Baker! I thought, with no reason to suppose Baker was Beryl's client.

"Maryann Macready," Beryl said. "I'll give you her telephone number. She admires your work. But don't try too hard to shock her. She's still very young."

I knew for a fact that Maryann Macready was at least a year older than I.

I could barely contain myself until I got off the tube at Hampstead – only the Heath was a big enough setting for my emotions.

"I'm a real actor," I cried to the grey sky. "I'm going to have a career!" An hour later I was still leaping up and down hills. "'Silent now is the wild and lonely glen,'" I bellowed at a harrier gliding past, bringing a fleeting bleak smile to his fanatical face.

That night, sitting in the bathtub trying to make a pair of dungarees look worn, scrubbing at them until the tub turned blue and the walls were splattered with blue suds, I began to wonder how long Beryl had known about my getting the part. An outrageous notion occurred to me: she'd phoned me so early in the morning that she'd probably known since yesterday and waited overnight to tell me. Would she ever have contacted me again if the film people hadn't wanted me?

"This is Daniel Henry."

"Hello?" Maryann Macready sounded puzzled.

The pause lengthened. I wouldn't let myself be intimidated into breaking it.

"Oh yes. Of course. Beryl –"

"Hello. I wondered if you'd like to come to next week's matinee of *Romeo and Juliet*? I think there's still time to get tickets. It's usually easy to get tickets for the Old Vic. If you haven't already seen it."

"Yes. Oh no, I haven't. I just finished in a play." Maryann's perfect Kensington elocution sounded at odds with the bewilderment she was projecting – though the effect was to rivet my attention. "Yes, I'd love to. Let me see. No, I have nothing else planned for that day."

"I'll ring you again if I can't get tickets," I said. "Otherwise I'll meet you at the theatre. Whereabouts?"

"Meet me at the stage door," Maryann said, suddenly in charge. "Fifteen minutes before curtain. My uncle works backstage and I'll pay him a quick visit."

With contacts like that, I thought, how easy it must be to get on the stage.

Maryann Macready was the twenty-year-old discovery who'd just finished playing the ingenue in a wafer-thin moonlit Anouilh comedy about Time, Memory and Love Regained. Her publicity had been tremendous, her notices wildly divergent. She was 'ethereal,' 'enchanting,' and 'the heaviest young actress, emotionally speaking, on the West End stage.' Much had been made of her inheriting the talent of the legendary William Charles Macready, who her publicity claimed was an ancestor. I don't think anyone had bothered to investigate her family tree: new young actresses were allowed such charming conceits. I was unimpressed, proud to despise the nepotism that drove so much English theatrical success.

It ought to have been a triumphant vindication to announce myself to the same stage doorkeeper who'd turned me away six months ago. But I cared so little now that I forgot to check if it was the same man. Maryann emerged from inside the theatre as soon as I appeared in the doorway, moving towards me with the energetic hesitation that drew attention to her on the stage. I wondered if I was in on the beginning of an old new look: she wore a faded-looking floral print frock, a dark fur stole and a small velvet hat perched on one side of her blonde hair.

The business of meeting took care of the nerves I'd wasted time fretting over.

"Shall we have a drink before we go in?" I asked.

"Let's go in. I hate being stared at," Maryann said, her icy elocution totally at odds with her shy manner.

I wondered why a stage actress had to worry about being recognised when no one ever noticed a television actor like myself. After we settled in the eighth row of the stalls it was I who kept glancing round to see if anyone was watching. Maryann read the program or stared at her knees. I was pleased to note that makeup couldn't hide two small acne pimples beside her left nostril. Someone else would suffer with me until they found a cure.

The expensive Zeffirelli production of *Romeo and Juliet* had been lavishly heralded and poorly reviewed. It looked wonderful, with rich costumes bathed in golden Renaissance light, but the actors seemed mostly left to their own devices.

"Should they have done that?" I asked Maryann in the interval. "I mean the way they left oranges from one scene near the footlights during the following scene?"

"Yes, I was wondering," Maryann said, and appeared to ponder the matter further. "Yes, I think so. It's more existentialist." She pronounced it "existawnshalist," which I was certain was wrong.

I thought the acting not much better than in the school plays that had filled every moment of the winter term for my last three years in grammar school, but I was afraid of saying so in case I was wildly off base and Maryann told on me.

"I know a saloon bar where the company goes," Maryann said after the play. "By the way, thank you for bringing me.

I'm very pleased to have seen it, though I think Zeffirelli should stick to opera."

"I agree," I said stoutly.

No recognisable member of the Old Vic appeared in the saloon bar while we huddled over ham and potato salad in a drafty corner. The first encounter of two young stars at the beginning of their careers: it occurred to me that this meeting might get written about some day. I was courtly and protective and normal – I imitated Michael Baker. When I couldn't stop myself glancing at an attractive man in the bar I dulled my eyes and looked hostile. It would certainly be convenient if Maryann and I were a couple. I'd seen *Room at the Top*: I wondered if I was corrupt enough to make love to a woman for ambition's sake.

Maryann enjoyed her food, cutting and chewing with absorbed efficiency until she noticed me watching her. She laid down her knife for a moment.

"I was in rep for a year," she explained, glancing apologetically at her plate. "My parents weren't madly keen on my becoming an actress, so I was determined to show them I could make a go of it on my own. I almost starved. I'll always remember the night before payday counting the coppers in my purse to see if I had enough to buy a bar of Cadburys Milk Tray at the sweet shop next to the theatre. Have you ever been poor?"

I flushed. "Sometimes. When I was washing dishes at the hotel at least I got my meals."

"What do your parents think of you becoming an actor?"

I hesitated over how much to reveal, and chose to give away as little as possible. "They don't have an opinion. Did I tell you I got Norrie in the film of *Boxing Day Hill*?"

"No! That's wonderful!" Maryann breathed, her eyes widening. "I was up for the film of *Look Back in Anger*, but they cast it from a theatrical clique."

"I know," I said hotly. "An angry young man director from the Royal Court makes a film and he casts it with middle-aged Shakespearian actors. It's outrageous!"

When Maryann finished eating she rotated her glass of sweet Vermouth, clearly framing a question. "What do you think of Stanislavski?" she finally asked.

"I do concentration exercises for fifteen minutes as soon as I get up in the morning," I reported, "then I practice improvising psycho-physical actions."

Maryann looked frightened.

"I wanted to ask you a question about doing the Anouilh," I said, confident that I'd established my credentials. "Did you go into character two or three minutes before your entrances? Did you do what she'd been doing even before the audience actually saw her?"

"I tried to," Maryann said. "But there was one scene where she appears to him as an apparition in his memory. No matter how hard I tried I couldn't imagine what an apparition does before it appears."

"Certainly not in Anouilh," I agreed. "If it was in Shakespeare you could imagine being in hell. It's the playwright's fault, not the actor's, if he insists on creating apparitions with no subtext to help us."

"The subtext of an apparition," Maryann said thoughtfully in her clear superior voice.

I glanced at her sharply to see if she was making fun of me. We stared at each other, then on cue began to giggle in affectionate acknowledgment that we were self-absorbed freaks indeed.

Maryann peered at the clock but seemed to have trouble seeing that far. "What time is it?" she asked. "I should go. I told my parents I'd be home by seven. Would you like to come and meet them?"

I wanted to, but I'd begun to realise that Londoners, even colleagues like Maryann, did not always mean what they said. "Do you really want me to?"

"Yes. It would help." Maryann looked up at me from under sketchily darkened lashes, seeming almost to plead. "They're very protective. It helps if I can show them who I've been with." In the taxi she turned and laid a hand on my arm. "I have trouble telling the time or my left from my right. Mathematics is a lost cause. My parents educated me at home."

I shrugged to indicate that such eccentricities must be

expected in an artist.

She took out a tiny purse and began unfolding ten shilling notes. "Let me pay you for my ticket and the meal."

"No, no," I said. "I wouldn't hear of it." Where I came from it was unheard of to let the woman pay. Then I quickly calculated the afternoon's cost. "I'll let you pay for the taxi," I conceded, blushing.

The taxi burrowed deeper into night past narrow terraces until we stopped outside a small closed eccentric shop with dusty windows. There were lights behind curtains on the second floor.

"My parents sell herbal remedies," Maryann explained as she unlocked a side door, her mouth twisted in what looked oddly like shame.

In the booklined upstairs living room Maryann's voice softened to blend with her parents' unobtrusive suburban accents. Her mother betrayed her.

"I hear Beryl got you a part in a film," Mrs. Macready said rather hungrily.

Maryann's face reddened. Her elaborate surprise at my news had been phoney.

"Is this agent any good, do you think?" her father asked. "We had her here for drinks and I couldn't pin her down on anything."

"I honestly don't know, Mr. Macready," I said.

"Fawcett," he said.

I stared at him.

Maryann reddened further. "I took my ancestor's surname as my stage name," she explained airily over her shoulder.

I knew how an Ulsterman unwilling to make allowances for the artistic temperament would have judged her: Maryann Macready was affected.

TWO

His name was Jonathan Samuels. We met only once, except that a year after our meeting we found ourselves face to face in the crush of Piccadilly. I started to smile but his eyes jerked away, tense and blank.

A note – 'Dress casually' – on the card Kinross sent me, and the time – nine o'clock on Saturday night – suggested exactly what kind of party I was invited to. It came at the right time. I was desperate to lose my virginity, even if it had to be with a man not quite as glorious as Gordon Bennett or Michael Baker.

Kinross barely had time to acknowledge me when he opened the door. No chance for me to register any signs of censure over my thieving. But I noticed that the study door was firmly shut and the rooms that were open for the party had been cleared of pocketable objects.

Men drifted across patterned patches of light from lamps with scarves draped over them. I helped myself to some potent punch and found a dark wall to lean against, lapsing into a kind of dream while I waited for Gordon's or Michael's face to appear before me. The records the guests danced to were of female singers, German or French or Greek, all of them asserting a plangent bittersweet strength. I greatly admired a black boat-neck shirt one man was wearing. The rest wore sweaters, like me, or open-necked dress shirts, a few with cravats, and slacks, like actors in a sports committee scene from an English film – noble Trevor Howards, the pride of English manhood that Ulster folk despised as sissified.

When Colin, the blond man in the boat-necked shirt, asked me to dance, he had no way of knowing he was the first man I'd put my arms around since I was an infant. I certainly wasn't going to tell him.

It seemed to come naturally to me. There was only one right way to fit my body against his bony frame so that we could move to the smoky music. The boat-neck shirt was new, or freshly-laundered. Colin had no smell except for the shampoo scent on his slightly sweaty hair. I almost jerked away when my crotch bumped against his, but the lump in Colin's trousers continued to thrust discreetly: you were clearly supposed to let yourself touch your partner down there, at least while the dance lasted. It felt so right that I immediately took it for granted.

"What do the words mean?" I asked, my mouth touching Colin's ear.

"I don't know," Colin said, elongating the vowels of the simple words, just like the Queen of England. Then he pursed his lips and twinkled, as if an admission of ignorance was the same thing as wit.

I found myself eyeing other men over Colin's shoulder.

"So you're an actor then," Colin announced out of the blue, although I hadn't mentioned my profession.

"Yes. What do you do?"

"I'm a wine merchant." Colin pursed his lips and twinkled. But he left me as soon as the song ended, clearly not fooled by my attempts to look interested.

Five minutes later I caught the eye of Jonathan Samuels, who came and leaned gratefully against the wall beside me. In his grey three-piece suit he looked as if he'd come straight from work. His longish hair was slicked down like Gordon's, though the colour was lighter, and his body considerably frailer.

"What is she singing about?" I asked.

Jonathan knew the song. "Wherever she goes she always leaves a suitcase in Berlin." His voice was educated, but mercifully free of a braying tone and inhuman vowels. "It helps her believe that she'll always go back to the city she loves."

I was immensely attracted to the notion of leading a fateful cosmopolitan life in the old stone capitals of Europe. Drink had loosened me enough to let me look directly at Jonathan and show him how moved I was by the song – almost the same as being moved by Jonathan. Our eyes locked. Jonathan gave a small warm troubled smile.

I watched myself being led from the party, relaxing my shoulders in order not to betray that I was the prisoner of a great event, wanting to look as if I was used to leaving

37

parties with another man I was about to make love to. In the chilly taxi on the way to his Knightsbridge flat, Jonathan politely provided the usual information to identify himself: he'd gone to Harrow and Cambridge and was a copywriter at Mather & Crowther. "What do you write copy about?" I asked.

"A soap powder," Jonathan said, "and a car."

"They should give you a free car," I said.

"I saw your play," Jonathan said.

"I'm glad." I thought it would be provincial to inquire if he'd liked it, or to confess how good it was to finally meet people willing to admit they recognised me.

I would see many more ambitious young men's flats like Jonathan's: an excellent address, three or four small rooms, fitted carpets, one or two pieces of good furniture – a leather-topped writing desk, an solid table – and a frugal absence of colour and comfort.

"I think there's some Scotch," Jonathan said.

"No thank you." I waited for him to show me what to do. I thought it was probably time to fall into one another's arms. But Jonathan had been remote and distracted since we'd left the party. While I remained standing in the living room, he puttered away into the kitchen and then the bathroom. I sat down, examined the room again, then picked up a magazine and moved closer to the one lit lamp to flip through it.

Jonathan reappeared in his shirtsleeves, looking surprised and disparaging. "Shall we go to bed?" he asked briskly.

"Yes," I said, hopping to my feet.

Both of us kept our underpants on. The bed was so cold that it seemed natural to scuttle into each other's arms. Jonathan's skin was warm and I was making it warmer with my own body. For an intoxicating moment I let myself feel longings fulfilled. I wallowed in the uncomplicated smell of his skin while I buried my face against the boyish chest, my heart and cock filling with uncomplicated lust at the thought of Jonathan taking off his cotton underpants. Clinging to him against the cold, I slid my mouth up to Jonathan's neck and then his chin, then closed my eyes and pulled his mouth against mine. The press of willing lips was said to give joy, but for the moment I was too busy learning the mechanics of opening my mouth, my teeth, where to put my tongue. Jonathan was preoccupied with another project, kicking off his underpants. I immediately reached down and slipped off my own underpants, looking under the sheets with furtive intense curiosity for a glimpse of his cock. I saw the hard small purple circumcised cock next to my thigh, then felt it prod my belly, the little pouch under it settling against my skin.

I thrust my body closer against Jonathan's. I knew no way of telling him what I felt without giving away the secret that this was my first time. I was deeply unwilling to entrust that much information to a stranger: I wouldn't admit that I was still a boy. So I was afraid to moan, or try to tell how my heart was glad and grateful, or praise Jonathan's beauty, because I didn't know if that was what a man did in these circumstances, and I wanted most of all to appear to be an experienced man. It was enough to lie locked under Jonathan's body, now and then pushing up against his flat belly with my cock, which was ready to erupt, though I didn't care about that. I could masturbate any time. Far more urgently I wanted to hold another man in my arms, nudge his body with my nose and mouth, explore his back with my fingers, even reach down and tentatively cup his buttocks. I was romantic: I wondered what dreams and disappointments this body hid, what small heartstopping quirks it had, that I could only learn if I were admitted to its intimate routine.

Then Jonathan sat up, straddling my hips, his cock no longer quite at attention. I began to stroke his chest, and shyly looked to him for guidance as to what we did next. But he gave an impatient and dismissive toss of his head.

"You're not queer," he said, refusing to show disappointment.

"Yes I am," I said immediately. I moved my hand and touched his cock for the first time, as if that proved I was queer.

The movement only seemed to confirm his judgment.

39

He watched me for only a moment, then gave up. "You're not queer," he said.

"Yes I am," I persisted. But he'd already lifted himself away and turned his back to me. I snuggled up behind him and laid a hand on his side. It was ignored.

✳ ✳ ✳ ✳ ✳

Boxing Day Hill, an ensemble play about an infantry company trapped in a bunker during the last days of the Korean War, brought an angry cynical anti-Establishment point of view to an ancient storytelling convention, the cross section of characters in crisis. There were no patriotic sentiments in this war play. The main character was a brutal self-destructive sergeant driven by expediency, his subordinates ignorant pawns manipulated by the military and the government. Everybody died at the end, though mostly offstage. My character Norrie, the raw private goaded to invent stories of his sexual experiences, died first. It was a plum role: the character was onstage continually until his sudden emotional explosion in the middle of the third act, when he threatens one of his tormentors with a bayonet. He is interrupted by another explosion: a grenade drops into the bunker, bounces off Norrie's helmet, then blows away the lower half of his body.

The star who played the sergeant in the film version, a former underwear model who'd scored a huge hit in a thriller based on a comic strip, still had a Scots burr to his voice, though he was fast losing it to accommodate himself to international stardom. That was why I was cast as the character who'd originally been a Scot: someone had decided it would be inappropriate to have an unashamed Scots accent in the cast.

The private lives of the other actors spilled onto the set: a baby was sick, they took calls from girlfriends and agents, the order of shooting had to be rearranged to meet their other commitments. I had nothing to do but look after the interests of my character, and became so absorbed in Norrie that my moves might have been dictated by his spirit. The star, and the large cast of character actors, some of whom had once been young film stars, behaved well. Nicholas Sherwood (who must have made up his too perfect name), the twenty-seven-year-old actor who played Norrie's friend and supporter, came closest to resembling the kind of affected actor you saw in the plays of Noel Coward, that frivolous playwright who'd gone out of fashion. Nicholas uttered light bon mots then beamed around as if they hung in the air, expecting applause, six inches from his nose.

The sets at Shepperton were surprisingly small: life-size segments of the bunker and tunnels that would be six times larger when they were projected in black and white Panavision on a West End screen. I read Thackeray and Proust as I waited for my scenes, so unwittingly tense that I grew drowsy and was grateful when the crew woke me up with conflicting news and instructions. The star gave interviews to a stream of nervous dowdy men and women who could take their revenge with an envious flick of the pen. I was asked for interviews only to get my comments on working with the star.

The best fun was learning about the low grade explosives camouflaged on my specially made trousers and detonated by remote control to simulate the grenade explosion. I pleaded against the use of a stand-in, and insisted the scene would be more realistic if the blast also blew off my helmet. On the screen, the five second shot with postsynchronized sound effects would be shatteringly effective. On the set I had to scream my agony in a totally silent corner of the sound stage – the explosives on my trousers detonated like cap guns while a technician on the platform above me jerked on a wire to tear off my helmet.

The blast was supposed to blow me against my chief tormentor, played by the star, who in a moment of self-revelation disbelievingly watches his own hand move to comfort the dying soldier.

"Eons ago I played a messenger in a comedy at the Belfast Empire," the star told me while we waited for the interminable technical setups.

41

"My class went to see Donald Wolfit as Shylock at the Belfast Opera House," I said shyly. "In his curtain speech he said the way we booed him was music to his ears. My classmates were too naive to understand what he meant."

The camera rolled for the first take with the back of my dying head resting on the star's shoulder.

"I just want to say something," the star told the camera. "Daniel, please don't kiss me. I just got married again and my wife is extremely jealous."

I/Norrie couldn't believe my ears until I heard shrieks from the crew. I waited until I felt comfortable speaking.

"Let me know when you're ready to start working," I said, and settled my head against his shoulder to wait.

"I'm hit," I/Norrie croaked. "It isn't deep. Is anybody else hit?"

I let chill death flow from the bloody mess of what was left of my toes until it filled my head and pressed on my eyelids and I floated into the void.

"Daniel darling," the director called. "Um – I'm just thinking aloud – when you die next time, could you just slump a little or something?"

I came back to life and sat up. "I will if you really want me to," I said. "But it's a cliché to slump when you die. I bet almost nobody slumps when he dies."

The week after filming ended I had to report to the Labour Exchange near my new flat in Kensington High Street to explain why I was buying twenty-four self-employed insurance stamps all at once – the Post Office refused to sell me that many all at one time. I waited on a wooden bench to be seen by a clerk, miserable in the heart of one of London's hierarchies of humiliation. I was of course publicly disrespectful of authority, but I knew to my shame that the disrespect hid bottomless layers of self-doubt. Nearly everyone in England seemed to be ashamed of who they were, of their 'place,' and took it out on those beneath them. In a pub near the Inns of Court that I'd wandered into after my first meeting with the accountant Beryl had recommended, a polite Indian – his accent mimicking upper-class English so impeccably that it drew cruel attention to an outside attempting to fit in – asked if he could join some other junior barristers at the next table. One of them, unwilling to risk an openly racist slur, ignored him except to embarrass him by flaunting his sexual conquests.

"I'm only exhausted next day if she's one of the ones who makes a fuss about it." The high contemptuous voice flung words like knives. "Some women take hours to seduce."

As I waited at the Labour Exchange to explain my infraction I could imagine other actors using such an occasion to give a performance. They'd assume a gentle eccentric helplessness, a bewildered inability to comprehend why the stamps couldn't be purchased in clumps, all the while intending to subvert the values that allowed minor officials to function. I somehow couldn't summon up the energy to contribute more humiliation to the overloaded system. Performances belonged on the set.

This time being made to wait was the only recrimination. I paid my money and had my card marked by an inattentive clerk. As I made a getaway I caught the eye of a dark-haired man in a floral print shirt – obviously an American – waiting by a notice board. I smiled vaguely and walked on into the street. The man fell in beside me.

"Hi," he said, holding out his hand as if he had a reason to introduce himself. "I'm Peter McCracken". The voice was deep, easy – definitely American – though the man clearly had to make an effort to seem at ease.

I shook the strong hand, but remained aloof. I had no idea what was going on, and I kept space between us to ward off the suspicions of the respectable shoppers. The enthusiastic stranger only moved closer when I backed away.

"You're American," I said, hoping to encourage him to tell me what he wanted.

"Canadian," Peter said. "I'm from Toronto."

I was disappointed. Canada was a bland country that suffered badly from its proximity to dazzling America. I glanced at my watch. "I'm going to be late for my class."

"Are you in school?" Peter asked.

"I take private acting lessons," I said.

43

Peter looked immensely relieved. "I'm an actor too," he said. "I teach theatre in Toronto." Then he set aside his geniality and stared me down, raising an eyebrow, almost glaring. "Would you like to have a drink at the Salisbury?" His question clearly contained a coded challenge.

The late spring sunshine glinted on his hair and skin. He was darker, glossier, more muscular than the English.

"All right," I said.

"Six o'clock," Peter said, turning away.

"You mean tonight?"

"Yes," Peter said.

He didn't show up. At five to six I pushed through the crowded pub, my expectant look making it clear I was searching for a prearranged face. The show of purpose backfired. By 6:20 it was clear that I'd been stood up. It was no good pretending the crowd didn't notice, because I caught people eyeing me when I looked up from the *Standard* I'd buried myself in. I was beginning to get a better idea how to carry myself, how to hold my head to display my face and show self-respect, but it was hard to show your face to the world when you were humiliated.

The second my watch hit 6:40 I fled. I checked the alley next door in case Peter was waiting there, then lingered a few more moments outside the dirty bookstore across the street, a narrow slot in the wall that sought to disguise its true nature by crowding scientific studies alongside queer autobiographies and novels: grubby copies of Kraft-Ebbing and *The Kinsey Report* as well as *Against the Law*, *The Verdict of You All*, *The Heart in Exile* and *Aubade*.

This part of town had other attractions for me. The office crowds had gone home to the suburbs and the theatre crowds hadn't arrived. The streets glowed in the last of the sun and the neon coming into its own. Overhead the birds that lived in the monuments inked their last noisy arcs. Outside the theatres were life-size Zoe Dominic and Angus McBean portraits of the players, and reviews painted in black and gold on cardboard and wood. It was almost enough to be Daniel Henry alone, walking through the ambitious air, dreaming about the parts I'd play and the things I'd see.

The phone rang that night while I was making an omelette. We had not made omelettes in my part of Belfast: they'd have curdled in the lard we kept half an inch thick in the black frying pan. This time I was daring to add chopped cooked ham to a difficult cooking adventure that only turned out edible half the time, though I ate the results even when they were burnt and greasy.

"Where were you?" Peter asked. "I waited till 6:30."

"I waited until twenty to seven," I countered. Not that it mattered now: we were clearly going to meet again.

"I don't understand," Peter said. His drawl, isolated from the rest of him by the telephone, suggested good-natured bewilderment where an Englishman might have sounded icily indignant.

"I don't understand how I missed you," I said. "Did you wait *outside* the pub?"

"I waited outside the theatre," Peter said.

"What theatre?"

"Wyndham's Theatre."

"You said to meet you at the Salisbury."

"I don't like the Salisbury," Peter said.

I was too relieved to waste any more time on the mis-understanding. "I'm glad I didn't get an ex-directory number," I said. "Where are you now?"

"In South Kensington."

"Would you like to come round for drinks?" I used the phrase I'd picked up from invitations.

"I'll be right along," Peter said.

He arrived an hour later, long after I'd cleaned the toilet bowl and vacuumed my new dark brown bedroom quality fitted carpet.

"I had a lot of trouble finding you," he complained, sounding not quite so good-natured from the shadows of the porch.

My flat was in a clearly signposted garden square directly off the High Street, but I was too relieved to question him.

"It's vast," Peter said. Then, perhaps with marginally

45

less enthusiasm, "It's like a stage set."

The furniture I'd bought – a brass bed, spot lamps, dining table and chairs, a big sofa and two armchairs still uncovered – wasn't enough to make the flat look inhabited. Once three large rooms, it had been converted into one high-ceilinged space with cubbyhole kitchen and bathroom and a balcony overlooking the trees in the basement garden. There were no paintings on the walls because the only paintings whose quality I was sure of cost fifty times more than I could afford.

I cleared the *Hamlet* books off the sofa so that Peter would have a choice where to sit.

"Why do you have a private teacher?" he asked. "Why don't you go to drama school?"

"I already do what they're supposed to teach you in drama school," I said apologetically. "I've been lucky."

He chose to sit on the sofa, the way an actor in a drawing room comedy would sit: one arm stretched along the back, the opposite leg thrust out behind him, his attention apparently riveted on me, who sat next to him. I knew that civilians were more physically withdrawn, their attention troubled and scattered.

Peter hadn't heard me. "I don't think you have a hope of getting to read for the commercial theatre unless you've been to drama school," he warned.

"When did you arrive in London?" I asked.

"Four months ago."

That explained it. I gently filled him in on my career so far. He'd never heard of *The Tin Islands*, and *Boxing Day Hill* wouldn't be released until November.

"My friend Maryann Macready got turned down by all the drama schools," I said to clinch my argument.

I watched Peter's attention turn electric while admiration fought a stubborn resistance to the possibility of breaking the rules.

"How old are you?" he asked.

"I'll be twenty soon. How old are you?"

"Thirty-one." He shook his head and gave a rather wild laugh. "I guess they do things differently in London."

46

Again taking in the size of the flat: "I thought your family was rich."

"They aren't."

I was comfortable taking charge in my own home, doing for the first time what I would do with other men: sitting sideways to face them on my sofa, drink in hand, wondering if they were attracted to me, wondering if I was really attracted to them, wondering who would make the first move – which was never easy until the moment it was made, when it seemed remarkably easy.

"Are you teaching theatre in London?" I asked.

I think Peter was ashamed of what he was doing, but he hid it well after a brief panicky grin. "I've been working as a substitute teacher," he said, sounding purposeful. "I start again in September."

"Are you in England for good?"

Peter hesitated. "I don't know." Then, unhappily, "I'm leaving for Europe on Saturday night. I'll be gone seven weeks."

I felt my face turn scarlet. We found ourselves exchanging suddenly urgent glances. Peter's left eyebrow arched.

"Have another drink," I said. When I stood up with the glasses he followed me.

"You could use a few brass rubbings on your walls," he said at my elbow. "I made dozens at Salisbury Cathedral. They're really spectacular."

I turned with the drinks and my hand bumped into his chest. He was staring at me, both eyebrows arched now, his face several shades darker. I lost control. I looked down for his hand to push the glass into it, saw his cord trousers, which seemed to be swimming in heat, forced myself to look into his challenging expectant face, and fell into his arms.

Peter's body felt strong and beefy, exactly what I wanted. We tongue kissed, which was what I knew you were supposed to do, but I got more enjoyment out of affectionately poking my tongue into the dimpled knob on the point of his chin and nuzzling the stubbled flesh under his jaw. Peter moved methodically, documenting each move with a significant look; I wanted to close my eyes

47

and lose myself. I opened Peter's shirt and buried my face in the black chest hair.

"Shall we go to bed?" I croaked for the first time in my life. ('Men just jump into bed with each other,' a judgemental bluestocking who worked for a director complained to me a year later.)

We stepped out of our clothes – I'd never seen patterned boxer shorts before – and fell onto the bed. I was beginning to get a notion of some of the things two men might do, but I was too inexperienced to fully execute any of them. I worked my way down his body to his cock, which looked enormous, and took it in my mouth and sucked it. It was smooth as rubber and tasted squeaky clean, as if all traces of the liquids it dispersed had been scrubbed away. I even licked Peter's groin. Then I moved up in the bed again and lay back against the pillow to see what happened next. If I hadn't known there was supposed to be a lot more to come it would have been enough to feel the wonderful weight of Peter's body on me. I shuddered as his tongue travelled down my body and saw the head of my cock disappearing into his mouth. But only for what seemed a second. Then Peter was coming back up to cover me again, looking as if he'd swallowed a hair. I hoped my cock didn't taste bad: it was leaking from excitement.

I'd have enjoyed just swooning under Peter's weight. But he thrust his cock against my belly, poking it with the head. It was a hard dry uncomfortable movement. If I'd trusted my instincts I'd have told him to relax.

"I need Brilliantine," Peter said.

"What?"

"To put on Daddy," Peter said.

It took me a moment to understand. "I haven't got any," I said, and racked my brains for a substitute. "Butter?"

"Uh-uh," Peter said, disgruntled.

He reached down and bundled the two cocks in one hand, thrusting his cock hard against mine. Between the thrusts I tried to sneak in the gentler movements that made my cock feel good. Peter's cock looked like a huge antiseptic weapon, coloured a uniform pastel purple; my own paler cock was deep red at the slit, which swam in liquid that oozed onto my belly. I didn't understand why Peter was working so hard, but I supposed there was a lot I didn't know about sex. At last, because his hip bone was digging into my thigh, I reached down and took over the handling of my own cock, burying my face in his armpit. I came a minute later. Peter looked disconcerted. I liked the way he jutted his chin when he didn't seem to know what to do next.

On my way back from the bathroom I collected the drinks we hadn't drunk. Peter was sitting up smoking. I cuddled against him, resting my glass on his stomach.

"Do you live in your own flat?" I asked.

"In Toronto. My mom's taking care of it for me. I rent a room in South Kensington from Hank and Bev. They're a couple I know from back home. Every year Hank says let's go home, and Bev says one more year."

"You could move your things in here before you go abroad," I said in a small voice. As an added inducement: "You'd save money while you're away."

After a moment Peter turned his head and gazed down at me, his face warming. He moved an arm so that I could snuggle closer. "Sweet boy," he said.

By the time Peter left on Saturday it was established that we were in love, though we didn't meet again till early on Saturday when I helped him get his trunks into a taxi and carry them into the flat. On Thursday night Peter had a school meeting, on Friday he was having farewell drinks with Canadian friends. But by Saturday morning we were a couple. Most of our talk on the phone in between was to celebrate our new status, which we'd settled when we woke up rumpled and sweaty on our first morning together.

"Are you excited about Europe?" I'd asked.

"Yes," Peter said. A pause. "But I don't want to be the sort of person who spends his life travelling the world alone."

I said, somehow confident of my reception: "You never need to be alone again."

I watched Peter unpack his trunks in order to pack his two suitcases. In his toilet case I saw for the first time a man's deodorant stick. He sorted through cords, chinos,

49

cavalry twill trousers, trying to decide what to take with him.

"Don't you wear blue jeans?" I asked. "I can never get mine to look the way they do in American films."

Peter wrinkled his nose disapprovingly. "I don't like cheap trousers."

He had three glossy ten-by-eight photographs, one smiling, one serious, one looking over his shoulder with a provocative eyebrow arched as high as it would go, all confidently engaging the camera. In pictures from a university production of *As You Like It* he was clearly having the time of his life as Malvolio, his skin resisting the makeup's attempt to age it.

"Do the teachers appear in the plays with the students?" I asked innocently.

"Sometimes," Peter said.

"Come to bed," I said when the cases were packed. Peter's eyes took on their charged look, promising inflammatory things to come. But I only wanted to lie in his strong arms on the white sheets in the sunlight that sliced through the shutters.

"Now I know what Bradley was talking about," Peter said. "He said he could stay in bed with Hernando the whole weekend."

But we only had ten minutes.

"I need to take a bath, sweet boy, or I'll miss my train."

"We could take a bath together," I said.

Peter backed off bashfully. "We don't have time."

I waited, and discovered that being half of a couple created small pockets of empty time.

Five minutes before he had to call a taxi to Victoria Station Peter panicked: he couldn't find his passport. There wasn't time to unpack everything. He snapped open his suitcases and jabbed through the layers of clothing. I found the passport almost immediately under a sweater in one of the trunks he was leaving behind.

I kept it out of sight behind my back. "Guess what I'll give you if you give me a kiss," I said, my eyes bright.

Peter groaned with relief and kissed me.

50

"I'll give you another kiss back," I said.

Peter stopped smiling. He laughed uncertainly.

I had the good sense to hand him the passport.

As the train started moving we locked eyes dense with meaning. I reached out and grabbed Peter's hand and held it till the train pulled my lover away. We knew we were observed – a porter on the platform looked over his shoulder at us with a curiosity that seemed to stop short of censure. On this occasion neither of us cared. We were playing an essential scene. The love promised to men and women had come true with another man.

✳ ✳ ✳ ✳ ✳

I stayed busy on weekdays during the day. Twice a week I worked on roles with Julian Lambert, an expensive demanding teacher I'd been lucky to persuade to take me on. For the last six weeks it had been Hamlet, with no end in sight. I played the prince, Julian played everyone else, except when he made me switch roles to help me understand another actor's task. Julian had a brilliant reputation as a teacher, but he'd played only minor roles in the theatre, years ago. I assumed I knew why: he was 5'6". His only references to his private life were sentimental, disappointed, an astonishing contrast to his steely approach to work.

We took *Hamlet* apart word by word. At first I'd say: "I can understand what he's feeling. At school in Belfast –"

A flick of Julian's hand dismissed my insight. "Without even thinking about it you will bring all your own experience to the role, all your unique qualities. What you must learn to do is saturate yourself in the unique experience of this particular man in his particular world at this particular time. You must decide why the prince is saying each of these lines, why he is choosing these words. Is it because Shakespeare liked to write poetry?"

"A lot of the time that *is* the only reason for a line's existence," I protested. "Shakespeare was a journeyman playwright as well as a genius."

"But you must always suppose there is a better reason. You're on stage to create the illusion of a human being infinitely grander and more varied than the members of the audience feel themselves to be. You must have purpose. You must throw no line away."

After the day's work I wanted to hear Julian tell me I was destined for greatness. I got no praise, only insistent encouragement to try harder. It suited me to be disciplined, not to beg for approval. Each morning I still worked through my Stanislavski exercises, but the line between them and what I did with Julian blurred. He deflated me by telling me that English actors had used Stanislavski since the 30s. I still preferred to associate the Russian teacher with the virile new American actors.

I'd told Beryl I wanted to audition for every decent role I was remotely suited for, though I knew that might be a mistake. I didn't understand my success so far: I thought I was only extraordinarily lucky. I thought there was a danger in making myself so available they'd see my limitations. I'd lose the special reputation I had from *The Tin Islands* and the upcoming *Boxing Day Hill*, in which I knew people thought I was good. From the way the cast and crew had treated me, from what they didn't say to me, I knew they talked about me when I wasn't there.

Or maybe it was my imagination. And maybe I didn't have a special reputation. The truth was I had no idea what was going on. I'd have liked to hide behind my (imaginary?) specialness. But what happened if no work arrived before the money ran out?

I chose to demonstrate that I was serious, so that I could blame fortune, not myself, if there was never any more work. Sometimes I'd go to two auditions in a week, then three weeks went by without a nibble. Almost everything was out of my control – nothing I did seemed to make a difference, from the first auditions when I was so nervous I misunderstood everything that was said to me, to later auditions when discouragement made me brittle and flippant and ashamed of myself afterwards.

You had to be what they were looking for, and I thought

52

they probably knew if I was right the moment I stepped into their office or onto the audition stage. Anything I did merely confirmed their prejudices.

Most of the producers and directors and playwrights I read for treated me well. I sensed they were at least intrigued by me as a phenomenon. One or two went out of their way to humiliate me.

"You are a little provincial, you know," a director drawled. I waited a moment, dead-eyed, killing my feelings, then turned insolent eyes on him. "Yes I am," I said, making my accent sound even blunter. "Definitely."

I'd decided with Julian to retain my accent but add some Southern Irish softness.

"But you have absolutely no stage experience," a director said incredulously, pretending to suddenly uncover an unsuspected failing in me.

I had a standard reply. "*The Tin Islands* was live experience. A lot more depends on a live television transmission going right than any single performance in a theatre."

I was turned down by the Shakespeare Memorial Theatre, dismissed as if it was outrageous of me to offer myself. Yet sometimes I thought I heard envy in the voices of the men I auditioned for. Or perhaps I hadn't a clue what was really going on.

After training by myself for a month, I joined a harriers' club that met at the bottom of Parliament Hill Fields on Sunday mornings. Running in all weathers – getting caught in rainstorms and splashing through puddles, feeling my skin bake on hot days – was glorious fun, though motorists and pedestrians clearly thought I was mad. At first I had so much trouble keeping up with the other harriers that conversation was out of the question. When I was able to engage in brief panting exchanges I found that these teachers and clerks and draughtsmen and civil servants shut up for a while when they heard I was an actor. It didn't seem to cross their minds that I might be queer: I was already exotic enough. I evaded questions about girlfriends, blushing, but refusing to lie.

53

Enthusiastic postcards began to arrive, sometimes two a day, describing the Rococo and Baroque glories Peter encountered in Europe. Soon there was a long letter portraying the fabulous people he'd encountered.

"But without you," he wrote, "I am still the lonely wanderer, a stranger everywhere I go."

I took the letter with me to class and to auditions, and used it as a bookmark in the Penguin Classics I read in the evenings, when I was usually alone. Occasionally I went to the theatre with Tom or Hugh or Maryann. Often I went alone to old films at one of the Classics. After the letdown of discovering that no one seemed to recognise me, I gave up looking around to see who was paying attention and did exactly what I wanted.

*****

Real life began the moment Peter got off the train. Back at the flat he kissed and hugged me ('Sweet boy!'), then sat down to read a letter from his mom. I put dinner in the oven – shepherd's pie, made from scratch according to a cookbook, and served by itself because I thought the potatoes and other vegetables in the pie would be enough. Peter laughed uproariously as he read his mom's account of some domestic upheaval.

"She sold an article to the *Reader's Digest*," he boasted, and showed me the clipping of a five-line domestic anecdote.

"Dinky's angry," he told me in bed that night, referring to the dark-red slit in the head of my cock – perhaps it got that colour from over use, since I'd been masturbating a lot in the weeks I was alone. We strained together, Peter on top, until I couldn't wait any longer and brought myself off. Peter came too, delivering one small glob of semen that lay on my belly like a drop of glue.

"That's our baby," Peter said. "Perfect rhythm," he added, his eyes tearing. "Some couples try all their lives to come at the same time."

I turned on my side to go to sleep, thinking that this was happiness and I should never want anything more.

Peter farted. While I wondered how to respond the bed started to shake. I turned on my back again, careful not to put my nose under the sheet. Peter was shaking with suppressed laughter.

"I didn't notice I done it," he said, sticking a finger in his mouth and pulling a simpleton's face.

The sheets had to be washed more often now that two people were sleeping in them.

It hadn't occurred to me that my routine would have to change, or that once I learned to make changes Peter might not appreciate them. I decided it was my duty to get up early to make breakfast for Peter, but after the first day or two he never had time for a proper breakfast before he left for school.

I'd been happy to eat dinner on a tray in front of the news on the box. One night I came home to find the table set for dinner, with flowers from the garden for a centrepiece. It seemed that Peter wanted to make a proper home.

After we sat down our different urgencies collided. Peter, who never mentioned the children he taught, wanted to talk about the exploits of his colleagues. I, who thought schoolteachers were minor eccentrics, wanted to talk about the play I'd discovered at the library, *The Green Bay Tree*.

"The word's never mentioned, but it's far more about being queer than *Tea and Sympathy* or *Cat on a Hot Tin Roof*. Even the author's name is queer – Mordaunt Shairp! Women are the absolute enemy to him. The characters are stereotypical queers, of course, but the play was produced in 1933. Laurence Olivier played the languid young man in New York."

Peter was impatient for me to finish. "I invited Frank." Frank was an art teacher.

"What night?"

"Tonight."

I frowned, ready to be irritated. I'd wanted to spend the evening learning more about making love.

Frank, a middle-aged bachelor, seemed innocuous until I mentioned something Tynan had written, and then I felt his rage at people who got paid to air their opinions.

55

"I don't see the function of theatre and film critics," Frank said furiously. "Why do they have them? Why can't we be allowed to make up our own minds?"

I couldn't understand why Peter was nodding sympathetically.

At eleven, when Frank showed no signs of leaving, I said goodnight and went to bed. A blanket pulled over my ears didn't completely muffle the sound of their talk.

Peter getting into bed woke me.

"Is he queer?" I mumbled.

"I don't know," came a reply that sounded hard and distant.

Next morning my lover stared disapprovingly at me when I stumbled to the kitchen where he was eating toast.

"You had a nightmare last night."

"I don't remember a thing," I said carelessly.

Peter was determined to make me care. "You sat up in bed screaming. Screaming! You were soaked in sweat." He shuddered.

I shrugged. Something felt wrong about Peter's need to insist that the nightmare was unwholesome, and I somehow to blame for an involuntary act.

"Frank told me what you did," Peter said.

I was bewildered. "I never saw him before last night."

"He told me what you did at the end of *The Tin Islands*."

I'd been wondering when to tell him. I was beginning to be modestly proud of the way I'd drawn attention to our way of life.

But he was glaring at me. "How could you? How could you?"

He never elaborated. I didn't know whether he blamed me for being unprofessional or blatantly queer, but he seemed to enjoy the blaming.

Once a week another Canadian arrived at the flat full of a tourist's woes. I got tired of being made to feel unemployed by commonwealth visitors who asked me what I was acting in now.

A stylish woman burst into tears because she'd got lost at the wrong moment, when her feet were dying from the cobblestones.

"But your historic buildings are wonderful," she said. "Some of them must be nearly two hundred years old."

I, a foreigner myself, couldn't hide a superior smile.

"She says you're beautiful enough to be a girl," Peter reported.

Which I guessed was not meant kindly, and may have been the visitor's way of indicating she knew exactly what was going on, though we played resolutely normal in front of anyone who'd report back to Peter's family.

"Did you see the way she stared at my balls?" Peter asked incredulously. "She knew about us. Women can always tell when a man is queer." He touched his fingers to his temples. "Queer men have smooth skin at the corner of the eyes."

I thought of checking in the mirror, but supposed I was too young for the rule to be relevant.

The first time Peter didn't come home till eleven I rushed to meet him in a temper.

On this occasion he chose to think the best. "You were worried something had happened to me. I told you I was meeting some of the guys from school."

"No, you didn't," I cried.

I'd assumed that as a couple we'd spend our free time together. Soon, unless we'd arranged to go to a film or play, I learned not to expect him home early on weeknights. My hurt wasn't sexual. It never occurred to me that Peter might be having sex with other men – we'd promised to be faithful. I was bewildered why he'd want to spend an evening with Frank instead of being with his lover.

More than once, when it was Peter's turn to buy the tickets for a play, we arrived on the wrong night because he'd got the dates mixed up, or late, because I couldn't get him out of the house in time. However late we were, he was a stickler for correct form. As the taxi drew up to the Globe fifteen minutes after curtain time Peter held me back, making me wait until the doorman came and opened the door for us.

One Sunday we went to see *Two Men and a Wardrobe* at

57

the Chelsea Classic.

"It was fabulous," Peter said, "but I didn't understand what it was trying to say."

I wasn't certain either, but I had ideas. "All they were doing was carrying a wardrobe around, and just for that they got treated worse than the people who were beating up other people. Though I don't understand why they came out of the sea."

Peter shook his head admiringly as if he'd had a revelation (which must be a popular phrase in Canada, he used it so much) about how smart I was.

We went to see a double bill of *Autumn Leaves* and *Cat on a Hot Tin Roof*.

"Liz Taylor must be dikey," Peter said. "Even I got the hots for her."

I told him that he looked like Cliff Robertson.

"A friend of mine went through exactly the same thing with a younger man," Peter said gloomily.

"You mean she paid for him to get treated in a mental hospital?" I asked. "Did he come back to her afterwards?"

Peter shook his head with what looked to me like considerable enjoyment.

On Saturdays we did the laundry. "This is a real proof of love," Peter said, sorting through my dirty underpants.

Sometimes I was able to drag him into bed on a weekend afternoon. One day, when he'd had been labouring over me for so long, rubbing his cock against the small of my back, that I stopped pretending it was interesting, I reached out for the latest *Picturegoer* and flipped through it lying on my stomach while my lover worked away. There was still enough good humour between us for Peter to laugh.

"Times are bummy, gettin' bummier, Ain't we got fun," he'd sing, high-kicking through the door like a chorus girl.

We began to argue over money as soon as the bills started coming in. We argued over who ate more food, used more hot water. Peter insisted it was cheaper to heat a saucepan of water with the gas on medium. I'd go into the kitchen to find a kettle still hadn't boiled because he'd turned down the gas. Neither of us came close to articulating one cause of the tension between us: I lived off the savings I'd earned acting, Peter taught theatre in Canada but had never made a non-academic cent from it.

Even so I was humbler about the realities of an actor's life. "I'll wash dishes again if I have to," I said at the end of a busy week of failing to get work.

Peter's nose wrinkled disapprovingly. "That's isn't a quality decision," he said.

At the same time he expected to share in my good fortune. He lived rent free until the beginning of the first calendar month we were together, when I told him how much his half would be. He stared at me, then shook his head over something he couldn't begin to utter. Half-an-hour later he came out of the bedroom with a cheque, presenting it with a flourish whose meaning was clearly intended to be obvious to me. While I was making dinner one evening I heard the phone and called to Peter to answer it. Five minutes later I came into the living room where he was correcting exercise books.

"Who rang?" I asked. Then I saw the phone lying off the hook.

Peter looked up. "I thought you heard me call you. It was your agent."

I picked up the phone, but Beryl had hung up. My mouth snapped open before the cold challenge in Peter's eyes made me think twice.

I began to expect disapproval from my lover. He found me in the kitchen drinking milk straight from the bottle. "Sometimes I wonder where you really come from," he said disgustedly.

I wanted to give a cocktail party, and Peter agreed enthusiastically. When I compared my guest list with Peter's list I discovered a misunderstanding.

"I want to give a queer party," I said. I didn't say that I couldn't imagine Tom Finlay or Lord Kinross wanting to meet Frank.

I rushed home from class on the afternoon of the party to find the flat a sea of white. Peter had put paper napkins on every surface in the flat where anyone might be expected to set an ashtray or a glass. I'd been to enough parties to know that upper-class queer Londoners did not protect their furniture when they gave a cocktail party. I blushed scarlet at the thought of social catastrophe, then began rushing around snatching up the napkins. Peter watched openmouthed.

The need to avert disaster made me careless of my lover's feelings. "It looks so – so bloody provincial!" I cried.

It was much easier to give a party than go to one. I was in my element greeting my guests expansively, making introductions, trying to control who talked to whom. Peter got high, eyes glittering, head tilted to perform. But he laughed too loudly and talked a little too emphatically. I felt alone. Once or twice, pretending to listen to a guest, I glanced around to see how my lover was doing. He seemed to have forgotten me. I found myself cherishing my well-behaved respectful guests, who even knew exactly when to leave. By a quarter to eight only Julian (who was discussing Canadian theatre with Peter) and Hugh were left.

I walked Hugh to his car to cool down, then asked if I could get in.

"I'm unhappy," I said, and found myself in Hugh's arms. As if my situation wasn't interesting enough, I repeated a phrase stolen from a play or book: "I don't like to leave a lover unless I have another to go to."

Hugh's immediate display of hungry adoration wasn't enough to make up for his blubbery kisses.

Peter and I stared at each other when I got back to the flat, searching each other's faces for confirmation of our own reactions to the party, then we fell into each other's arms. Our affection had to do with pulling off a successful party.

Maryann invited us to the first night of a play directed by her director in the Anouilh. Kay, this week's visitor from Canada, made up the foursome: another academic, another single smart attractive thirtyish woman who hung around Peter in self-destructive puzzlement. Or perhaps her important emotions were invested elsewhere. After the play we brought them back to the flat for drinks. Peter, high on the first night, disappeared for five minutes then danced in from the bathroom naked, doing the Can-Can.

"I think I'd better call you a taxi," I told Maryann, and bustled her into the street to wait for it. When she'd gone I found Peter, still naked, bent over a fully clothed Kay in what he clearly wanted to be a passionate embrace. His cock remained soft, but he started banging his left foot on the floor, as if that would bring the cock to life. I headed for the bathroom.

It seemed a long time before I heard goodbyes at the front door.

Peter appeared in the bathroom doorway, still naked.

"At least she'll have something to talk about when she gets back to Canada," I said.

The air was charged, too dangerous for anger. Peter pushed past me, hunting through his shaving things.

"Where is my everlasting blade?" he demanded.

"I don't know," I said. "I threw out an old blade when I was cleaning the bathroom. Was that it?"

"You threw out my blade!" he yelled. "That was my everlasting blade."

"I didn't know it was anything special," I said, almost in tears from temper I was afraid to let loose. I picked up my toothbrush. "We don't have everlasting blades in England."

"I can't get another one," Peter said, too quietly.

I found that my hand was shaking and I was afraid to look at him. "I said I was sorry. I didn't know." I turned my face away, ashamed because I didn't seem to be able to get the cap off the toothpaste. "Just leave me alone, Peter!"

He swung me around with enough force to knock the toothbrush from my hand. His fist landed on my cheekbone and I immediately buried my face in my forearms – I had an audition the next day.

"Speak to me with respect!" Peter roared, pummelling my body.

"I'd speak to you with respect if I respected you," I gasped, my breaking voice muffled by my arms as I sank to the floor.

"Speak to me with respect!" Peter bellowed, pounding on the top of my skull because he no longer had easy access to the rest of my body with his fists. From behind

61

my arms I saw him raise a foot. Maybe he was going to kick me, but something changed his mind. He turned on his heel and left the bathroom. I jumped at the door and locked it, fought myself not to cry, started sobbing.

A little later, while I soaked in the bathtub, trying to wash off humiliation, Peter pounded on the locked door.

"I'm sorry, Daniel, I'm sorry."

"Go away," I shouted.

Twenty minutes later I came into the bedroom long enough to collect a blanket, then headed for the sofa. Peter laughed uncertainly. "I'll be glad to have the bed to myself," he called.

"I slammed into the wall of the squash court," I volunteered at the audition next morning, to explain my swollen face.

That night Peter came home long enough to wash a sweater and change to go out again. I ignored him, my back turned to him as I pretended to read in an armchair. I heard him go to the front door, but then he came back.

"I said I was sorry. But –" His voice was rough with resentment.

"Leave me alone," I said.

"We'll talk when I get home," Peter said carelessly.

Later in the evening I ran a bath, and discovered that Peter had draped the sweater to dry on the last clean towel. I lifted the sweater to feel the towel: it was too soaked to use.

By now I could predict when rows would erupt.

"You moved my sweater," Peter accused me when he came home late that night. "Why can't you leave my things alone?"

I started to explain, but saw only another argument ahead. I slept on the sofa another night.

In the morning I came and stood in the kitchen doorway while he was making his instant coffee. I leaned against the door for support.

"I want you to find someplace else to live. I'll give you back your share of this month's rent."

It felt easier than I'd feared, though I hated the weakness in my voice. Peter nodded and grinned, as if at his own shrewdness, as if he'd known all along how badly I would treat him.

He said to the kettle with rehearsed clarity: "I don't think you'll ever know how much you've hurt me."

I had to be certain he meant to leave. "If you don't leave soon," I said, "or if you ever touch me again, I'll call the police." I walked away keeping a determined look on my face to stop myself crying.

That day's mail brought a love letter in which Hugh poured out his heart and hopes, making me feel guilty and dishonest as well as defeated.

I replied by letter: "I'm deeply sorry you were the one who happened to be there when I was so unhappy, and that I may have misled you. It will be a long time before I can sort out my feelings or feel ready to trust another person. I just need to spend a lot of time alone."

More words borrowed from plays or books. They seemed to cheapen what was happening to me, like the official account of a complex event, like an actor whose life becomes a performance. But I was disappointed when I heard nothing more from Hugh, when he didn't pursue me further.

I stayed out as late as I could the day I asked Peter to move. When I got home there was no sign he'd been back to the flat since morning. I couldn't sleep for listening for the sound of his key in the lock. Then I woke up to find that it was morning and Peter had never come home. I didn't see him again till eleven o'clock that night, when I heard him opening the front door. I lay tensed, waiting to jump out of bed if he tried to get in beside me. But he was walking back and forth, pulling out drawers, making more noise than he needed to, I thought getting ready for another row. Then I heard him leave again.

When I came home from the Sunday run his trunks and suitcases were gone. I scoured the flat for anything that belonged to him and found two coat hangers, brown wrapping paper and an envelope that had contained a letter from his mom. I buried them in the rubbish. Then I realised I hadn't found his keys. Before I went to bed that night I pushed an armchair in front of the door. On

63

Monday morning I called the landlord and ordered him to change the lock.

On the first day that I knew I was safe I slept till noon and spent the rest of the day unwilling to move from the silent flat. Peter had done a good job of clearing out, but we hadn't managed to remove all traces of him. I kept finding the small things – buttons, collar stays, small tubes of specialised ointments – that become unpleasant detritus when the person who used them has gone. I tried to read but couldn't concentrate – I'd come to in the middle of angry ruminations. I was angry that I hadn't fought back when Peter hit me, that I'd been turned down for work perhaps thirty times in the last six months, that my Aunt Peggy from Belfast was coming to visit me, that the flat already felt contaminated after I'd just painted and furnished it.

After a week or two, when it was clear that Peter had no intention of reappearing, I began to cry in bed at night – because I was lonely, because he was gone for good, because I knew he was lonely too.

THREE

Aunt Peggy plodded towards me through Leicester
Square, expecting the worst, immune to joy. To protect
herself from the London drizzle, she'd donned matching
pieces of cream-coloured plastic weatherwear, from a pixie
hat that covered her ears to bootees pulled over her modest
heels and tied around her ankles. The only flesh visible
was the circle of her face and an inch of leg beneath the
hem of her raincoat. All morning I'd felt myself tightening,
but I couldn't help grinning at the sight of her. She allowed
her eyes to shine at me, then read my mind and retrenched
into prudish caution.

"I'm not going to risk spending my days in London in
bed with a cold," she scolded. "I am not."

"The rain has stopped, Aunt Peggy," I said. I found
myself towering over her, enjoyed it for a moment, then
gave in to the irresistible pull to stoop down and make
myself her size.

She compromised by pulling off her mittens and tucking
them safely in her large homemade handbag. I'd watched
the size and homeliness of Aunt Peggy's handbags increase
as she progressed from young womanhood to middle age.

At the Corner House before we sat down, I made her
watch omelettes being made behind the glass while I tried
to anticipate every xenophobic doubt.

"I've had an omelette," she objected, moving us on. "Do
you not remember the time we had lunch at Flemings?"

But I saw her checking over her shoulder to make sure
they hadn't introduced some germ-laden new trick into the
process. The time Aunt Peggy brought me to London for
five penny-pinching days during the Festival of Britain, we
wandered into Flemings on some boastful neighbour's
recommendation without checking the prices. I embarrassed
my aunt by demanding ice in my glass of water, making it
clear I wasn't accustomed to refrigerators.

She settled for bacon and eggs and a cup of tea. I knew
that even in a grander restaurant she'd have insisted on tea

with her meal instead of following the London custom of waiting for coffee after dessert.

Sitting down we were equals. She surveyed my face and coloured at the intimacy she was about to utter: "I'd have thought all your spots would be gone by this time."

I shut down. I knew she wanted me to be the perfection of young manhood. I knew Aunt Peggy had suffered from no one ever caring enough to examine her face. But I shut down. Because she had another motive: to ruthlessly insist on her right to a place in my heart.

"I got your postcard from Paris," she said. "So you finally used that passport that caused all the fuss and bother."

I stiffened further, shook my head to warn her that I wouldn't let her touch that topic. The skin on her cheekbones turned pink again as she prepared to express a radical opinion. "I thought Paris was disappointing so I did." Her eyes brimmed with the effort it took to disagree with every civilized person. And I was stymied. Moved, because I knew Paris had been disappointing to Aunt Peggy on her one trip abroad years ago because she was as full of romantic dreams as myself but none of them would come true; blocked, because I could never hurt her by letting on I knew why Paris had been disappointing (once, when I was a child eight or nine years ago, I'd called her an old spinster, and her tears had almost broken my own heart); foiled, because she'd engaged my sympathy and made it harder for me not to let her treat my life as family territory to be trodden at will. There was something else. In Belfast she'd never mentioned the most desperate thing of all because it had never occurred to her that it was relevant. I was certain she felt she had good reason to mention it now.

She held up her fork, inspected it, then wiped it with her handkerchief. "Did I tell you what Mrs. Macpherson did?" she asked. "After Willie died? She put a notice in the *Telegraph*. 'Sadly missed by all,' it said."

I roared so loudly that people looked up from their plates and Aunt Peggy had to shush me. "At least I made you laugh," she said. "And did you know Margaret

66

Conway had a blue baby? The poor wee thing." Her eyes filled although she loathed Margaret Conway.

She polished off the eggs and bacon, but I couldn't persuade her to order the fruit salad. Why wouldn't she eat more when she had a chance?

"I wanted to tackle you about something," she said, visibly preparing herself to get down to business.

I waited, wary, though somehow this didn't seem like the way she'd broach the subject of queerness.

"Mary would never ask you herself," Aunt Peggy said, "but she could do with a bit of financial help."

"Do they need money for something in particular?"

Aunt Peggy hedged, weighing the probability of an immediate windfall against long-term insurance. "No, though they can always use anything they get."

"I sent them money at Christmas, you know."

"It was a drop in the bucket."

"That's strange," I said, "because it wasn't a drop in the bucket to me. There are three of you and one of me."

"Aye but you know the situation in Belfast. We didn't have the advantages you did."

Six years at a free grammar school. But even buying my uniform had been a sacrifice.

She couldn't say the other thing she'd come to say as long as she was facing me. She waited till we were in the street, as we threaded through the crowds on our way towards the Temple. The kind of pansy I never gave a second look in London glided past us, his painted face grimly nonchalant, giving Aunt Peggy her excuse.

"You remember that painted woman we saw on the tube when we were here in '51? You said that's not a woman, Aunt Peggy, that's a man."

I frowned. To smile would be to side with bigotry.

"You know I'm broad-minded," she continued doggedly, "but the one thing that fills me with disgust is two men –" Her upper lip curled. "Anything else but that. That's the one thing that disgusts me."

I straightened up, wondering how long she'd rehearsed the little speech. Its effect was to confirm that we lived in

67

different universes.

"I remember that," she said, pointing to the Festival Hall across the steaming oily river.

I'd taken her to sit in the sun on the Embankment. She wiped the bench quite dry and sat on her pixie hat for double protection.

"Isn't that where we saw those 3-D films?"

"Nearby," I said. "I think we saw them in the building that became the National Film Theatre."

"Do you ever think what you'd do if you never got another role?" she asked. She had a way of identifying my fears.

"All the time," I said.

"Do you ever think it might be a good idea to train for some other profession, just for insurance?" She was directing my life again.

"I could train as an accountant," I said brightly. "I'm sure they'd let me off three or four times a week to go to auditions."

She scowled, trying to think of a retort. But she gave in to the sun enough to lift her skirt half an inch to feel its warmth on her shins.

"Actually," I said, relaxing into naughtiness, "what I'll do after I win the Oscar is convert to Catholicism and become a priest."

Aunt Peggy's mouth tightened. She knew she was being provoked, but lacked the ideological resources to launch a major counterattack.

"I don't think you know," she said, picking up halfway through an argument that had been following its subterranean course between us without a word being said, "how much you mean to Mary and Harry. They think the sun rises and sets on you and they always tried to give you the best of everything." She hesitated, then took a small step into dangerous territory, her voice trembling. "I'd hate to think where you'd be without them."

I'd been looking at the river, thinking that most of the events I'd been educated about had occurred nearby. It seemed to me a lot easier to play one of history's kings or peasants than to struggle to keep a sense of myself as I wanted to be.

It wasn't until Aunt Peggy hunted for a tiny hand-kerchief and blew her nose that I realised she'd been crying. Not over anything I'd said, but over thoughts she attributed to me. I fought not to let guilt soften me: she was crying, after all, because she found it harder and harder to get a say in shaping my life.

I pretended I hadn't noticed her tears and went on watching the river and the passersby. Finally I forced myself to say: "We have to be going. I have an appointment later in the afternoon."

She always brightened after shedding tears. "Did I tell you about Winnie Agnew?" she asked as we walked up Villiers Street. "That man she married after she picked him up on the seafront at Portrush? Just a common pickup." She shook her head wonderingly. "Their country seat has a helicopter port. When they send out invitations they assume their guests will arrive by private helicopter."

Once she got going on a brighter topic she could allow herself to bask a little in my success. "Do you ever think people are going to recognise you in a place like the Corner House?"

"Yes, but they don't," I said sadly. "Anyway, if they do I have nothing to hide. I'm an actor, not an escaped convict."

I invited her to dinner the following night. I couldn't wait for Aunt Peggy to see my flat. One Christmas ten or twelve years ago, when I'd helped make the Christmas decorations, I was told by my mother, and by Aunt Peggy more authoritatively, that strips of blue and green crepe paper did not go next to each other, even after I proved that they did by pointing out the ready-made decorations in Woolworths' window. The first present I'd bought myself from the *Tin Islands* money was a blue and green striped pullover. I'd painted the walls of my flat, following the old division into three large rooms, in great alternating blue and green areas.

She looked a little stunned when she walked into my flat, but made no comment. I thought we parted as friends.

69

Five days after she went back to Belfast a letter arrived from my mother. It had to be serious news, because my mother usually excused herself from reading and writing by claiming she'd left her glasses upstairs.

She asked me to write and apologise to my Aunt Peggy. "I'm ashamed of you, Daniel. She says you treated her as if she's not good enough for you now, you don't want anything to do with provincial people like us."

The letter stung: I was young enough to assume I deserved every rebuke.

❊ ❊ ❊ ❊ ❊

I was asked to meet the producer of a new film to be based on Edgar Allan Poe's *William Wilson*. My imagination took off before I was halfway through reading the tale. There wasn't time to get Julian Lambert's advice on how to nail the part. I didn't want Julian's advice. I had to play William Wilson, and I proceeded instinctively: I was going to lay my passion in front of whoever had the power to give me the role. I had to win it with my intensity.

The first person I saw when I walked into the producer's office was Cliff, my director on *The Tin Islands*, who'd cut me the last two times we met.

"I don't have a chance," I thought, and the unfairness of it turned me sullen with disappointment.

I shook hands with the producer, who was from somewhere in Eastern Europe, one of the foreigners who were becoming powerful in London and whose foreignness was ignored by the English, at least to their faces, as if that was the most tactful thing you could do for them.

When I turned to Cliff he was staring at me with a worried intent look. At least the outraged hostility seemed to be gone.

"Are you directing?" I asked grimly.

He nodded. "Didn't Beryl tell you? It's my first feature film." So perhaps he'd asked to see me after all.

I sat down. The producer was already sitting behind his desk.

Cliff perched on the corner of the desk and asked: "Have you read Poe's story?"

"Oh yes," I said. "I have indeed read Poe's tale. Many times." And saw that I'd got their attention. So I paused, and gazed at each of them in turn. Then I waited, looking as if I had a lot to say. A pulse pounded in my temple. I felt so excited I was worried I'd faint. Only purpose kept me conscious.

"What did you think?" Cliff asked, laughing at the impatience I'd created in him.

"I want to play William Wilson," I said.

Cliff and the producer nodded, as if that was to be expected.

I took my time, getting ready to justify my desire.

"Why?" Cliff finally demanded.

I didn't do it the way I wanted to. I wasn't precise or ordered. All I could do was let my thoughts spill out. "Obviously it's a dream role for an actor. I get to play two different parts. In appearance as well as inside. It's really important that we do it that way. He says his alter ego, his doppelganger, gradually becomes more like him. So when I first appear as the double I should look so different that the audience will think I'm another actor. Then I slowly grow to resemble the hero more and more and then suddenly wham! we're physical doubles. Only nobody but the hero notices how alike these two people are, right?"

The producer opened his mouth to object, but instead looked at Cliff.

Cliff looked perplexed. "Those early scenes take place in school. We'll be using child actors for those scenes."

"You can't use child actors," I said, thinking aloud, not protesting, just being sensible. "Children couldn't handle a plot like that. They don't have the emotional depth. You don't need any childhood scenes. You could start with them as adolescents at Eton, if you really insist."

"Why wouldn't we start at Eton?" Cliff asked, worried again.

"I'm not sure," I said. "It's in the story, though I don't think Poe knew anything at all about Eton. He was an

American. Are audiences these days really going to sympathise with a hero who goes to Eton? It's too – it's too – too *specific*. Somehow. Is the script finished?"

Cliff and the producer exchanged glances.

"We have a script," Cliff said.

"You could set the whole thing at Oxford," I said. "You could get away with Oxford, particularly if it's still period. It's not modern dress, is it?"

"No," Cliff said. "It's 19th century. Just 19th century. We're not trying for anything more specific. Actually we're planning to start with a prologue from *King Pest*."

"I'll have to read that again," I said. "I read it, but I didn't really get into it."

"Not the plot of *King Pest*, just the setting," Cliff said. "London during the Plague. Dockland alleys. We have to show what happens to William Wilson, but we want to end with the murder and the mirror."

"You mean after he murders his doppelganger he sees himself all bloody in the mirror and realises it was his best self he murdered – you're not going to go back and show us a real body the way Poe does, are you? Because this really all could be William Wilson's fantasy, couldn't it?"

"No –" Cliff glanced at the producer again, as if asking for permission.

"I mean if you do," I said, noticing that I was resorting to Method shrugs and hand mannerisms and telling myself to stop, "then you have to explain how he got away with murdering a real person, and if it's his doppelganger, then having a second body doesn't really make sense anyway. You could have a voice-over as he stares at himself in the mirror. His conscience at last: 'Henceforth you are dead to heaven and to hope,' something like that."

Cliff suddenly looked overwhelmed. "Yes. No," he said mildly. "Well, we know he somehow did get away with the murder because at the beginning we have William Wilson dying in some horrible plague-infested alley and he breaks into a boarded-up tavern so that he can steal his last drink."

"And as he's slurping the booze you dissolve to him when he was a young man at Oxford," I said. "There's something else. I thought of the wrong way to do this film. You could just have a rather virtuous young leading man play the role, who's gradually overwhelmed by vice, but that's going to make it dull. You need William Wilson to be a complex character. Poe says he's ardent and capricious and self-willed and ambitious and passionate, and he hates having his will interfered with. If you use an upper middle-class English actor for the role you'll lose the audience's sympathy, that with the combination of it being set at Oxford. But if you use a working-class English actor he'll seem out of place in 19th century Oxford. You need an actor who can play *character* and who's a little different, a little – foreign."

I swallowed, blushing furiously, though my face already felt red from concentration. "You need me."

I had nothing left to say. I sat back, beginning to be shocked by my own vehemence.

"Well," Cliff said. He stood up, and I was sure I'd gone too far. "We'll get in touch with Beryl."

What did that mean? Shy again, I hadn't the courage to ask.

The producer spoke at last. "Good to meet you," he said, shaking hands again.

"Good to meet you," I said enthusiastically. And found myself walking down the Charing Cross Road in the rain. My confidence was fading, but I was still high as a kite.

When I got home I phoned Beryl. She'd heard nothing, but promised to phone Cliff. I could think of only two ways of getting through the leftover day. I wanted to fall into bed with a drink to put me to sleep. Instead I went running in a drizzle that didn't stop before I reached home again, perhaps hours later, pushing myself with leftover purpose down to the river, across Battersea Bridge and through the park, back across Chelsea Bridge and along the Embankment. My body, steaming in the soaked white cotton shorts, attracted the attention of an assortment of men and women. Once or twice I smiled in acknowledgment. But I was possessed by a more rigorous obsession that made lust seem trivial. After I got home and bathed I reread *King Pest*

73

and *William Wilson* to see if I'd missed anything.

Julian blinked when he opened his front door to me the next afternoon: my energy was palpable. I told him the plot of *William Wilson*, and told him my ideas for playing the part. Then I wondered how I could possibly play an older man dying of the plague.

"It won't work if they put grey on my hair and give me whiskers," I said, already desperately worried. "It always looks ridiculous when they do that. Unless they can put convincing wrinkles on my skin I'm going to insist that they leave me looking young. They can make me look *sick*. I'll *play* old."

Julian gave up hope of working on Shakespeare that day. He listened – proud, amused, dismayed – made a couple of weak suggestions, and sent me home.

It was almost an anticlimax – I felt an initial surge, but I'd exhausted strong feelings for a while – when Beryl called a week later to say that filming began in October, that I would be starring in *William Wilson*. I whooped and jumped in the air, then wondered what to do with myself till then.

In the weeks before *Boxing Day Hill's* premiere I gave a dozen dutiful interviews to magazines and newspapers. I might as well have posted them answers to a questionnaire. The reporters already knew what they were going to write: I was a star of tomorrow getting my big chance in a major film with today's number one box office star after just one controversial television appearance. To the inevitable question: "What was it like acting with –?" I tried to tell them what it was really like: the waiting around, the apprehension that this would be the time I wouldn't manage to get it right, the effort of having to jolt myself from lethargy into instantaneous life, the grateful warmth between two people trying to create an honest action. The reporters' eyes glazed, but I refused to give them the clichés they wanted.

The interviews they wrote could have turned my head. If you believed the popular press *Boxing Day Hill* had two stars, and I was one of them. I couldn't help basking in that illusion. But I knew I was getting the interviews, while seasoned character actors were ignored, because I was a fresh face. It seemed that to get attention you had to be new, or a star proving yourself all over again.

I took Maryann to the premiere in a limousine sent by the distributor. She also had a part in a new film, a May-September romance starring a British actor who'd spent ten years in Hollywood and was now reduced to smaller budget British films and European co-productions.

"Has he made a pass at you?" I asked.

"Oh yes," she sighed. "He smells so foul. You always smell so nice, Daniel."

I wondered in passing if the antiseptic compliment was a declaration of sexual interest, but was afraid to ask. I'd chosen to be authentic, to stick to men.

As we got out of our limousine at the Carlton in the Haymarket a Hollywood blonde bombshell with grotesque swollen lips was posing for photographers on the strip of red carpet. To prolong her moment in the limelight she held up a hand and displayed green fingernails to the crowd. Maryann and I had to head for the foyer through the disgusted jeers her hands provoked. I wondered if you were supposed to wave at a crowd that showed no sign of recognising you, and looked to Maryann for guidance. She was smiling modestly in the direction of the photographers, and threw the crowd only one brief unassuming glance.

Maryann gave a little chuckle when I appeared on the screen.

"My right foot is rotting," I said.

I'd been too proud to ask for a screening, so it was the first time I'd seen the film. I was overwhelmed by how big I looked on a screen that turned my small moments into a huge product. I had to stop myself cringing at my callow movements and unpolished speech – at the same time that I kept a mask of pleasant heightened interest on my face in case I was watched watching myself. But what I did suited the character. I had to remind myself I'd chosen to play Norrie that way. I just wasn't sure the camera would have let me move and speak any differently.

The notices were good. I was singled out as 'honest,' 'strong,' 'moving.' But films no longer had the impact of the years of my childhood, when the pages of even the Ulster editions of the national newspapers were bordered with display ads for the London West End showings of twenty films. The popular papers devoted three or four paragraphs to reviewing *Boxing Day Hill*. The heavy Sundays floated a sociological or political balloon of an idea about the film, giving short shrift to the actors. Star power made the film a modest hit, which these days meant that it ran for four weeks in the West End. In the provinces it kept cinemas busy on Saturday night; the rest of the week they might as well not have bothered to open.

To my surprise the frugal and secluded Sunday morning harriers knew about the film. Runners I'd never talked to made a point of nodding, their faces briefly brightening before they returned to the aches and pains of overused tendons. Ben, a social worker who ran a settlement house in South-East London, drew abreast of me in the North Wood and invited me to his visitors' day the following Saturday. I made polite non-committal sounds. But he phoned me on Friday to remind me, and I chose not to think up an excuse.

The settlement house was a dilapidated grey Victorian house like a schoolhouse or parsonage, its overgrown grounds cleared for a vegetable garden next to the gateway. The house was an anomaly in that district, pasted onto an entirely different picture: it stood isolated on the perimeter of black tenement buildings, regular rectangles set in concrete all the way to a sulky horizon. In Belfast, where the slums were flimsy redbrick terraces, you could at least see the green sometimes sunny hills.

When I took in the small crowd I knew where I was – back at the Coronation Day street party in Belfast when, because I was well-spoken, I found myself making or seconding too many speeches. None of the other visitors looked as if they lived in the tenements, not the mums in floral aprons setting out plates of sandwiches and cakes, or the grander females in important hats, the men in white shirts and grey flannels, or kids too dressed up to have fun at what was essentially a women's meeting, because it had to do with social concerns.

I decided I'd eat a sandwich, make a quick tour of the house, and be out of here in half an hour.

"Our famous guest is here," Ben remarked to the group he was with, detaching himself to come up to me. "Now we can begin," he said, grinning.

My face fell as my heart sank. I was expected to participate.

Ben gripped my arm while he called for attention. "I'm Ben Talbot, the warden of your settlement house. I'd like to introduce Gillian Kingham, my assistant, who's in charge of the hostel program we just inaugurated three months ago."

He indicated a self-possessed blonde who'd come to stand on my right and was scrutinising me with irritating amusement.

"So far we're the only staff members," Ben said, sounding modestly in charge. "We couldn't run things without all the voluntary helpers like yourselves. We're here to answer your questions and listen to your ideas. If you don't come and talk to us we'll come and talk to you."

The women smiled, the men and kids began to look wary.

"Now, we have a celebrity guest this afternoon. It so happens that I belong to the same harriers' club as a star of screen and television. I know you've all heard about Daniel Henry's latest film, *Boxing Day Hill*. He very kindly consented to come here today and declare our visitors' day open. So please welcome Mr. Henry."

Ben let go of my arm, I think finally assured that it was too late for me to escape. Someone in the crowd la-laed the first few bars of the theme song from the thriller the real star of *Boxing Day Hill* was famous for. Laughter and applause.

I blushed no more than I'd blushed on Coronation Day. "Ladies and gentlemen," I began, and gave Ben a dirty look. "I wasn't expecting this." Some laughter. I discovered what was in my head as I heard myself speak. "I firmly

77

believe that actors should stick to acting, and I'm about to demonstrate why that should be the case. You see, I have no idea what people say when they declare a visitors' day open, and since no one has written my lines for me, I don't know what to say." A fair amount of laughter. "But I do feel like an imposter, because I think it should be one of you speaking, instead of an unimportant actor like me."

I looked around at good-natured or preoccupied smiles. A few were clearly dazzled by my celebrity. It seemed to me that a lot of the young women were pregnant.

Nerves, and relief that I really didn't need to say much more, nudged me into honesty. "It occurs to me that I'm not such an outsider here. Because I grew up in an area of Belfast very much like this."

To my great surprise, I heard my voice break. I waited until I was sure I had an optimistic new voice at my command. "I wish the settlement house many years of useful work, and I'm happy to declare your visitors' day open."

My confession touched some eyes in the crowd. I thought some of the dignitaries stiffened at the news of my heritage. I became resolutely cheerful, having revealed too much of myself for one day, and turned to lecture Ben on false pretenses. But he'd darted off on business.

"Ben should be shot," Gillian said in a creamy upper-class voice. "I take it you had no idea what was expected of you."

"None at all," I said. "What kind of hostel do you run? For homeless families?"

"For unmarried mothers," Gillian said.

"That's very interesting," I said.

*****

I was ready to play angry with Ben at the next day's run, but he didn't show up. Three days later he phoned me.

"I wanted to thank you for your speech. You made quite an impression."

I grunted.

"I hope it wasn't too boring for you."

"No, of course not," I said. "But I meant it about feeling a total fraud. I'm not Princess Margaret."

"She'd have been much more of a total fraud," Ben said briskly. "You're not a fraud if you attract interest in the settlement house. I wondered if you could get me a couple of tickets for a show?"

I was puzzled. "I don't have any particular pull. Which show? I don't think it's hard to get seats for anything these days."

"I suppose you've seen almost everything," Ben said.

"Almost," I said. "Did you want me to recommend something? You'd probably like something at the Court or at Stratford East."

Ben demurred. "They sometimes send us comps. I'd prefer something cheerful in the West End."

"You could try one of those English musicals," I said, sounding doubtful enough to distance myself from such a recommendation.

"Well, when are you free?" Ben asked, finally making his purpose clear.

The musical I got tickets for was a soulless tuneless attempt to create a folk opera about London dockers. I thought rather bitterly that the man who'd designed the articulated wooden blocks of the huge set had merely created another good reason not to pay attention to the actors.

"I bet the entire audience is wondering if the set will fall down and crush the actors," I said in the interval.

Ben was inclined to be kinder to the play, but for social worker reasons.

"It's totally fake," I objected. "An opportunistic Shaftesbury Avenue attempt to glorify the working class because it's fashionable."

"A short while ago it wasn't even fashionable," Ben said.

"It won't last," I said, enjoying myself more than I'd expected on this duty outing. It felt good to have a normal civilian friend. "I liked Gillian," I told Ben. "I wish you'd brought her. They used to make films about people like the two of you. With Walter Pidgeon and Anna Neagle or Greer Garson."

That made Ben grin. He was two or three inches shorter than I, so I stooped a little in the pushy crowd. "I expect it isn't noble at all," I said. "I mean I'm sure it doesn't feel noble on a day-to-day basis. Do you ever even notice yourselves making a difference? Maybe in small ways? The way I'll finally figure out how to say two lines of Shakespeare that have been baffling me."

"The changes in people occur over such a long time that you can't possibly notice them on a daily basis," Ben said. "On a daily basis the work can be so discouraging that the smallest thing turns out to be the last straw. One day last week Gillian got home to her flat and switched on the hall light. But the bulb had gone. She burst into tears." He glanced around at the confident indifferent public faces. "You know it's arrogant of us to expect change. All we can do is suggest possible choices. We have no right to think we know best. And often there are no choices available. There's no retraining available for people who've lost their jobs, there's nowhere to go to get away from a husband who beats his wife and children. Some days I think I'm lucky if I've just managed to persuade the electricity board not to turn off the power in someone's flat."

"It feels very strange to be talking about such things in a West End theatre," I said when we were back in our seats. "Does what I do seem very superficial to you?"

"God no. Everybody should be like you. You're blessed. You can't know what it was like for my people to meet you. I'm sure they thought actors were royalty who lived in Rolls-Royces and penthouses. Just seeing you in the flesh as an ordinary person might convince them that they have a chance too."

"I'm the one who still believes actors live in Rolls-Royces and penthouses," I suddenly confessed, learning something about myself as I spoke. "It's all seemed just as unlikely to me as it would to one of your people in those tenements. *The Tin Islands* and the film felt totally unreal. I thought it was happening to someone else. But now I have a new film

80

coming up and I *worked* to get the part. I'm just starting to feel this is my own life I'm living."

The confession left me feeling warm and sleepy during the second act. Afterwards, on the pavement outside the theatre, I'd have been happy to say good night.

"How about coming back for a sandwich?" Ben asked.

I hesitated. "To the settlement house?"

He nodded. "I have a flat on the top floor."

My own flat was no farther from the West End, but it seemed closer and more hospitable.

"Why don't I make us an omelette and open a bottle of wine?" I offered. "And let's find a taxi. I expect you have to work early tomorrow." I imagined that Ben worked as rigorous a schedule as any Russian party worker.

"I brought my car," Ben said. "I'm parked near Green Park."

He seemed puzzled about something, but kept silent as we threaded through the crowds, which I was used to negotiating alone. I tended to make way for other people, then get annoyed when they took advantage and pushed past me.

"Did you take a taxi to the theatre tonight?" Ben asked as we headed west in his Ford Popular.

"I took the tube," I said. Then I thought I understood his puzzlement. "I do have a car, but it's a fourteen-year-old MG TC and I think the engine's going to blow up at any moment."

"What would you have done tonight if you'd been by yourself?" he asked.

I wasn't entirely pleased by his assumption that I was unattached. "You mean if I'd gone to the theatre by myself? Afterwards I'd probably have eaten braised steak or Spam fritters and chips and peas at that stand-up place in Leicester Square. It used to be a luxury for me and it's still my favourite food."

"Why didn't you tell me?" Ben asked. "We could have gone there."

"Well –" I struggled to explain. "You know how it is when you go out with somebody. It's an occasion, so you

81

think you should go someplace better than you'd go to if you were by yourself."

His silence made me think the explanation lacked something.

"I'm still learning how to do everything," I complained. "Half the time I don't know what I'm doing, if you really want to know the truth."

"You could have fooled me. You know enough to be a film star who travels on the tube and eats at stand-up grills and keeps both feet on the ground."

"I'm not a film star," I said crossly. "I'm an actor. I started out wanting to be a film star, but now I want to be an actor."

For Ben I thought it best to play down the amount of living space I occupied. "It's not as big as it looks," I apologised as he halted just inside the door. "It just isn't divided into smaller rooms." I gestured towards the bare walls that I'd painted so carefully. "They're waiting for all the paintings I'm going to buy with my *William Wilson* money."

I found two sweaters and tossed one of them to Ben. "Wear that till the place warms up."

"All that money on paintings?" he asked.

"No, of course not. I save a third for taxes. A third of the rest is what I live on next year. The other third is what I live on the year after next if I don't get any more work."

Ben grinned and shook his head. "You're a hard wee laddie."

The Scots burr was the fourth accent I'd heard him assay. Once he got going about ideas his educated London accent disappeared under a mix of generic working-class English and a democratic American softness.

"You live alone in all this space?" Ben asked from the kitchen doorway.

I flushed, and felt more comfortable directing my answer at the omelette pan. "There was somebody living here. But he's gone now."

I heard Ben's voice: "Your boyfriend?"

I stiffened. The glance I threw over my shoulder – Ben

seemed to be trying to look as if he'd asked a perfectly normal question – was fairly hostile. Social workers presumably were neutral about sexual matters, but I hated feeling on the defensive, having to monitor myself not to sound apologetic about behaviour that was against the law and public opinion.

"He was," I said harshly, and turned and handed Ben his plate with an angry look for cornering me.

"Good omelette," Ben said into the unhappy silence that descended on us.

I cleared my throat and swallowed. "I gave you the best one. My cooking still fluctuates."

"Look, I thought you'd be open about it," Ben burst out, trying to clear the air. "Everyone who saw that TV play probably thinks you had an affair with Michael Baker."

"Not queers in the business. They know him better than that." It was getting easier to talk about it. "It would be hard to find another actor who hates queers as much as Michael Baker. That's why I kissed him." Which was another discovery for me, as I heard what I was saying. "I live in two totally separate worlds, one where it's accepted, and the other, one that's much bigger and all around us. Which includes South-East London settlement houses and Hampstead Heath harriers' clubs. It's like having dual citizenship of countries that don't even have a common border."

"I'm sure they do touch each other," Ben said earnestly. "They do overlap."

"Yeah, but only because I'm in both of them," I said grimly.

He started to speak, perhaps to reassure me that I couldn't possibly be alone, but he changed his mind.

We finished eating in silence. I poured the rest of the wine but made a point of not suggesting we leave the table, which might prolong the evening.

"What do you do when you're not working?" Ben asked, clearly determined to lighten the atmosphere.

"I do my acting exercises. I attend class. I audition. I read. I exercise."

83

"You keep busy," Ben said approvingly.

I heard a judgment that most actors were lazy and decadent, saving their energy for showing off before an audience. But I wanted to be honest with him. "Just now it's very hard to do any of those things. *William Wilson* starts in three weeks and the waiting is exhausting me. I feel as if I've thought about it too much already. But I know I won't feel like that when filming starts. The problems that come up on the set are things that never occurred to me, even though I think I've thought of everything."

Politeness dictated that I turn the conversation to Ben's work. "Do you work regular office hours? What time do you start work in the morning?"

"Don't worry, I'm going," Ben said, starting to rise.

"Oh, I didn't –" But I was too tired to protest strenuously. "It's cold outside," I said. "Keep the sweater on under your jacket. Give it back on Sunday."

Ben held out his hand, suddenly shy. I wondered why a man of thirty or more would still be impressed by me. He turned his head to me, our faces inches away, as I reached past him to open the front door.

"I thought actors –" he said.

I waited, not knowing what might be coming.

But Ben shrugged and turned away and allowed himself to be let out of the flat.

It wasn't until I was falling asleep that it occurred to me that he might be queer, and then I wondered why I hadn't thought of it sooner.

He didn't show up for Sunday's run.

❋ ❋ ❋ ❋ ❋

While I waited for filming to begin with a week's location work in Oxford, I worried about the script. I still hadn't seen it because they were rewriting it yet again. Would it turn out to be nothing but a Hammer horror film with a slightly bigger budget? Had they lied to me when they agreed to get rid of the scenes with a child actor? Was it all going to be ridiculous and overblown? Would audiences be given an irresistible opportunity to laugh at me in all the wrong places?

Alone in my flat, I discovered myself rehearsing angry accusatory arguments with Cliff over promises broken and a script that was going to kill my career. How could Beryl have let me sign a contract without seeing a script? What kind of fool would chose a job where you had to rely on the quality of other people's work, had to fight and beg for parts though you were the one audiences came to see and judged in the final product?

The script arrived by messenger one morning when I'd just got back from running in the park. Now I put off the moment I'd been agonising over. I took a long bath. I read the paper thoroughly over breakfast. It was after eleven before I sat down in an armchair and forced myself to turn to page one.

I thought it was wonderful. Poe had written only three major scenes that could be adapted almost unchanged: the scene where Wilson holds a lamp to his sleeping rival's face and realises that the man isn't just a tormenting imitator but truly his double; the gambling scene where the double unmasks Wilson as a cheat; and the final murder. Poe told the rest of the story in inflated rhetoric about the aftermath of events he didn't directly describe.

The screenwriter had fashioned a coherent plot in a series of short scenes set in an Oxford library, a gymnasium, the rooms of Wilson's tutor, developing the story from Wilson's first meeting with the young man who vaguely resembles him to his realisation that the man is becoming his physical double, to his final paranoid conviction that there is nowhere he can go to escape the doppelganger.

The script introduced a love story with a dying woman, the tutor's daughter.

"Thank God," I muttered to myself. "I finally get to play emotional scenes with a woman."

Both my characters fell in love with the tutor's daughter, who was initially attracted to Wilson but more and more drawn to the goodness of his double. By the time the heroine lay dying Wilson was forbidden from seeing her.

Infuriated by rejection and grief, he impersonated his double in order to gain entry to the sick room and see her one last time, only to have her shudder and watch her eyes fade into death as she realises it is Wilson she is seeing.

I phoned Cliff, who sounded near the end of his tether. "It's great. It's wonderful. It's far better than I could have hoped."

Cliff's grunt sounded relieved but wary.

"There are just a few things. Can I tell you about them?"

"Of course, dear boy," Cliff said wearily.

I'd jotted down a list. "I think you were right to drop Poe's notion of the doppelganger also being called William Wilson. It might have drawn all kinds of laughter in the wrong places. But *does he have to have a name at all*? I mean you could cut out the scene where everybody is introducing everybody to everybody else and just cut to the meat of the scene. And you could still have the scene towards the end where William Wilson goes to his double's rooms to borrow the book he wants to read and finds his own name written in it. It would make it all so much more dreamlike. Or nightmarish."

"I think that may be a very good idea," Cliff said cautiously.

"And in the *King Pest* bit at the beginning," I said. "Would you let me not guzzle the booze I steal when I break into the tavern? Could that all be more romantic? I mean he knows he's dying, he's softened, he's almost welcoming death. Could I drink that drink gratefully, as if it was food or medicine?"

"Of course, dear boy."

"And just one last thing," I said. "Where is the opening scene in the plague-infested alley being filmed?"

"We're building a set," Cliff said stiffly.

"Could we do it in a real alley?" I asked.

"I'm afraid that's impossible."

"Why?" I demanded.

"When we work outdoors we have to worry about the weather and matching shots."

"I know that, but it takes place at night," I said. "In fog.

We want bad weather."

"We'd have to match the fog."

"Look Cliff, it's going to end up looking like a scene from *Oliver Twist* if you do it in the studio. I know it is. I mean you're going to the trouble of shooting exteriors in Oxford. This is the first scene in the film. You want it to look realistic. Couldn't you please find a real alley in Wapping or somewhere?"

"I'll think about it," Cliff said dully.

"Other than that," I said fervently, "everything is wonderful. Thank you for giving me such a wonderful opportunity."

"Are you fit?" Cliff asked, finally voicing his own concerns. "This will be an arduous shoot. We have a very tight schedule."

"I'm fit as a boxer in training," I said. "Or a long distance runner. See you in Oxford." I wondered if other actors gave their directors so much trouble.

Ben missed another Sunday's run but was there the following Sunday, talking in a group when I arrived. He felt my gaze on his neck and turned to half wave, half smile, as if we barely knew each other, then turned back to the group. Once we started I fell in behind him, making sure I kept him in sight. Non-runners might have supposed I was the one with the ideal runner's body, long legs to cover more ground, but not so. Most good runners had Ben's compact frame, though he was more muscular than the best harriers, who put in so much mileage that it stripped muscle from their bodies.

When I reached Spaniard's Road and saw Ben ahead of me, running alone, I accelerated and came abreast of him.

He smiled, scarcely glancing to see who it was, as if he'd been expecting me, but his eyes remained cautious under the helmet of brown hair. What he said told me we might still be friends.

"I forgot your sweater. I'm afraid I like it so much I've been wearing it around the house. If you like we could go back and get it afterwards."

87

"I can't," I said.

Ben's face closed down. I thought he was on the verge of accelerating to leave me behind.

"I have a train to catch," I explained quickly. "Filming starts tomorrow in Oxford."

He couldn't stop himself smiling. "Doubtless you travel second class."

"First class in the train today," I said. "I need peace and quiet. But when I went to Paris I tried to book a second-class plane ticket."

Ben broke into a grin. I'd won him over again.

"I should be back by next Sunday," I offered. "I could come and get my sweater then."

"It's a date," Ben said. Of course we both knew he could have brought the sweater with him to next Sunday's run.

✵ ✵ ✵ ✵ ✵

The production company had taken over an Oxford college for a week, and hired students from OUDS as extras. I'd dreamed of belonging to a society of privileged young men dedicated to discovering the truth about work and art and love, and always supposed I'd be forever excluded from such a society. Now I hardly had time to recognise that I'd somehow outstripped the world I'd yearned for, without ever belonging to it. I appeared in its midst carrying a film on my shoulders, the centre of attention, with all kinds of privilege available to me if I'd asked for it. The students were impressed, though one or two jeered at the film people loudly enough for me to hear an awful upper-class whinny.

Most of them looked very raw to me. Once or twice I caught darkened eyes watching me with a special interest. I smiled, but my attention was needed elsewhere. I had to stay inside myself to concentrate on what I was doing.

The location scenes were carefully blocked exteriors in which I played only William Wilson. I'd play the same scenes later as the doppelganger on a special sound-stage at Shepperton. Even when I was only crossing the quad or examining a notice board I had to know what William Wilson was feeling at that particular stage of his complicated development from self-absorbed hedonism to haunted fury. I also had to know exactly what the absent double was feeling, see his expression and movements, how close he'd come to resembling Wilson. It was an obstacle course hazardous with the prospect of terribly expensive failure, and I soon realised it was easier to stop playing as if – instead I started seeing the double beside me, performing as I'd perform later.

At the end of each day I forced myself to change into running kit and run through the town. I met some stares and whispers, sometimes a second of uncomplicated acknowledgment from an athlete running in the opposite direction. At the close of the first day's filming I joined the other actors for dinner in the hotel dining room, but I almost fell asleep from the effort of trying to talk to them. For the rest of the week I ordered dinner in my room and ate it while I studied the couple of pages of script for the next day. Then I fell into bed. Rather than feel alone, I imagined curling up behind Ben, my arm hooked over his chest as we slept.

✴ ✴ ✴ ✴ ✴

On Sunday we merely signalled to each other at the end of the run. As I drove up to the settlement house Ben was unlocking the door.

He held it open for me with an overcourteous gesture. "The star returns," he said.

My temper flared. "Stop it!" I cried. "Just stop it!" And I found myself staring at Ben, panting, appalled at myself.

Ben, equally startled, opened his mouth to justify himself, but decided not to.

The house looked even smaller and more ramshackle after a week at the Oxford colleges. Ben seemed smaller – no one had a physical presence as large as the presence of Ben that had started looming in my head – but far more interesting. I'd remembered the muscles of his legs as he

89

was running, but not the width of his mouth and cheek-bones that made his brown eyes seem close-set, or the fascinating unknown history, and thoughts about me, hidden behind those intelligent eyes.

He led the way across bare wood floors through wood-panelled rooms into a big empty kitchen.

"My kitchen doesn't have a fridge," he explained, handing me eggs and bacon and milk and margarine from an otherwise empty refrigerator.

I put them all on a counter.

"We can go," Ben said, and waited for me to pick up some of the groceries again.

"Oh. We're not cooking here," I said sullenly, feeling slow-witted, still ashamed of my outburst.

Ben's flat was in the attic, four small rooms with slanting ceilings, and a skylight and a fireplace in the living room.

"You'd like a fire," he said, not waiting for confirmation.

"I really like your flat," I said.

It felt like a retreat from the world, but the posters on the walls and records and books – on the Russian revolutionaries and the Fabian Society, on apartheid and nuclear disarmament, with rows of economics and political and social work texts – all spoke of Ben's commitment to his egalitarian internationalist beliefs.

I went and stood beside him until we were sure the fire had caught, then followed him into the kitchen and watched him frying bacon. The promise of warmth and food pushed me into wanting to be conciliatory – in truth I'd never wanted to be anything else.

"There's a Communist bookstore in Belfast," I said. "When I was in the sixth form I got my courage up to go there and buy the *Daily Worker*. I read it very ostentatiously on the tram on the way home, expecting to be stoned at any moment."

"At most they thought you were a harmless eccentric," Ben said, "or a schoolboy who hadn't had the corners knocked off. It's hard to shock people with ideas. They're too busy scraping a living."

"I really expected the FBI to come and arrest me," I said.

90

"I don't know what I thought the FBI were doing in Belfast, but the only film about Communists I ever saw was made in America."

"You didn't talk about politics in your home," Ben said.

"How did you know that?" I asked, astonished.

Ben turned the oven on and left the door open to warm the kitchen while we ate. I noticed the strong taste of the bacon and eggs – usually I was thinking about anything but the food when I ate alone. I was comfortably tired from the morning's run in the cold and expectations and emotions I couldn't identify. There were so many things I wanted to talk to Ben about that I didn't know where to start, so eating was an excuse for delay. Ben, unreadable to me, was a careful presence who made me happy.

When we finished eating he turned the oven off and we took mugs of tea into the living room and sat in ratty armchairs in front of the fire. I found myself stealing glances at Ben, so I turned my body to face him, to force myself to be open with him.

"Fires seem to be a luxury in rich Londoners' flats," I said. "In Belfast they were a necessity. It was how we heated the water."

Ben's eyes were cloudy. "Do you miss Belfast?"

"Not for a second. Never for a moment since I stepped on the boat."

"Did somebody hurt you?" Ben asked.

The notion was foreign to my way of thinking. "No," I said promptly. I didn't like it when Ben asked social worker questions. They drew attention to differences in knowledge and experience as well as the ten or twelve-year difference in our ages.

He visibly prepared himself to raise a touchy subject. "Why didn't you like being called a star?"

I flushed, at the memory of my outburst, at being forced into perilous territory.

"I thought you were making fun of me," I said lamely.

"I wasn't," Ben said, and waited.

Both of us were dissatisfied with my explanation. I forced myself further. "I thought you were only interested in me because I'm an actor." My eyes challenged Ben's in misery and pride.

"It would be hard to imagine Daniel Henry without the actor part of him," Ben said softly.

The explanation sounded reasonable and somehow dishonest.

"Isn't that why you wanted to be an actor?" Ben asked. "So that people would pay attention?"

"I don't know why I wanted to be an actor," I said. "A very little of that sort of attention goes a very long way." I realised that I was picking at the frayed welting on the chair arm.

I hadn't managed to keep looking at Ben, who finally asked harshly: "What sort of attention do you want?"

His eyes caught the firelight and burned my forehead, forcing me to look up. I trembled, overwhelmed, feeling impossibly green. "Maybe the sort of attention you don't want to give me," I said miserably, my voice breaking.

Ben leapt from his chair and was on his knees in front of me, holding my face in his hands and planting kisses on it in a flurry of amazed grateful emotions.

"I didn't think you wanted my attentions," he said, the words spilling out. "That night I came to your flat. You just wanted to get rid of me." He sat back, catching his breath, eager for my response.

"It never occurred to me you were queer," I said, shocked and shy to find myself suddenly physically entangled with a flesh and blood Ben.

My eyes overflowed and ashamed I hid them behind my fists while I tried to think of a way of demonstrating that I wasn't really crying.

But Ben pulled away my fists and started kissing my eyes.

"I love you," he said.

It was too much for me to handle: I burst into serious tears.

Ben, still kneeling, moved and somehow amused, which I didn't like, held me, my face buried in his shoulder.

"Why?" he asked. "There's no reason to cry, Daniel. Do

you still think you're the only queer in the harriers' club? Do you still think you and I are the only queers in the harriers' club?"

Curiosity about who the other queers were was almost enough to stop me crying, but I cried some more, out of leftover chagrin that I'd cried at all. How long could Ben go on loving a cry baby?

He stood up and raised me to my feet and motioned towards the bedroom. When we got to the bed I made to take off my sweater but Ben stopped me.

"Your shoes," he said, taking off his own shoes and pulling back the striped Spanish blanket he used as a bedspread.

We lay in each other's arms, bodies stretched tight against each other, feeling the beginning of our cocks' urgent stirring at the same time that I, worried that Ben hadn't already guessed it, whispered "I love you" in his ear and, exhausted, fell asleep in my lover's arms.

The first moment of waking coincided with the necessity to be naked together. But I couldn't get at Ben's clothes because of what he was doing to me. He'd already pulled off my sweater and shirt and was licking my chest, nuzzling my armpit, lapping at my nipples and then guzzling them. As he moved further down my body I made one last effort to get a hold on Ben's shirt but he threw off my hands and tore at my belt. I fell back against the pillow, for the moment giving in to my lover. But hadn't I a duty to give pleasure to Ben instead of just receiving it? He was licking my cock still inside the jockey shorts, his breath and tongue wetting the cloth until the cock showed pink through the steaming cloth. I reached down to get rid of the shorts but Ben pushed my hands away and started to suck on the head of the cock through the shorts and then pushed his tongue past the cloth to my groin. Once again I made myself submit to receiving pleasure.

When Ben at last released my cock from the shorts there was a moment of dead silence while he examined it. I was scared to keep watching him in case he looked disappointed – Peter had his reservations about my cock –

but I heard a satisfied grunt.

"You have the biggest balls I've ever seen," Ben said, sounding admiringly amazed.

I sighed with relief. I was afraid to ask what he thought of my cock, but was soon convinced that he admired that too. He relinquished a mouthful of balls long enough to say "I used to run ahead of you and look behind at your shorts, I couldn't believe what I was seeing" before he took the cock in his mouth.

It seemed to go in far further than I'd previously believed there was room in someone's mouth for it to go, but I could be unselfish no longer. I sat up, which pulled my cock out of Ben's mouth, and set about undressing him.

My only guide to giving Ben pleasure was to do to him exactly what he had done to me. I went through the movements a bit perfunctorily, dutifully, afraid of skipping anything. I knew at once that this would get better, that I had a lot to learn. The lovemaking didn't match the emotional intensity of being in love because I hadn't allowed myself to fully experience the pleasure of Ben making love to me, and so couldn't share Ben's pleasure in being made love to. But I really wanted to get down to Ben's cock, which was brown and, in my limited experience, medium-sized. It fitted perfectly in my mouth. Ben's balls seemed to be smaller than my own, but I didn't care what size his balls were.

Ben soon insisted on swinging his body round so that we could suck each other at the same time. It wasn't an exact fit: when one cock was all the way in one of our mouths the other cock couldn't get all the way in the other mouth, which had to suck and lick at the shaft and the balls of it. I forced democratic procedures on Ben: each cock got exactly the same amount of full mouth treatment and loving fondling. Once I registered Ben's slurps and grunts and moans I started making the same sounds when I was in the same position. I was slurping down on Ben's cock, cocooning it in a swimming mass of warm mucous membrane, when I felt my cock start to explode in Ben's fingers. I wallowed in my own primitive cries as I started to come, then jerked my head off Ben's cock just in time to see my own come spurting onto Ben's neck. Ben finished himself off before I could start sucking him again and came over his belly in a few seconds. The puddles of come from both our bodies looked fluorescent against his skin, which was browner than mine. We both laughed at the same moment, sighed with heartfelt relief and triumph.

"Perfect rhythm," I couldn't resist saying.

Ben was the first to move, to get a towel, because the come became cold and the bedroom air was chilly on our bodies. But I wouldn't let him go. I pulled him against me and crushed the come-splattered parts of his body against my own. It felt wet and slimy and we had to manoeuvre quickly to stop it sliding onto the sheets, but we were determined to be happy and body heat soon dried out the sliminess.

When we were warm again, heads nestling together, I said: "I love you. You're the most beautiful man in the world."

"I love you," Ben said. "You're the most beautiful man in the world. Even if you did do your best to break my heart these last few weeks."

I realised that explanations and protestations would have to wait. "It's almost my bedtime," I said.

Ben glanced at the clock, uncomprehending.

"They're sending the car for me at six in the morning," I explained. "I have time to drive home and eat and then it will be time to go to bed. I have to get up at five o'clock."

The bath that Ben ran for us was shallow because the tub was really too small for the two of us. We had to be careful not to knock our hands or elbows against the taps as we soaped each other, but we managed to stay warm by leaving on a trickle of hot water. I was sleepy again, overwhelmed by the prospect of happiness and fulfilling the duties of a lover, but beginning to be nagged by thoughts about the scene I had to play tomorrow. Ben seemed carefree, smirking and purring as I emptied warm water from my cupped hands over his head.

Towelling me dry, he placed a hand on one of my

95

cheeks, pulled it aside and firmly wiped my arse dry.

"He knows I belong to him," I thought. But I couldn't stop myself seeking reassurance as Ben walked me to the front door. "Keep the weekend free?" I asked, my voice cracking.

"From lunchtime on Saturday," Ben said, searching my eyes for the answer to a question he didn't need to ask.

✻ ✻ ✻ ✻ ✻

He showed up on Saturday afternoon in my sweater, bunched at his wrists and waist. We'd forgotten all about it on Sunday.

"I really am bringing it back," he said. "It was colder out than I thought." He made to take it off as soon as he got into the flat but I pinned down his arms and pulled our bodies together.

I could tell he'd taken a bath before he left home because his hair was still damp. He smelled soapy and un-complicated and incredibly sexy. I nuzzled past the frayed collar of the grey shirt he wore under the sweater and guzzled on his neck, my body stirring at the notion of Ben's body clothed in that particular sweater. "Keep it on," I said hoarsely. "It's not very warm in here."

Ben looked wary, a bit at a loss. I realised that both of us were frightened I'd start crying again.

"I'll make some tea," I said, kissing him on the mouth then moving to disengage.

"You look tired," Ben said, following me to the kitchen.

"I haven't got over the week," I said. "I didn't get up till nearly eleven today." I put the kettle on, looked around the cramped space for what to do next, then caught Ben's eye and grabbed him hungrily. "Oh Ben," I moaned into my lover's mouth, my body bursting with love.

Ben reached over and turned off the gas.

Our need was so great that I had no chance to apply my self-imposed rule of give and take. After the first frenzy of clinging and desperate heartfelt assurances Ben suddenly stuffed a pillow under my head and buried his cock in my mouth. I gagged once or twice but once I got the hang of Ben plunging back and forth along my tongue I started bringing myself off. Quite soon – I had no reason to expect it because Ben hadn't made any special sound – I smelled or tasted a split second of nastiness, then Ben grunted and his come spilled into my throat. I came as I swallowed the come, not wanting to taste it first in case I didn't like it. Water was spilling out of my eyes and nose. I wiped my eyes with my fists as Ben retrieved his cock, his torso looking hard and triumphant while he still loomed over me. Then I held up my arms, begging to be held, and Ben's brown body folded onto mine, wanting just as much to be loved.

"Did you ever do that before?" Ben asked as I sniffed away the liquid in my nose.

"Nobody ever came in my mouth before," I said.

"What did I taste like?" Ben urged, greedy and proprietorial.

"I hardly got a chance to taste it," I said. "It tasted sweeter than I thought it would."

Ben made a satisfied sound and kissed me in gratitude.

"I'll get a towel and make that tea," I said, other urgencies taking over. "If I don't get out of bed I won't sleep tonight. Can we eat at home tonight? Would that be all right? I could get a roast at Sainsburys, but I should go soon or there'll be nothing left."

"Anything you say," Ben said lazily.

I never knew what I was going to say to Ben: it depended on what I couldn't help letting out first under the pressure of a lifetime's things waiting to be shared. In Belfast, except for the experimental tin of Nescafe, we'd drunk nothing but tea, the pot always left stewing over a low gas until it was finally judged too strong to drink. I'd assumed that Londoners drank only coffee, but learned that tea was considered an elegant afternoon drink. Tea in bed with Ben at three in the afternoon was a comfortable proletarian drink. All this ran through my head as I made the tea, but I didn't know how to start talking about it. "How was your week?" I asked politely when we snuggled up again.

Ben sighed.

"Tell me," I insisted, and Ben shook his head as if to clear it. "Were you very busy?" I prompted.

"No. Maybe. I don't know." Ben forced himself to make sense. "It would be very easy to fool myself that I was busy, trying to make contacts and set up programs for clients who don't exist. The problem is that most of the clients who do show up are really beyond our help. They're bombsite drunks or addicts or mentally ill and looking for nothing but a handout. They already know what resources are available and if they wanted to make use of them they wouldn't come to us. So if a filthy drunk shows up it takes a disproportionate amount of time to get rid of him and he always arrives at the same time as a client I could really do something for and manages to scare her off."

"The drunks are always men and the potential real clients are always women?" I asked.

Ben smiled. "You're smart to take me up on that. Actually the falling down drunks are about two to one men to women, when they get to that final street phase. In the city at large men who are heavy drinkers seem to greatly outnumber women, but that may be because women are more likely to be secret drinkers. The clients who come to us are almost always women, though the presenting complaint is usually about their husband. He can't find work or he deserted them and won't pay child support. We can put them in touch with existing services, let them know exactly what they're entitled to, help cut through red tape. There are all sorts of pilot social service programs scattered all over London and theoretically most of our clients should qualify for some of them, but often trying to get into them turns out to be more trouble than it's worth to the client. And I have to spend a lot of time away from the settlement house just finding out what's going on elsewhere."

"It sounds very frustrating," I said sympathetically.

"And it's not the main reason we're supposed to be there," Ben said. "We're supposed to create a sense of community, organise groups where women can learn coping skills from each other to function better in the community, if there is a community amongst those bloody tenements. But that's very slow starting. And all our volunteers are coming from outside, middle-class students and housewives testing the waters for a career. We have one volunteer from the neighbourhood, a nosy narrow-minded do-gooder whom I loathe."

"So sometimes you wonder if it's worth doing?" I asked.

"Yes," Ben said. "Though I was trained not to expect fieldwork to live up to my own expectations." He pushed aside the sheet, oddly shy at being naked again. "Come on. Let's go. We don't need a car."

I persisted in trying to comfort him as we dressed, touching him as I reached past him for my clothes, as we knocked into each other, sometimes deliberately.

"The hostel for unmarried mothers certainly seems to be a success," I suggested.

"Oh yes," Ben sighed. "But by its very nature the clients aren't part of the community. They come to the hostel from other areas because their families can't bear the shame of keeping them at home. That's the difference between them and you and I, Daniel. When they have sex they pay the consequences, probably for the rest of their lives. When you and I make love it has no consequences except for the two of us."

"That doesn't mean the consequences aren't important," I said quietly. I thought of another objection: "If we got caught it would have consequences. Your career would come to an end, and that would affect you and your clients."

The shops in the High Street were ready for Christmas. I found myself enjoying the decorations' extravagant promise without cynicism or dread, perhaps for the first time since I was small.

The shoppers in the food stores were almost all women. As we queued in Sainsburys I spotted another male couple, two middle-aged men in identical sheepskin jackets. I watched the one who was taking a fussy interest in the cuts of meat until I realised his partner was watching me, and then I blanked my eyes and quickly turned away.

"Do you want a beer?" Ben asked as we passed a mews pub on the way home.

It seemed to me that we stuck out just as much in the pub, sitting at a table with our shopping bag while the regulars stood at the bar with their drinks while dinner was presumably being prepared for them by women. I thought even strong Ben's face looked paler and more fragile here, oppressed by unspoken judgments. But as I looked at him I began to burn with thoughts of Ben in his jockey shorts, white against his skin. I thought of stealing a pair to snuggle up to on the nights he wasn't with me.

"Cheers!" Ben said, knocking his mug against mine. "Why was *your* week so bad?"

"Not bad," I said. "Hard. I rang you on Tuesday and Wednesday night, but there was no answer."

"Let's see. Tuesday night I had to give a report to the committee. Wednesday night I gave a talk to Gillian's unmarried mothers."

"What do you say to them?" I asked.

"The one thing they all want to know is what men will think of them. They're almost all giving up the baby, so they want to know if they should tell any future man in their life what they did."

"So you have to pretend to be normal and explain what you'd prefer if they were your girlfriend?"

"No," Ben said. "I suppose I do have to pretend to be normal, but all I do is lay out the options they have, and the possible psychological consequences."

"Does Gillian know you're queer?" I asked.

"She doesn't *know* I'm queer because we've never talked about it. I don't know what she *thinks*. I think she has other things to think about. She's being psychoanalyzed on the National Health to discover why she wants to do this kind of work. So far only about six people have ever managed to get psychoanalyzed on the National Health."

I'd started to feel jealous about all those women thinking Ben was normal; I'd have felt more secure if Gillian knew that Ben was queer.

"You still haven't told me why your week was so hard,"

100

Ben reminded me.

"I was miserable because I didn't get a chance to talk to you," I admitted. "I started to think I'd imagined you."

Ben nodded, in his eyes a mixture of lust and approval that I was learning to talk to him. He tried to give me the gift of reassurance: "I never have to wonder whether I imagined you," he said, and then his face darkened as he realised he'd reached a point of no return. He went on almost resentfully: "I only have to look at my collection of Daniel Henry press cuttings."

I couldn't believe my ears.

He checked over his shoulder to make sure we couldn't be overheard. "I've had the hots for you ever since the first time I saw you on a run," Ben confessed, pretending to be resentful. "Did you really think I wouldn't keep the pictures that were there every time I opened a newspaper?"

"Then I want a photo of you," I said.

"I'll get you one. But you're going to be seeing plenty of me. You won't need a photograph."

"I had to work so hard," I complained as we started back to the flat. "On Monday I was in a rosy glow after Sunday with you. I was actually stopping to talk to people on the set. I couldn't talk about you, but I could talk about the weather. And then I realised my work was being affected. I wasn't focused. I'm going to get this terrible reputation for being distant and swollen-headed. But if I don't stay in character, whichever of these characters I'm playing, and don't keep up with what my other character is supposed to be feeling, I get completely lost. I won't fake it. Do you know I have a double who sometimes plays one of my characters in a scene and sometimes plays the other? They vary the scenes by sometimes shooting the back of my double's head. That's worse than talking to thin air, because he's forty years old, with this wig that's made to look like my hair. So when I'm acting with him I have to blank him out before I can imagine me standing there playing my other character."

Ben seemed lost for words. "The perils of being an actor," he said inadequately when I finally stopped talking.

Ben insisted on peeling the potatoes that were to go in with the roast, although two people filled every inch of the tiny kitchen. I thought I'd been thinking only about how happy I was, but I heard myself start up again.

"It's a smaller film than I thought it would be. There are a lot of close-ups, which are cheaper and easier for Cliff to do than the process work. I expected it to be more visually sweeping somehow. But every scene in any film always feels quite small when you're in it. Maybe it will look bigger on the screen. There are some scenes I wish were smaller. I had to walk all the way across an Oxford quadrangle having this animated conversation with somebody who wasn't there."

Ben's neck looked red; I suddenly was certain that my lover was going to walk out on me, exasperated with having to listen to self-absorbed nonsense about making films. When I opened the oven door to put in the roast the blast of heat sent both of us reeling back, but we had only each other to fall against.

I quickly shut the door. "We're done."

Ben walked away while I cleaned up the counter.

I found him on the sofa in front of the TV, which was on, though Ben was leafing through the paper. I sat in an armchair, to give him some room, and kept checking on him out of the corner of my eye while I pretended to watch the box. What was he thinking? What was happening between us at this moment – if anything? The silence lasted long enough, and was tiring enough, for me to start paying attention to the TV.

"What are you doing over there?" Ben asked when he'd finished with the paper.

I gave him a hard look to make sure he wanted what I thought he wanted, then leapt out of my chair and dove onto the sofa, landing my face in Ben's lap. I rooted and buried my face in the sweater, digging my hands behind Ben's back.

"How do you like it?" Ben asked.

"What?" I asked, worried again that I'd seem slow-witted.

"Your meat," Ben said.

The only way we roasted meat in Ulster was to reduce it to half its original size, with a delicious burnt shell.

"Well cooked," I ventured.

"Good," Ben said. "So do I." He fiddled gently with my hair. "What's wrong?"

"Nothing," I said too quickly. Then, after reburying my face, feeding on Ben's warmth, I raised my head.

He was looking mildly disbelieving.

"I'm afraid you'll get bored listening to me talk about acting," I said. "I think you'd rather talk about world revolution."

Ben rearranged the position of his upper body to lay his chin against the top of my head, kissing it briefly. "Don't you know you're a shining example of how I'd like society to be? Real art will be important in the world revolution, far more basic to society than the ridiculous Shaftesbury Avenue comedies that milk laughter from superficial class differences. I'd like everyone to be allowed to achieve their potential without the help of money or connections."

I'd later suspect, though I never dared say it, that Ben distrusted the ability of the British worker to run the country and was secretly glad that total revolution seemed likely to confine itself to Eastern Europe and the third world. It took me a long time to raise with Ben the issue of the international brotherhood's hostility to homosexuals.

Meanwhile, I took comfort in basking against my lover's belly. Learning a little more about Ben only revealed how little I knew. Being in love was hard work.

❋ ❋ ❋ ❋ ❋

At the *William Wilson* wrap party I felt profoundly unreal, forced to emerge from inside my head into a world whose rules I didn't control. I'd made no friends during the filming, had stayed remarkably withdrawn during the interminable hours of waiting for shots to be set up. I gulped at my drink as Cliff made a thank you speech that moved fairly methodically up the hierarchy of talent involved in the production. But he had no words of praise for me. Instead he called on me to speak, and I, unprepared, was forced to speak the truth.

"Is this what it's like to be an actor?" I asked, forcing myself to throw my shoulders back instead of huddling over my glass. "This feeling of total unreality when the film is over?" I put a hand behind me to steady myself against a table, missed, and for a moment seemed about to fall over. I heard uncertain laughter, perhaps not all sympathetic.

"Is this the price we pay for creating a satisfactory illusion? I realise that I know hardly any of you except as the characters you play or in the essential tasks you perform, and that's because I've been working so hard at getting to know the two William Wilsons."

The little speech was judged to be charming or pretentious, depending on how much you liked me. People were no easier to talk to afterwards. I felt as if I was emerging from another performance.

In the car that drove me home for the last time I curled up in the back seat and watched through tinted glass as a foreign world performed its mysterious manoeuvres.

That was on a Thursday. On Friday at noon, while I sat up in bed eating scrambled eggs like a patient at the beginning of a long convalescence, Cliff phoned and told me I was needed back at the studio on Monday to redo some of the process shots. I threw the tray on the floor and curled up under the blanket again, trembling with rage I was too exhausted to let out.

Ben took one look at me on Saturday and insisted on driving me into the country for dinner. We ate in silence, commenting only on the food and the other diners, as if we'd been together twenty years. As soon as we got home I needed to lie down, and promptly fell asleep. I woke up on Sunday morning with no memory of Ben undressing me.

During the retakes, which spilled over into Tuesday, then Wednesday, I could only concentrate on the movements I was required to make. The characters had died in me.

✼ ✼ ✼ ✼ ✼

Ben told me to take a holiday, but he couldn't afford to take time off himself, and I wouldn't go without him.

"Why don't you go back to Belfast for a week?" Ben asked.

"I can't do that," I said.

He couldn't press me because he didn't like to talk about his own parents, who were divorced. All I knew was that his mother had remarried and lived in York, and his father was bitterly disappointed by his son's choice of a career, which he considered a job for a do-gooder spinster.

I'd given Ben a key to my flat, where he now stayed every weekend (I'd told him it would be bad for his career if I was seen to be staying overnight at the settlement house) and at least one night a week now that filming was over.

"You're the one who's quiet now," I said over Saturday dinner. I looked for the cause in myself. "I know I've been impossible these last few weeks."

"Not impossible," Ben said. "I was worried about you. You're tough, but I thought you were going to crack under the strain. You've rebounded amazingly well."

I doubted if I was so tough, but pride made me accept Ben's assessment. "It was necessary strain. No matter how seriously you take a role, on top of everything you still have to look almost as if you're walking through it. Otherwise on film it comes across as too much."

When we met again at the flat after a day or two apart our bodies would clamp together and we'd begin to undress each other, taking the other's hunger for granted. When we got into bed at the end of a day we'd spent together we had to pay more attention to what the other wanted – sometimes we'd spent so much time making love earlier that the touch of the other's skin felt painful. We'd learned what signs to respond to: the length of kisses, a proprietary arm trapping the other's chest, a cock's thrust against the thigh.

Tonight Ben moved so purposefully that he hardly waited for my responses. We committed the full length of our bodies to each other, reaffirming all our promises, then Ben straddled my chest and pulled my mouth over his cock. I'd learned to tease the underside with my tongue while I sucked, but I'd hardly got going when Ben pulled out and went down on me. I moved to swing round so that we could suck each other, but Ben stopped me with a hand on my chest. I knew he had a different purpose in mind tonight because he gave my cock only a few efficient sucks and then he moved down to my balls and groin. Again he moved on quickly. He pushed against my hamstrings with the palms of his hands and licked the seam of skin between my balls and my arsehole, and then his tongue started exploring the hole itself. If it had been any other tongue I'd have been busy forcing myself to pretend I wasn't shocked and disgusted. Since it was Ben's tongue the act had to be good. It took only moments of observing my arsehole being licked before I allowed myself to feel it. As the tip of Ben's tongue teased then probed deeper inside me I discovered an urgent need I'd never imagined existed. I wanted to open up more of my insides to Ben's tongue and had to force myself not to because I was afraid I'd fart. My bottom was getting cold sticking up in the air, except for that tender previously ignored and shameful area that was so warm and wet, revealed to another man and taken care of by him.

Ben sat back on his haunches. "Turn over," he said.

I obeyed immediately, giving Ben a grateful look. If I lay on my stomach Ben might be able to get his tongue further inside me. My lover's face was red and his eyes spilled the way my eyes spilled when he pushed his cock down my throat. I stretched out on my stomach, my head sideways on the pillow, and Ben covered me with his body, pulling the clothes over both of us. The warmth made my gratitude overflow.

"I love you, Ben."

Ben nuzzled the back of my neck. "I love you, Daniel." But he sounded preoccupied. His cock lay along the base of my spine, and I pushed up against it to feel closer as I kissed Ben's hand on the pillow beside me. He raised his body on one elbow and reached down with one hand – maybe to push off his socks, though I thought he'd already taken them off. Then he sat up completely, leaving me cold again. I gave a humorous complaining moan. I heard a pressured squelch and Ben pushed something cold and wet against my arsehole. I tensed, then right away made myself relax, wanting to show Ben that I trusted him. I snuggled one side of my face against the pillow, showing the other side to Ben as he pushed a wet finger into my arsehole, working it in and pushing against the sides. I gave a little yelp as Ben pulled his finger out and my arsehole closed with a pop. By the time I heard more of the pressured squelch maybe I guessed what was coming, from old appalled jokes and disgusted speculation about what homos did. But I still wasn't certain what was happening. The speculations I half-acknowledged to myself suddenly seemed unfounded, because Ben gathered the bedclothes around his shoulders and fell down on top of me again. I got ready to snuggle gratefully. But he didn't come down completely. He stopped halfway, leaning on one elbow. I felt his hand brush my bottom, his knuckles pushing the cheeks aside, and then pressure against my arsehole, as if Ben was somehow trying to push it in on itself.

Ben seemed to pull away – I couldn't really tell what he was doing – and then I felt my arsehole probed by a slick object that pushed through my insides.

I cried out and raised my head in panic but the probe was relentless, pushing through me like metal, opening me up far more than I could possibly endure before it suddenly stopped. My arsehole was completely plugged with Ben's cock, inside me before I was certain what it was. It didn't feel like his cock, it felt like a heavy foreign object. I only knew it was his cock from the position of Ben's legs against my body and the feel of his balls pressed against my balls. I didn't start to tremble until I was absolutely certain what he was doing to me. I opened my mouth to cry out again and then Ben's face came down to me, kissing my ears and neck, and he pushed his hands under my chest – though not until he was certain that our lower bodies were firmly anchored.

"It's all right," he crooned. "Just lie still. Relax. I love you. Beautiful Daniel. I love beautiful Daniel."

I lay frozen, scared to move, but my eyes filled with tears, because Ben loved me and because I felt uniquely vulnerable.

"Beautiful Daniel." Ben flexed his cock and I grunted: my insides felt so crammed and raw that a pulse in the cock felt like a sudden stab.

"Just relax. I won't hurt you." Ben moved his upper body to cover more of me, warming my shoulders, covering my neck with kisses.

"I've wanted to be inside you for so long," he murmured, then seemed impelled to confess more. "I was scared to start anything while you were making the film because you were so close to the edge. You were so fragile I was scared you'd break." Ben's voice broke as he finally let himself complain: "You were like a stranger."

I groaned. "I thought you knew," I said in a small voice that was all I could summon, "you were what got me through it. I thought I saw you deliberately giving me strength."

In an enthusiasm of loving gratitude Ben shifted to kiss my face and his cock shifted inside me, making me yelp.

"I'm sorry, Daniel, I'm sorry."

I lay still, assessing what was happening to my body before I committed myself. "Actually that was more of a yelp about what I expected to feel when you moved. I don't think it hurt so much that time."

"It shouldn't hurt at all," Ben murmured ardently.

I took the initiative. "You stay still and let me –" I'd realised that for both of us to lie still was not what this activity was about. Very gingerly, I bore down on Ben's cock. But I never got a chance to find out how that movement would feel by itself because Ben couldn't resist thrusting a little deeper up inside me.

I grunted, a little more happily. I felt as if my lower body had been spiked on a thick blunt object that was crushed against my tenderest parts. But I wasn't in pain – I felt threatened because my body seemed on the *verge* of massive invasive pain.

108

Ben needed no more encouragement. He anchored my hips with his hands then began thrusting inside me, but with our bodies locked so tightly that he seemed to be pushing along with me rather than thrusting his cock any deeper. I couldn't feel any more invaded, because my arsehole was already full. But I gritted my teeth, soon using my grunts and squeaks to tell Ben to finish, because the pounding made my arsehole feel raw and about to split around his cock.

Then Ben gave a thrust that made me shout and see red, then he shouted and froze. I wasn't sure, but thought that perhaps I felt Ben's come spurting against my insides. He collapsed on me, showering my shoulders with kisses and then lying still, his heart thudding.

Both our watches were ticking furiously. The pressure and pain were gone. I felt drained – I'd been through an arduous ordeal – but my arsehole now felt just pleasantly full of a part of my lover, the rest of whose body surrounded my body, glued to it by a light sweat. I was even able to push against Ben's cock to feel it still inside me. I wasn't sure if I was up to letting Ben put me through this every night of our lives.

I'd have liked even more gratitude from Ben, who seemed to have fallen asleep, his hands on the pillow on either side of my head. But his regular breathing suddenly stopped and his body jerked, his startled head rearing. When he knew where he was he kissed the back of my head.

"We need a towel," he said. He raised himself on his hands and in one slow smooth movement pulled his cock out of me. It felt as if he was pulling my insides out after it. I gasped and cried, stunned by the movement while it lasted, but it lasted only a long moment. While Ben went to the bathroom I was left to feel empty. My body was already cold by the time he returned with a hot wet towel. He laid it across my bottom, and pushed it into the crack, using a finger to wipe it against the arsehole.

After he gave my bottom a last wipe he pretended to examine the towel. "No blood," he said teasingly. "Are you sure you were a virgin, Daniel?"

109

Already cold and empty, I felt demeaned and abandoned. I pulled the bedclothes over me while Ben took the towel back to the bathroom. When he climbed back into bed I made no move to meet the body that wrapped itself around me to steal my warmth.

Ben, sleepy and exhausted, took a little time to get the message. "It'll start to get much easier," he whispered in my ear. "I wouldn't want to hurt my baby for all the world."

"Why should you care if you weren't the first?" I asked harshly into the pillow.

"What?" Ben asked, starting to wake up.

"Why should you care if you weren't the first?" I repeated, miserably trying to shrug off my lover's body.

"I thought I was the first," Ben said, bewildered. He tightened his hold on my arms and chest. "What are you saying?"

"That was the first time that ever happened to me in my life," I complained, "and you made a joke out of it."

Ben sighed with relief. "Oh Daniel." He leaned over and kissed my face. "I know I was the first. I'm sorry. I didn't mcan to spoil it."

I considered holding out for more reassurances, but saw no future in it. I turned around and delivered myself to Ben's body.

"I love my baby more than anything else in the whole world," Ben whispered.

"I love you too, Ben," I said, and arranged my chin on top of his head to go to sleep.

He had an afterthought: "If you ever let anybody else do that to you I'll kill both of you."

"I'll never let anyone else do anything to me," I vowed sleepily.

When I went to the bathroom next morning my arsehole seemed to be tightly pushed in on itself. Nothing came out, but I wiped it anyway and learned how sore it was. All I'd managed to eject was a light brown cream that looked as if it came mostly from Ben. Later that morning, when I landed more heavily than usual leaping over a ditch, I felt a sharp contraction. It didn't worry me: I was merely discovering

110

the unaccustomed aftereffects of what I'd done to give my lover pleasure.

Ben usually stayed at the flat until Monday unless he had an unusually early meeting. When we went to bed that night, after we'd lain quietly together long enough to get the reassurance each of us always needed from the other's body, that it was still generously loving, that it wouldn't go away, I said dutifully, though I wasn't sure my arsehole was up to it: "You can do it again, you know."

Ben kissed my forehead: "My baby needs a rest. Is it sore?"

"A little bit," I admitted.

"It'll be better by tomorrow," Ben promised.

By Monday my arsehole no longer felt tender and my bowel movements had returned to normal.

We arranged to see each other on Wednesday night. Without discussing it we were sticking to the weekends plus one night a week schedule that had worked while I was filming. But now I had time on my hands for the first time since I met Ben. I'd started classes again with Julian and told Beryl I was ready to audition again, though now I wanted to be more selective, and definitely wanted to do a play. But I had no work prospects. I didn't *want* to work. I had so little energy that I thought I might be sick, except that I started each weekday morning with an hour's run in one of the parks.

On Monday I drove into the country to try out the three-year-old Austin-Healey Sprite I'd just bought. In the dark drizzling weather all I wanted was to find some place warm to eat before starting back in time to miss the rush hour. On Tuesday morning Beryl's secretary phoned to offer me comp theatre tickets for that night. Ben was free, but we parted after the play because he had an early meeting.

On Wednesday night I had dinner ready before Ben arrived, except for the vegetables he was bringing from his garden at the settlement house. He'd never been late before. He answered the phone immediately when I phoned his private number.

111

"Dinner's ready," I complained.

"What?" Ben's voice was high-pitched and flustered.

"Dinner's ready," I said.

"I thought you cancelled tonight because we went out last night," Ben said.

My temper flared. "I cancelled nothing. We didn't spend the night together."

"I can't come round tonight," Ben said. "Or maybe later. I'll try to call you later."

"Don't bother," I yelled, slamming down the phone. And immediately regretted it, because I was left to myself, so I got angrier at Ben for making me angry. How could he think last night counted as one of our nights when we hadn't slept together? I thought of him carefully allotting a portion of each week to me, so uneager to see me that our time together could never be expanded.

Dinner, a *carbonnade de boeuf* that I'd made for the first time, tasted good. I ate more than usual and shovelled the salad I'd made for two into my mouth while I stared sightlessly at the TV. I left the flat immediately after dinner with one purpose in mind: not to be there when Ben phoned, which he surely would.

By the time I got back from the cinema I'd cooled down, had reckoned that not losing Ben was worth abject apologies for losing my temper. Then I started feeling hurt again because Ben wasn't waiting for me at the flat, because the phone didn't ring immediately I came in the door. The moment I crawled into bed I dialled Ben's number. The longer it rang unanswered the angrier I got, until finally I banged down the receiver, my eyes brimming. I could be alone again; Daniel Henry didn't need anyone.

Next morning, convinced that I'd been abandoned, I got out of the flat early, hurrying in case Ben phoned and proved me wrong. I spent the morning at the V & A, lunched at the *Salisbury*, so busy redesigning my prospects that I forgot to notice who else was there, then went to a film I knew Ben would want to see with me.

He phoned soon after I got home.

I pretended my heart hadn't leapt. "Hello," I said coldly.

"I've been ringing you all day," Ben said. "I rang you twice last night. Where were you?"

"Out," I said.

"Stop it, Daniel," Ben ordered. "Stop it. Right now. Do you hear me?"

I stopped myself banging down the receiver. "Yes," I said, my voice cracking. My own obedience astounded me. There was a silence that I wanted to rush to fill, but I didn't want to admit I'd been totally stupid.

"I told you I was sorry about last night," Ben complained. "I meant it. Do you understand?"

"Yes," I said before I had time to think about it. "I'm sorry too. Where were you?"

"I'll tell you when I see you on Saturday," Ben said.

Friday's *Evening Standard* contained a photograph of Ben, heartbreakingly earnest and handsome, and an interview about the unmarried mothers hostel. Thank goodness, I thought. Now I can pretend he's as famous as me.

Although Ben had a key he always rang the bell when he arrived at the flat and waited for me to open the door. He showed up on Saturday looking mischievous as well as stern, as if he wanted to be lighthearted but knew he might have some work to do. I felt sheepish: I trusted him not to remind me I'd been jealous and difficult, but I kept reminding myself.

We seemed to come to independent agreement about the easiest way to break the tension between us. Ten minutes after Ben arrived he was fucking me again.

This time I knew what to expect and wanted it, but I still dreaded Ben pushing into my arsehole. The moment he started to push into me I tensed and opened my mouth to cry out for him to wait. But he was already inside me. The only pain I felt was the memory of the moment's thrust through tender tissue, though I felt as if I wanted to shit. I lay pinned, silent, astounded, while Ben waited for a sign that he could start serious fucking.

Having him inside me opened up my emotions. "I'm sorry I was such a baby," I apologised into the pillow.

Ben replied by flexing his cock, which pulled an

113

immediate grunt out of me.

"You've got to learn to trust me," Ben said, and didn't wait for confirmation before he pushed his knees between my legs and began working resolutely towards his goal. The second time seemed to take less time, though he still reduced me to helpless squawks and gurgles as he thrust harder towards his climax. This time, moments after he came, Ben worried about me coming. I knew how to take care of it. I lifted my arsehole – making sure Ben stayed inside me – high enough to slide a hand onto my cock. It took twenty seconds before I squirted onto my fingers, and then I let Ben's weight push me flat against the bed again.

"Did you see the *Standard*?" Ben asked as we drowsed in each other's arms.

"What about the *Standard*?" I asked, sounding perfectly casual.

I felt Ben blinking with disappointment.

"There was a –"

But I couldn't stop myself laughing, and knew my shaking body would give me away. I exploded into Ben's armpit: "Of course I saw the *Standard*. The picture was beautiful. Don't dare answer any of the fan letters even if they pretend to be interested in social work. Though I don't understand why she interviewed you instead of Gillian, since it was about the hostel."

"The pecking order," Ben said. "It would have caused Gillian more trouble than it was worth if she'd let herself be singled out instead of the warden."

"How did they find out about you?"

"I phoned them," Ben said nonchalantly. "We need all the help we can get."

"Good for you." But I couldn't resist tormenting him. "Even *I* don't ring up newspapers asking for publicity."

"You don't have to," Ben said. "They're a lot more interested in actors than in settlement houses."

I got out of bed and brought him my scrapbook with the *Standard* piece about him already pasted alongside the early *William Wilson* interviews. "Now it's *our* scrapbook."

One Saturday afternoon Maryann Macready phoned to invite me to a party the next day. Only after I said I'd be there and asked if I could bring a friend did Maryann say, as if it were an afterthought but in a small voice that thrilled with triumph: "I want you to meet my husband." Next day's papers contained a pale smudged photograph of the young star and her childhood sweetheart Gary Sloat, the manager of a building firm.

I asked Ben if he'd like to drive us to the party in the Sprite, ostensibly to let him try it out, really because I got nervous at the thought of having his life in my hands.

Maryann's modest new flat was three streets away from her parents' house. When she pointed him out across the room her husband looked like an awkward public school boy in his dark grey suit and mop of red hair; when I went up to him he seemed more like a working-class tough who didn't even know how to handle congratulations. The hand that crunched mine had been scrubbed raw in an attempt to remove the dirt.

"Were you really childhood sweethearts?" I asked. "Or did the *Standard* make that up?"

"I grew up down the road," Gary said with a directness that made me think he was merely feeling intensely out of place in his own home. He turned away to his mates and I had no more contact with him.

The party was a family affair with several small children, no other actors, and only Beryl and the director and script-girl from Maryann's new film representing the profession. I introduced Ben to Beryl with a pride that announced I had a life worth living quite apart from the work she might arrange for me, and left them together while I went to congratulate Mr. and Mrs. Fawcett. But Maryann intercepted me, looking full of a secret she might be persuaded to divulge. She wore a shiny peach frock that looked wrong in ways I couldn't begin to analyse, but her face had lost its pudginess and her skin and hair had come to life.

"We've lived here three months," she said, apologising

115

for the half-furnished rooms, "but I've been so busy."

"What did your parents think about you not being married?"

"Officially I was living alone. But I wouldn't go to bed with Gary unless he was living with me. So he moved in with his suitcase one Friday night and I spent most of the night in my nightgown in the bushes next to the back entrance."

"What if someone had seen you?" I cried, shocked and delighted. "You're a film star!"

"I know everyone would have thought I was doing it for publicity, but I was terrified." She paused, then decided to make a confession. "I was a virgin." She gave a wry little shrug, searching my face as if she expected me to call her a liar. "Gary was so disgusted he left me to it, but then he got worried and came down to get me. He said someone would call the police and that persuaded me. But halfway up the back stairs I thought of *sexual intercourse* again and got frightened again and ran back to the bushes. My teeth were chattering and my feet were filthy and finally I got so cold that I thought that if I went to bed with him I'd at least get warm. Next morning his parents told my mother and father we were living together, and that started another crisis. I began to wonder if it was all worth it."

Maryann told her story with more sparkle and wit than usual, but she still sounded abstracted, as if she were summarising the plot of someone else's life. "Is Ben your boyfriend?" she asked suddenly, politely demanding one confidence for another.

I blushed violently. "Yes."

She waited, her look urging me to tell more.

I wanted to share very little of what I felt for Ben. "He's the warden of a settlement house," I said proudly. "He's made me the happiest man in the world."

"He's beautiful," Maryann said with cool enthusiasm.

I found myself talking to Gary's sister Dorothy, who frankly confessed to being one of my fans. "My girlfriends and I couldn't take our eyes off you in *Boxing Day Hill*. We kept on at Maryann to introduce you to us. We always thought she was going to marry you." As she talked she had to work continuously to keep grumpy three-year-old twins in check. "I admire you," she said. "You know what you want and how to get it."

I decided it was part of my duty not to spoil her illusions. It was time to go home and re-establish what was important to me. As I moved through a group of people towards Ben, I just missed the impact of a blow to my stomach. It stopped short of hitting me because the man who aimed it – either Dorothy's husband or Gary's brother, both of whose faces were twisted unnaturally away from me when I looked around to see who'd tried to hit me – hadn't been able to use a full range of motion in case he was observed.

As I started the car I told Ben what had happened. "Why?" I asked. "Why did they want to beat me up?"

"They envy you," Ben said sadly. "They knew everybody was thinking you'd be a much more suitable match for Maryann."

"But I wouldn't be," I protested. "I'm queer. They have no reason to envy me. I come from a worse background than they do. So much for your workers' solidarity. What's your theory for dealing with that kind of attack?"

"In any society that's still based on privilege," Ben said rather wearily, "there's only one way that doesn't make matters worse. Talk to them. Let them know who you really are."

"Why should it be my responsibility to educate thugs? I'd like to see them behind bars."

"You don't really mean that," Ben said.

"Yes I do."

It was clear to both of us that I was going to get angry at Ben for not taking my side, so he tried to distract me. "I liked Beryl. She'd read the *Standard* piece. She was really interested in the settlement house."

"Beryl is interested in nothing but the business," I snapped.

"I think you're wrong," Ben said gently. "By the way, Gary really is one of the workers. He's a labourer. He isn't

117

a manager and never has been."

"You're kidding," I said, starting to enjoy myself again. "Maryann really does like a bit of rough."

"When's the baby due?" Ben asked.

I was slow on the uptake. "What baby? You don't –No!"

"Yes!" Ben said. "Of course she's pregnant."

"How do you know? What makes you think so?"

"It's obvious. You must have been the only one in that room who didn't know Maryann is pregnant."

I flushed. I still didn't enjoy Ben thinking I was ever less than omniscient. To prove that I was trusted with extraordinarily intimate information, not common gossip, I started to tell Ben the story of Maryann in her nightgown in the bushes.

*****

David, a psychologist friend of Ben's, had arranged for an influential psychiatrist to meet four queer men in the hope of persuading him to back a change in the law. "The only homosexuals he meets are patients with mental problems," David explained.

"He must move in a very small circle," I said smartly.

The other guinea pigs were also a couple, a clerk and a schoolteacher from Streatham, three or four years older than me. I warmed to them instantly because the lives they lived were what I could once have reasonably looked forward to. I guessed the intimate details of the two men's lives, how much they could afford to spend on food and clothes, though they largely ignored me, as if I belonged to another world. Ben drew a warmer response from them. I'd grown used to seeing people who were wary of me relaxing with Ben. He never seemed to have to do anything to earn it.

The room in Golders Green, lit only by table lamps, could have been in the desert or an East End slum. Tapestries on the walls disguised its true shape and location. I had to fight myself not to feel like a patient. The psychiatrist was tense, weighted by responsibility. Though his face seemed to lighten in recognition when he saw me, he could give me no special acknowledgment, since David introduced us by our first names only. The psychiatrist's wife, the sister of the most famous violinist in the world, served mugs of vegetarian stew and glasses of beer, then left us alone.

I wondered how willingly the psychiatrist had been drawn into this exercise – he seemed to wish he was somewhere else. He volunteered nothing and let David do the work while he watched us with what looked like impatience or distaste. David, his skin and hair beginning to be bleached by age, was scrupulous, tired, and slightly prissy. I thought no one ought to be so lonely, have to strive so hard to overcome the prejudice of strangers, on behalf of strangers.

David threw out questions from a list he'd written down, letting whoever wanted be the first to answer, trying to get everyone to make some attempt to answer every question.

"I didn't really admit what I was until I finished at LSE," Ben said. "I always had girlfriends while I was a student. I knew it wasn't enough somehow, but I was very hide-bound. I didn't want my contemporaries to know what was really going on inside me."

I loved it when Ben admitted to being vulnerable, but I could only show it by giving him a quick glance, my eyes starting to brim. Howard and Robert, the other couple, were sitting close together on a sofa, thighs and hands brushing. I sensed that Ben didn't want that kind of demonstration from me: it seemed redundant, a show put on for the others.

"Then the summer I graduated I discovered queer pubs," Ben said. "Once I knew how to find what I wanted I allowed myself to admit what I wanted."

"I think I could very easily have turned out normal," I agreed quickly. "There were two girls at school I had all kinds of exotic fantasies about. 'Pillowed upon my fair love's ripening breast,' that kind of thing. I was definitely thinking about the breast of one of the girls, if I could get her to go up Cave Hill with me. But both of them turned

119

me down, on the same day. I always wanted middle-class girls, and I was too poor for them. But I also think I've been queer since I was five years old. I caused a scandal by trying to get Frankie, the little boy next door, to put my penis in his mouth. 'It wasn't me,' I insisted when they caught me. 'Don't you remember, Frankie? I saw you down the entry with that other boy, but it wasn't me.'"

David was fidgeting, but the psychiatrist caught him. "Please," he said, holding up a hand. "Let's call a – spade a spade."

"I had these feverish fantasies about peeing in his mouth," I added, encouraged.

"I've always known I was a qu – homosexual," Howard said. "I was never interested in girls." After a pause, at a loss for anything else, he appealed to his lover: "I know he's the same."

"Yes," Robert said. "I've always known I was a homosexual."

Ben took it upon himself to tackle the unspoken agenda of the meeting. "Every individual should have the right to determine his own destiny without the artificial restraints of what society says is right at that particular time in history," he argued. "It's society that's sick, not homosexuals. People who call us sick are uneducated people. They have a very limited historical perspective."

"My parents hate queers," Robert said. "They go on and on about what ought to be done to queers when something appears in the papers or on the telly."

"But his parents love me," Howard said.

"They love him," Robert said. "They gave us furniture for our flat, though they don't want to visit us. They always remember his birthday and he's always invited for Christmas. His own parents don't want to know him. They found a book he was reading and he'd have been living in the street if he hadn't had his Aunt Iris to take him in."

"I feel normal," I said, "and I also feel queer. Queer is normal for me. All the things I've been discovering about sex with Ben seem totally natural to me. They're things that have been waiting inside me, waiting to be uncovered. But lately I've been very conscious of what people think of me as a queer. Well, I always was. Where I grew up it was the worst deadly sin. It was so terrible people got upset even when they joked about it. I'm really conscious of what most people really think of queers. What upsets me is that there's not much I can do about it, except perhaps what we're doing tonight. You can't start an angry confrontation every time somebody says something nasty about queers."

"Why not?" Ben asked sharply.

"All right," I said. "Maybe you can. You start it and I'll back you up."

"I think the trouble is that we're not courageous enough," Ben said. "We know there's nothing wrong with what we do. But nobody who grows up in our society can help incorporating the message that homosexuals are sick. So we have to fight that ingrained belief every moment of our lives, even though we know that what we're doing is perfectly natural."

I enjoyed arguing with him in public. "That can have its good side. I've learned not to believe a word anybody tells me about anything. If they can be wrong about something so important to me as being queer, they can be wrong about everything else."

Ben nodded approvingly. "Being queer can be a revolutionary act."

David had a question he needed answered for himself. "How long do you think you'll be together as couples?" he asked, though he must have known what we'd say.

"I hope Howard and I will be together the rest of our lives," Robert said. "If he can put up with me."

"I'd want to kill myself if I didn't have Robert," Howard said.

I blushed as soon as I opened my mouth. "Ben is the most important thing in my life. He's far more important to me than my career, though I'm sure he doesn't believe that."

The declarations of love brought the meeting to an abrupt end. The psychiatrist and David glanced at each other and nodded.

I forced myself to speak. "There's something I'd like to

121

say. I don't know how to say it."

"You'll think of a way," David said gently, and everyone laughed.

I pressed on, blushing all the more. "If indeed being queer is normal human behaviour, and it's society that's wrong, then there's something peculiar about what we've been doing here."

Ben nodded and smiled and shook his head, recognising what I was going to say. I realised that my lover was proud of me.

"We've been on our very best behaviour," I said. "It's as if David handpicked us to find homosexual specimens who would tell you what we thought you wanted to hear. So we all have respectable jobs, except perhaps for me, and we all have faithful relationships. None of us are queens or thieves or compulsively promiscuous. We don't fiddle with little boys. But if homosexuals are as normal as everyone else, then we have as much right to be promiscuous as normal people, and as much right to be unemployed, and as much right to have emotional problems. We shouldn't have to be on our best behaviour all the time just to prove that society is wrong about us."

"Hear! Hear!" Ben said softly.

For the first time the psychiatrist looked as if he might be about to argue, but he let it go. He politely shook hands with each of us, offering no reassurances.

"That was strictly a one-way street," I complained outside the house. "I felt like a lab specimen. How would he like it if the tables were turned and we treated him like that?"

Ben had met Ronnie Laing and was unimpressed by orthodox psychiatry. "Psychiatrists don't dare engage in discussion except with each other. Their opinions are based on Freudian mumbo jumbo that couldn't survive scientific scrutiny. But they've been given this power to hurt us."

I invited everyone back for a drink, but only David accepted; the invitation seemed to panic Robert and Howard, who scurried away.

"I liked them," I said as we headed for our cars, knowing I would probably never meet the couple again.

"They almost split up recently," David said. "They came to see me about some problems they were having. I discovered the wrong one was playing the passive role in bed."

I'd not yet learned to apply such an analysis to sexual matters. Ben caught the suddenly enlightened speculative look on my face and frowned and looked preoccupied.

"David ought to be shot," he said that night as we jockeyed for space in the bathroom. "He should know better than to reveal what two clients told him in confidence."

"I talked too much," I said. "Did I talk too much?"

"You're always going to talk," Ben said impatiently. "You need to get used to who you are and accept it."

"I'm shy without you," I objected. "It's being with you that gives me confidence."

Ben didn't look convinced.

❋❋❋❋❋

Ben asked if Gillian could spend Christmas Day with us.

"Of course," I said, trying to hide my disappointment. "We'll have to watch how we behave in front of her."

At the last minute Gillian softened towards her family and chose to go home for Christmas. Ben and I had four days alone together, which was exactly what I wanted. I felt we never had enough time together, particularly time to do nothing. Ben always had one foot in the wider world, but I'd stopped thinking about the things I was missing if I stayed at home.

I bought Ben two pullovers for Christmas, one from Harrods, one from Jaeger. Ben bought me *The Decline of the West*, which we planned to discuss critically, and a biography of a French avant-garde actor. Without telling him I bought and decorated a Christmas tree on Christmas Eve morning. We'd arranged to meet that evening at a small party at Julian's. The tree was waiting, already lit, when we got back to the flat. I watched Ben's face as we walked through the door. He saw the tree and smiled, delighted to be home.

I made sandwiches and after we ate I curled up on the sofa, my head in Ben's lap. "I never knew whether to admire or despise the actors I met when I was growing up," I told him out of the blue. "Rather I admired them because they were everything I wanted to be, but they were everything I'd been taught to despise. They were worse off than we were. We rented a house. They lived in boardinghouses. But they were always smartly dressed, interestingly dressed, and they had this optimism, this openness that made them totally unlike other Ulstermen. I was taught to despise it because it had no basis in reality, it wasn't practical. What was the point of living in the moment, treating everything and everyone as if they *mattered*, when life was a struggle? Any actor who lived in Belfast was doomed to poverty. What they were doing was whistling in the dark to keep their spirits up." I raised my head to take a swallow of eggnog, then nuzzled Ben's crotch, breathing on it, then feeling the heat against my nose.

"Why did you suddenly start telling me about those Ulster actors?" Ben asked gently.

"I don't know," I said, wondering if I should fish out Ben's cock. But I sensed he was waiting for me to stop thinking sloppily, to come clean. "I was thinking that it's all right if all this doesn't last," I admitted. "Actors are *supposed* to be poor. It goes with the profession."

"That's what I thought you were thinking," Ben said. "You don't know how good you are. You deserve to be a success."

"Being a good actor has nothing to do with being a successful actor," I said. "Anyway, I have enough to live on for three or four years."

Ben played with my hair, as if to soften what he was going to say: "Have you ever thought of taking up some sideline for when you aren't working? Starting a business? You could take photographs. You could sell photographs of other actors."

"Or run a stall in the Portobello Road," I said disgustedly. "You sound like Aunt Peggy. I'm still training to be an actor. If I took full-time lessons from Julian for the next five years

124

I still wouldn't know all I want to know. You know what my life is like. Just going to class and looking for work is a full-time job."

"The amount of energy you have increases with the amount of work you have to do," Ben suggested mildly.

But the suggestion that I could ever be a part-time actor upset me more than the prospect of being frequently out of work. "Maybe in five years time," I said to please Ben. "When I've learned my craft."

"You can at least be aware of what's going on in the world," Ben said. "You have time for that. Most people are grossly ill-informed about what goes on outside their jobs and homes. They're too busy scraping a living. That's why they're easily swayed by political slogans and images. You have time to be well-informed."

"I promise to be well-informed," I said. "With your help. Did I ever tell you about James Young?"

"Who was James Young?" Ben asked dutifully.

"There used to be a weekly radio show from Belfast called *The McCooeys* starring and written by James Young, who was an Ulster comedian. The whole of Ulster tuned in once a week for that fifteen minutes. Everybody's face would be purple from laughing. I couldn't explain to you what was funny about it. There were lots of catchphrases, like *ITMA*, and double entendres. It was very domestic and regional and working-class. That was part of what made it funny. People who pretended to be middle-class were shamed into laughing at themselves when they recognised their own sayings and behaviour. But it was also queer humour, whole subtexts of it. James Young was queer, and so was at least one of his sidekicks. I know because I saw them when I went to buy tickets for their shows. They did a sold-out summer season every year. James Young used to sell tickets himself at the box office during the day. He was only about thirty, his skin very white and unhealthy looking without makeup. Have you ever noticed that a lot of popular comedians are grungy looking offstage, as if they don't wash very often?"

"I've never met any popular comedians," Ben said.

125

"The stage shows were riotous," I went on, "and they went just as far as they could go. The climax of one skit was when James Young threw open his raincoat to show that he was only wearing a very skimpy pair of underpants. I think he had a hard-on. I'm sure he loved the thought of parading nearly naked in front of an audience. The house went wild. Just the mention of queerness was enough to get a laugh, but there was something else going on. What made it so near the bone, what really aroused the audience, was that James Young was treading very dangerous water. Even if they didn't know he was queer they sensed he was queer. And I think what made them laugh that much louder was that it nudged their denial of their own fascination with queerness. At one point in the show James Young always used to throw chocolate bars out at the audience. He very deliberately threw a couple into the lap of a young man sitting at the front. They gave each other this conspiratorial look. I'm sure he was his current boyfriend. I happened to look at a woman in the audience who was also watching them. She knew exactly what was going on. She was smiling because James Young was giving her a good time, and at the same time she was judging him. On some future occasion she'd be happy to see him brought down."

"There have always been queers all around us," Ben said. "I had a science teacher I'm sure was queer. I was one of his favourites. I always had strict instructions never to come to his house, no matter what. I think he lived there with his lover."

"We were surrounded by queers," I echoed, "but it was never enough. We still felt as if we were the only one. Think what it must have been like for someone like James Young, living in lodgings for the summer, trying to manoeuvre that young man up to his room, scared the landlady might walk in at any minute."

I looked at the Christmas tree, then up at Ben, who sensed what was coming. His eyes softened.

"I remember the red lights on the first Christmas tree I ever saw," I said. "After that, Christmas was all downhill. One terrible Christmas I lost the five pound note that was

126

to buy the turkey and pudding." I put an arm around Ben's neck and hoisted myself up to his face. "Thank God I met you," I whispered. "We're always going to be together, aren't we? No matter what?"

"Yes," Ben promised.

I kissed him and returned my head to his lap, reassured. "Would you still love me if I was horribly disfigured in a car accident and never got another acting job?"

I waited for the answer I was certain I'd hear, but nothing came. When I saw Ben's red scrunched up face I thought he was crying. He was holding the back of his hand against his mouth and nose, like a barrier against tears. Then I saw his body shaking.

"You pig!" I cried. "What's funny about me being horribly disfigured?"

Ben let out a riotous squawk and fell back helplessly on the sofa. "I'm – I'm –" But at every attempt to speak his body doubled up and he clutched his belly and gasped for the breath that laughter was forcing out of him.

"Very funny," I said.

"I'm laughing," Ben gasped, "I'm laughing – because – you make me – so happy." He rolled off the sofa onto the floor and gave in to the heaving laughter.

I straddled him and lightly pummeled his bottom with my fists. "Do you really think –" Now I was seized by laughter. "Do you really think – that I'll let you – let you have your way with me after this –" I choked on the next word, which seemed to me the most hilarious in the language. "This – *unconscionable* display?" As I spluttered out the last words I fell on top of Ben and both of us squealed helplessly into the carpet.

"Yes," Ben gasped, tears running down his face. "Yes, I think you probably will let me have my way with you."

"I think you're probably right," I gasped.

❊ ❊ ❊ ❊ ❊

Our bodies gave in to the holiday and slept until ten o'clock on Christmas morning. As I floated up from sleep I checked

127

for Ben's position in the bed – we'd been sleeping four inches apart, Ben's hand on my hip – and then I saw the time and rolled over on my back, intentionally nudging Ben awake. He always slept with his nose held high, frowning slightly as if he was trying to solve a complicated maths puzzle.

The day outside seemed inhospitable without the hum of traffic from the High Street. "I've got to get up and make the stuffing," I groaned. "We won't eat dinner till five or six as it is."

Ben started to guzzle on my shoulder, growling villainously and pretending to take chunky bites out of me.

"Merry Christmas," I said. I kissed his forehead and leapt out of bed.

I had no stomach for handling the ingredients of the turkey innards stuffings in the English cookbooks, so I was making the Christmas stuffing I remembered from home, fresh bread crumbs, onions, parsley, milk and egg, guessing at the amounts and consistency.

Ben hovered outside the kitchen with his morning cup of tea, already dressed for our run, hurrying me along. Finally he snuggled up behind me, pressing his crotch against my arse and laughing at himself before he spoke: "Let's do some stuffing of our own."

"Whatever you may think," I said distractedly, "I am not a turkey."

The brief light was sharp in the cold streets. Couples carrying bright boxes stepped directly from blocks of flats into cars. Lonely people, I guessed from experience, hid in their rooms, praying not to be discovered until the day was over. Apart from dogs and their owners, Ben and I had the streets and parks to ourselves; even other runners, eccentric as they were, had stayed home.

By the time we reached Kensington Gardens the usual transformation of our bodies and spirits had begun, that made each determined stumbling out into forbidding weather always feel worthwhile. The heart lifted, the blood sang, telling us we were invincible: the changes occurred so gradually that we noticed the effects suddenly, after we'd been thinking about something else.

When we ran any distance together we ended up talking about everything – even the disproportionate hurts over niggling slights or impossible people that we'd been taught it was unmanly to admit to. Except that we didn't talk about our families: Ben and I had put them in a box and thrown away the key almost as soon as we gained entrance to each other's hearts and minds.

"When I was growing up," I said, methodically relaxing my upper body so that I wouldn't pant as I talked, "I always pretended I was starring in a film. I'd be swinging from a tree or speeding down the hill from Stormont on my bike, or just coming down the stairs at home, and just before I started I'd say 'Shoot' under my breath. I never told anybody what I was doing, so they thought I had this stupid habit of going 'Shhhh' all the time for no reason."

"How was school?" Ben asked, looking worried.

"Awful," I said.

He didn't wait to see if I intended to elaborate. "When I was growing up there were two boys I envied more than anyone," Ben said. "Bobby Carruthers and his friend Gerald. They were inseparable. I thought to have such a friendship was the only happiness worth having. One summer Gerald went away for two weeks, and Bobby and I picked up together. For exactly two weeks. We both knew all along that we'd stop going around together as soon as Gerald got back. I was never more than a fair substitute. Their loyalty could never have accommodated a third friend."

"What did Bobby Carruthers look like?" I asked, suddenly intuitive.

"He had blond curly hair," Ben said.

My intuition had been wrong.

"But Gerald looked like you," Ben said.

We ran in silence for minutes. I reached inside for something to give Ben, to match what he'd shared with me.

"When I was fourteen," I said, "I used to take the tram across Belfast to the Mayfair, which was a small cinema across from the Ritz that played sensational foreign films – war atrocities and prostitutes. The main excitement of

129

going there was trying to pass for sixteen in order to get in. The films always promised more than they were allowed to deliver. One particular night the blond man sitting next to me had his raincoat over his knees, and he very soon started moving his knee towards mine. I just moved slightly towards him and his leg clamped against my leg. I thought: If it's happening it must be natural. But then I thought: Suppose somebody from school sees me? The man leaned over and whispered: 'Will you let me see it?' It was too great a step to take. I got up and rushed out of the cinema. But in the foyer a woman spat at me: 'There's that thing there!' I ran out without looking at her, but burning with shame at the thought of being found out. How could there not have been someone who knew me in the audience? In Belfast there was always somebody who knew you. But I wanted to kill her: how dare some ignorant prurient bystander judge me and dare to fling that judgment at me? I grew up cautious because I knew ignorant people would judge me. I was so well-mannered, so frozen behind my good manners. I never learned to tell people what was going on inside me. When I eventually did go to bed with a man for the first time it was a few moments of intense confirming joy, and then questions and problems and a feeling of failure because I wasn't willing to admit it was my first time."

We ran on, Ben's silence according an appropriate weight to what I'd told him.

"Do you remember a heavyweight boxer called Bruce Woodcock?" he asked suddenly.

"Of course," I said.

"I used to have fantasies about him."

I grunted approvingly, recalling the boxer's sweaty curly hair and big chest.

"I used to imagine that Woodcock's manager transported him from fight to fight on a baggage car," Ben said, "roped to a slab of ice, wearing nothing but his boxing shorts."

He glanced at me to make sure I wasn't laughing at him, so I gave another appreciative grunt. He grinned to himself. "I could never explain to myself why the ice didn't

130

melt, or why Woodcock didn't die of cold."

"It's very English public schoolboyish, don't you know?" I barked, putting on a clipped military accent to break the mood, my breath streaming into the prickly air like evidence. "All this gung ho emphasis on exercise that you and I share. A sound mind in a sound body. I don't know why I chose to go this way. Maybe because athletics was the only sport I was good at, and it was cheap."

"The emphasis on team sports is one of the ways they brainwash generations of schoolboys to accept British values," Ben said. "Do your duty. Don't question your leaders. The workers feel seedy because they don't have the opportunity to be brainwashed the same way. Do you know how ignorant most people are? The workers and the leaders? On how little basis in fact great decisions get made that affect the lives of millions? Decisions made on just an assumption that someone from the right set couldn't be wrong?"

I didn't feel like pursuing such depressing theoretical matters. "I'll race you over the Serpentine Bridge," I cried. "Ready?"

Our sprints were all-out duels, but no consistent winner ever emerged. When it looked like I was winning too often, I held back. I sometimes wondered if Ben did the same, but I would never ask.

"I didn't want to imitate my betters," I said as we turned for home. "I wanted to be James Dean. Every young actor still wants to be James Dean. It just doesn't seem to fit somehow into the work that's available in England. But after *East of Eden* came out I wanted to hang around brothels and get drunk."

Ben started to speak, then paused to reframe what he was about to say. "You don't do so badly sometimes."

"What do you mean?" I asked. It took me a moment to work out what he was saying. "Are you saying I drink too much?"

"Sometimes," Ben said.

"I do not," I protested, and got no immediate reaction from Ben, who hesitated even longer over what to say next.

131

"Drink was meant to be a social relaxer," he ventured, throwing me a look that begged me not to take offense. "Not a way to drown your sorrows."

What sorrows? I was torn between wanting to show Ben that I could listen to criticism, and wanting not to have any faults.

He heard my dilemma. "I'm not going to love you any less just because you have one too many occasionally. You're Irish. It's in your blood."

I kept watching him, to make sure he meant what he said. "I'll be scared to have anything to drink ever again," I complained, mollified.

We ran on, listening to each other's breathing, adjusting through some subterranean process to each other's pace, each knowing the other was wondering what he could expect next from the lover who engrossed him. In public we hid our affection, engaging in spirited disagreements as if that proved we couldn't possibly be lovers, relying for reassurance on secret demonstrations of the sixth sense that was growing between us: a look that signalled agreement on what was happening around us; showing up at the other's elbow, which meant it was time to go. But I knew that no one seeing us running in that skeletal grey park – each oblivious to anything but what the other was feeling, our faces rapt, the difference in our ages remarkable but disappearing as we strained to meet each other, bodies darkening our sweatshirts with identical stains – could have doubted that we shared an extraordinary friendship. That was a gift I thought would be enough in itself. I didn't know it was inseparable from love and sex.

The flat already smelled of roasting turkey and warm onion. After I basted the bird I brought two mugs of hot sweet tea to the bathroom and joined Ben in the tub, our limbs getting so tangled underwater that we soaped and sponged flesh without knowing or caring who it belonged to. We became sleepy and forgetful of each other, as if we owed our happiness to the water, not to our lover, and towelled each other dry absentmindedly, no longer together. When we needed to make allowances, when there were urgencies we didn't share, when sex seemed mechanical or ungrateful, it seemed to me that Ben made the necessary adjustments automatically. For me they were an opportunity to demonstrate, to both of us, that I was growing up.

After breakfast Ben spread himself on the sofa with last Sunday's papers and the latest *New Society* while I made certain I'd taken care of everything in the kitchen. Then I settled down with Spengler. When I got up to turn on the Queen's speech I saw that Ben had fallen asleep. I woke him up with kisses, kneeling beside the sofa and insinuating my hands under his warm shoulders.

I listened to the speech with a self-conscious new awareness of the issues the monarch smoothed over blithely, as if her empty assurances were enough to take the sting from injustice and calamity.

Ben listened with good-natured scorn. "I wonder," he said, "if she's ever bothered by any inkling of her great good fortune, of her material advantages and her intellectual shortcomings?"

I soothed him back to sleep with promises to wake him for dinner.

But Ben awakened by himself in time to set the table.

"Are we allowed wine with dinner?" I asked innocently.

"Don't be obnoxious, Daniel," Ben snapped, cranky from daytime sleep. "Of course you're allowed wine with dinner."

Which made me a little cool towards my lover until the sight and smell of the turkey on the table reminded me how grateful I should be.

"So I'm obnoxious," I whispered that night when I curled up to Ben in bed.

"I suppose I'll never live that down," he grumbled.

Both of us were lethargic from too much food and too little news from the world outside, which seemed to have died that day. But in the middle of the night Ben woke me with his urgent need and found me ready to respond as urgently. We coupled hungrily and relentlessly, noisily shouting our love for each other as if to reassert possession of a territory we were secretly afraid of losing.

✾ ✾ ✾ ✾ ✾

In March Beryl arranged for me to read for Oswald in a new Tennent's production of *Ghosts*. I knew I didn't stand a chance of making my first stage appearance in a West End production of Ibsen. But the play merited a good audition, and I wanted to make myself known to Tennent's. At least I had a week to study the play, though not in the new translation that would be used. Normally I was told so little about the character I was reading for that it was impossible to formulate an approach to acting him. It seemed to me that the theatre cast types as much as any film producer, not giving me a chance to show that I could really act different characters.

On first reading *Ghosts* seemed solid, enormously theatrical in an old-fashioned way, and Oswald an opportunity to portray strong emotions. I realised immediately I wouldn't get the part: I was five years too young. I read the play again before I went to Julian to work on the character, and it took hold of my imagination. I thought I'd never come across a play that said so much in so little time. Every line was there for a reason that didn't become apparent until later in the play. To read it a third time was to uncover even more of the characters' secrets. I understood what I could aspire to as an actor.

The audition was on stage at the Globe, on a set already in place for the first act of the Graham Greene comedy playing there. The director introduced only himself, but there were others watching from the stalls. I caught just one shadowy presence – a pale attentive overwrought myopic ghost. Without making out her features I knew it had to be Charlotte Ritchie, the star of many Tennent's productions, who would play Mrs. Alving.

I began to read from my character's first entrance, simple lines that could not be acted authoritatively unless you knew that Oswald, forcing himself to go through the motions of a long-lost son greeting old acquaintances, was actually in shock, alternating between denial of his illness and bitter terror of what lay in store for him.

134

Oswald: "Excuse me, I thought you were in the study. Good morning, Pastor Manders. – Yes, I really am the Prodigal Son. – Or at least the son come back again."

Manders: "Doubtless there are people who can stay uncorrupted even in places like that."

Oswald: "I hope so."

The audition was going well: I was able to see with Oswald's eyes, yet direct myself to enter the character, and watch both of us in action.

After five minutes I skipped to the lines that closed the play, shrinking, irrevocably lost to human connection: "The sun. The sun."

"Thank you very much."

At the sound of the director's voice I tried to snap back to Daniel, but Oswald held onto me. I blinked and shook my head. All at once I was fighting to come to, trying to reach air by breaking a surface that retreated as fast as I struggled towards it.

I heard the director speaking at a distance. "I wonder, do you have any ideas – could you help us with the meaning of those last lines?"

I reconnected with him through sheer will. "No one can know what those lines mean," I said, still giddy. "They're Oswald's private vision, and he has moved beyond communication. The words may mean something totally different from our understanding of them. He may not even be able to match what he sees with the appropriate words. That's the final terrible thing Mrs. Alving has to face." I directed an acknowledging glance towards the presence in the shadows behind the director. A thought struck me. "Or maybe Oswald is reaching out one last time for all that he's losing. His life's work – his paintings – which were filled with sunlight."

"Thank you very much," the director said again. "Of course we still have a long time to finish casting. We don't go into rehearsal until September. Are you contracted for a film in the autumn?"

At least they knew who I was. "No I'm not," I said. "That would be good. It would give me lots of time to

135

think about Oswald."

As I turned to go I stole another look at Charlotte Ritchie. Her white wraith of a face smiled, brimmed, fluorescent in the shadows.

Ten days later I was rehearsing a Restoration comedy at the Royal Court. I never learned if another actor had dropped out – even the gossip at rehearsals was desperately perfunctory – but probably not: I think my casting was another makeshift decision in a project that seemed to have started from scratch four weeks before it was due to open.

Why a Restoration comedy at the Court? Because they wanted to show the English Stage Company wasn't limited to kitchen sink dramas and could repeat the success of *The Country Wife*. Why Colley Cibber's *The Careless Husband*, which nobody but academics had ever heard of? The choice was an implicit criticism of the narrow revival repertoire available at theatres in the nation's capital.

Ben conceived another theory when he read the play. As part of his duties as my lover, he read my scripts; as part of my duties, I read *New Society*. Ben drew my attention to some of Cibber's lines – 'the veriest fool of a beauty shall make an ass of a statesman' – and told me the rumours flying around London about a cabinet minister and a prostitute.

"How do you hear these things?" I cried enviously.

"People talk," Ben said. "I knew Patrick Kinross was queer long before you introduced me to him. And it was normal men I heard talking about him, over lunch at a social workers' workshop. By the way, if you get the Ibsen role, don't let Binkie Beaumont lay a hand on you."

He was ahead of me again: I'd just learned from Nick Sherwood, the actor from *Boxing Day Hill* who'd turned out to be queer, that Beaumont, the head of Tennent's, was also queer. Ben also told me how the Beaverbrook press relayed gossip that was considered too inflammatory to print. Unrelated stories about the figures involved, or photographs of them, would be printed side by side on the front page, encouraging savvy readers to draw their own conclusions.

At the first reading at the Court the actors seemed

lethargic and depressed. When I looked at the frightened girl next to me, an actress who'd been plucked from nowhere and won awards as the waif heroine of a heartbreaking film, I somehow recalled that innocent animals were the first to sense an impending earthquake.

The reading seemed to last all day. Comic speeches that were twenty lines on the page took seven or eight minutes to get through. I had a line at the beginning of Act V: "Oh, we are pretty safe here. Well, you were speaking of Lady Betty." As I read it, it struck me as probably the dullest, most awkward line ever written by a playwright. But I had only instinct to tell me that stage actors weren't supposed to feel this way at the beginning of rehearsals.

"We may have to cut," the director said as the last actor finished. Everyone laughed.

I turned to Mary, the actress who played the servant Edging. Both of us were at least five years too young for our roles, but we had to be grateful: if the play had been cast more carefully we wouldn't have got the work.

I whispered in her ear: "Where does the prompter sit?"

She turned panic-stricken eyes to me. We read each other's thoughts, and on cue burst into uncontrollable giggles. When I got home I set my alarm clock for six in the morning. It wasn't one of Ben's nights, so I was going to get up early and learn my lines.

Three weeks never passed so quickly; three weeks never passed so slowly. Each day it became clearer that the play would not be ready in time. The gloomy dread I felt at the thought of opening night accumulated relentlessly. The director, coming off a huge success with a bawdy costume film, hadn't directed a play since he came down from Cambridge. He concentrated on choreographing the actors' movements – certainly an essential task since the play contained little physical action except entrances and exits – as a ceaseless dance of fashion, the players coquetting, pirouetting, fanning, clutching their private parts to indicate lust, or reeling giddily in the thrust and parry of the high stakes game of reputation and seduction.

The director was so busy choreographing that most of us

were left to develop our own interpretation of our characters. The actor playing Lord Foppington, my character's rival for the attentions of Lady Betty Modish, preened and insinuated and squawked and leered like a dissolute Roman emperor in a CinemaScope epic. He was normal, which I supposed made him feel secure enough to camp it up so senselessly. It seemed to me a wearying display, but perhaps I was jealous because I had the less showy role.

My character, the worthy and rather dull Lord Morelove, the only virtuous male character, had for years loved Lady Betty, who preferred to exercise her power to torment him. I felt abandoned by the director, perhaps because Morelove was staid and needed less choreography than anyone else. On my own I developed a reaction of dizziness, taking one step back and furtively laying the back of a hand against my brow, in response to the ceaseless whirl around me.

I found professional reasons to be grateful for being queer. I didn't see how a normal actor could find much comedy in Morelove: normal actors would take it for granted that it was normal to be besotted with a woman. To me it was a forgotten emotion. I refused to draw on my experience of wanting men – instead I found comic distance by playing normal emotions as if they were the most extraordinary things in the play. My Morelove was a bit thick: it never occurred to him that he was the only character to whom honour and devotion came naturally.

Morelove had joined the fashionable season after spending time with 'books and solitude.' I decided that he'd learned much of his behaviour from those books.

Morelove: "Ha! Is't possible? Can you own so much? Oh, my transported heart!"

One performance got attention from the director, because the actress demanded it. Lady Betty Modish was played by the radical darling of the Royal Court, a thirty-year-old actress who'd been acclaimed for her spirited working-class heroines. She fought consistently for attention.

"Can we just stop a minute and analyse what's happening here? Can we talk about my intentions here? Because they seem pretty confusing!"

138

A sudden businesslike appeal to the other actors for support: "I mean if he's doing this then why am I doing this? Do you think we should be blocking these moves this early on?"

Sometimes the attention she demanded spilled over to the other actors, and I wondered if I should perhaps be grateful to her. But I didn't trust her. The first time she set eyes on me her face froze for an appalled moment. Every time our eyes met in rehearsals she looked worried and irritated and impatient, on the verge of sparking into a rage. But she never came out with what concerned her.

I guessed the ten-year difference in our ages contributed to the problem: it could help the play, add to the subtext of the complicated games that masked the search for love and sex in a superficial society. Or it could make her ridiculous. Her looks were best described as *jolie laide*.

When she managed to get the director to pay attention to the details of our scenes together, she'd barely glance in my direction, and never consult me directly: "Suppose I move towards him like this, and he could –"

She was directing me. I had trouble not showing how humiliated I felt, and started ignoring her when I could. But something gave me considerable satisfaction. Her ease of technique and vocal range were far superior to mine, but I was dulling the effect of her performance. Lady Betty would have seemed more delicious if Morelove had been played as a clod. My Morelove's bewilderment that anyone should even hesitate before choosing virtue was funny, and made Lady Betty seem more superficial than the actress would have liked. No one could argue with my interpretation: the Court wanted the play to be seen as an indictment of a frivolous England under a Tory government.

Sometimes I worried that I was imagining the leading lady's hostility, but then I saw the way she treated the young film actress, whose face was known throughout the world, but who hadn't a clue how to act on stage. She paid her charming acknowledgment the first day, then brisk attention, then almost immediately contempt. Mary was relentlessly choreographed like everyone else, but no one seemed to be teaching her what she needed most – to learn to command the audience's attention, not to try to hide every time she came on stage.

Or at least no one talked to her about it at rehearsals. Things were going on that I was excluded from: lines were cut, moves changed, without telling me. I found myself waiting for cues that no longer existed. At first I felt foolish. I couldn't believe that anyone was deliberately trying to hurt my performance. Then I started to get angry without admitting it to myself.

On the Monday morning of the third week of rehearsals I moved from sullen patience to inchoate fury in a second.

"Look," I suddenly shouted at the director, "if you want to do this bloody play without me I'll be happy to walk out and not come back." I discovered that my chest was heaving, my knees about to give way. "Either let me know what's going on or –" My voice gave out under the weight of tears I was fighting to keep in check. I gasped for breath. I made an involuntary movement towards the wings, searching for some kind of relief.

"Darling, of course we want you in the play," the director cried. "We couldn't do without you."

I didn't believe a word of it, but I found myself relieved to still have a job. "Then let's get on with it. Would somebody tell me what – what my cue is?" My voice was a gasping croak.

The other actors, more startled than I was by my outburst, pretended not to notice that I couldn't produce a voice for my lines. Mary couldn't take her huge eyes off me. The leading lady watched closely, smiling a sharp little smile. I thought she was probably calculating if there was a way to use the incident to get rid of me.

The dress rehearsal ran four and a half hours. All of us still had trouble remembering our lines, they'd been cut and rearranged so often. I overhead Sir Charles and Lady Easy whispering that the leading lady had asked the director to postpone the opening. But he told us to return at ten in the morning, when cuts would be handed out for another complete dress rehearsal before the seven o'clock opening. My part wasn't likely to be cut much more, since most of my scenes were with the leading lady. I thought: in twenty-eight hours the worst will be over.

It was fortunate I had no time to think about the cuts, which would have confused me utterly if I'd been able to sit down to study them in the quiet of my flat. I wasn't sure the play made sense any more. But we got through the second dress rehearsal by practicing a form of selective amnesia: you went from A to C trying to forget you'd once learned you were supposed to stop at B. The second dress rehearsal still ran four hours. Forty minutes after it ended the audience began to arrive for the first performance.

In the dressing room we shared, Lord Foppington asked me if I wanted to smoke some pot. I was dying to try the exotic substance, but this was the wrong time. I wondered if Lord Foppington would contribute to the catastrophe by losing his mind in the middle of a scene.

Ben arrived to wish me well, and Lord Foppington, who was still supposed to be normal, started flirting with him. Ben ignored him and directed all his attention to his stricken lover, who wanted most of all to be curled up in bed against Ben's body with the blanket pulled over our heads.

Yet to be a coward and unworthy of Ben was unthinkable.

"You're going to be wonderful," Ben said, burning with proud helpless love. I tore into his arms and got a tight hug and a peck on the lips. Even that much of a kiss meant that I had to wipe my makeup off Ben's mouth.

As I waited to go on I was certain the audience was a black monster waiting to devour me. It had been presumptuous indeed of me to ever suppose I could be a real actor, as opposed to some kind of model endlessly repeating tiny bits of behaviour before a camera. I have no explanation for where my nerves and cowardice went to. I think I willed my entrance with a toss of my aristocratic character's head. What happened was another inexplicable gift.

My entrance felt like stepping into a tropical ocean after a long journey from a northern city.

Morelove: "Dear Charles! – Nay, I did not think of coming myself, but I found myself not very well in London."

Perhaps the warmth of the light reassured me. The light bathed the audience as well: a man in the front row wore a black suit that looked singularly shiny and threadbare. Perhaps he was an imposter too, as imperfect and unprepared as I. Before I devoted all my attention to my character, it occurred to me that we deserved sympathy, like these parasites in dusty finery who'd go back to the library after this brief resurrection.

The play came to only fitful life. Nobody remembered all the cuts and changes. In an ensemble scene a bewildered actor went on playing a passage that had been cut while the rest of us ad libbed and the scene ground to a halt. Lady Betty took control, skipping forward to a long speech that gave the other players time to find their bearings. Lord Foppington seemed more desperately energetic than ever, and Mary clearly wanted to be anywhere but here. But it went better than expected. I sensed a generous good humour in my scenes with Lady Betty; her eyes were warm, willing to be convinced of the sanity of loving me. The performance ran an interminable four hours and a lot of the audience left well before the final curtain.

Only one notice called the production a disaster for the English Stage Company. Most critics agreed that one inadequate production didn't unduly weight the scales in the ongoing argument about whether to take seriously the Court's attempts at the classics. The production was judged to be intermittently funny and stylish, but slapdash and far too busy. 'The director appears to have so little faith in the play that he instructed the players to do anything to divert the audience's attention from their lines.'

Lady Betty's notices were respectful ('The final verdict on whether she has the ability to play high comedy will have to await a far better production than the present one'); Lord Foppington's notices were bad; Mary was advised to go back to films (one reviewer dissected her performance in vicious detail but made a point of not mentioning her name in order, he said, not to embarrass her). My notices were good. 'Young Mr. Henry provides a welcome note of stability and good sense in the midst of the general busyness.' But another reviewer pointed out that I couldn't help looking good in the presence of the production's other representative from the film business. I was pleased with myself, but thought the notices were too short and superficial.

As I drove to the theatre for the second night I worried over whether it was good form to talk about the notices. Outside our dressing room door I heard Lord Foppington giving a malicious imitation of my Morelove. The loud female laughter turned out to be Mary's. She froze when she saw me, her mouth open, her eyes glittering.

I pointed to my chair where she was sitting. "I need to get ready, Mary."

She gave me a stricken defiant look and bolted.

As I fumbled with stuff on my dressing table I considered what to do next. I turned to Foppington in a half-temper, ready to take him on, and caught him watching me with an insolent grin, spoiling for a fight.

I studied him for a moment, directed a sweet blind smile at him, then turned to my mirror and began to fiddle with my makeup, my hands trembling. So much for idealistic nonsense about actors working together to create art. It occurred to me to wonder how much rage and envy I'd ignored on the sets of *Boxing Day Hill* and *William Wilson*.

Mary lasted two more nights, never speaking to me, scurrying past me backstage. Her understudy played the fifth performance, and the next day's papers carried the news that Mary had left the cast, suffering from shingles, which were attributed to her disastrous notices. The tabloids devoted ten times more space to her leaving the play than they'd given to reviewing it.

I didn't speak to Foppington again. Why nourish betrayal? He was out with flu the first Saturday, and missed the entire third week, the last of the run. I wasn't sure how I got on with Lady Betty. At times I felt we were almost allies, guardians of professionalism; at other times I caught the same sharp angry look in her shrewd eyes. But each night I couldn't wait to get out on the stage; anything was

143

better than the hostility in my dressing room. I learned to accept the uncertainties of working with under-rehearsed understudies as part of the job of keeping the play afloat. I tried to plot ways of mesmerizing the dwindling audiences into believing they were being vastly entertained. Some nights I got laughs that kept me awake half the night wondering what I'd said or done that was funny. Some nights laughter seemed to die an early death and was never resuscitated.

I was still sentimental: I believed in a sense of occasion, that turning points should be marked. But *The Careless Husband* petered out. By the middle of the second week the actors had lost energy, most of us in various stages of colds or flu. I had to force myself to go to work the last Saturday. When Ben came backstage for me after the final performance I was sitting waiting for him, my bag packed. He took me home and put me to bed, waking me up long enough to eat the eggs and bacon he'd cooked for me. Next morning he had to leave early for a workshop. I spent most of the day in bed.

I didn't see him again until Wednesday night. As I waited for him I made a weekend shopping list from cookery books. I hadn't cooked for him in nearly two months.

He still rang the bell, to warn me he'd arrived, but now he let himself in without waiting for me to come to the door. The minute the door was closed I pulled him into my arms and held him, waiting for his strength to seep into my own body.

"I missed you," I said, which was what I always said when I hadn't seen him for even two days in a row.

"I've missed you," Ben said in a close approximation of his normal manner.

I stiffened. "What's wrong?"

He looked glum, his eyelashes suspiciously moist. He pulled away and headed for the kitchen. "Finish what you were doing," he said over his shoulder.

It took me twenty seconds to finish the list, then I went and stood in the kitchen doorway, leaving Ben room to move in the tiny space. "What's wrong?" I asked.

144

Ben threw me a puzzled wounded loving look, then concentrated on opening a packet of tea. "You're back," he muttered, looking bewildered.

"It's me front you're talkin' to, not me back," I said with the best Ulster accent I could manage.

But Ben threw me the squinty look that meant he was hurt or angry or desperate for reassurance.

"Will you tell me what's wrong?" I demanded.

Ben looked down at his hands.

"What do you mean I'm back? I haven't been anywhere," I cried.

"Yes you have," Ben said grimly. "Go inside. Let me make the tea and I'll come and talk to you."

I stared at him, genuinely bewildered. Yet I had an inkling, like a memory of a memory, that I ought to know what he was talking about. I went into the living room and sat down on the sofa and waited. I was rested, almost lighthearted now that the awful play was over, but I had a feeling I was about to take a test I'd better pass.

Ben set the tray on the table and came and sat beside me. "You've been like a stranger," he said, his voice rising more complainingly than he'd intended. He shook his head as if to clear it, the way he did when his body let him down or gave him away, then he turned to look me in the eye. "It's been like living with a stranger."

He threw me one last pale devastated look before he turned his head away again to hide his face.

I felt dizzy and slipping away. Only Ben's presence kept me grounded. I wanted to touch him, to get a better purchase on reality and to comfort him, but I knew that was the easy solution and he'd be disappointed in me. I wanted to play for time, open my mouth and say "But we don't live together anyway," but that would be a superficial response. I didn't know what to do, because I still didn't really know what Ben was talking about. Only the shadow of a memory nagged.

Ben saved me. He stole a glance at me, looked harder when he registered my stricken face, frowned with what looked like impatience, but then reached out and took my

145

hand. At once I gratefully tried to move into his arms but he held up his free hand to stop me, still not permitting easy solutions. "Do you really not know what I'm talking about?"

"No!" I cried. "I know I've been preoccupied, but you never said anything when we were together. We've been making *love*."

"You were somewhere else," Ben said, his face ugly. "You were going through the motions but you weren't there!"

I felt my temper start to flare. "Yes I was there! That's a terrible thing to say. What are you telling me? That I was thinking about something else? I wouldn't have been able to get through the last two months without you. Don't you know that?"

Ben pulled away his hand. "That's what you always say."

"Well it's true!" I recognised that it would be a mistake to argue any further. "The thing is, I have an inkling of what you're telling me. Since the play finished I've felt as if I was coming out of a bad dream. I didn't realise how bad it was until it was over. If I'd admitted to myself how bad it was I'd never have been able to go back to the theatre."

"Two of the actors dropped out," Ben conceded.

"Yes they did," I exclaimed, as if I was finally letting myself understand how bad the experience had been for all of us. "But the whole time I kept looking forward to seeing you. I thought, in three hours I'll be seeing Ben again. I was so grateful to see you I didn't realise I was treating you any differently."

"You've changed in all sorts of ways since you started working in Chelsea," Ben said sadly.

Now I was absolutely bewildered. "What's Chelsea got to do with it?" I asked.

"You began behaving like a Chelsea person," Ben said.

"What's that?" I cried. "What's so different between Chelsea and Kensington? You and I eat in Chelsea once or twice a week."

"What's different about Chelsea," Ben said disgustedly, "is that one of my clients, a seventeen-year-old apprentice, goes to a party at [he mentioned the names of a composer of musicals and a vivacious pop singer] and comes home

146

with gonorrhea and possibly a drug habit."

"That's terrible," I said automatically, but again I felt as if things were slipping away from me. We sat in silence, drained of energy by problems we'd never anticipated.

"Let's – let's just –" I pointed to the tray. "Let's have some tea."

I sniggered immediately at my Celia Johnson solution, and Ben finally smiled a wan smile.

We both got up. Standing at the dining table, handing Ben a cup of lukewarm tea, I thought I saw my lover as he must look to outsiders, colleagues I'd never met who'd never be given the privilege of sharing his body and his heart. He was principled, stubbornly idealistic, extraordinarily handsome. I wondered how many men and women pursued him in the world I couldn't enter. Ben came backstage; I didn't go to social work seminars. I knew I didn't deserve Ben: he was another inexplicable gift that could be taken away from me. I shivered. "I'll turn on the fire."

I sat down in one of the armchairs by the fire. "Maybe all this is a warning," I said. "Maybe I'm not cut out to do plays. I wasn't very good anyway."

Ben was still standing. His shoulders twitched impatiently.

"No, I mean it," I protested. "I thought I was just as involved in *William Wilson*, but you didn't complain then."

"I'm not complaining," Ben said.

"Maybe not now, but you were," I insisted. "Yes you were. Don't call what you were doing not complaining. And you have a right to complain. If I'm your lover you have a right to my attention. Maybe I should stick to films."

"For God's sake, Daniel," Ben cried, slamming down his saucer. "You're a man. You have to do everything you want in your career."

"Not if it means losing you."

"You're not going to lose me. Can't we –" Ben bit his tongue. "You're not going to lose me," he repeated.

I believed him, but felt no less miserable. "That's what I wanted to hear. But you were afraid you'd lost me. And

147

that's the same thing. Next time will you tell me what I'm doing so that I can change it?"

"Yes," Ben said. "I didn't try, because I felt it would have been like talking to a stranger. But yes, you're right. I should have talked to you. I was worried if I started in on you you'd never be able to finish the run."

"The play doesn't matter!" I cried. "The bloody plays don't matter. They're just what I do."

Ben grinned an involuntary grin.

"And don't laugh at me! You could start believing what I say for a change, instead of always thinking you know me better than I know myself."

Ben shook his head, with the look that meant I was sometimes beyond him. "Are we going out to dinner?" he asked.

"Yes. No. How about eating spaghetti and salad here?" I was still sitting in the armchair. I was embarrassed to ask Ben to touch me after he'd refused me once. I got up and headed for the bathroom but as I passed Ben I stopped. We moved towards each other at different moments and misread what the other wanted. Each of us turned away, thinking he'd been rejected. We had to start again before we reached each other's arms.

"This is better than anything," I said thankfully as I held onto Ben. "This is better than anything. Do you believe me?" I leaned back, still holding on, to look him in the eye.

He nodded curtly, his face almost clear. "Yes," he said.

Even that reassurance left us wary of each other for the rest of the night. We kept each other in sight, at a respectful distance, connecting now and then to make minor decisions. After dinner each of us was too shy to be the first to suggest it was time to go to bed.

When we finally moved into each other's arms in bed – Ben's skin felt cold and new – he made the first move to initiate sex. But I clung even closer, trying to blend into him so that he could never threaten me with separation.

"If I just have you to hold me I won't care about anything," I said. "You thought of leaving me, didn't you?"

Ben took too long to answer. "No," he said. "As soon as I

148

imagined what it would be like without you I realised that wasn't an option."

I stopped myself saying: "So you did think of leaving me."

"May I ask you a question?" Ben asked, moving into a sleeping position once it seemed we weren't going to make love.

"Of course."

"Do you ever think of using what happens between us in your acting?"

I wanted to scoff "Of course not," but realised in time that I'd better be seen to give the question careful consideration. "I don't usually think much about acting when I'm with you, Ben. I have enough trouble keeping up with you."

"But afterwards," he persisted. "When you're rehearsing do you ever remember something that happened between us and think it would be just right for the character you're playing?"

"I think about you all the time at rehearsals, but what I'm thinking is that if I didn't have you the work would seem that much more difficult and not so worthwhile. Why? What are you asking? Have you noticed me using anything that came from us?"

"Once or twice," he said hesitantly.

"What? What did you notice?"

"It's hard to pin down. I don't remember now."

"I've got to draw on my feelings," I reasoned. "I know about love. I know about responsibility. I know about caring for someone else more than I care about myself. Some of that has to come out in my acting if it's appropriate to the role. I just hope I don't start calling the other characters 'Ben.' At least not on the stage. We could always do another take if it was a film." I was ready to laugh, but felt no response from Ben. "When you have a client who's twenty years old," I said, "don't you sometimes see me in him and give him a little more attention?"

"I didn't think of it that way," Ben said.

Sensing that I had his sympathy, I chose that moment to ask him a question I'd been rehearsing for ages. "Can I fuck you?"

Ben gave a quick embarrassed grin that immediately turned knowing. "I knew this was coming," he growled. "I know how ambitious you are."

"It just occurred to me thirty seconds ago," I lied, nuzzling his ear. It was no time to question his infuriating ability to predict my behaviour.

"An idea out of nowhere," Ben said drily. "I suppose it never once occurred to you to do to me what I do to you three or four times a week."

"No," I said, then sniggered to let him know I was lying outrageously.

"You can fuck me if you want to," Ben said. But he had an unexpected caveat. "After the last time I got fucked I couldn't get a hard-on till I went to bed with a woman."

After that sank in I rolled over on my back, lust and even curiosity checked. I didn't know which was worse: the possibility of Ben's cock not working, or the thought of him having to fuck a woman to fix it.

"That threw you," he said with some satisfaction. When he heard nothing from me for an unusually long time he raised himself on an elbow. "You're the one who wants to do the fucking. I don't know why that should upset *you*. I'd be the one who couldn't get a hard-on."

He reached over and stroked the bridge of my nose, but I wouldn't look at him: I didn't want him to know I was fighting not to betray a sudden self-pity that struck me as so childish I was ashamed of it.

"You can fuck me if you want to," Ben said. "I'd been considering suggesting it."

I rolled myself into Ben's arms and buried my face in his neck, starting to feel it might be a lot easier to maintain the status quo.

"What is it? What is it, Daniel?"

"Nothing." My voice was an unconvincing croak.

"Out with it," Ben said. "How come you're suddenly lost for words when most of the time you're so good with them?"

I'd started to feel abused, and a sense of injustice made me fight back. I rolled onto my back again, away from the

150

body that gave me so much pleasure, and surprised myself by calmly vengefully bringing brought out a list of complaints.

"My feelings were hurt. The thought of you going to bed with a woman gave me a sinking feeling in my stomach. The thought of you going to bed with anybody gives me a sinking feeling. You knew I was upset. You knew that was why I was lost for words. So you didn't have to make a joke of it. You didn't have to hide behind words, because you knew exactly what I was feeling. You could have told me you understood."

Getting it out gave me the courage to look Ben in the eye. I was already thinking it was time to make up, but Ben looked humbled, felled by reason, so I pushed my advantage.

"A lot of the time I don't think you take me seriously. It's as if you've assigned a role to me, and you react to that instead of listening or reacting to what I'm really saying or doing. I suppose it's easier to do that than pay attention all the time. I do it to you sometimes. When I'm excited about something or preoccupied I react to my notion of Ben instead of reacting to what Ben is actually doing or saying now. Ben now is always different, at least slightly, from my memory of Ben or my notion of how he's going to behave."

I realised that inside a minute my message had gone from riveting to theoretical to boring. Neither of us could find any more emotion to invest in it. I'd left us feeling stranded.

"However I behave," Ben said, "never believe that I don't take you seriously."

"I know that," I said. "I know that underneath everything. That's what I don't understand. I trust you and I know you love me. I know you'd move heaven and earth for me. So I don't understand why we end up having these conversations."

"Let me ask you something," Ben said, reaching out and laying a hand on my hip. "I mean this very seriously." He stared at me until he had all of my attention, then grinned a sudden dazzling grin. "Do you still want to fuck me?

151

Because if you do, I'm yours."

I held out my arms but shook my head. "Another time. I just want to snuggle up to you." I reached out to stop him taking off his vest. "Don't take it off. I love the feel of your body through the vest."

When we were comfortable I murmured in Ben's ear: "And I'm not ambitious. I just want to do good work."

*****

Not long afterwards I decided it was finally time for me to fuck Ben.

"I want you," I told him one night, and didn't wait for an answer. I gave his cock an expert suck then reached for the KY.

"Turn over." I reached out to give his body a push in the right direction but he moved so quickly and obediently that my heart and chest swelled with love. Until my cock took control again.

Ben's arse was a work of art, two small tight globes set off from the rest of his body by a tan line that magically persisted from the one or two times a month he took time to sunbathe. For a moment I was checked from my purpose by the panic I always felt when I thought of how he sunbathed – on a twelve-inch ledge outside his bedroom window at the settlement house. All he had to do was fall asleep in the sun and roll over and he'd be killed. The thought of Ben in peril made me kiss the cheeks of his arse in gratitude that he was here, and lick the little clump of hair at the base of his spine.

Lust got the better of me again. I knew I should separate Ben's cheeks with my fingers and lick his arsehole. I owed it to him for all the pleasure he'd given me that always made me beg him to get inside me. But my cock was so urgently needy that I only took time to plant one more kiss on each cheek and nibble on one of them – it still had the athletic taste and smell of the pool where Ben sometimes swam on his way home from work – before I squished KY onto a finger and inserted it in Ben's arsehole.

152

He jerked. "Careful! Watch your fingernail!"

"Oh shit! Did I –?"

"No. I believe in yelling before I'm hurt. But be careful, Daniel!" Then he laid his face trustingly back on the pillow.

I wasn't sure if I'd lubricated his arsehole well enough with my finger, but I moved on to squirting KY on my cock. At least that didn't have a sharp fingernail attached to it. Ben lay waiting, so vulnerable, heartbreakingly willing to give himself over to my needs. His body secreted memories of our months of intimacy and learning from every pore. But I discovered that my urgency almost made me indifferent to him. I straddled him and pushed my cock roughly into his arsehole, amazed and guilty over my own lack of concern for his feelings. His arsehole felt soft and open, so I plunged.

Ben reared. "Wait!"

I grabbed his hips and held fast.

"Jesus!" His face turned purple.

For a prolonged moment I thought he was going to fight to get away from me, but then he seemed to force his body to relax and he stopped gritting his teeth. He took charge, but didn't expel me.

"Hold on!" he commanded, his head already dropping back on the pillow, his face friendly, almost self-mocking in its willingness to accept what was happening to him, though I noticed that his shoulders had dampened with sweat.

"It's been a long time," he muttered, more as a comment than a complaint.

I eased myself down on him, keeping my cock anchored inside his arsehole but covering his body and kissing his shoulders and neck the way Ben always kissed mine. The dampness on his shoulders, traces of the effort and upheaval I was putting him through, warmed my heart and excited my cock even further. The hairline on his neck was wet, as if he'd been running; the side of his face looked wan, as if he was tired from an exacting ordeal he'd committed himself to on principle. Protective love surged back into me, my body started trembling with it, but I was also

153

overwhelmed by lust. I gave a firm limited exploratory thrust of my cock.

Ben grunted but his arsehole didn't retreat.

"I love you," I whispered, overcome by gratitude. "I love you so much."

Ben's answer was to relax even further, inviting me to sink deeper into him, which seemed the natural thing to do – his arsehole, a warm firm sheath, felt made for my cock.

As I began the serious fucking I lost myself and Ben: I started seeing my semen shooting into a tunnel in space and floating away. My last ten or twelve thrusts were mechanical and brutal, desperate for the explosion in the arsehole that I shamefully exposed by pulling aside Ben's cheeks to get even deeper inside it. Ben, his body shunting with each thrust, grunted in a sort of subdued panic at the same time that he pushed back against me, consenting, demanding more.

Coming was a huge cold impersonal moment. As my semen pumped into Ben's body, I faced a terrifying choice: to live with my loneliness now that I'd used Ben's body (and the weary indifference I felt the moment my semen spurted made that seem the honest choice) or to make amends to the body I'd used. Ben lay exhausted, possibly abandoned, beneath me. I felt a split second's contempt for him. And then momentous love.

"May I ask you something?" I murmured as we lay ready to drift into sleep.

"What?" Ben asked grumpily, a little shy of me, temporarily fragile. He'd had trouble looking me in the eye, but he also had trouble not smirking, he was so proud of me.

"I just wanted to know something," I said. "It's okay either way."

"What's okay?" Ben complained.

"Does it still work?" I asked in a concerned voice.

After a moment he groaned.

"Or is it too soon to tell?" I continued politely.

"Shut up!" Ben growled. "Just shut up!"

"Are you sure you wouldn't like me to test it?" I continued. "It would only take a minute. I think it's best to know these things, don't you?"

"If you don't shut up I'm going home," Ben said.

I tightened my arms. "Don't ever say that, not even as a joke. This is your home."

✻ ✻ ✻ ✻ ✻

I became more protective of my lover than ever. Once I knew I was capable of mistreating him, I sensed it would be a bad idea for me to try to fuck Ben often. Ben needed to be able to pin me down, to feel my dependence on him, to possess the reality of me at this time when mechanical images of me were beginning to proliferate in cinemas and in the newspapers. But the possibility that I would insist on fucking him added to the tension between us as we fought to be ourselves and still give the other what he needed – learned to live with the inevitability of finding the other in every corner of our lives, coming to terms with moments of claustrophobia and boredom, accepting them willingly as the smallest of prices to pay for what we'd been given.

✻ ✻ ✻ ✻ ✻

When I heard I'd won Oswald in the Tennent's revival of *Ghosts* the first thing I thought about was when to tell Ben. I was trying to be more restrained in the way I talked about my career. I cut back on the blow-by-blow accounts of what happened at each audition or on Julian's tactless dismissals of my insights into a character, focusing instead on Ben and whatever we happened to be doing together. Putting Ben first still sometimes felt like a conscious exercise, though it calmed me down, made me feel that I was mature.

I decided to save the news about *Ghosts* till halfway through dinner. I'd drop it casually, then wait for Ben's joyous explosion, because I knew he'd behave as if his own dreams were coming true.

The first thing I noticed was that he looked worried and tired. I thought he had bad news about the settlement house. Maybe funding had been cut.

He wouldn't talk until we were comfortable on the sofa and I'd pretended to tell him about my day.

"They called this morning and said they were going to offer me the job," he said at last. "I said I'd take it."

"I'm glad you finally decided," I said, trying to sound happier than I felt.

He was to be the first overseer of an LCC program to fund settlement house services throughout the city, including starting up more hostels for unmarried mothers. He'd been meeting officials but had no idea a decision was imminent.

We'd worried endlessly over the pros and cons. Ben loved casework, but he'd always known that if he wanted promotion to policy making he'd have to forego one-on-one contact with clients almost as soon as his career began. He felt most authentic when he was working at grass roots level, but even his job at the settlement house had become more and more administrative as his programs expanded.

"You couldn't have made any other decision," I said. "Now you'll have a chance to push for the things you believe in."

"I'll be wearing a suit instead of a sports coat," Ben said ruefully, trying to find something to laugh at. "I'd like a drink."

"I'll get it for you," I said.

We'd reached a compromise over my liking for booze and Ben's concern that I drank too much: We drank a bottle of wine with dinner, and sometimes one drink before dinner, but only when Ben suggested it, because I was afraid of Ben thinking I was a drunk if I suggested it first. On the nights when I was alone I drank rather more.

"I have some news too," I said when we were settled with our drinks.

"What's that?" Ben asked abstractedly. I watched him shifting gears to give me the attention I deserved.

"I got Oswald," I said casually.

Ben stared at me until he was certain what he'd heard, then his face registered more than the great news: he realised I'd held it back to give his news its due.

156

"That's wonderful," he said. His eyes filled. "Come here," he said hoarsely.

I obeyed gladly. He kissed me with concentrated ardour, and then I snuggled happily against his chest, rooting for the day's smells on his shirt.

"That role is the best thing that could happen to you at this stage in your career," Ben said gruffly.

"I know. I never thought I'd get it."

"I had a feeling you'd get it," Ben said. "I didn't want you to be disappointed if I was wrong."

"I'm too young for the part," I objected.

He surprised me with a remark of the sort that made me feel he was calculating the moves in my career far more shrewdly than I was able to. "Your being so young is an advantage for the star. Charlotte Ritchie won't have to act her age to be convincing as your mother."

I was more concerned about whether I'd see my name in lights. "They haven't settled on the billing," I said. "I get third, or else 'and Daniel Henry' after all the other actors."

I decided he still needed cheering up. "Did I tell you the one about the actor who lobbied incessantly to have 'and' put before his name at the end of the cast list so that he wouldn't appear to be the least important member of the cast? He thought he'd won until the posters came out. He was set off from the rest of the cast all right, but instead of 'and' it said 'but.'"

I didn't tell Ben that my first feeling when Beryl phoned with the news was a sinking panic that I wasn't ready for the role. The gap between who I felt I was and what I was becoming had never seemed so great. I calmed myself by reading the play again, and let ambition persuade me it was inevitable I should play Oswald. Like him I was an artist from a northern city who'd gone into the world early, leaving a family and its secrets behind me. *Ghosts* drew me into it again, setting off depth charges that I welcomed without fully understanding their effects on me.

Ben had to give up his flat in the settlement house as soon as his replacement was appointed. Once again we sought in subdued hopeless tones to find a way to live

157

together. I told him it was impossible, but I still worried away at it. I blamed myself for being twelve years younger than Ben – that was what would draw attention to us, even more than my semi-stardom. I blamed myself for not being a civil engineer. Many civil engineers were doubtlessly queer, but they weren't perceived to be. Sooner or later, Ben's career would be ruined if he lived with me.

"There's no way we could keep it secret," I protested, as if Ben were putting up much of an argument. "I'd have to stay away when you brought your colleagues home. I'd have to clear away all traces of you before I let an interviewer into the house. We'd have to have separate telephone numbers. One of us would be sure to pick up the wrong phone when the wrong person was on the other end."

It was always I who voiced all the arguments against us living together; Ben listened in silent miserable assent. I longed for him to suddenly shout that we were going to live together at any cost, but I knew it wouldn't happen; I didn't even know what my own reaction would be if it did happen.

"It's ridiculous," I cried. "The LCC ought to *want* a queer to oversee their hostels for unmarried mothers. At least you aren't likely to get them pregnant."

"The Catholic church wouldn't let eunuchs be priests," Ben said. "It's the same principle at work. They need to suppose I'm battling and overcoming my baser instincts to serve as a moral example."

Ben ended up taking a dark flat in a mansion block two streets away from me. I wanted him to wait and find something more interesting, but he didn't seem to care. I was still wondering how to broach the subject of giving or lending him money to furnish the flat when he told me he'd arranged for family furniture to be taken out of storage. It turned out to be solid expensive dull Kensington mansion block furniture.

Two weeks after Ben moved in I was still waiting to be given a key to the flat. I sickened with hurt even as an assortment of my books and clothes collected in Ben's flat from all the time I spent there.

The hurt finally exploded one night in bed. I turned away from him in tears and he had to coax the reason out of me.

"I've been wondering what misguided tact was keeping you from using your key," he said. "Look in the top right-hand drawer of your dresser. I put the key there the day after I signed the lease. I showed you what I was doing before I left that morning. You must have been still asleep."

I took a moment to examine whether there was any way I could still blame him for at least part of my misery, then groaned with self-disgust. "All I had to do was mention it to you. I'm an idiot. How can you stand me?"

"No," Ben said gently, "I understand. I wouldn't like you if I wasn't capable of hurting you."

✱ ✱ ✱ ✱ ✱

William Wilson opened at the Leicester Square Theatre without a charity premiere, so my worries about how Ben could go to the premiere were wasted. We couldn't have gone together without women. It was probably too risky to be photographed arriving together even with women. My idea had been that we could arrive and leave as separate couples, but sit together.

In the end we slipped into a back row just as the lights went down one afternoon for the magazine showing at Studio One. The major illusion worked from the start – even I sometimes forgot that the same actor was playing both parts. I put it down to the excellent special effects rather than my own acting, which I thought was good but limited by the trickery inherent in the production. I'd always had to think too much about the technical aspects of what I was doing, I seldom had another actor to play off. The film took its time, and seemed long even to me, who was engrossed in evaluating the execution of every detail. Ben was quiet as we slipped out of the cinema and headed round the corner for Carnaby Street, where I wanted to buy a pair of bell-bottoms.

"You can do anything now," he said, his face shining as if a load had been lifted from his soul. "Your reviews are going to be marvellous."

159

"Did you like the *film*?"

"Yes, but I liked you even better."

"If my notices all turn out to be marvellous," I said, "then I'm not as good an actor as you think I am. If I were really marvellous, there'd be a lot more disagreement about how good I am."

"Nonsense," Ben said staunchly. "You just haven't had a chance to show your stuff."

My notices were indeed wonderful. Some critics also thought the film extraordinary, but cold, uninvolving. I slipped into an afternoon performance during the third and last week of the run at the Leicester Square Theatre. I couldn't believe my eyes – the stalls were empty. I knew business hadn't been great, but how could a film that attracted so much notice fail to attract an audience? For a moment I felt as insubstantial as my image on the screen. I was never going to be a popular star. I thought ruefully that perhaps I was going to get exactly what I said I wanted: the chance to do good work without the hindrances of great wealth or fame. Which was just as well. My private life could never have survived that much scrutiny; unless I'd invented an elaborate charade, I'd have had to pretend I didn't have one.

✳ ✳ ✳ ✳ ✳

Six weeks before *Ghosts* went into rehearsal I was offered another play at the Court. The run of *Cleaning* would overlap the *Ghosts* rehearsals, so at first I demurred.

"You should consider it," Beryl said. "It could be different this time."

The Court was in fact far less of an ideological and cultural entity than the public or I supposed – working conditions varied with whichever team was working there. I accepted the role, partly because *Cleaning* was a new ensemble work by a working class writer that gave me a chance to show I hadn't become a superficial film actor, partly because I wanted to prove to Ben I could work harder than anybody.

I played one of four prisoners who take over the governor's quarters of a maximum security prison while his family and a group of politicians are visiting. The prisoners talk throughout in profane scatological shorthand; the governor and visitors talk in eerie verbose bureaucratese. The play ends in a prolonged bloodbath when the prisoners torture the visitors until the tables are turned by guards. I could hardly wait for Ben to read my copy of the script.

Each day's rehearsals began with a movement class for the entire cast, then a session when we were picked at random to improvise the reactions of other actors' characters. Which gave me problems, because I had trouble distinguishing the character I played from the other three prisoners. Rehearsals seemed more like a collaborative attempt to explore the play than an effort to get something in shape for opening night. The production stayed in flux until the opening and beyond it. But this time the mood was buoyant instead of gloomy.

I froze when I found myself at the first improvisation session sitting on the floor next to Foppington, who was now playing the governor's son. I was ready for anything, but he greeted me so casually we might never have exchanged an ugly look. At least, I reminded myself, one set of terrible notices wasn't enough to kill a stage career.

Another of the four actors playing prisoners was queer. Lenny was a frail thirty-year-old whose sad-eyed crumpled face and stained skin seemed the legacy of dirty air and bad nutrition. His childhood in East End foster homes had been far more desperate than mine. I sought him out to compare notes, and we discovered we'd eaten the same biscuits and sweets when we were children. Five minutes after I talked to him I overheard him talking to another actor – now he was camp, jaded, brittle, 'West End.'

✳✳✳✳✳

"You like *Ghosts* much better than *Cleaning*, don't you?" Ben said two days after *Cleaning* opened.

I was brought to a halt, confronted with an incorrect attitude. "No," I stammered. "I don't know."

"You love *Ghosts*," Ben persisted. "You know, being infatuated with Ibsen is nothing to be ashamed of."

"I love *Cleaning*," I protested. "Or I like it very much. Or I admire it tremendously."

"That's what you think you're supposed to think. What do you really think?"

"I like and admire it tremendously."

"But?" Ben prompted.

I thought better of protesting any further: Ben clearly intended to force me to work. "All right. I'm not sure if I can put my finger on it."

"Try."

"I'm *going* to try! Just give me a chance to think. First of all I'm not certain it's really good. There's something wrong with it."

Ben opened his mouth then shut it, waiting to give me a chance to elaborate.

"It sort of seems like a translation, far more than *Ghosts*."

Ben picked up one of the notices waiting to be pasted into my scrapbook. "It's been praised for its 'densely poetic use of the vernacular'," he countered.

"Some of it *is* densely poetic," I said. "But the talk of the bureaucrats is like a Brecht translation." I felt my face redden as I found the courage to voice an opinion that had just struck me. "I'm not sure the prisoners' talk is densely poetic. It's theatrical and effective, but I think it may just be a clever trick. Once you learn how to do it, you can just keep on doing it without much effort."

Ben was starting to look pleased, but still dubious, as if I'd have to work harder to convince him.

"It's very repetitive," I offered. "It builds, that's true, and the violence is shattering, but all it is is more and more of the same thing at higher levels of violence and rage."

"It 'achieves the intensity and purity that modern dance usually only aspires to'," Ben quoted.

"That's nonsense," I cried, blushing again as if I was contradicting Ben instead of a critic. "Compared to dance it's lumpy and static. I wish critics would learn to criticise plays as plays instead of something else."

"A lot of people think the future of drama lies in embracing dance and music and ritual again."

"*Cleaning* isn't one of those plays," I said. "It's heightened realism." The argument was becoming less involving but still heady, as both of us strove to keep it afloat.

"You still haven't explained why you like it less than *Ghosts*," Ben said.

"It doesn't convince me the way *Ghosts* convinces me. By the way, why should I have to justify my liking something?"

Ben shrugged away my attempt to sidetrack the argument. "Does drama have to be convincing?" he asked. "Isn't it artificial by definition?"

"It has to convince you of its artistic truth in its own terms. Otherwise you won't remember it or go back to it. Despite all the controversy and the publicity we're playing to half-empty houses."

Ben scoffed. "You're playing to half-empty houses because the Establishment that makes up the London theatre audience won't go near any play that challenges its beliefs. They'll come to see *Ghosts*, all right, and congratulate themselves on doing something rather daring, even though it was written eighty years ago."

"Are you saying that the ideas in Ghosts are no longer valid?" I asked softly, sniffing a victory to come.

"They're valid," Ben said, "but not hot off the presses, not the way *Cleaning* confronts us with the rage that's all around us in modern Britain, though our 'leaders' are doing their best to pretend it doesn't exist, or treating it as criminal behaviour when it can't be ignored."

"It often is criminal behaviour," I said, though I felt disloyal siding with the Establishment for even a moment. "But I want to read you something."

I picked up my marked copy of *Ghosts*. "This is Manders: 'What you're talking about is unsanctioned relations! Nothing less than free love! How can the authorities tolerate such things? Your son has been keeping company where immorality is honoured, as if displaying it for

163

everyone to see wasn't enough!'

"Oswald: 'I've often been invited to these illicit homes on Sundays and never witnessed anything you could possibly call immoral.'"

Ben couldn't help smiling at the aptness of the quotations, but he shrugged off their relevance: "He wasn't writing about homosexuals."

"Are you sure?" I demanded. "Does it matter? When people hear those lines two months from now in the West End quite a lot of the audience is going to think how aptly they describe the Establishment's attitude towards homosexuality today. I don't understand why you always want to fight other people's battles instead of your own. Do you really like listening to the way the prisoners in *Cleaning* call each other queers as if it were the worst thing you could say about anyone?"

Ben gave an apologetic little nod. "He's attacking the dehumanising effects of capitalism and a class-ridden society. When people become less dehumanised they'll learn to respect everyone's right to live as they choose."

"In the meantime you, Ben Talbot, have to hide who you really are in order to win the right to fight for other people. Maybe we should be fighting for our own rights first."

"We do fight for our own rights, Daniel," Ben said, suddenly weary. "We are trying. There's a very good chance the law will be changed in the near future."

"In five years," I said disgustedly. "What I object to is the way they're presenting the need for change. 'Homosexuals are lonely men who will never know the happiness of family and children. Let's not make their miserable lot worse by prosecuting them as criminals.'"

"I know," Ben said. "But let's get the law changed first, before we do anything else."

"We're letting even our friends patronise us! You talk about the dehumanising effects of capitalism. What about the dehumanising effects of being called sick and unhappy? It's amazing that you and I ever found each other and managed to stick together."

Ben visibly turned inside himself for strength, then

directed at me one of the wise loving looks that made my heart swell.

But I was inspired: "That's what's wrong with *Cleaning*! It doesn't respect its characters! They're caricatures!"

"No," Ben said firmly. "In order to show how society dehumanises the individual he takes his argument to its logical extreme and makes the characters inhuman."

"There's something patronising about that. There's something – that doesn't feel right about it. If he really cared about people he wouldn't portray them as ugly automatons with no free will at all. A really great playwright would at least have shown them as human beings before he turned them into pigs."

"Now you're trying to dictate the dramatist's plot to him. Artists have to be ruthless."

Both of us were running out of steam. Though neither would concede defeat, I wasn't sure Ben hadn't taken his initial position to give me a chance to sharpen my wits.

"Every play doesn't have to be a great play," he said.

"But doesn't every playwright set out to write a great play?"

"I don't know. But *Cleaning* has already served its purpose. It opened a debate that's still raging."

"Even though nobody is going to see it."

"The ideas will trickle down."

I'd been pacing up and down, as if movement would help me pluck ideas out of the air. I wanted to add a private complaint to the argument, and thought it wise to sit beside Ben and take his hand before I spoke again.

"I still think he somehow patronises the people whose rights he claims to be fighting for. It's as if he knows in advance they're not good enough to hear his argument, so the avant-garde and the intellectuals will take care of the discussion for them until some day the people are raised up to their level. Which nobody believes will ever really happen."

My courage almost deserted me: the rest came out in a very small squeezed voice. "The way you expect a lot more from me than from the people you work so hard to help."

"What?" Ben cried, turning a pained amused look on me. "Are you feeling sorry for yourself, Daniel?"

That got me going again. "You don't go around advocating hostels for homosexual actors! You push me every minute of our lives together. You never let me get away with a bloody thing."

"From each according to his abilities," Ben murmured.

I found I'd lost interest in complaining the moment I started. I leaned over and licked Ben's ear. "Why don't you shut up and fuck me?" I whispered, and couldn't believe my ears, which had started to burn before I finished speaking.

Ben pulled me closer. "Good idea. These days it's the only way I can keep you in your place," he said proudly.

*****

For the first few days of *Ghosts* I fully expected to be sacked. The other actors at the Court delighted in regaling me with stories of Tennent's firing its young male actors (Richard Burton from *Adventure Story*, Tim Seely from *Variation on a Theme*). I supposed I'd be forced to arrive for a performance knowing the rest of the cast had already read in the evening papers about my losing my other job. But I was so frantically busy that I concentrated on doing my best and stopped worrying. I'd already ordered my priorities: I would always be fully present for Ben if he came to pick me up after the performance, whatever was going on with either play.

Ben had made me aware that the action of *Ghosts* reflected the great dramas seething in the capitals of Europe at the time it was written. My Oswald was to be an intensely ardent child of revolution, only made cynical by the injustice of his destruction. I'd done my reading – I expected the air at rehearsals to be thick with the momentous ideas of mid-19th century Europe. But when I started talking of Oswald as an heir to the 1848 rebellions I ran into a wall of amiable English silence. In my more feverish ambitious dreams I imagined asking the director if he thought we were doing a minor domestic drama.

I'd half expected to have to hide patronising thoughts about Charlotte Ritchie as a relic of the bad old days of plays carefully tailored to a Shaftesbury Avenue audience. Instead I found myself mesmerised. When we were introduced Charlotte paused, weighting my palm with a long thin scented hand, while she peered at me with the famous blue eyes. Perhaps they were myopic or distraught; perhaps they were subjecting me to intense astute scrutiny.

I wore chinos to rehearsal. Charlotte wore the kinds of skirts and blouses that were designed by British dress designers everyone knew to be queer, but who were written about without a hint of innuendo in the popular press, sometimes by columnists whom everyone knew to be queer.

Charlotte moved in a tasteful buzz of extraneous activity that had to do with the arduous duties of a West End star. Her secretary had appointments to juggle and decisions to be approved, her chauffeur's movements had to be co-ordinated and accommodated. When she spoke to me, so matter-of-fact, so eager for my advice, I couldn't help being grateful that she'd found the time. I wondered where the money for the retinue came from, since Charlotte's career consisted of a six-month run every year or two. She was usually considered too actressy for films. Ben reminded me that the husband she'd recently shed was a merchant banker.

While a secretary handled abandoned cigarettes and cups of tea with honey, Charlotte frowned at the script through monstrous horn-rimmed glasses, sometimes clutching it reverently, sometimes waving it over her head as if she wished it could be rewritten from start to finish – and came up with her canny insights. I'd guessed she would be wonderful with the comedy and irony, but rather wondered how she could play anyone's tragic mother. As rehearsals progressed I began to be convinced that it was her frail self-conscious presence, her broken sibilance echoing the tragediennes of the past who'd tried every trick in the book, that gave the production the strangeness it needed to be more than just a solid English production of a foreign classic.

Charlotte drew me out, her eyes gleaming when I won through at rehearsals. She supported me when I skirmished with the director over the melodramatic transitions Oswald had to make.

"'Oh yes, I see it now!'" I read. "Do we have to have all these exclamations, all these 'Ohs'? It's only a translation, it's not as if we'd be cutting Ibsen's own lines."

The director wanted me to work with the lines as written. I floundered, exasperated, then retreated into Oswald and stopped worrying about being laughed at. Charlotte had her own melodramatic transitions to handle: the closer I got to uncovering Oswald the more she opened to me. I couldn't remember ever depending so much on the approval of another actor. Usually I liked to perform independently, checking for respect out of the corner of my eye.

I also fell head over heels in love with Oswald. Ben had seen it coming, and seemed to approve: "We're a threesome now, at least for the run of the play," he said.

*****

The Sunday after *Cleaning* closed Ben drove me to Brighton, where *Ghosts* was trying out for a week. That night we had dinner with Charlotte at her hotel.

"She loves you," I said as we walked back along the deserted promenade inside a bell of fog. "Everyone loves you."

"She dislikes me intensely," Ben said. "As much as I dislike her."

I was thunderstruck. "Why? I don't believe you!"

Ben shook his head, tight-lipped. "Did you know that she gambles, and has to be periodically rescued from impending ruin by her ex-husband?"

"Where do you *hear* these things?" I wailed. But I still couldn't believe that Charlotte disliked Ben.

I moved closer to him and slipped a hand into his coat pocket. "Let's go for a dip," I suggested, shivering at even the mention of the inhospitable black ocean.

Ben astonished me: "All right."

I wouldn't let him call my bluff. I turned towards the beach, pulling him with me.

On my first trip to Brighton I'd been amazed and disgusted at the sight of a beach with no sand. Now I swore as the shingle cut into my freezing feet. We took off our clothes under the wall and then I took small gingerly steps towards the water. Ben dashed past me, plopped onto the water and disappeared under the fog.

The water was suddenly deep just a few steps into it, and it moved as heavily as tar under the surface foam. I knelt tentatively, new inches of skin assaulted by the cold, and was buried by a crash of pungent surf as the undertow dragged my feet from under me. It took all my strength to struggle back and find my feet again. I panicked almost immediately when I turned back towards the ocean. It had turned into a foaming treacherous pit.

"Ben! Ben!"

The surf flattened the sound of my voice against my ears.

I waited only a second, then began to scream Ben's name over and over again, scanning the surf under the fog for a sign of him being tossed back to me.

He re-emerged luminous. His cock, darkened and shrunk by the cold, looked vastly appealing to me.

"Let's go back!" I shouted, terrified he'd disappear again.

Ben wasn't ready to argue.

"Why do you listen to my stupid ideas?" I scolded him. As we struggled into our clothes, unable to accurately locate our own frozen limbs in the dark under the wall, I shouted an imaginary headline: "'Actor and friend caught naked in ocean.'"

"You'll never make a headline writer," Ben shouted. "How about 'Film Star Nude on Brighton Beach'?"

A week after the West End opening of *Ghosts* at the Queen's Ben phoned me at the theatre. "I changed my mind. I'd like to get together tonight after all."

"Good," I said.

"Come round here," Ben said. "I should be waiting for you. My meeting should be finished by nine at the latest."

169

As I let myself into the flat that night Ben came into the hall.

"Any change?" I asked automatically.

Ben shook his head. I demanded his mouth for the kind of long kiss that neither of us, now that we'd grown so busy and used to each other, sought at the moment of meeting unless he wanted to initiate sex. Tonight I didn't want sex. My eyes filled with tears – of gratitude, and a certain resignation.

"Do you want something to eat?" Ben asked.

"No. I'd like a scotch." For once I wasn't reluctant to ask for a drink, and I assumed Ben would also want one. "Let's take our drinks to bed," I said.

I thought that once we were in bed we'd want to talk. But the bedroom was chilly and we had trouble propping ourselves on our elbows to drink and keeping our shoulders covered at the same time. The sheets smelled of a combination of Ben's particular smells and a certain staleness.

Ben's face as it caught the lamplight seemed at a loss. It was a night when I might have looked to him for answers. Instead my heart was touched, and that was enough.

"Let's snuggle up," I said, draining my glass. We stretched out naked, folding our bodies together. "I love you," I said, hoping that love burned in my eyes through the darkness. "I'll love you till the day I die."

"I'll always love you," Ben echoed.

I settled myself, wondering what I wanted to say next. But almost immediately I fell into the exhausted sleep I'd slept since *Ghosts* opened.

Noise woke me in the half-light that meant daylight in Ben's bedroom. Just the recognition that I was waking up was good news, before I felt Ben's arms relaxing and heard what he was repeating along with the radio announcer.

"They turned back," Ben said.

"Thank God," I said, and lifted my head to cover Ben's face with joyful kisses. The Cuban crisis was resolved: the ships with Kruschev's missiles had turned back to Russia.

"A playwright would have done it differently," I said that weekend, recalling what we'd done the night we

170

thought we might not live to see morning. "A playwright would have had to put words in our mouths to show what we were feeling."

"If a playwright put the two of us in bed together," Ben said, "worrying about our dialog would be the least of his problems!"

* * * * *

One of my adolescent crushes was on a centre-forward for the Blues who never wore a jock strap under his shorts. The footballer himself seemed as interested as I was in the sight of his genitals bouncing against the tight thin cotton – he kept glancing down to check on what he was exposing. He was a handsome unmarried wildly popular player who never realised his full potential in the game. From listening to my friends you'd have thought the footballer was popular because he was a skilled and personable man's man. My instincts told me he was popular because he showed off his cock and balls, touching off some wild longing in the male fans that they'd never be able to admit to except in dreams or extreme drunkenness.

In the middle of my passion for Ben I discovered I'd become obsessed with another mercurial dark-haired footballer, this time an Englishman who became as much the rage as any pop star. The night I learned the extent of my obsession I was shaken to the core: I found myself pretending Ben's cock belonged to the footballer. I wasn't too devastated to finish what I was doing, in case Ben started to wonder what was wrong, but afterwards I lay in my lover's arms as guilt-ridden as if I'd committed adultery.

How could I be dishonest enough to pretend I was making love to Ben when I was thinking about somebody else? Did my secret passion mean that I didn't really love Ben? Did it mean that all homosexuals except Ben were really as promiscuous as everybody said? Or was I just one of the bad ones? How could I set aside Ben's love for thoughts of the skin and sexy grin and shorts of a man who'd be as indifferent to me as I was to the fans who

171

wrote me letters that always suggested, as an apparent afterthought, a meeting to discuss the crisis in the modern theatre?

I had no one to talk to. I'd never confess to anyone that my union with Ben was less than perfect, and to tell Ben about my secret infidelity seemed like confessing I wanted a divorce. I supposed I must be the queer equivalent of a nymphomaniac and wondered if I should consult a psychiatrist. I'd been greatly attracted to uncovering the secret conflicts in my unconscious mind ever since I saw *Spellbound*, but it was safe to assume the psychiatrist would want to cure me of my homosexuality, not my male nymphomania.

The more I lusted after the footballer, the fresher, the more virile, the more glowingly desirable Ben seemed to me, so that every thought of the footballer brought tearing guilt and fears that Ben would read my mind and leave me. I remembered how in the fifth form at school I helped concoct a plea for help to an agony column from a fictional fourteen-year-old girl. It contained every sexual catastrophe schoolboys could think of: VD, pregnancy, and the continued insistence of Uncle Harry on having his way while her parents were out of the house. Three months later the letter was reprinted by the *Woman's Own* advice columnist. Her response sent us into fits: 'My heart goes out to you, my dear,' it began.

Now I wished for the impossible: that there was a magazine that published an advice column for queers.

One Saturday morning before our run I froze, horrified, as I ran a comb through my hair while Ben stood peeing beside me. I checked and rechecked what I saw, hoping to erase it.

"I'm going bald!" I wailed to Ben. "Look! I'm going bald!"

Ben finished peeing, shook his cock, tucked it inside his shorts, then inspected my scalp for only a moment. "It's receding a bit at the temples. Every man's hair does that. It won't show unless you brush your hair straight back." It mattered so little to him that he left me and headed for the living room.

172

I couldn't take my eyes away from the mirror. "What happens if I have to brush it back for a role I'm playing?" I demanded.

"It's normal," Ben said mildly. "It's supposed to look like that. Come on. Let's go!"

"I'm going bald," I repeated dully.

"Come on!" Ben cried. "My hair would look far worse than that if I brushed it straight back."

"Your hairstyle wouldn't suit me," I complained. "And you're twelve years older than me."

Halfway through our run I came out of myself enough to notice that Ben was being unusually tight-lipped. It occurred to me that my lover might not regard being thirty-two as an undiluted advantage. I couldn't imagine how it felt to be that old, so I treated Ben as if he were twenty, like me, but stronger and more experienced.

"How did you feel when you noticed your hair was receding a little?" I asked with what I thought was superb tact.

"I don't remember. I don't remember a first time when I noticed it. It seems to me I always just assumed it was happening."

My efforts to placate him put him in a little better humour. "It will do you good to be less than perfect," he grunted. "Teach you a little humility."

I grinned. I liked to hear him complain about me.

During the rest of the run I had time to consider that one of the advantages of having a wonderful lover was not having to worry about the future when you started to go bald. I discovered that my cock had swollen in gratitude.

The minute we got back inside the flat I pulled Ben towards me. "Let's go back to bed."

He made only a token protest. This time I didn't think about the footballer.

❋ ❋ ❋ ❋ ❋

For the run of *Ghosts* I led the sedate life of a dedicated successful actor: I showed up for work exercised, rested and sober; I joined in an Arts Council reading of Irish poetry (most of it by Catholic poets from the south, but it never occurred to the English that I might be an inappropriate reader) and performed in a Restoration tragedy on the Third Programme. I still saw Julian twice a week, still working our way through Shakespeare. Ben and I slept together on Tuesday or Wednesday night and one of us arrived at the other's flat late on Friday and stayed until Monday morning.

I longed for the impossible: to live together all the time. I thought how good it would be to spend so much time together that we had a chance to grow a little bored and irritated with each other. Instead a familiar stranger descended twice a week: I noticed anew how he smelled and how handsome he was. We spent a lot of time catching up with each other and never quite managed to.

We no longer rushed to tear each other's clothes off. Our need had become a normal appetite that sometimes still amazed us with its sudden sharpness. On Sundays we went about our own business in each other's flats, nudging in passing, never far apart, rarely looking directly into the other's eyes except across a dining table or in bed.

"Guess where I was on Thursday night," I demanded one Sunday after we ordered early dinner at a country inn where Londoners came to dine with other Londoners.

Ben grinned in anticipation: he knew he was never disappointed when I announced momentous or delicious news.

"Kensington Palace," I said lightly, pretending to concentrate on buttering a roll while the news sank in.

"He came to photograph you," Ben said. He was impressed, though I could feel him mentally rehearsing his class struggle polemic.

"He came to photograph me at the theatre, and afterwards he took me home on the back of his motorbike to meet the wife."

"Isn't he surrounded by policemen?"

"No. He's in touch with them by walkie-talkie. He says they could be there in a minute if he needed them."

"Did he make a pass at you?" Ben asked, not sounding as joking as he wanted to.

174

"No."

"He must really love her," Ben said. "Why else would he give up all hope of having a private life? And she's such a – fettered personality. Trying so hard to break out from the rigid narrow values all that privilege endowed her with. You'd think that at least they'd give them a decent education. But she has the dreams of a starstruck shop assistant."

It was not lost on me that Ben was talking about someone he'd never met. The marriage, in accounts that ranged from the purportedly intimate to the glamorised, was still the talk of the land.

"I think there was one policeman at the gate," I said. "Maybe they were all hiding in the bushes. We walked right in with not a servant in sight. She was sitting on the floor in a cream-coloured housecoat putting photos into a scrapbook. She's smaller and much prettier than in the photographs. Much finer-boned." I began to be ashamed of how enthusiastic I sounded. "But not very bright. After we got there a journalist and her husband arrived for a drink."

"What paper did she work for?" Ben asked sharply.

"Television. She's working with him on a documentary about what happens to prisoners after they're released. They mentioned they'd eaten cod and chips in a caff in Islington the day before. 'What's cod?' she asked, making it a multisyllable word, like Lady Bracknell and 'handbag'."

Ben nodded, hearing what he'd expected to hear.

"I think it was real ignorance," I continued. "She wasn't sending herself up. She was proud of her ignorance, as if it was somehow a mark of sophistication. She kept missing the point of everything we were saying. When we talked about *Ghosts* it got to the point where I had to let it go, otherwise I'd have been contradicting everything she said. I'm not sure how he stands that. Living with someone who's not very bright, who just hasn't been exposed to the real world. He kept offering me drinks and cold chicken, as if that made up for it."

"It was his way of sharing the wealth with someone he thought deserved it," Ben said.

"The journalist kept calling her 'ma'am'," I said incredu-

175

lously. "Her husband, who's some kind of writer, didn't."

"What did you call her?"

"Nothing, of course," I said indignantly. "He struck me two ways. He seems very competent and efficient and out to get what he wants. But he also seemed detached from it all, as if he was wondering what he'd got himself into."

Ben sighed, half-amused. "Well, you've received the final accolade modern Britain can bestow on its meritocracy."

"You can't help feeling good in their presence," I said apologetically. "For a minute you're fooled into thinking you have all that wealth and privilege to fall back on yourself. If I'd known in advance it was going to happen I'd have been nervous, but it all happened so quickly and naturally I just felt sort of heightened. There was a lot of light in that large room, just like a stage. And a lot of furniture and really deep comfortable rugs. Everything was really shining and clean and well-lit." I made a rueful face. Ben and I hated to clean our flats, and neither of us used a char, Ben because he couldn't afford it, I because the idea hadn't crossed my mind.

"I'm sure they rotate the rugs regularly, just as the Queen turns the sheets to get the most wear out of them," Ben said sarcastically, referring to a widely-mocked report that portrayed the Queen as a diligent home economist.

Despite our mild contempt for the Royals, despite our pride in our own achievements, that evening Ben and I hunted in vain for another topic half as interesting while we finished dinner.

❋ ❋ ❋ ❋ ❋

Charlotte Ritchie left *Ghosts* after five months and was replaced by a former J. Arthur Rank film star who'd turned to the stage when film roles were no longer available to her. She was competent, amiable, and out of touch with the character of Mrs. Alving. *Ghosts* ran another six weeks, and then I was out of work for two years.

176

FOUR

Part of it was my own fault. It was hard not to show a certain amount of contempt for the work I was offered. After *Ghosts* and *William Wilson* and *Cleaning* I had, after all, standards to keep up, and most of what the British film industry and London theatre produced was worthy of anyone's contempt. But one of the plays I might well have been right for later won the *Evening Standard* Award. The pages I was given to read seemed slovenly and boring to me on the particular day I auditioned. I didn't even try, and made it clear to the director I wasn't interested in trying.

I recognised my mistakes and changed my attitude. At twenty-one I couldn't live on past glories. But then it seemed to me I was no longer given the opportunity to try out for decent work. Sometimes I found it hard to keep my temper with Beryl, who was like part of the wall that prevented me doing what I wanted to do, and Julian, who nagged me to work even harder to hone skills no one would let me use.

My demoralisation proceeded in tiny steps. After all, an actor's duty was to be optimistic and grateful even for the opportunity to be turned down for a role. But sometimes I was overwhelmed by the futility of it. I never had good news for Ben any more. Each audition was a fresh tale to tell, but all my tales had the same ending. It was hard to keep pretending to be optimistic for Ben in the face of relentless disappointment. He provided the only pleasure and support I had, but I began to wonder what I had to give him. He got more press coverage than I did now, his life a series of important meetings. He bought a Ford Consul, became a little set in his ways. He had a separate social life in which he played the bachelor for his colleagues.

Some weeks I did almost nothing from the time I said goodbye to him on Monday morning until I greeted him on Tuesday or Wednesday night, except to air my flat at the last minute as if it had grown stuffy from my lethargy. Since Ben didn't have time to cook, we always spent our midweek night together at my flat and I always cooked dinner. Since I had the time, it seemed sensible to offer to pick up Ben's laundry each week. One night Ben found he had no shirts because I hadn't had time to fetch his laundry after an audition that ran late. He showed a hint of impatience, and I exploded with rage.

"I'm not your bloody servant!"

"You're mad," Ben cried, and walked out.

I poured a drink, put the dinner in the fridge because I had no stomach for it, then took it out again and started stuffing myself while my mind raced with contingencies. I wouldn't pick up the phone if it rang, I could afford not to work for years if I had to, I could afford to be alone, which was probably a more suitable condition for an artist.

Our silence lasted until Saturday. I made sure I was out of the flat early that morning. I shopped for two, but told myself the food would keep if Ben wasn't there to eat it. He was waiting in the flat when I got back. I tried to hide my relief, from him and from myself: of course Ben had come back, he was supposed to come back to where he belonged.

"Let's sit down and talk," he said, looking worried.

I made it to the kitchen to put on the kettle, then I burst into awful stormy tears.

"I know how hard it is for you not to be working," Ben said later. "You've been handling it very well. All I can suggest is that you find something else to do while you're waiting. Have you ever thought of taking extension classes towards a degree?"

I shook my head. "This is what it's supposed to be like for an actor. This is how it is for nearly all actors. I was incredibly lucky. I had no right to expect my luck would last for ever."

"You have every right," Ben insisted. "I keep telling you you don't know how good you are. If you don't start realising how good you are, it will be harder for you to find work."

"England is full of good actors," I said. Then I decided to tell him more of the truth. "You know what? Sometimes I'm not sure I even want to act any more. I just can't think of anything else I could do."

We adjusted to each other again. I tried not to blame myself for not getting work, Ben tried not to take me for granted. But days felt too long, though months and even years felt as if they'd passed quickly once they were over. Christmas and birthday celebrations were somehow forced, as if we were making ourselves forget how bad times were. In truth I was always grateful, because I had Ben, but my failures cast a shadow on him that made me angry at myself.

The night I told Ben I had a part in a play again his face lit up; the next time I saw him I thought he looked five years younger.

The start of the audition had felt as unpromising as every other audition I'd been to lately – worse, because I was reading for a notoriously difficult role. I was so busy avoiding the traps in the lines I was reading that there was a lag between what I was doing and my realising I was doing it with unusual grace. Nothing special was said to me when I finished reading, but I felt certain I'd at least be called back. I'd had the same feeling after the audition for *Ghosts*, but I couldn't let myself be absolutely certain. If I was wrong I'd never trust my judgment again – I'd know failure had contaminated it.

My role was the extraordinary impossible part of Marchbanks in Shaw's *Candida*, in a production at the Lyric Hammersmith that only got off the ground because the star of a television series was playing the heroine.

"It's my first comedy," I told Ben excitedly. "I'm too old to play an eighteen-year-old, but the actor who was first choice for Marchbanks in the original production was thirty-eight!"

The character's combination of delicate shrinking torment and physical cowardice and emotional vehemence seemed unplayable to me. I could see myself making a mess of it, darting all over the stage, tripping over myself with contradictory movements. In the end I tried to see the world through Marchbanks' eyes and let the exterior business take care of itself. What I came up with contained some of the way I'd felt at Tom Finlay's party that night when I was eighteen and every movement and light and sound in the room overloaded my nerves, and the way I felt, raw and threatened, my head jangling at the thought of being hurt again, when I was beaten up by Peter. For Marchbanks' emotional certainty I borrowed from my own belief in my right to be queer and an actor, though my belief in my calling had lately been under siege.

I toned down one aspect of the role that I thought would make the audience laugh at me instead of with Marchbanks: his effeminacy. I rationalised by telling myself that Shaw hadn't intended effeminate gestures so much as a feminine sensibility. In truth I thought a normal actor might have been more comfortable playing an effeminate man.

I always felt that Marchbanks eluded me, and I was unimpressed with my performance and the production as a whole. But when the play opened three of my notices were raves. 'Mr. Henry is an underrated treasure,' the *Daily Telegraph* critic wrote. 'For how much longer are we going to dismiss the performances of this very young, dedicated and passionate actor as well-directed flukes?'

I'd had my share of good notices and didn't feel my triumph until I saw it shining in Ben's eyes.

"You've arrived," Ben said.

"You've told me that at least twice before," I reminded him happily. "Rather long ago."

"You were right," he said. "I can see you being out of work for *five* years and coming back as if you'd never been away. But I still think you ought to at least buy an interest in a business."

Candida transferred to Wyndham's for a six-week run. Shortly after it closed I started riding lessons in Richmond, getting ready to play a medieval prince in a Samuel Bronston epic to be filmed in Spain.

When I got the offer I went through the motions of discussing it with Ben. "I'd never leave *my* husband to do a Broadway play," I'd told Ben a year ago when Maryann Macready left for America with her infant son – the play flopped, but Maryann was now living in Hollywood with its star, a middle-aged Method actor. Both of us knew I had to take the part, for the sake of our morale and my bank account. Ben would come to Spain for his summer holiday.

"A year from now," I said, "you'll be seeing my face thirty feet high in Super Technirama-70 at the Dominion or the Astoria."

I spent four lethargic months at various locations in Spain, getting up before dawn to go running before the real heat started up again, spending the rest of the day half asleep on huge sets or on a horse in front of a crowd of extras. The film had lots of fanfares and processions and marches, during which all I was able to do in the way of acting was to get from A to B without sneezing or fainting in my heavy costumes or falling off my horse. The American star who played my father was reputed to be a good actor, but he was too eager to please: in moments of high emotion he smirked and talked as if he had plums in his mouth. For the first two weeks of shooting I often saw him with a young man who I supposed was his son. But the young man disappeared when the star's wife and children arrived. I finally got the picture when he reappeared after the family returned to America.

The Italian star who played the heroine lived in a dust storm of press, dispensing earthy wisdom about the joys of family. Her husband and daughter showed up obediently for photo sessions. Perhaps they really did have a private life back at the hotel. As an actress she was marvellously decorative and able to be still, and sometimes good at suggesting elemental emotions. But she had trouble with her lines, pausing against the sense when she had more than five consecutive words to utter. She particularly loved to swirl and sweep her long robes, posing on parapets or at the top of long flights of steps. I remembered how I'd posed at the top of the short staircase at home when I was small, pretending to be shooting a scene for which I was unable to imagine a script.

This script didn't make sense to me. It seemed to me that the main reason the characters kept making enemies and fighting was because the film was a roadshow attraction that ran three hours. But I invented an inner life for my doomed

181

prince, with dreams and wracking disappointments, and hoped that some of it would show on the screen. When I wasn't needed on the set I became an anonymous tourist, wearing a wide-brimmed straw hat and long-sleeved shirts to keep an even tan and avoid screwing up matching shots. I sent Ben postcards with pictures of lonely castles, and several letters in which I reaffirmed my love for him, still trying to find a reason for my good luck in finding him. Ben would thrive in the Spanish sun.

But he wrote to say that he couldn't get away for a holiday, and suggested instead that I come back to London for two or three days during a break in filming. I preferred to sulk. Perhaps my unhappiness made me look available, for I suddenly found myself exchanging burning glances on the set with a handsome Spanish actor. We met at my hotel one afternoon. I'd forgotten the excitement of wanting a new body, the intoxication of the first touch of new skin, the pleasure of the deliberately slow uncovering of the other's body. The Spaniard wanted his muscular bottom fucked, and I took my time methodically giving him exactly what he wanted. He got up and left, immediately indifferent, the moment I came inside him. On the set we were strangers again. I was still too disappointed with Ben to admit that I felt guilty, but I resolved it was the last time I'd be unfaithful. The cynical emptiness after a quick fix was no match for the deep ebb and flow of my feelings for Ben.

My pale lover met me at Heathrow. He looked blinded and dazed even after our eyes met. Probably I did too, until we assured ourselves that the stranger was our lover. We allowed ourselves to touch each other on the shoulder in this public place.

"Te echo de menos constantemente," I recited carefully. Ben, still looking dazed, seemed hardly to register that I was talking in a foreign language. He moved stiffly.

It was already winter in London. When we were safely inside the car I stole into his arms.

"You managed to get a lot of sun after all," Ben said, blinking as if his nose itched or he wanted to cry. "Did you learn a lot of Spanish?"

182

"Hardly any. I intended to, but the boredom got to me. By midday all I wanted to do was sleep. I'm not sure I got the tense right in what I said to you. But it's true anyway, past or present. Did you understand what I said?"

"I think so," Ben said. "Do you want to stop somewhere and buy milk and eggs? I haven't managed to stop by your flat the last few days."

The Consul was chilly until the heater started doing its work. I kept a hand in Ben's coat pocket all the way into town, talking about his work rather than Spain – everybody had heard more than enough about the boredom of filming on location.

The letterbox inside the main front door had filled since the last time Ben came round. Inside the flat, letters he hadn't thought worth forwarding were neatly piled on the living room table beside the bills he'd paid for me. Otherwise the flat seemed exactly as I'd left it.

I grabbed Ben and held him tight. "You feel different," I said. "It feels as if you've put on a bit of weight." I got down on my knees for a minute and nuzzled his belly. "More Ben. Yummy. Haven't you been running while I was away?"

"Not as much," Ben said ruefully. "I told you work has been horrendous."

"I'm not going to unpack tonight," I said, breaking away. "Except for your presents."

I opened a new suitcase and produced parcel after parcel, pretending each one was the last then uncovering another, dumping them in Ben's arms until he sat down, holding the pile together with his chin, looking somehow shamed by my generosity.

"I'm going to take a quick bath," I said. "Do you want to go out to dinner?"

Ben shook his head, easing the parcels onto a table. "I'll make omelettes for us. Yell when you're nearly ready."

He came into the bathroom holding a shirt against his chest while I was still in the bath. "It's beautiful," he said, hesitated, then sank to his knees to kiss me as if it was an unusual thing to do.

183

"Would you sponge my back?" I asked opportunistically. When I stood up in the bath, Ben stood up too, trying to look me in the eye, but his eyes kept dropping to my cock. I was fully aroused before I'd finished drying myself. I reached out and guided Ben's head down on me.

I'd learned some moves from the Spaniard who'd bucked and reared under me. When I pulled Ben into bed I pushed my arse onto his cock and pushed and heaved so that the cock was the recipient of my arsehole rather than the invader. I felt safe in taking such an initiative. Ben would assume the innovations were inspired by four months' hunger, not by lessons learned from another man. Would I ever tell Ben about the Spaniard? Probably not, at least not for ten years or so.

"Do you know how much I admire you?" Ben asked when I lay peaceful in his arms.

"That's a funny thing to say," I whispered sleepily. "But I'm flattered. You know me inside out." I sniggered. "In more ways than one, and you still admire me. *I* admire *you*, but that makes sense."

"There's something we have to talk about," Ben said, sounding distracted, when I called him at the office on Friday to make plans for the weekend.

"I can't wait," I said.

I was reading the paper, waiting for the day to begin, when Ben arrived on Saturday. I immediately gave him my full attention, as I'd trained myself to do. Now that I was back I wanted him to feel he was at the centre of my life.

"Let's not leave the city, even for dinner," I pleaded. "I've been in too many planes and cars. I want to hear your news. Do you want some coffee or tea?"

"Yes. No." As if he were overwhelmed, Ben held up his hands to put a brake on my energy. "We have to talk. Sit down."

"All right." I plunked down on the sofa and patted the spot beside me.

Ben hesitated, then sat a little farther away than I wanted him to. I reached out for his shoulder and pulled myself over to kiss his neck and ruffle his hair. I almost plucked at

184

a grey hair but decided it would be prudent not to mention it. Ben's face had grown rounder while I was away.

"What is it?" I asked. "Talk."

Ben stole a glance at me, and I realised that my lover was terrified.

"Are you ill?" I asked. "Were you ill while I was away?" I pulled myself even closer.

"For God's sake, Daniel!" Ben shouted, flailing his arms to throw off my hands as if there were ten of them tugging at him. He stood up, scowling. I saw dread in his face, even more than anger.

My future became clear to me, but I immediately made myself forget what I foresaw, so that everything started to have an eerie feeling of deja vu.

Ben was struggling to speak but could only make an ugly spluttering sound. It occurred to him to seek my help in what he was about to do.

"Daniel," he said ingratiatingly, turning to plead with me. Then he recognised the incongruity of what he was doing and turned away again, disgusted with himself.

I looked at the stranger looming over me, older, suddenly solid and unapproachable. He wore suits to work and changed the way institutions were run. I wondered how it could have been so easy for us to decide we belonged together.

"What?" I asked, shivering.

Ben turned back to me, took one step forward, then stepped sideways, raised a hand to the back of his head, then touched his neck, then let the hand fall again. Movement clearly wouldn't help. He stared at me, his mouth twisting. I knew he was enraged at the evidence that I had so much power over him, since he was about to deny that power still existed. He made a decision, then spoke with enormous ugly-looking effort.

"I'm getting married," he said, then looked relieved, then as if he was about to cry.

"You're already married," I said quickly, quietly. I already knew with certainty that the years with Ben were over, but I had to convince myself that it was not inevitable, that

185

words could make a difference.

Ben shook his head impatiently, though he clearly felt I had a point. "I'm getting married next month to a woman I met," he said hoarsely. He glared at me, then pity overtook him. He moved towards me, changed his mind, then moved again, and came and sat beside me.

As Ben put an arm around me I forced myself to look into his face: perhaps the last close-up of Ben's face I would ever see. It was tense with anxiety, the pores coarser, the lines deeper than I remembered seeing them.

"I desperately want to try and help you understand," Ben said.

"All right," I said, my voice cracking. "Help me."

I was moving underwater in slow deep calm, feeling profoundly unreal. But I still found the energy to shrug off Ben's arm, which felt like deadweight anyway. He seemed grateful to get back his hand and started kneading the knuckles against the palm of his other hand. He must have rehearsed what he would say, but I think his memory was failing him.

"I don't like the life we've been living," he complained, then screwed up his face distastefully as if even he thought his excuse sounded thin. "I don't like living a lie, pretending to be what I'm not. I don't like hiding my private life."

I recognised the words because I'd heard them before countless times, though I'd pretended I didn't hear them: they echoed Ben's thoughts that I'd heard and ignored. Easy to deny them – they were contradicted by everything he'd said for the three years and more we'd been together.

In a small voice I stated the obvious: "But you didn't have to hide who you were with me. Who you were with me was who you really were."

"No," Ben lied.

"Yes," I insisted. "But you didn't hide anything, you know. I knew what you were thinking, and I never admitted it to myself."

Ben nodded, desperate to find common ground with me. He cleared his throat. "Then you understand."

"No I don't understand," I said firmly, feeling briefly

real again. "I think you have a choice and I think you've chosen to pretend to be what you're not."

Ben shook his head vehemently. "I don't have a choice, Daniel. I'm doing what I want to do."

"You're doing what you think you should do," I said. "You're giving in."

"I will always do anything I can to help homosexuals," Ben said stoutly.

I sniggered. "The best way you could help homosexuals was to be one," I said. I noted my use of the past tense, but struggled on. "This is what I don't understand, Ben. I understand you. It's myself I don't understand. I've known you've had this struggle since the day I met you. That night we went to try to persuade that psychiatrist to back a change in the law I felt as if you were doing your duty, I didn't think you really wanted to be there. I recognise everything you're saying. Yet if anybody else had suggested these things about you I'd have said they were mad. I managed to totally lock them out of my mind."

"It's a struggle a lot of people have," Ben said, glad to agree with me. "That's how you recognised it in me."

"But nothing you said or did –"

"I hid it from myself," Ben said, trying to be gentle with himself, but looking shifty.

"You're marrying Gillian," I said, almost gratefully – for Ben to marry the woman he'd worked with for four years would clearly be a marriage of convenience, not of passion.

"No," Ben said. "Her name is Jenny." He suddenly looked especially uncomfortable. "She wrote that *Evening Standard* piece about me."

"Jesus," I cried, "we can't get away from the bloody newspapers. Have you been seeing her ever since and not telling me?"

"She phoned me for some background information when I got my new job," Ben said.

"Like hell!" I exclaimed. "She was after you."

Ben's face twitched irritably. "I took her to lunch with my superior. I thought it would be good for both of them to know one another. We started seeing each other while you

187

were away."

"Of course," I said disgustedly. "I'll hate that bloody film till the day I die."

"I want children," Ben said, as if he'd come up with the one unassailable reason for what he was doing.

"How old is she?" I shot back.

"Twenty-six," Ben said, almost apologetically.

I was somehow pleased that Ben was marrying a woman older than me. But bitterness seeped through. "Are you sure she can have children? If she's in Fleet Street she's probably already had two abortions."

"Don't!" Ben warned sharply. "Don't start attacking Jenny or I'll leave now."

My rancour was easy to curb: I kept feeling flickers of life, but then I went back underwater. "Why do you need more children," I asked, "when you have me to take care of?"

Ben shrugged impatiently. "Don't waste my time with that nonsense. You're a man and I've always treated you like one."

I thought about it. "When I had you I was able to pretend I knew what I was doing."

Ben looked blank, so determined not to weaken that he couldn't afford to consider subtleties.

For a moment it seemed that both of us had run out of things to say. I panicked: What if Ben left now and I never saw him again?

"Did it really all happen this summer?" I asked quickly. "I think it was brewing all that time I was out of work."

"I didn't start seeing Jenny till a month after you left," Ben said, sounding ludicrously loyal. "I would never have left you – I would never have let anything happen while you were out of work."

"I'm out of work now," I said.

Ben's impatience flared. "You know what I mean. I didn't understand what an actor's life is like."

He checked his annoyance and made a conciliatory move, turning his body towards me on the sofa. I think he had a prepared list of things to get through. "I want to

188

make sure you understand. I won't leave you until you do. You've got to understand. I wouldn't hurt you for the world. But I've got to do this."

"I'm *trying* to understand what's happening," I complained. "Are you going to walk out of here five or ten or twenty minutes from now and never see me again? We made love two nights ago. You fucked me as if you'd never want anybody else. Do you want her the way you've wanted me? Do you like her smell as much as mine? Have you ever made love to her?"

"Of course," Ben said, looking pleased with himself and furtive at the same time. "I won't discuss her with you, Daniel. I just want to make sure you're going to be all right."

I knew that Ben would leave me. I knew I had to try to keep him. His face next to me, as it prepared to retreat from me for ever, looked massive, trembling with life.

I started to plead with him, dully, complainingly. "If you knew what you were doing to me you wouldn't leave me. I know you can't allow yourself to think about it or you'd never leave me. You must have grown tired of me."

"No," Ben sighed. "It was what I wanted for a long time. Now I want something different."

"What are you going to do?" I asked the floor. "Are you going to leave here now and never come back?"

I darted a glance at him – he couldn't speak. Despite all his talk, it was exactly what he intended to do.

"Let's have a farewell drink," I suggested.

"Keep off the sauce, Daniel," Ben warned quickly, betraying a specific fear.

"No," I said, "let's have one last drink. I want to keep you for another five or ten minutes. There are things I've never asked. All kinds of things we never talked about, because I thought we had a lot of time."

Ben got up when I got up and went over and stood by the mantelpiece. As I poured the drinks I hit the bottle against a glass and he flinched. He must have been living on his nerves thinking of this day. I handed him a glass and held out my glass to touch his. Our eyes met and softened. Briefly, we were friends again.

189

"Have you told her about me?" I asked.

Ben hesitated, then decided to tell the truth. "No."

He read what flashed through my mind then, that I could cause him endless trouble with the woman he was about to marry, spoil the innocence of their beginning. Then I saw relief in his eyes. He knew I wouldn't do it: he'd taught me that part of our freedom as men was to choose not to hurt the other.

"I'm glad you didn't tell her," I said. "Don't."

I began to examine the mantelpiece. "Where are you going to live?" I asked.

"We're buying a house in Canonbury," Ben said. "You should buy a house, Daniel."

My knees chose that moment to buckle. Only my hand on the mantelpiece kept me from falling. Ben didn't see that I was ill, or couldn't afford to see. I gulped at my drink then forced myself to talk, though the sound of my voice became a part of the whirling that was going on inside my head.

"If something about me had been different, would you have stayed?" I asked. I thought my voice would sound abnormally forceful, using it as I was to cling to consciousness, but it seemed to be coming from someplace outside my mouth.

"No," Ben said. He sneaked a look at his watch. Now he had someplace else to go on Saturday.

"There must have been something," I persisted, more to stay in touch with reality than from curiosity.

Ben was starting to get impatient. "I never expected you to be perfect," he said. "I never wanted you to be."

I gulped the last of my drink. I was running out of props. "Were you always faithful to me? Before Jenny, I mean."

"Yes," I heard Ben say.

"I wasn't faithful to you," I said. "A couple of weeks ago I was fucking a Spanish actor in Madrid."

I saw Ben's face turn suddenly furiously red, then he banged his glass on the mantelpiece and darted away from me. To move, to keep from fainting, I found myself wandering loopily to the shelf where I kept the liquor and managed to pour myself another drink, my movements grossly off target. When I focused again Ben was wildly stuffing clothes into the kit bag he kept at my flat, his face still a dangerous shadowy red. The bag was open, overflowing, when he hoisted it under his arm. He came a little closer, but still kept a distance.

"If you're ever in need, Daniel," he tried to say calmly, but his voice heaved, "all you have to do is ask, and I'll do anything I can."

His face broke into what looked like a smirk, as if he'd done all that duty demanded. He reached into a trouser pocket, turned away, and reached towards a shelf on his way to the door, snapping the key against the wood so that I couldn't miss what he was doing. He'd taken it off his key ring so that he wouldn't have to fiddle with it in front of me.

"Wait!" I cried, back in reality.

There were whirlwind movements at the door, then it slammed behind Ben. I was so used to fitting my actions to Ben's behaviour that I waited to see what would happen next. Just as it began to dawn on me that my point of reference was gone, I felt my mouth fill with salt. I lurched to the bathroom, glass still in hand. The moment I dropped on my knees in front of the toilet bowl my breakfast slid up through my chest and out of my mouth and nose in one slick lump. I set the glass on the floor and waited, staring at the vomit, to see if there was more on the way. When my stomach felt steady again, I hauled myself back on my feet and supported myself on one hand to splash water on my face. I headed for the bed as instinctively as an animal heading towards hibernation. Sleep to blank out pain and a misery I couldn't let myself feel even the beginning of.

I woke up clearheaded and hungry with two simultaneous thoughts: "Is Ben in bed with me or did he already get up?" and "Ben is gone." It was four o'clock, already dusk outside. The notion that Ben had left me was so outrageous I could invest no emotion in it: it was a conceit, as abstract as a move in chess, the game that Ben was still teaching me. I got up energetically, almost cheerfully, and put the kettle on before I went into the bathroom to rinse my mouth and face. Ben's toothbrush was still there, but not his razor. I couldn't remember Ben going into the bathroom to get it before he left yesterday. No, today. This morning. Today was still Saturday.

It was like one of the days between Ben's days when I had no work or prospect of it. I turned on the tube and sat down with my mug of tea and glanced through the *Radio Times* to see what was on later. The page blurred, but I blinked and refocused. I felt detached, unalarmed. I noticed myself get up abruptly, leaving my tea untouched, the TV on. I had to get to the shops to buy food for the weekend before they closed.

I noticed that I was getting from place to place with no memory of the journey. Once again Kensington High Street wore the shameless advertisements for Christmas that cheered then immediately disheartened me. In the late shopping crowds there were faces that recognised me but tried hard to pretend they hadn't. How despicable! I thought. Without giving it a second thought I bought enough food for two people.

The smells and warmth of cooking made the flat a haven for me. I drank two drinks before dinner, then opened a bottle of wine. Before I knew it I was dozing over a magazine in front of the TV. It seemed like a good idea to go to bed, and not worth the trouble to brush my teeth first. Immediate sleep again, that lasted till morning.

I woke up thinking that Ben would show up for the harriers' club run. A few words exchanged as we ran on the Heath would solve our problems.

When I arrived he wasn't amongst the men running in place, testing stiffnesses and minor injuries, impatient to get started. But we'd always arrived separately and only ran together when we could make it look as if we'd met up by accident. The runners who came abreast of me were never Ben, so I let them move ahead into the muddy shade without acknowledgment. Driving home I caught myself still feeling optimistic that Ben would show up for the run – I was having trouble catching up with myself, coming up with another plan. Maybe he'd show up next Sunday, but that was a week away, a canyon of time. Of course – Ben was bound to show up at the flat long before then.

I'd forgotten how long Sunday could be. The feeling of well-being after I bathed away the mud and effort didn't dispel the cloud I moved in: objects were blurring, and larger than I expected them to be. I kept bumping into them. My breakfast mug as I raised it to my lips looked unnaturally bright. I had difficulty concentrating even on the theatre and film reviews.

I knew I wasn't fit to drive long distances, but I thought I could get safely to Notting Hill if I made myself concentrate on what I was doing. I got one of the last seats for a dubbed Joe Levine Hercules film at the Gaumont and had to watch from a cramped seat next to a pillar. The impossible events on the screen, made even more unconvincing by the scrupulously polite dubbed voices, somehow fit my mood. The cheapness of each succeeding special effect didn't diminish my hope that the next would be truly spectacular. I liked the actors' muscles.

When the film got out it was still afternoon, so I headed down the street to the Classic. The film there was *Maytime*, and it got me in trouble. I'd always loved extravagant Hollywood sentiment about love lost forever – Ben liked Westerns, I liked MGM dramas and musicals – but this time I couldn't shed an easy tear. I sat stunned, appalled, while the soft-focus actors, their voices thinned by time, tried to move me with transparent effects. A kind of daring curiosity made me stay to the end, for I wanted to find out how near I could allow myself to get to the avalanche of feeling whose roar I heard in my ears.

When I got back to the flat Ben was not waiting for me. There was no note pushed through the letterbox. He did not phone. Once again I created a warm cocoon for myself with food and wine and the TV. That evening I began to entertain two contradictory thoughts that would war in my head for years: it would soon be over, Ben would come back and everything would be well again; Ben no longer loved me, so he would never return.

FIVE

Nick Sherwood, the actor from *Boxing Day Hill*, invited me to Sunday tea at his maisonette in Earl's Court, and commiserated with me that I wasn't being exploited into the popular stardom my career seemed to justify. On my way back from the bathroom I was met in the hall by Nick's Indian boyfriend, who laid a hand on my arm, gazed up at me with melting eyes, then pulled me into the kitchen to arrange a time and a place. Before I left I also made a date with Nick to look at some paintings. Within a week I'd been to bed with both of them.

Going to bed with someone because they seemed to expect it felt clinical, like taking your clothes off for the doctor or learning a new skill.

"I was really annoyed with Gibreel for getting you first," Nick confessed, sharing a mildly affectionate emotional revelation after being fucked.

I thought my only interest in the affected Nick was as a point of reference to track the progress of my own career. But eventually I used him to catch up on the information about clubs and pubs and baths and cruising areas – Speakers Corner, the Heath where I ran, but at different times of day, the Serpentine in summer – that I'd ignored during the years with Ben.

It never occurred to me that being seen in queer haunts might hurt my career. Speculation about their sexual leanings didn't hurt Cliff Richard or Paul McCartney, and I thought other queers had as much to lose as I if they talked about me to normals. When I discovered that queers hid their queerness by gossiping about other queers, I chose to ignore the risk: I felt my right to be authentic would protect me. Everywhere I went I looked for Ben, which meant that my mind was never on what I was doing, and I doomed myself to always ending up with the wrong man, however invigorating it might feel to arrive at a new place or face for the first time.

A million queers went about their illegal lives, mostly behind closed doors, most of the time able to delude themselves that they moved freely. Only a few ever got into trouble with the law. One night as I followed a stranger up a tiny staircase to a toy flat above a photographer's studio in Covent Garden, the photographer ran into the hall below.

"I warned you I don't want you turning this house into a brothel," he shouted, his face contorted.

"I pay my rent on time," my temporary friend shot back. "If you won't let a law abiding tenant have visitors, perhaps I'd better report you to the police."

I remembered the huge amount of newspaper space devoted to the photographer's trial on charges that he'd solicited a plainclothes policeman to perform unnatural acts.

The police had so much power to destroy lives that stories about bobbies turning out to be queer had the same narcotic effect as speculation about members of the Royal Family: "I was so drunk I didn't even see who I was picking up. The first thing I saw when I woke up the next morning was a policeman's helmet on the nightstand."

My confidence had been shattered. I trusted my judgment about nothing that happened outside the self-referential worlds – miniature gardens inside sealed jars – of stage and film. Nobody I met beyond this world was as he seemed. It turned out that the sensitive dark-suited Swede at the Rockingham sold sheets at Harrods, was ashamed to let you see where he lived, and believed in flying saucers. The stocky man in a tattered T-shirt at the Coleherne was a dance critic. He told me how he'd seduced a telephone repairman by showing him a book of erotic drawings of men and women, then offering to relieve his swollen cock by sucking it. "My wife doesn't do that," the repairman groaned. He was disgusted when the critic's tongue moved to his arsehole, but learned to endure it. The bodybuilder in a black leather jacket who invited me onto his Chelsea houseboat as I ran past was a senior clerk who liked to passively cuddle and guzzle beer till he passed out.

My revived career had given Ben the excuse he needed to leave me, so I despised it and resolved not to draw attention to it. "I act," I said when people asked me what I did, and immediately changed the subject. Then it occurred to me that I didn't have to tell the truth. Except for theatre books and programmes my flat wasn't decorated to celebrate my career – I'd always worried that walls covered with framed photographs and posters would seem to diminish Ben's achievements. Now if a man I brought home noticed that there were a lot of theatre books I invented a drama student flatmate who'd gone abroad. I became, if the mood took me after a double Scotch or pint of bitter, a medical student at St. Thomas's, a trainee nuclear physicist, a visiting Harvard mathematics fellow (if I softened my consonants my accent sounded closer to American than to English), an English teacher (too easy to be any fun), an IRA rebel who hated all Ulstermen, a plainclothes policeman who was normal but wanted to see what all the fuss and risk were about, a husband whose wife and children were visiting her family, a solicitor's clerk who one night a week had to prostitute himself with his elderly employer, for undisclosed reasons that everyone I tried the character on seemed to accept without needing further explanation.

If I wanted to get on with the sex or was drunk or tired I often had trouble keeping my story straight. Some men tumbled to me right away, but they didn't seem to mind. I think they recognised me and assumed I had good reason to protect my reputation. Some men became more bewildered as the night went on, hypnotised by my improvisations but sensing that everything was wrong.

I thought nothing I did in the night hours mattered: it wasn't work; Ben would come back and real life would begin again. But the encounters that fuelled the life of the bars and clubs had a social foundation: friends went hunting together, people you picked up picked each other up and compared notes. Confronted once or twice as an outright liar, I introduced myself and explained I'd been rehearsing for an audition.

One day I tried to analyse my behaviour with the methods I used to analyse a character in a play. It didn't work. I didn't know why I was doing what I did. But neither did anyone else know why they did what they did. Few men I met were what they wanted to seem. It wasn't just the posturing, the public school men dressed like lorry drivers, the shop assistants pretending they could afford Kensington, the bruisable heart in the butch clothes. Queerness had a dislocation at its heart: however brave you were, the best you could do to stop internalising society's scorn was to recreate your own courage each moment you lived. Nobody was strong enough to do that all the time, even those with clear evidence that our enemies had feet of clay. It seemed to me that almost everyone in England, normal or queer, was ashamed of his father, and pretended to more class privilege than he possessed. Class privilege was better, even though it was unearned or you didn't really have it anyway.

I began to tell other tales to the men I picked up – of boyfriends tucked up in bed back at the flat, of families visiting – so that I could see where they lived. Sometimes it was in a pied-a-terre above a Harley Street practice or a flat in Eaton Square. Usually it was in bedsitters or in shared bedrooms of flats where four people lived. London starved its children to punish them for leaving the manageable institution of the family. Like everyone else, queers clung to their hard-earned possessions. In some smoky suburb I was forced to sleep between two men I'd picked up at the Coleherne, to prevent me getting up in the night and stealing their modest belongings. I was taken to rooms that smelled of boiled eggs where that day's shirt was hung to drip dry overnight so that it could be worn again tomorrow. Unless I blew my money I was secure for three or four years. But I knew I was destined for poverty again, and knew that when that happened my great good luck would not repeat itself.

Then it seemed that the years of studying Shakespeare with Julian were going to pay off. I was invited to meet a producer who was planning to mount a West End production of *Romeo and Juliet*.

"His wife is playing Juliet," Beryl reported drily.

I'd seen her in a comedy at the Duke of York's. She was

197

Canadian, and ever since Peter I'd dismissed all things Canadian as readily as I now disbelieved everything I read in the *Evening Standard*. I found it in myself to give her the benefit of the doubt.

She appeared from the children's room of the Mayfair flat, dark-haired and petite, her face dull and puffy in daylight, though it could be high-spirited on the stage. Until she arrived the conversation with her husband had been halting.

"My teacher has been encouraging me to push for Mercutio," I told them. "I tend to agree with him." The actress nodded sympathetically, as if she'd have made the same choice in my position. "I'm afraid my husband has his heart set on you playing Romeo."

The producer spread apologetic hands on cue. I discovered that I wasn't disappointed.

"Now all we have to do is find the money," the actress said with a little sigh.

"Finding the money is not a problem," her husband told both of us. "It's only a question of when."

❋ ❋ ❋ ❋ ❋

A Beaverbrook editor – I pressed him, but he knew nothing about Ben's wife – invited me for early Sunday drinks at his flat on the Embankment and fell down drunk in his bathroom before noon. "That would make some woman happy," he said when he recovered, referring to my cock in his hand.

One Sunday afternoon, at a loss for what to do with myself, I walked to Speakers Corner. A tall lean Jamaican kept positioning himself in my line of sight until I had to smile.

"Is it my colour?" he asked, smiling with willed ease when I turned him down.

"No, of course not," I lied. I liked to look at black-skinned people, but had no desire to touch. This man's poverty – the lines of his sleek suit doing double duty as Sunday best were unspoiled by anything in the pockets –

felt too close to home.

"You will say yes to me one day, I know it," the man grinned.

I wondered if he was right. Later, in the dark under the trees, I invited someone whose face I couldn't see to come home with me. He declined. "You'll find someone," he said in consolation.

"I'd like to see you again," I told an American journalist I'd introduced to Gertrude Lawrence's records and John Horne Burns' *A Cry of Children*.

"I'm no good at that," said the American, who was in London to write a book about the Beatles. "I'd only let you down."

Each time a man turned me down, daring to presume that I wanted more than sex from him, I was outraged, and stewed for days.

The man under me in the soft and pillowed bed lifted his knees in the air as he broke a capsule under my nose. My brain flooded with euphoria and the man's arsehole turned slurpy and insatiable.

I decided I'd been unforgivably backward in experimenting with drugs. A forty-year-old heart surgeon who couldn't get an erection so fascinated me with his tales of mystical LSD trips that I kept phoning him to try and schedule a trip for myself. He turned disapproving, implying that only a member of the medical profession was trained to handle the rigours of such a trip. Three months later, when I ran into him in a pub in Belgravia, I pretended I wasn't Daniel Henry.

Out of the blue I received a note from Harold Brookman, one of the quintet of senior Englishmen whose performances defined the art of acting for the stage. He had an offer that he thought might suit me. "If you're interested, please telephone me to arrange a meeting." Brookman was not currently associated with any of the permanent companies, but I knew he was about to direct a play for Michael Codron.

I waited until the afternoon of the day I received the letter to phone him, less nervous than the occasion

199

demanded because I expected to run a gauntlet of servants and secretaries before I had to deal with Brookman.

"May I speak to Mr. Brookman?"

"Yes?" Even the monosyllable was mellifluous enough to be recognisable.

"Is that Mr. Brookman?"

"Yes?"

"This is Daniel Henry." Pause. Keep your mouth shut, Daniel.

"Bless my soul! You can't be ringing about my letter! I thought I just posted it this morning!"

"That's what I'm ringing about."

"Would you like to come and see me?"

"Name a time."

"Luncheon on Thursday here at my house?" Thursday was the day after tomorrow. It appeared that Brookman was nearly as eager as me.

He lived in a Kensington crescent substantial enough to give any events that occurred there automatic weight. To my amazement Brookman himself opened the heavy black door – I couldn't believe that anyone so famous would let himself be so accessible. Famous pale blue eyes in a proud head squinted at me through old-fashioned glasses that he might have got on the National Health. He was fifty, and nearly bald, and notoriously queer. It was the queerness that stopped him intimidating me, because it made him vulnerable.

The talk on the stairs to the first floor living room, about whether I had difficulty finding the street where Brookman lived in relation to the street where I lived, was hackneyed enough to shame anyone of less consequence.

"What will you drink?"

One of my rules was never to drink at lunchtime, but I glanced at the sparse liquor tray and at the empty glass next to Brookman's armchair. "Oh, I don't know. What are you drinking?"

"Scotch and dry ginger?"

"That will be perfect."

"I'm an admirer, you know," Brookman said when he

200

brought me my drink.

I'd been examining a Keith Vaughan on the wall next to the library. "Yes, he's very fine."

Brookman laughed, or chortled, throwing his head back, his cheeks turning rosier in an already rosy face. "Of your acting, Mr. Henry," he said.

I blushed. "Daniel. Please."

"Of your acting, Daniel," Brookman said, and sucked noisily at his drink before setting it down and easing his body into the armchair.

I sat down on a sofa facing him. "I'm extremely flattered. And very surprised."

"I don't know why you would be surprised!" Brookman exclaimed with a haughty toss of his head. He squinted shrewdly, benignly down his nose at me.

"It never occurred to me that you'd even know my work," I confessed.

"My dear boy!" Brookman cried. "I do keep up, you know."

I began to feel as if I was already on my second drink. "You do know most of my role was cut from the Bronston film? I could have filmed it in two weeks instead of four months."

"I don't think we can complain too much about what the film people do to us," Brookman said expansively. "They know as well as we do that we only take their money to finance our stage work. Films bought this house, and my cottage in the country. If it hadn't been for the film money I saved I'd have been destitute during my dry period."

I nodded sympathetically, understanding that Brookman's 'dry period' referred to a well-publicised bout with debilitating stage fright that turned him towards directing. I still couldn't believe my ears: Brookman talked as if he included me in his own league.

"You do save, don't you?" he asked rhetorically. He didn't wait for an answer, and I suspected he assumed it was too much to hope of any young actor. "It's still the only way an actor can survive in this philistine country."

I heard him swirl a mouthful of drink while he appeared

to contemplate the tall window behind my head. Then his eyes swivelled and narrowed and fixed on me with a benevolent stare. "What's the work look like at the moment, Danny?"

I was certain I knew what Brookman was leading up to. "Kaplan wants me for Romeo. He's –"

"Do you think he's going to bring that off?" Brookman interrupted. "I'm not so sure, you know. Of course he'd do anything for her, but a Shakespeare production from scratch in the West End can't be done for peanuts. Unless they skimp."

"Even if they skimp," I said.

Brookman, whose eyes had returned to the window as he pronounced his opinion, fastened another sharp stare on me. Then he laughed. "Yes, *even* if they skimp. You're so right. Do you think it's going to come off?"

"I've no idea. I hope so. At least I think I hope so." I decided to be charmingly in awe of him. "I can't help but fail, of course. How do you feel? How does it feel to the definitive Romeo of his generation to meet one of the upstarts who wants to try it his way?"

Brookman smiled at the window, was quiet, then shifted in his chair so that it would be harder for him to look away from me. I had the feeling that I was finally being seen as myself, rather than a generic ambitious good young actor. "You couldn't do it my way even if you wanted to," Brookman said mildly. "You're too young to have seen me do it. I suppose your parents didn't bring you to London theatres when you were a toddler?"

"No indeed," I said unnecessarily. I persisted: "But how does it feel to meet someone who's trying to follow in your footsteps? Do you feel sorry for me? Do you wish you were twenty-five or thirty again so that you could do it exactly right, knowing what you know now?"

Brookman's face went blank for a second. I thought I saw a shadow of irritation or umbrage, and I went cold thinking I'd been too familiar.

But he beamed at me, his cheeks rosier than ever. "Bless my soul, I certainly don't feel sorry for you! You're going to

202

have an opportunity to make your mark." He fitted a cigarette into a holder then offered the box to me as an afterthought. I shook my head. I'd been smoking too much and hurting when I ran.

"I couldn't play Romeo now, you know, not with my present-day consciousness, even if my body were somehow transported back in a time machine." He spoke coolly, with an utter lack of nostalgia. "Experience has led me to think about other things. So you have to play these roles when you get the opportunity."

A small woman had appeared in the doorway, blinking and shaking her head. Brookman took his time finishing what he had to say before acknowledging her.

"Luncheon is served, sir."

"Thank you, Mrs. Pugh," Brookman said.

"I'll be going now, sir. I did what you asked me to."

"Till Monday, then," Brookman said mildly and turned back to me. "Shall we go down? You can bring your drink if you haven't finished it."

Mrs. Pugh preceded us down the stairs at a kind of trot. When she'd disappeared into the back of the house, Brookman made an exasperated face at me.

"Absolutely dotty," he said, rolling his eyes.

The dining room was big and chilly, the pattern on the plates cobwebbed with wear. I found myself grateful for the thin sunlight that made a bright puddle on the carpet by my chair.

My host's manners forced me into awkwardness. Instead of assuming that I wanted some of everything and letting me help myself, Brookman made a fuss of exposing each dish separately, then offering it to me.

"Would you like some bread, Danny? How about some vegetables? Are you ready for some of this wine?"

I could think of nothing to say about the bread, the vegetables and the wine except "Yes, please" and "Thank you," all the while feeling like the gardener's son invited to Christmas dinner at the great house. The main dish, barely enough of it for two, was a mildly spiced beef casserole.

"It's delicious," I said before Brookman could inquire

whether I liked it.

"It is rather delicious, isn't it?" Brookman remarked.

It seemed that the high and mighty invested energy and enthusiasm in small talk that their inferiors would not have ventured on without a certain self-protective irony.

I tried to make the food on my plate last, but it was soon gone. Brookman, by sinking into thought as he sucked at his wine, kept food on his plate much longer.

"I suspect your Romeo would be rather less poetic than mine," he suddenly announced, fixing me again with the shrewd look that I'd begun to suspect was a useful mannerism not always laden with meaning.

"I think you're right," I said lamely. It was hard to conceive of any Romeo being as poetic as Brookman's was reputed to have been.

His manner changed abruptly. "Let's get down to business, Danny."

I sprang to attention, hoping that I looked respectful, worthy and not too eager all at the same time. I'd want to know all about the part in the new play before I turned the business details over to Beryl.

When I heard what Brookman had to offer I was so bitterly disappointed that I had to fight to keep my lower lip from trembling. He'd been asked to nominate candidates for actor-in-residence at the drama department of an American university, and wondered if I'd be interested.

"Of course," I lied. I'd resolved never to leave London again for more than two or three days as long as Ben lived here. "But wouldn't they want someone older? And wouldn't a drama department want someone who at least went to drama school? Who spoke their language?"

"Oh, I don't know," Brookman said. "I think it might be a refreshing change for academics to work with an actor who came up through the ranks. Americans do tend to be too academic about everything. Well, Mr. Daniel Henry? Do you want me to propose you?"

"Of course," I lied again.

"I shall need a *vita*, of course."

"I'll send you one."

The food was gone and there was no dessert, but there was still wine left to drink at the table. "Now tell me, dear boy," Brookman said through teeth clenched on his cigarette holder, "what do your parents think of all the hullabaloo?"

I wasn't up to describing the mix of shy pride and uncomprehending moralistic dread I sensed in my family. "It's all like a foreign country to them."

"Why is that?"

"The height of their ambition was for me to be a schoolteacher."

Brookman sucked on his wine. "I meant the homosexual hullaballoo, Danny."

I felt great relief that the other important thing I shared with Brookman was out in the open.

"That's not talked about. I'm sure they know it in their bones, but they won't let it into consciousness. I'm sure my mother prays every night that God will arrange for me to meet a nice girl and settle down. But she doesn't admit to herself why she's praying so hard for that to happen."

"How could they not admit it? I mean after *The Tin Islands* flap?"

"Oh, that was a TV play. That has nothing to do with real life. Not in Ulster."

"But how could they ignore it? I remember the papers even reporting that famous kiss was your own idea. You were the talk of the town for at least a week."

"*One* paper said I initiated the kiss, and that paper isn't available in Belfast. If they'd asked me, which they didn't, I'd have said I thought the part demanded it. That would be quite enough to shut them up."

Brookman's eyes narrowed – he was unconvinced. "It all sounds *very* strange to me, Danny. You talk as if somehow they were your children, not the other way around."

I thought he was talking through his hat, but tried to stay respectful. "People don't behave the way they're supposed to," I said. "I mean characters in Shaftesbury Avenue plays have to be consistent if they're to be believable. When they do something surprising we have to be told something we didn't already know to make it

205

credible. But people aren't like that in real life. They don't do what you think they're going to. There's too much going on in people's lives for anyone to predict what anyone else is going to do."

"That's certainly an interesting theory," Brookman said sceptically.

"I wish I'd known I was the talk of the town when I was eighteen," I said. "I could have used the attention. I was living in two rooms in Swiss Cottage."

"Some of the fraternity were very angry, you know," Brookman confided. "They don't like the public's nose rubbed in it. It might make the authorities more vigilant. Also I think for them there's a certain *cachet* in being underground. And when somebody very young does it, it's even more maddening. Because your elders shouldn't be made to suffer for what you do."

His face brightened with a glee that surprised me. "Some of us were thrilled. It was a very daring, reckless thing to do, Danny. It could have destroyed your career completely. But it didn't. You came through."

It was years since anyone had talked to me about *The Tin Islands*, which I thought had been forgotten. "I wish I'd known all this at the time," I said. "It would have given me some confidence."

"How *could* we tell you?" Brookman exclaimed. "None of us knew you. There's this mysterious young actor who pops up regularly in marvellous parts in plays and films and then disappears again."

"You could have come backstage."

"There are people one visits backstage, and people one doesn't visit."

"And I'm one of the latter?"

"Very much so."

"I don't know why," I protested. "I shop at Sainsbury's like everyone else. I go to the bars."

Brookman's eyes flickered, as if to avoid information that didn't fit the picture he preferred of me.

"I heard another rumour," he said, smirking as if he might not be persuaded to tell.

206

"What was that?"

He appeared to consider, then beamed at me, choosing to reveal it. "I heard that you were quite mad."

It had long since occurred to me that Brookman seemed more fascinated by me than I was impressed by him: in person an overweight older man couldn't hope to match the glories of his stage performances. I wasn't used to such attention. I craved it, but believed that to solicit it would demonstrate a lack of seriousness. I certainly couldn't allow myself to be upset by the rumours strangers spread about me.

"What do they think?" I asked irritably. "That I have keepers who wheel me out of a padded room when it's time for me to say my lines?"

Brookman chortled. "Something like that. Of course if you were a little more gregarious it would be harder for people to slander you."

"I hardly ever get invited anywhere," I said, which was the truth.

"One rumour I've heard rather a lot," Brookman said with a haughty toss of his head that might well be a cover for shyness, "is that you live with a government official and have every reason to keep your private life private."

I think I lost all awareness of what room in what house I was in. I forgot that I wanted to impress the older actor.

"I did live with someone for a long time," I snapped icily. "He wasn't a government official. We're not together any more."

I found my fury increasing instead of subsiding. I was just managing to stop myself leaping out of the chair. Perhaps only a second passed. When I was able to refocus my eyes and my attention, I saw that Brookman looked appalled.

"Come upstairs and have a brandy," he said quickly. It seemed to be all he could think of.

I remembered my ambitions and knew I'd better show him I was still capable of modulating my emotions.

"I didn't come here to talk about me," I said charmingly, as Brookman poured us another drink. "This is a heaven-sent opportunity for me to learn from you."

He stared at me, then visibly chose to believe my temper was normal.

"I'm not sure I can tell you anything useful, except by example," he said, his head bouncing at the flattery as he fitted a cigarette into the holder. He was clearly ready to make the attempt.

"You've heard there are two schools of thought about how much acting you should do when you're very young? Some people say you should pick your parts. Others say you should take just about anything you're offered, that it's an actor's job to act, and the work will help you find your own level."

"But you picked your parts," I said confidently.

"You know, dear boy, I'm not so sure I did. When I was with Lilian or at Stratford I suppose I had a few options. But I was never offered bad parts in the commercial theatre or in films because I wasn't suited to that kind of thing. The film people knew I wouldn't pull in the crowds, so I was only asked to appear in prestige films. Luck is very important. To be available when the right part comes along. Some people have no luck, so they have to take anything they can get."

"I've had a lot of luck," I said.

He nodded. "It *might* help to have family money. But actors never do. We're nearly always vagabonds born to penniless parents."

There were, I knew, degrees of penury. Brookman had gone to Eton and Cambridge.

"But you must have been offered the occasional seedy part," I argued. "And you never took it."

"Not according to some of my critics," Brookman said, smiling with some irony. "One or two of them claim I've given some *very* seedy performances."

"When you're great they try to tear you down," I said sadly. "That's why I've never had any really rotten notices."

Brookman erupted into laughter, his body shaking so hard that brandy washed against the inside of his glass. "I think it's a little early to count yourself out, Danny," he said, beaming.

I had a strong feeling that I should go now. Anything else that happened here would not be what I wanted. But the brandy, and the shame I felt after my outburst, and a feeling that I had to somehow bury the part of me I'd revealed to Brookman, made me linger. And I had nothing to do that afternoon.

"Would you like to see the rest of the house, Danny?" Brookman asked, as I'd known he would.

"Yes, I would," I said, trying to sound faintly surprised and flattered.

It was furnished like the houses of most of the rich people I'd met – not the way they'd do it if they started from scratch, because they had a lot of stuff to begin with. As we chatted in front of a Duncan Grant, Brookman's suddenly silent stare drew me to turn to meet it.

"How about a kiss, Danny?" he asked.

He was a little drunk, but even so it was clearly harder for him to say than he pretended. Though he was no taller than I, I had the feeling I was approaching a looming father figure for an adult reward, one I might not value.

The brandy in his mouth tasted like a temporary coating over depths of dryness. His tongue was intrusive, cramming into my mouth until I couldn't move my own tongue except against his.

I had many doubts about the moves I was allowing myself to be led into. My options were to reject at the last minute one of the most distinguished actors in the world, which I considered inadvisable for my career, or find a way to back off until I learned to string him along without ever intending to go to bed with him – a dreary alternative I didn't have the patience to endure. I thought the choice I made was honest and generous.

But it was hard to pretend I wanted to get Brookman's clothes off or torment my lust by lingering over doing it. We became matter-of-fact and retreated to opposite sides of the bed to undress. The sight of his bulky stomach stretching the waistband of baby blue boxer shorts made my heart sink. His sheets were blood red. I jumped between them and waited for him like a whore.

It could have been worse. The first touch of anyone's body, before we feel pleasure or indifference or disgust, reminds us that we're alive. But in Harold's embrace I felt soft flesh where I longed for muscle. His skin was white and dry and vast. Since his body held no prospect of pleasure for me, I thought I'd try to get it over with. I went down on him and gave his cock a perfunctory suck, and then a series of them, that probably felt to him like one fairly long suck. His off-white cock stayed resolutely flaccid while he lay still and silent like a beached unconscious whale.

When I came up again his head on the pillow still looked noble. He buried his mouth on mine as if to taste himself on me was the ultimate intimacy, and then he went down on me, on cue. I moaned in fairly genuine appreciation.

"What do you think, Danny sweetie?" Brookman suddenly asked, addressing my cock. "Do you think we might do this again?"

"Of course, Harold," I said.

He got up on his knees and started beating on his cock. "Turn over," he said with sudden ferocity.

Which I did quite willingly: his cock up my arse would be enough to distract me from almost everything else about Harold, a satisfactory way out of a dicey situation.

But Harold couldn't get hard enough to push inside me. We ended up masturbating ourselves, Harold insisting on stale kisses. I came; he didn't.

"You take terrible care of your clothes," Harold said as we lay together resting.

It had never occurred to me not to drop my clothes on the floor when I took them off.

He added out of the blue: "Michael Baker had it coming to him, what you did to him. He's probably had trouble making love to his wife ever since." His loose torso shook with snorting spluttering laughter. "He's such a limited actor."

❊ ❊ ❊ ❊ ❊

"We all piss in the same pot," Tom Finlay said, as if hearing about Harold and I constituted definitive proof of that

210

truth. "I'd love to be there when you tell him you never loved him."

Tom's vindictiveness surprised me: he'd once claimed an acquaintance with Harold. I suspected his invitations had been rebuffed. I didn't challenge Tom's assumption that I would someday tell Harold I didn't love him – I enjoyed trying out the role of a high-class whore. With Tom as well as strangers I sometimes now drifted into the prevailing way of talking: one expressed simple opinions as emphatically as possible or told humorous anecdotes, pretending to be helpless or bewildered in the face of life's complexities. To be allowed seriousness, one must be a success of the moment. One kept it light, or hid from sight.

The first time I got out of Harold's bed I went home, took a bath, and dressed to go out and pick up a man my own age. I went on seeing him because I thought he could help my career – he must have influence with the resident companies – and because I enjoyed imagining how hurt Ben would be to hear what I was doing: "You see what I've become, Ben? I told you nothing would ever come to any good for me again."

I stayed with Harold because I could never quite work out how to leave him. A new lover sweeping me off my feet seemed to be the only unassailable excuse I could come up with, but I never thought of inventing one, despite my other feverish inventions of the night.

Closeness to the trappings of Harold's life – the house, the cottage in Surrey with the dark pond he claimed he couldn't afford to drain, the public standing he'd achieved despite his vulnerability to scandal – made me feel secure, though much of his social life was closed to me, sometimes on the basis of distinctions too fine for me to fathom. Harold took me to dinner at the White Tower, but not to lunch at the Garrick, was seen shopping with me at Aquascutum (where I called him 'Uncle' in front of the sales assistants) but made a string of unconvincing excuses to keep me from coming to rehearsals of the new play he was directing. Of course I wasn't taken to official functions, the invitations to which lined Harold's mantelpiece. Some

211

out-of-touch hostesses even requested the presence of 'Mr. and Mrs. Harold Brookman.' A lot of my shyness had returned now that Ben was gone, but such occasions would have held no terrors for me. You dressed up for them and behaved as stiffly as everyone else. An admiral's opening gambit to Harold at a Lord Mayor's banquet: "Gold plate makes the soup cold, what?"

Harold saw that I basked a little in reflected glory and couldn't understand it. "This is what I have to show for thirty years of work, some of them very spotty. When I was your age my career hadn't begun."

But he was grateful for whatever kept me with him. "Are you faithful to me, Danny Wanny?" he once asked me after some tepid sex.

"Of course," I said automatically, with no attempt at conviction. He didn't ask me again.

It was magical to talk to him about actors and plays, to test my instincts against his experience. When I arrived at Harold's house I could pretend I had a place in the world, but it was hard for me to keep up the performance that earned me that place. If I'd been more cunning I could have had him as a friend, snaring him with the possibility of more. Instead I'd trapped myself: if we stopped being lovers the relationship would end in bitterness.

Perhaps I did my best to end it. After the conversation and the food we had to go to bed together. I gave as little as I could, and grew more and more disgusted at the thought of giving anything. Only a man who was infatuated would have settled for a lover who tried to avoid him in bed.

"Do you love me a little, Danny?" Harold asked after we got into bed one night.

"Of course I do," I said. "I love you a lot."

And I turned over to go to sleep, to get away from his flesh, which my imagination had made clammy.

Three weeks before the opening of the play he was directing Harold asked me which two places in the world I'd like to visit most.

"New York and Moscow," I replied.

He proposed that we fly to Nice for three nights, to clear

his head and to get to know each other better.

I said I didn't feel like spending money on a trip.

Harold burst into the blustering laugh he used to contain a number of emotions. "I really hadn't thought of asking you to pay your own way, Danny," he cried.

We weren't equals after all.

I'd been sulking. There was a medium-sized young man's role in the play. As I read it I assumed Harold would offer me the role. I'd decided I'd decline, because the part wasn't strong enough or large enough, but at the back of my mind I was open to being persuaded. I thought Harold held off offering me the role to torment me: he knew I was out of work and in all the talk of auditions and casting he never mentioned who was being considered for the role.

Two days before rehearsals started Nick Sherwood told me he'd been cast.

Just before we flew to Nice I received a three sentence letter from the university drama department in America declining to offer me the post of actor-in-residence. I'd known they'd never accept me, and I believed Harold had always known my chances were slim. He'd used the nomination as a chance to meet me. I felt doubly betrayed.

On our second day we ate a late lunch at a restaurant off the Croisette in Cannes, empty except for one other couple. I watched them over Harold's shoulder: an ugly middle-aged businessman who wore a large diamond ring, and a girl even younger than me, *gamine*, her face half-alert, half-cynical. She caught my eye, took in Harold, and we smiled. We were platonic conspirators straight out of a Sagan novel, destroying our souls for the chance to eat fresh baked sardines at a restaurant in the South of France. For a moment it seemed to me a good idea that we should take off together.

After lunch Harold and I walked along the deserted Croisette. Empty white hotels sparkled in the sun. He told me the sting in the air was from the mistral that would soon begin to blow even harder. The sound of the wind's name, the moments I spent imagining its journey to this place I'd come to against my better judgment, were the most romantic

213

moments of my stay. I began to imagine my salvation lay in the solitary pursuit of adventure in far countries.

During our siesta, when Harold came up behind me and made amorous moves with his groin and hands, I said I had tummy trouble, which was true, but still an excuse. He persisted, getting angry, and it occurred to me that he thought he'd bought rights to my body. A lot of his anger was at his own cock, which could not be relied on to get hard, and then only with the help of Harold's hand.

His bad humour persisted during drinks at the hotel bar and in the side street restaurant where queers were said to congregate. I thought the restaurant's reputation must be exaggerated: impossible to believe that all these men were queer.

Harold fitted a cigarette into his holder for a quick smoke before the food arrived. "Why do you never talk about your parents, Danny?" he asked.

He looked sulky and determined in the candlelight that darkened his eye sockets and the pouches under them. I knew at once that we'd arrived at some sort of reckoning.

I tried to shrug off the question as I examined the other diners. "There's nothing to talk about, Harold. They live in another country. I'm all grown up. I've looked after myself since I was seventeen." Two sentences too many.

How often had I shrugged off Ben? Almost never: I'd met him head on, given serious attention to every word he uttered.

Harold's eyes narrowed, his head as he sucked at the holder held so high that it seemed in danger of toppling backwards off his shoulders. "We don't escape our parents so easily, Danny. You aren't ashamed of them, are you?"

"Of course not," I said irritably, quickly, almost honestly. My father's occupation had become part of the Daniel Henry story that got dished out in the press releases.

"Then why do you never talk about them, sweetie?" he insisted, far from affectionately. "Our families can be the bane of our existence or a source of great comfort to us. Why do you pretend yours stopped existing the moment you set foot on the boat for England?"

Suddenly stung, I scowled, threw up my hands impatiently, then reached for my wineglass, ready to reward myself with a gulp as soon as I'd spoken. "Just tell me what it is you want to know. I'll be happy to tell you anything."

Harold snorted in my face. I felt the beginnings of a dull trapped anger. "You keep missing the point, Danny. I'm not the grand inquisitor. I'm only asking you to talk normally about who you are, the way normal people do in the course of normal conversation. All I've ever heard you talk about is plays and films and books and your career."

Cold anger helped me make a decision and welcome it. "You start," I said. "You tell me something about your parents, and I'll do the same."

"You're very good at wriggling out of tight corners, Danny," Harold said loftily.

"No. I promise to tell you ten times as much as you tell me. But the next time you start talking about normal and abnormal I'll leave and you'll never see me again." I was greatly attracted to exploring the bars of Nice and Cannes alone.

Harold was angry too. For a moment I thought he'd blow his chance to hear what he wanted to hear. But he controlled himself, merely snorting to indicate that he had plenty left unsaid. "Very well, Danny. My father's greatest ambition for me was that I go to Eton."

I tried not to smirk at his unquestioning acceptance that he was entitled to such privilege.

"I think it was more important to him than any good fortune that came his way in his own career. He was the son of emigres, and I think he believed my Eton education would make him an Englishman too. My mother didn't care one way or the other. I think she felt a public school education was an unnecessary torture England inflicted on its sons."

"Not all its sons, Harold," I couldn't resist saying.

The salade nicoise arrived as my turn came. I seldom wasted an opportunity to eat, so I talked between mouthfuls and directed much of my attention to my plate. I was beginning to recognise that Harold had become a means to

215

an end, a litmus test of other people's reaction to a story I'd never told to anyone.

"I don't know what my father's ambitions for me were," I began.

Harold jumped on me immediately, thinking I wasn't going to keep my side of the bargain. "You can do better than that, Danny."

"No, I really don't know what he wanted for me. If anything. We didn't talk very much."

"You can do better than that," Harold repeated stubbornly.

I glanced up at him long enough to see his eyes narrowed in irritation. "Do you want me to tell the truth?" I complained sullenly, "or do you want me to invent a well-made drama that meets all your expectations? He was a porter at Belfast railway station. How much do you think he had in common with a queer son who wanted to be an actor?"

"He raised you, Danny," Harold reminded me, somewhat mollified.

"Sort of," I said. "They let me raise myself."

Now he thought I was romancing. "You were dependent on your parents for the first sixteen or seventeen years of your life," he insisted. "All children are, however much they like to pretend they're gypsies' babies. There must have been *someone* who encouraged your ambitions. They didn't appear out of thin air."

"The BBC," I said. "Quite seriously. I used to sit in the kitchen with my ear glued to the radio."

"I think you're determined not to do your parents justice, Danny. You still have this adolescent determination to insist that you did it all yourself with no help from anyone. I think if you were honest you'd see that a lot of your ambitions were inherited."

Both of us were already rather drunk. Harold became more adamant; I grew sullen in the face of his arrogant assumptions. I couldn't believe how hard it was to say what I had to say.

"I don't know what my father's aspirations were,

because he never talked about them. But I'm positive they had nothing to do with the theatre." And then I started to mumble, though I was trying hard to be clear, to stay in control: "In any case I don't know who my father was."

The waiter took away my plate and set the entrée, whatever it was, in front of me. I gulped at my wine and directed the rest of what I had to say to the waiter's back. "I was adopted."

I was ashamed. Not, I thought, of the fact, but because I sounded as if I were ashamed. It had occurred to me that Harold might suspect I was inventing a romantic fiction. When I glanced at him, his expression was inscrutable, but probably disapproving. I noticed that my face was damp.

I went on talking as I ate, trying to keep my voice level, looking at Harold only enough to meet the minimum requirements of normal behaviour.

"My mother had a baby very late in life, very late, a total surprise to everybody, that died. I believe. I only have secondhand information to go on because it was never talked about. Never. The way I found out I was adopted was through a friend's spite. I had a friend, Roy, off and on when I was growing up. He was a tearaway, and everyone knew his family had adopted him. But my parents – my foster parents, my adoptive parents, whatever – I'm only used to calling them my parents – wanted my adoption kept secret. So everyone in Belfast who knew me and my family knew I was adopted. I was the only one who didn't know. But I *did* know, at some deep level. It was a surprise, but also like a confirmation, when Roy told me when I was twelve. I'd landed a big part in a radio play and the *Belfast Telegraph* ran a piece on me. Roy chose that moment to tell me the truth, though he'd been warned he'd get the hiding of his life if he ever told me."

I broke off to wolf some food. Harold was listening intently, almost smiling, but neutral at best, far from sympathetic. I thought he was trying to decide if I was dishonest enough to tell such a complex lie.

"And I realised I knew my mother when Roy told me who she was. She'd come to see us one day when I was four

217

or five and I remembered her as Mrs. O'Neill, a friend of the family who was never mentioned again after that one time, though I remember asking my mother when she was going to visit us again."

Harold allowed himself an exploratory caveat: "It's surprising that you remembered her, Danny."

I gave him a good long glare. "No, Harold, it isn't surprising. The atmosphere that day must have been heavy with secrets and caution. Everybody in the street knew that my real mother was visiting and that I wasn't to be told. Don't you think I got some very strange looks and wondered what they were all about even at that age?"

Harold retreated behind a flinty smile.

"When I met my mother again she'd just come back from Germany where she'd been working with displaced persons. Roy told me the gossip amongst people who really hated me was that my father was German. But the chronology was wrong for that. My mother had me before she went to Germany, and there were certainly no Germans in Belfast at the time I was born. She went to Germany to get over the shame of having me."

Harold opened his mouth to protest again, but the look I levelled at him made him think better of it. I'd realised I was on my own. His reaction to the story was somehow frivolous and shallow.

"Roy knew where my mother was," I continued. "All I had to do was look up her address in the phone book and take the train to Bangor, the town twelve miles from Belfast where she was living."

"You mean you ran away from home?" Harold asked unemotionally, as if he was conducting an official investigation.

"No. I just paid her a visit the next Saturday without telling anyone where I was going."

The occasion seemed to require from me some special effort at description, some extra emotional weight, but I was incapable of supplying it. I'd ridden the train grimly, not thinking about what was going to happen, and searched out the small terrace street where my mother lived. It was in the centre of town, five minutes from the railway station. The second I knew I'd found the right house my stomach sank and my knees felt wobbly but I pushed myself towards the front door.

"She answered the door. She looked exactly the way I remembered her. She looked like Maureen O'Hara, but heavier."

Harold's eyes flickered, dismissing my fondest memory of my mother as consoling fiction.

"She knew who I was. She'd seen the *Telegraph* article about the radio play. She just said 'Come in.' All my nerves went away the moment I saw her. She made me a cup of tea. It was flat, very ordinary."

Harold couldn't stop himself snorting a protest. "But Danny, she was seeing her son for the first time in six or seven years. It must have been a very emotional moment for her. And for you."

"Of course it was. But neither of us showed it. Not when we set eyes on each other. I didn't even feel it for a long time. We sat at the kitchen table and she launched into her story right away as if she'd been rehearsing it for years. She was very defensive and angry. I clearly wasn't allowed to question whether she ever had any alternative to giving me up.

"She told me she already had a son and daughter when I was born. She lived with her husband in a town called Newry on the other side of Belfast from Bangor. He was some kind of commercial traveller and they also had a small farm that she took care of with the help of an occasional part-time hand. She got close to one of those hands, and when she got pregnant with me her husband accused her of having an affair with the farmhand. She swore to him that it wasn't true, but he wouldn't believe her. She swore to me it wasn't true, and I still don't know if she was telling me the truth. But of course I didn't let her know I maybe didn't believe her.

"Her husband, perhaps my father, called in a Methodist minister and they forced a deal on her. The church would arrange for her to have the baby in Belfast and it would be adopted and afterwards she could come back to live with

219

her husband. I was born in the Midnight Mission in the Malone Road in Belfast –"

Harold couldn't stop himself bristling at such melodrama.

"It's on my birth certificate," I said, not bothering to hide my contempt. "I got a copy of my birth certificate without telling my adoptive parents, on the pretext that I'd need it if I ever wanted a passport. Not that I had any prospect of going anywhere. That way I was able to ask my adoptive parents why I'd been born in the Midnight Mission without giving Roy away. My mother – my real mother – claimed not to remember much about my birth. She said she was having a nervous breakdown through the whole thing. But she did keep control over the adoption instead of just giving me up to some anonymous person from an orphanage. A friend of a friend knew that my mother had lost her baby –"

"Your real mother?" Harold interrupted harshly.

I peered into his face to see if he was totally drunk. "My adoptive mother. She was the one who lost her baby and adopted me instead. So they sent her word that there was a baby available and she came to see my mother - - I suppose at the Midnight Mission — and it was arranged."

I helped Harold and myself to wine from the carafe and sat back, tired but feeling unassailable, almost triumphant with relief at getting it all out.

"That's quite a story, Danny," Harold said with a stern tight smile. He still wasn't sure that I wasn't an extravagant liar. "The reporters would have had a field day with that story if you'd told it to them."

"I was tempted to," I said. "They always get the stories so wrong that it ends up not mattering what they say. But I had two families to consider, and I couldn't hurt my mother, and my adoptive parents still think adoption is the most shameful thing that can happen to anyone. I think they always supposed the lie that we were blood relatives was the only thing that kept me from leaving them. Because I was different from them, as different as night and day."

Harold nodded to concede the logic of what I was saying, though not necessarily its truthfulness. "So you're still in touch with all of them?"

"My Aunt Peggy fights to hold on to me. She's my mother's spinster sister who lives five doors down from us. Roy told me there was even a rumour in the street that she was my real mother. My mother's solution to everything has always been to keep the house clean. When she finished at the bottom she started at the top again, and it was a very small house.

"Your real mother?" Harold interrupted.

"No, my adoptive mother," I said, beginning to wonder if Harold was even listening to me. "What I hear about what she really feels is relayed through Aunt Peggy, so I'm never sure whose message I'm really hearing. I saw my real mother two more times after I found her again, then not for five years until just before I came to England. That was how I got the money to come here. I'd have had to work in that shop a long time to save up £80. I asked my real mother to lend me some of her savings. I got the idea for that from *East of Eden*. The film, not the book."

Harold almost exploded. My mixing filmed melodrama with a story I claimed to be real was too much for him. He obviously suspected I was playing an outrageous hoax on him – at the same time he felt beguiled into believing me.

"'Talk to me, father,'" I pleaded in my best imitation of James Dean as Cal. "'I've gotta know who I am.'"

Harold's nostrils flared.

I couldn't resist directing an enigmatic smile at him over my wineglass. "I wish French desserts were gooier," I said blithely. "It's always fruit tarts and *pommes* and *poires*. I'd rather have something with cake and cream and chocolate sauce." I was taking my revenge for being forced to expose myself.

"I'd have thought you'd have wanted to stay close to your mother," Harold said over coffee, probing for a weak link in the story's logic.

"Which one?" I asked, pretending to be genuinely puzzled.

He controlled himself. "Your real mother. When you were twelve. After all the emotional trauma of finding her."

221

"She was very angry," I said. "At my father for destroying her life and mine. At the Methodist church. But she wanted more from me than I could give her. And there was too much going on. A whole new family. After I was born my mother went back to my father, if he was my father, and had another baby. But the marriage was destroyed. That was when she went to Germany, taking Ernie with her. The day she came to see us she brought him with her. So I also met my brother, or at least my half-brother, without knowing it. We hated each other on sight. He was whiney and pretty. He was the one who suffered most from all the upheaval, I think. When I met him again in Bangor he was in trouble with the police and my mother said he was still wetting the bed. And they were living with my older brother and his wife, who'd just got married and already didn't get on. All her children took her side against their father. My older sister had married a Jew. I think there was one Jewish family in that entire town, totally foreign and more segregated from both the Protestants and Catholics than the Protestants and Catholics were segregated from each other. My sister, of all people, had to marry into that family.

"At first a whole new family seemed very exciting, but it very soon became a lot more than I could handle. I just stopped visiting. I thought I'd get Christmas and birthday cards, but they never came. But when I went back for money she gave it to me. I repaid her out of my *Boxing Day Hill* money. Double."

"That must have been a traumatic scene," Harold said, "when you went back to get the money."

"No," I said. "You don't get it, Harold. What's traumatic is all the stuff you carry with you over the years. When you meet again you don't suddenly erupt in Greek drama. It's as if both of you know what's been going on inside the other and it doesn't need to be spoken. You just behave very ordinarily: 'You're taller,' you say. 'You've put on weight. Have you started smoking?'"

Now I was presuming to give a lecture on emotional truth to an artist whose performances were famous for it.

I think both of us wanted to get out of the restaurant as fast as possible. A smoky bar with a drag show was on the itinerary of all queer visitors, and we went straight there.

Even to queer theatre people the spectacle of raucous men in makeup and dresses was upsetting as well as exotic: the drag queens confronted us with the notion that to be queer was close to being a woman, at the same time that they challenged conventional ideas of what it meant to be a man. I think I know why we still crowded into that bar. The drag shows were as close to a public affirmation of our queerness as we could get. Even if they travestied our inner feelings, they were all we had. But that night I watched from a distance. The long angry self-justifying confession to Harold had left me euphoric as well as drained. I suggested we leave, much sooner than I normally wanted to leave when I was out with Harold. In bed, though I was too drunk and tired for sex, I impulsively pulled Harold on top of me and writhed with him for a few moments in what may have seemed to him like passion. It didn't last long, but it was the first time it occurred to me that anyone might take comfort from his flesh.

Next morning we took a local train to a small country station and were met by a chauffeur who drove us to a villa at Cap Ferrat. He stopped before we got to the house to show us the view that visitors so admired: a promontory with a stone seat, the grass and bushes warm and living even at this time of year, dark winter in England, and nothing else in view except the great sunlit ocean and the blue empty sky. I shook my head, faced with the limitations on where my wildest ambitions would get me. Even a Hollywood income wouldn't buy me such an expensive piece of the earth.

We lunched with an English lord who'd recently suffered a tragedy: three months earlier his boyfriend had lost control of his car on one of the hilly roads on the property and killed himself. The widower was pale and restrained and rather bored. We ate lunch at a small table in a huge white room – the lord was served steak, Harold and I ate pigeon that yielded barely a full forkful of meat. Before

223

lunch the lord's mother appeared and talked to us for a minute before returning to her quarters.

"The upper-class English are like that," I said on the train back to Nice. "They could live separate lives for ever in a huge house without ever connecting. When they get married they think the highest style is to treat each other with scathing contempt."

"You really are hell, Danny," Harold said quietly.

I said smartly: "If I'm such hell why are you in love with me?"

Harold hesitated. "And a little bit of heaven, Danny."

❊ ❊ ❊ ❊ ❊

Two days before the first night of the play he was directing, Harold was interviewed by the *Daily Express*. When the reporter arrived at Harold's house with a photographer he didn't even pretend to any interest in the play. Harold, caught off guard, chose to answer two or three questions truthfully, then ordered the *Express* men to leave. Next morning the William Hickey column reported that a guardsman facing trial for the murder of a QC had another even more famous mentor. Harold Brookman, the celebrated Shakespearean actor and director, had encouraged the guardsman's interest in the arts after being introduced to him by mutual friends. The implications were clear, though the William Hickey people thought so little of the story that they ran it third after news of a society divorce and a wedding.

"I knew he was quite mad," Harold told me. "I could tell from his eyes. Though it certainly never occurred to me that he was capable of murder."

The guardsman's obvious madness hadn't prevented Harold inviting him to the house more than once.

My own complicated reaction to the story disturbed me. Of course I felt sympathy and outrage. Harold's homosexuality was tolerated by London society only because it was never mentioned. He didn't know who would cut him now that it had been aired by Beaverbrook. I could only

224

guess at how much courage it took for him to walk into his club after the item appeared. But I had another reaction, a kind of gloating contempt for him for letting himself be exposed. I'd never been trapped, so I could still identify with the enemy.

The play was a failure, and Harold took more of the blame for it than he perhaps deserved. He was not a showy director, and critics had trouble identifying his contribution to a work. When the script was bad he was damned, when he had a good script to work with his direction was praised extravagantly.

I perhaps exaggerated the flop's effect on him because I hadn't his experience of living with the ebb and flow of a long career. He suddenly suggested that we go to Vienna for three days. I couldn't believe that he wanted to repeat the misery of the trip to Nice, then realised that the trip might not have been as miserable for him as it was for me. Or miserable in a different way. I know now that he was suffering madness of the heart. Vienna had been the setting of his greatest love affair when he was a young actor. Who else would he take but the man who passed for his current lover?

"Kiss every stone for me," said an actor we ran into at London airport. But I wouldn't allow myself to enjoy Schonbrunn because I couldn't believe the people who'd inhabited it deserved such architecture. The same evening, on the way to the Reisenrad in the Prater, Harold's cigarette brushed against a woman's coat. She turned to complain, took in the two of us, dismissed us with a knowing epithet Harold would not translate for me. We got to a bar on the Ringstrasse too early or on the wrong night, and found ourselves alone except for one other couple at a corner table: two dark-haired young men in black leather jackets, deep in conversation about serious matters, their bodies aching for each other. On the jukebox Nat King Cole sang *Stardust*. I couldn't take my eyes off what I'd lost, and didn't care that Harold had to watch my obsessive watching.

The next night, in a club frequented by expensive male

prostitutes, we got drunk with an old flame of Harold's and his young lover, at whom I made a pass at the urinal. He told his lover, who told Harold, who had to clean the rug I threw up on when we got back to the Hotel Am Stephansplatz.

"I don't think we have a future, do you, Danny?" Harold asked grimly at lunch the next day.

"If that's what you think," I said. Thank God, I thought, then began to dread that he would make one last attempt to reconcile that night in bed.

*****

Towards the end of my next lesson with Julian he told me he was retiring. I waited for him to say he'd make an exception for me, but he didn't. Lately we'd been clashing: I got exasperated when he jumped in with his suggestions instead of waiting to see what I'd do. We met for one more lesson. I wanted him to tell me how good I was, predict the course of my career. But we worked on a speech until another student arrived early. I started to tell him what he'd meant to me, but he almost pushed me out the door.

"We'll keep in touch," he said smoothly. "I hope you'll come to my Christmas party."

I read in Sidney Edwards' column in the *Standard* that *Romeo and Juliet* was finally going ahead. Romeo would be played by a Bristol Old Vic actor who was having a great success in a new film. Five minutes after I read the news I found myself worrying over how I'd speak one of Romeo's lines that I'd forgotten to ask Julian about – it seemed that when bad news came part of me denied its arrival.

Three months later I stole into a Wednesday matinee of what the papers were calling the 'Hammer Shakespeare,' because Montague and Capulet were played by two actors famous for their work in British horror films. I expected them to have trouble crossing the stage, but they turned out to be competent. In the interval I read that both had long careers, now forgotten, years ago at the Old Vic.

I wanted to be bored by the actor who played Romeo,

but I could hardly take my eyes off him. It stung to hear plausible line readings that hadn't occurred to me. His performance, the production as a whole, lacked a solid through line, a reason for its existence. They'd staged *Romeo and Juliet* because they were ambitious, not because they had anything to say. I would have done it better.

SIX

I'd heard nothing about Ben in the two years since he left me. He'd always kept me away from his family and colleagues, the few friends we had in common were queer men I'd introduced him to, and he disappeared from their lives the moment he disappeared from mine. With one exception – a grim November weekend when I'd agreed to drive down to Harold's musty cottage and he went on about the fragile green of the foliage in spring as if Oscar Wilde had never put the natural world in its place – I always ran with the harriers on Sunday morning, even in storms of thunder and snow. I thought this was where Ben would come if he wanted to see me again but was too proud or afraid to approach me directly.

We'd fall in beside each other on the path near Kenwood House, Ben looking heartbreakingly young in his white singlet. It was, after all, only polite to be civil after so long a time apart. At first we'd be formal because neither of us knew if his place in the other man's heart had been filled by someone else – but here my imaginings lost their delicacy because I was overcome with lust at the thought of Ben in running shorts, the cotton crinkled on either side of his crotch, the bulge pulling the cloth away from his thigh. That was what I longed for: his warmth and smell, so familiar that other men always felt like foreigners.

But Ben never showed up.

My days were rather empty now and I began serious training with the notion of working up to a London to Brighton one year. I usually started the day with a long run in Hyde Park or on the Heath, not too early. I was always on the lookout: who knew where or at what time Ben ran nowadays? In the evening another short run over one of the bridges to stop my craving for a cigarette. My diet had also changed: like the news of the dangers of smoking, information about what certain foods did to the body was finally filtering down to the public. Everything your mother said was good for you actually clogged your arteries. In Ulster we'd fried eggs and soda bread in lard.

I became thin and light-headed, my skin translucent on my bones, and developed numerous inexpensive addictions that filled the days now that my career seemed stalled – to the sweat of great exertion on my skin, to the feel of the sun and rain on my body, to the smell of my kit when it was clean and after it had shaped itself to my body on a long run. On an evening run along the Embankment I'd be lucky to see one other solitary fanatic. The general population left athletics behind with schooldays.

I didn't give up drinking or sex, though I regarded both as stopgaps to see me through till Ben showed up again. One night I fucked a visiting Dane, his brown body so hard and spare that it hurt to embrace him. We discovered a line of blood on the sheet under him. Six months later he showed up on my doorstep.

"You were the first," he said. Next day he left again, his painful emotions as tightly wrapped as his body.

An advertising man I picked up in Sloane Square managed to convey, by showing me a room where strips of rag were lying around, that he wanted to be bound to a chair. My rage when I started to beat him with a belt seemed like an old friend. I didn't stop beating him when he shouted for me to stop, but he managed to free a hand.

"I don't want to end up in the *News of the World*," he complained.

One night I found myself in bed with Tom Finlay, whom I saw no more than twice a year now. I'd learned to arrive rather late at his annual party in late September with two stiff drinks already inside me, introduce myself to strangers without needing a pretext, and leave quite soon. His small living room couldn't really hold more than twelve people comfortably; more and more of the well-dressed people I met there turned out to work in wine merchants. Once a year or so I met Tom for dinner and we did the bars rather half-heartedly, cramping each other's style. It was difficult to keep the conversation going for an evening after I became defensive about my career.

"There are always things in the works," I'd say, "but you

know how long it takes to get a project going. It's all a total seesaw. I wish I could make a living just running on Hampstead Heath." And then I'd change the subject.

But one night when I felt oppressed, jumpy from some threat I couldn't pin down, I asked Tom if I could come back to his flat for another drink. We began to play with each other's cocks, mildly curious, and that was the end of it. Tom's sexuality hinged on yearning after dangerous working-class youths.

The first time I got the clap I was naive enough to go to the VD clinic at St. Thomas's.

"It's gonorrhea all right," a depressed young doctor told me.

I sat there sickened, ashamed of my body.

"You people don't know what sort of epidemic you're starting. I suppose there's no way to trace who you got it from?"

"As far as I know I got it from an American journalist." I still had enough spirit to try to mislead him. "She's in Vietnam by now."

He raised his head from his notes long enough to give me a small contemptuous glare. "Your contact was male."

The next time I got the name of a queer doctor in Knightsbridge from Nick Sherwood.

"Did you really have an affair with Michael Baker when you were that young?" the doctor asked as he prepared a syringe.

✳ ✳ ✳ ✳ ✳

I spotted Charlotte Ritchie one afternoon in St. Martin's Lane and almost passed without speaking to her. She was swinging on the lapels of an older character actor, talking up into his face. But she saw me out of the corner of her eye.

"Daniel Henry!" she called, adding two syllables to my Christian name and peering at me as if I was barely discernible five feet away in the spring sunlight. "Promise to ring me and come to dinner."

I waited three days before I called her. Charlotte was

230

tentative at first, seeming not to remember her offer until I prompted her.

I thought I knew exactly what I was getting into.

Charlotte had created a living room in St. John's Wood that was a maze of independent nooks, with little space to stand or walk between them – the opposite of stage living rooms with their huge unlikely spaces. Charlotte, even tinier than I remembered her, served a cold dinner herself, salmon and chocolate mousse, sitting close to me at a corner of the dining table for what she called a tete-a-tete.

She blinked away the fact that I wasn't getting work. "I know all about it, dear boy!"

I wasn't allowed to entertain the notion that I might lack talent or drive. She seemed much more intrigued by the news that Ben had left me for a woman.

After dinner she gave me brandy in a screened recess. She smelled of silk and perfume. It was clear that I was supposed to make love to her, but she backed away an inch, looking startled, when I leaned over to kiss her.

"Dear boy!" she demurred.

I quite liked the taste of expensive makeup.

Charlotte led me to her bedroom and stopped me at the door with a finger to my chest.

"Join me in a moment, Daniel," she said, looking resolute and suddenly rather grim.

While I waited, rather drunk, for exactly five minutes, I had a brutal image of her cleaning the female plumbing that disgusted me. But if Ben could do it I could.

Her body was tinier than any I had rolled on top of, all fragile bones and very little flesh. When I moved my mouth dutifully down to her breasts I discovered that they'd disappeared, all but the leathery nipples, flattened against her chest. My cock hardened briefly at the strangeness of it all, but when I reached down to put it inside Charlotte – moving gingerly at the thought of touching her down there with my hand – I found I'd shrunk again. For the first time I confirmed, mortified, what I'd always heard: soft cock into vagina won't go. I concocted a flurry of passion with my mouth around Charlotte's nonexistent breasts, then tried

231

again. Still no luck.

I rolled onto my back. "I'm sorry. I've had too much to drink."

As I settled down to sleep it off I heard her calm voice from the depths of her pillow: "You must go now, Daniel."

✳✳✳✳✳

One July afternoon thirty minutes before closing time I sat in the Colville in the King's Road working my way though an early edition of the *Standard*. I'd tried eating a slice of veal and ham pie so distasteful that as usual I wondered why I ever tried. At best it was an excuse for eating French mustard. I'd drunk most of a pint of bitter, which after a long run earlier that day should have taken care of the residue of my hangover. But it hadn't.

Every day I searched the *Standard* for Ben's wife's byline and dissected her well-intentioned stories about social problems for grammatical errors and faulty logic. When all else failed I blamed her for not exposing the inadequacy of the remedies she publicised.

I was having trouble concentrating on the print. Sweat had sprung on my forehead and I wiped it off with a handkerchief, glancing around apologetically in case anyone was watching. I took a gulp of beer. For a reason I didn't want to think about it suddenly seemed imperative that I prove I could read the paper.

The lines of print were blurred. I blinked hard. The words became very clear, as if they were printed in bold type, but they didn't make sense. And then they began to dissolve before my eyes. Quite suddenly I felt as if a red hot poker had been pressed against my brain. I gasped and grabbed the table to stop myself falling to the floor. But the floor seemed to be dropping away.

I had to move to save myself. I poured the rest of the beer down my throat, pushed myself to my feet, both hands on the table for support, and staggered to the door, barely conscious, dragging each side of my body after its foot. Another patron smiled a cheerful goodbye. Then he took a second look at me.

The air on my face was a fleeting relief, but the sun felt too hot to be real. I knew I was going mad – I'd be locked up with no control over what happened to me. That fear was enough to make me do anything to prevent it. I stumbled along the street towards my car, stopping at shop windows to hide my unsteadiness, pretending to look inside so that I could cool my forehead against the glass. I caught a reflection: hollow-eyed, in desperate straits. I thought: If I can just get to my car it will prove that I'm still in control of what I'm doing, and that will mean I'm not mad.

When my heart slowed I realised how hard it had been pounding. It occurred to me that I might be feeling better, but the terrible inexplicable fear began to be replaced by a different fear, that the terrible fear would come again.

My new doctor would be able to see me at 5:30. I set my alarm, mixed a stiff vodka and tonic and took it to bed. Instinctively I felt there were certain places I'd be safe: in bed, probably anywhere in my flat, and while I was running. Crowded rooms and streets seemed the places to avoid.

The doctor was unimpressed by my symptoms. I knew my manner and appearance didn't plead my cause: however much I insisted I'd been scared to death, I was able to talk quite lucidly about the symptoms because I'd been free of them for hours.

"There's nothing wrong with your heart or lungs," he said.

I'd already guessed that.

"It sounds like a mild anxiety attack," he said. "I see much worse in some of my patients. It must be rather like the aura epileptics feel when an attack is coming on."

"I'm not your other patients," I complained. "To me it was the most frightening thing that ever happened to me, and I absolutely do not want to go through it ever again."

He wrote me a prescription for Valium. "Try this for a couple of weeks. It's a very mild tranquilliser."

The drug, or my fear of the fear, made my skin clammy. I felt all the time that I was sitting at a high window, watching what was happening to me down below.

One idle afternoon I went to the Odeon Kensington to see Michael Baker in a comedy that had opened without a critics' screening. It was filmed in black and white and took place entirely inside a courtroom, though there was no evidence in the credits that it was based on a play. The action had one premise: a barrister, played by Michael, found it impossible to deal with his learned friend because she was female. I still enjoyed looking at him, though he was getting jowly and he and the female star had been photographed to look powdery and constipated. Their voices sounded tinny and over-amplified in the empty cinema.

"Futile," I heard myself muttering.

The futility overwhelmed me. I gasped and bent forward in my seat, fear blossoming in my chest and pounding in my ears. I dove into a pocket for the envelope in which I carried an emergency supply of Valium and shoved three of them in my mouth. My head was going to explode, I was falling into red darkness. I crunched and sucked at the pills, willing relief to swim into my blood.

I stood up abruptly and stumbled up the aisle, as if I thought I could get away from myself.

"This film stinks!" I shouted, trying to counter the violence of what was happening to me with my own violence. I heard another patron, perhaps the only one in the cinema, cheer and clap agreement.

As I hurried along the street, panicky to get home safely, I noticed that I was moving in slow motion. Warm air nudged my skin in waves.

I phoned Nick Sherwood for the number of the psychiatrist he was seeing.

"I know somebody who needs to talk to an expert," I said, not fooling Nick.

I was stricken, apparently mentally ill, and certainly unhappy. I'd seen a reissue of *Spellbound* when I was nine and learned that just under the surface we were all a mass of conflicts that might erupt at any moment in frightening symptoms. I'd read *The Divided Self*, which struck a chord: we were victims of our families. I took it for granted that Dr. Scanlon, a specialist in the science of the mind, knew

234

what he was doing.

He was a slight blond man who betrayed little sympathy. There were even times when he seemed to find his work unsavory, but I thought he was too preoccupied with achieving an efficient cure to cultivate a bedside manner.

On the large heavy desk that separated us during our first session, he kept photos of his wife, also a psychiatrist, and their three children, two by his previous marriage. ("Psychiatrists always have at least one divorce behind them," Nick had informed me.) He prescribed Seconal in addition to the Valium, and I learned to crush the bitter capsules between my teeth when I felt an anxiety attack coming on.

"I'm queer," I told him matter-of-factly. "I don't believe that's sick or immature. Otherwise I'm neutral about it."

I heard my own turmoil: Being queer hadn't been good enough for Ben.

But it helped to talk. By the end of the first session I felt the same warm well-being I'd felt after I told Harold the adoption tale.

"One thing worries me," I told Scanlon. "I've done very well, with all my problems, or complexes, whatever they are."

He nodded. "Talent is a mysterious thing. What would you be if you hadn't become an actor? A clerk?"

"That's what worries me. Maybe my problems are what drives my talent. Maybe if you take away the problems you'll take away the talent."

"You should become more productive, not less, as you become healthier," he said.

What else could he say? I was willing to believe him.

"And your career appears to have ground to a halt."

"That's the nature of the business," I said carelessly. "It happens to every actor."

Scanlon looked dubious, and it occurred to me that he was perhaps not as knowledgeable as he thought.

He played a final card: "These anxiety attacks could be crippling if you were in a play."

235

"Oh no," I said, enormously confident. "They wouldn't happen while I was on the stage. I'd be safe if I was acting."

When I arrived for the next session he told me to lie down on a padded table. He was going to hypnotise me. I tried hard to relax and go under, but it didn't work.

"I did try," I insisted. "A stage hypnotist once tried to hypnotise me on the stage of the Belfast Hippodrome and it didn't work. I was the only one out of six people it didn't work on."

"I think you were resisting," Patrick said tightly. I called him Dr. Scanlon to his face, Patrick when I was comparing notes with Nick.

"No, I was really trying."

He took a small bag from his desk. "Pull up your sleeve. This is a very mild injection of Ritalin to help you relax. It has no after effects."

The drug rushed the same feeling throughout my body that psychotherapy took fifty minutes to achieve.

"I could get addicted to this," I said cheerfully.

Patrick sat well behind me, out of sight, usually silent until he announced the end of the session. I always knew when time was running out because I could feel the drug wear off, the dose timed almost to the minute. When I sat up, cold again, surprised not to feel groggy, Patrick would make some ordinary comment to sum up. It took on enormous weight for me because I'd handed over so much of myself.

As the talk flowed out of my mouth I heard what had shaped or still consumed me. As a child I'd been hovered over yet ignored, the parents wary of harming something that didn't belong to them, fearful of losing another baby, but already middle-aged and defeated, unable to cope with my energy.

"I always had this fear," I remembered, "that I'd be shut up under other people's control. My parents or Aunt Peggy would be able to visit me when they wanted and I'd be powerless to do anything but submit. In a hospital or sanatorium or somewhere." I made a sudden connection. "Or in an insane asylum."

236

"Were you very religious?" Patrick asked, as if he already knew the answer.

I wondered how he could possibly have guessed. "Briefly. I was converted when the evangelists came to town. The man I told about my decision invited me to his room for a talk and we knelt down beside his bed to pray. He was wearing grey flannels. It was the sexiest thing that had ever happened to me up to then."

The mixed messages of indifference and smothering were still being sent from home. My adoptive parents kept a respectful distance, but Aunt Peggy tried to run my life. Her letters sent me into a rage that brought on guilt and endless nagging thoughts that if I was really grownup I wouldn't care what she wrote.

On my fourth visit to Patrick I told him uncertainly that I thought I was going to cut her out of my life.

"For your sake I think that's a good idea," he said. But he salved his conscience: "I have to point out that she may not be deliberately setting out to have this effect on you."

"I know," I said. "She loves me, whatever that means. But love isn't always something you can put up with."

"Do you still hanker after Ben?" Patrick asked me coldly.

"No, of course not," I lied, convincing neither of us. Ben was out of bounds, even to a psychiatrist.

Patrick decided I was ready for an overnight LSD session at his home, a specialty of his I'd wanted to try since Nick told me how he'd regressed to the age of two and gone through his toilet training again.

Patrick's house in North London was pokier than I'd imagined it. No signs of his family or the other patients he treated with LSD on these weekend sessions. He led me to a tiny room at the top of the house and left me to undress. The waterproof sheet under its thin cotton cover made a crumpling sound as I got under the blanket – Nick had told me how Patrick protected his beds from incontinent patients, an awful detail that added to the seriousness of the treatment. I was surprised not to be hungrier: Patrick had instructed me not to eat dinner.

He returned with his little bag and painlessly injected

237

my arm with the LSD. Hypodermic needles seemed to have become thinner, or perhaps private doctors used more expensive needles.

"What can I expect?" I asked.

"Probably nothing for two or three hours," Patrick said, in a hurry to get away. He clearly regretted saying even that much, resolute in his scientific determination not to contaminate my insights. He showed me a button to push if I needed him, and left me alone.

It wasn't unpleasant to snuggle under the blanket to await the beginning of a medically regulated adventure. Across the Atlantic high school children were reportedly sharing the drug for lunch. But two or three hours was a long time to wait.

I raised my head, suddenly alert, though my body resisted movement. It was hard to see anything in that dark cubbyhole of a room. I thought perhaps the ghost of the lamplight from the street below stealing past the curtains made a rainbow rectangle, but by the time I noticed it was gone. Then I noticed that a small chest of drawers was shedding geometric shapes that marched towards the door. My head dropped back on the pillow – I was easily overwhelmed. The room was back to normal, except that I sensed it living an intense life of its own, which rooms were clearly entitled to. A lot was going on in corners, where I could tell that specks of dust were busy admiring themselves in the exceptionally polished wooden floor.

At some point Patrick came into the room, as detached and hard-working as ever.

"Not much is happening," I said, thinking I was telling him the truth.

He settled, notebook in hand, in a chair at the foot of the bed. No place here for him to hide.

The room and Patrick waited for me. I thought I was certain to disappoint them.

I was at the bottom of a well, looking up at myself when I was four or six years old, looking down at myself and feeling very sad.

"Patrick," I said, raising my head, eager to tell him what

238

was happening to me. But I'd been aware for some time that Patrick had gone to sleep. I'd heard his snores. I saw that his chin had dropped on his chest and his mouth hung open, his lower lip lax.

"Patrick," I called, louder, and he jumped and jerked back to holding his notebook at a professional angle as if I'd caught him stealing.

I began to talk, totally unable to get the words out fast enough, forgetting what I said as it spilled from my mouth. The pressure of all the words piling up faster than I could get them out brought me to a halt and I kept repeating the same word until I couldn't say even that.

Patrick darted from the room, I knew to get help, leaving me suspended, waiting so helplessly that panic seemed beside the point. He came back with a needle that brought relief as quickly as the Ritalin he injected in my arm once a week. I turned on my side and settled into sleep.

I was fully dressed, sitting on the edge of the bed eating the apple I'd brought with me, when Patrick came to wake me in the morning. He seemed to welcome my offer to find my own way downstairs and out of the house. I was given no chance to comment on last night's events. I fantasised that a patient made of weaker stuff than I had gone spectacularly mad during last night's LSD treatment and still needed all his attention.

I drove home not knowing what to think of what had happened to me. Most of North London was still enjoying its Saturday morning lie-in, but I got a chance to honk at a runner from the Sunday morning runs, grateful for the whiff of fresh air he brought me. I stopped for breakfast at my favourite place for food that was bad for me, Lyons Teashop in Kensington High Street. Excellent strong tea, two poached eggs on toast and two cold expensive strips of bacon.

I'd got less sleep than I thought. As I sat at home reading the paper I caught myself nodding off. I poured a large glass of sherry to help knock me out and took it to bed.

When I got up again and went into the bathroom my face and hair looked bleached. Out of habit I put on shorts and singlet and headed out the door for the park. But my stock way of bringing myself back to life didn't work as well as usual – I had to haul my body through its paces. For the rest of the weekend I stayed close to home, repairing myself with food and drink and rest.

On Monday morning the police called and said they wanted to talk to me about the two murders that had been committed in Earl's Court.

"I'd be delighted to help," I said, "though I don't see how I can." The call felt somehow inevitable, though I knew nothing about the murders.

Two detectives arrived an hour later – middle-aged, medium height, their bodies thickening in dark suits. Their eyes looked patient but pained, perhaps from deprivation, perhaps from all that they were forced to see. They'd learned to modulate their voices to hide their thoughts, but not to disguise humble accents.

I volunteered that I'd read about the murders in the *Kensington Post*. All I was thinking about was when and how they'd mention that the murder victims had been single men who frequented the Earl's Court queer pubs.

One of the detectives said he was interested in interviewing an Australian called John. "A friend of yours says he saw you talking to him at the Coleherne pub."

I searched my memory, genuinely trying to help.

"It's possible. I sometimes talk to a lot of people when I go out for a drink. But I don't remember talking to an Australian for any length of time. Australians and I tend not to enjoy each other's company. I find them gauche."

Which was true. I neglected to add that I lusted after Australian bodies.

My doorbell rang, and I excused myself.

A young woman stood on the front doorstep.

"I would like to introduce you to the Bible," she told me in a French accent.

I slammed the door in her face.

When I came into my flat again the detectives were going through my jackets and coats in the bedroom cupboard. They went on searching while I watched them.

240

"Do you have a blue suit?" one asked.

They mentioned several names to me, and several physical descriptions.

I could give them no help.

"On a busy night there are probably thirty men of medium height with brown hair wearing blue jeans at either of those Earl's Court pubs. I know hardly anybody's name. Someone will tell me his name and I'll promptly forget it and then I'll be too embarrassed to ask again. There are men in those pubs I've passed the time of day with for years and I still don't know their names."

"Your friends must be talking about the murders," a detective suggested.

"I've never heard anyone mention the murders. I mentioned them to someone –"

A detective looked alert. I anticipated his question.

"I don't know the name of the man I mentioned them to. He's tall and thin with thinning very blond hair. Almost albino. And he wasn't interested in talking about the murders. People go out to enjoy themselves, not to talk about getting murdered. And they're not really my friends. They're people who drink at the same pubs I do."

Just when I thought there was nothing more we could productively say to each other, the detectives exchanged glances.

"I think we should ask Mr. Henry to make a statement," one said to the other.

I felt somehow tricked, but I couldn't see any reason not to make a statement.

They let me follow them to the station in my own car. One of the detectives left me alone with his partner in a small windowless room like the rooms in *Z Cars*. He began to write out my statement for me, starting with my name, age, address and occupation.

"I saw you in *Ghosts*," he finally admitted. "A rather morbid play. Are you a homosexual, Mr. Henry?"

"Yes," I stammered, ashamed that my ears had started to burn. "Not that I think it's any of your business."

He nodded, and began to write down his account of

241

what I'd said in the interview, stopping now and then to check a detail with me. Then he read it to me from the beginning, in all its hilariously flat detail: "I first heard of the Earl's Court murders when I read about them in the *Kensington Post*. I don't enjoy the company of Australians because I find them gauche. I am a homosexual."

I signed the statement as soon as he finished reading it, and we shook hands like colleagues. All I felt at first was relief to be out of the station.

That night I went back to the Coleherne, wanting to bawl out whoever had given my name to the police, if I could identify him. It was a hopeless task: anyone who knew who I was could have fed my name to the police as a provocative tidbit. The pub was busy enough, though most of the familiar faces were absent. With one or two drinks inside me I found myself relating my adventures on LSD to a solicitor's clerk. His interest stalled at the name of the drug – he assumed I'd got it wrong. LSD meant money. I thought that some people had no idea what was going on in the world.

I caught the eye of a man who worked in the City and smiled to him to come over. He was a handsome man, and I'd been to bed with him, but a kind of utilitarian heartlessness seemed to affect even the way he had sex. He showed no feeling, his body like a sturdy rubber doll, his penis jerking out semen as mechanically as a tube yields toothpaste. Even his black hair, plastered to his scalp, felt dead. But he could be relied on to give selfish sensible advice.

"I should simply have told them I'd be happy to make a statement after I consulted my solicitor," he said immediately.

The simple solution confronted me with my own stupidity. I was still the provincial who believed he was at the mercy of the authorities, the child who acted guilty until he proved himself innocent. My anger at myself helped me identify some of the rest of the anger I'd managed to hide from myself.

✻ ✻ ✻ ✻ ✻

242

It felt good to confirm that Patrick couldn't read my mind. He seemed to notice nothing unusual as I greeted him, making sure my eye contact was as firm and trusting as usual, before I moved automatically to lie down and roll up my sleeve. The rush from the Ritalin wasn't quite as potent this time, probably because I'd made up my mind that I was going to have to learn to do without it. But the rush made it easier to tell Patrick what I'd decided.

First I wanted information and an admission from him.

"The thing I remember most about Friday night," I said, "is seeing myself when I was five or six years old standing staring down at myself at the bottom of a well. I was feeling very sorry for myself."

"You're not masochistic, are you?" Patrick asked disapprovingly.

"No," I said, not knowing if I was a masochist or not, and with no idea how he'd arrived at his interpretation.

"Did you know you fell asleep on me?" I asked teasingly, wishing I could turn my head to see his reaction.

A brief silence. "No," Patrick said.

"You fell asleep just after you came into my room and sat at the foot of the bed. You were snoring."

"I don't think so," Patrick said.

"But I saw you and heard you. Your notebook was about to fall to the floor when I woke you up." I tried to tell him that I didn't expect him to be perfect: "I'm not surprised. How could anybody be expected to stay awake all night looking after patients?"

"I think part of you is still rejecting treatment, trying to find excuses not to trust me," he said mildly.

What I was about to say would only confirm his interpretation. I was disappointed in him. He proved too predictable to be a worthy adversary.

"What else do you remember?" he continued smoothly.

"Not very much. I don't remember a thing I was saying when I got blocked and you gave me the injection."

He was on safer ground now. "It was just a small dose of Ritalin to relax you. It's normal to feel overwhelmed by the LSD treatment."

I seized my opportunity. "I didn't feel overwhelmed so much as attacked, invaded. My whole body took the weekend to get over it. I felt as if I were being really coerced by a chemical you'd put in my body."

"I'd encourage you to keep an open mind. We can discontinue LSD treatment if you don't feel comfortable with it. Though I never suggest we do it more than once a month."

"I've decided to stop treatment altogether," I said.

I was annoyed at how hard it was for me to tell him. For some reason I remembered Ben trying to tell me he was leaving me. "The thing is I've realised how easily I let myself be used by authority figures. By coincidence on Monday –"

I told him about the police. "A lot of people want to run my life. The police would love to use my homosexuality against me if they could, even though it looks as if what I do in my bedroom isn't going to be a crime much longer. I think you'd like me to stop being homosexual."

Patrick rushed in: "I would never want you to do anything you felt wasn't right for you."

"That's what you *say*." I tried to explain myself, to myself as well as Patrick. "What I really want is more of everything: more and more success, more and more happiness. And that's why I'm willing to put myself in the hands of people like you. Part of it is that I'm still this provincial child whose father earned less in a week than I pay you for fifty minutes. I still can't believe I'm who I am, so it's easy to believe that other people know better than I do what's good for me. The thing is that they don't have my talent. I never meet *anybody*, except maybe pop stars, who've done what I've done coming from my background. So how should anyone know how I should live my life? None of you could ever have predicted what I've done so far. Why should I want to change *anything* about myself? You'd get panic attacks if you didn't know if you were ever going to work again, if you lived in a foreign country full of strangers who still think you're some kind of a thing because you fall in love with other men. I need to learn to

244

be myself instead of trying to change."

I added weakly, to downplay the fear that had brought me to him in the first place: "I can control the panic attacks with Valium and Seconal."

I'd surprised myself, though I recognised the gap between what I said and what I'd feel when I left Patrick's consulting room, between a strong agenda and having to live it moment to moment.

Patrick couldn't argue with me without contradicting the non-authoritarian goals he claimed for his practice. "I hope you'll have a close relationship with at least one person," he allowed himself to say as I sat up to leave. He looked crushed.

I remembered other men and woman, ministers and teachers from my childhood, who'd surprised me by feeling betrayed when I didn't do what they wanted me to.

My emancipation from Patrick extended to a notion that I shouldn't have to pay his bill. I ignored his handwritten request for payment, but when a bill collector's letter arrived I was persuaded to pay up.

✳ ✳ ✳ ✳ ✳

I started pushing Beryl harder. I used all my technique to ignite a fire at auditions, but it didn't work. I couldn't fake the kind of passion I'd felt for Oswald or William Wilson. All I got was an offer to play the lead in an episode of a London Weekend horror anthology. I'd watched earlier episodes: it was the kind of thing in which the undistinguished spouses of famous actors were grateful to accept roles. I told Beryl icily that I'd be happy to do a really good television play, and in the meantime to please not let anyone suppose I might be interested in guest-starring in a series. She didn't argue with me, and as usual it was impossible to tell what she was thinking.

Was I a has-been? If LSE or Oxbridge had been willing to take me I'd have used the money I'd saved to read for a degree that might give me some kind of credentials if I never acted again. But I balked at having to study to retake my A-levels and wait another year or more. What I really wanted was to live the salad days that Ben had enjoyed and I had missed. I was already too old.

❊ ❊ ❊ ❊ ❊

"What I want to know," a BBC producer drawled as we talked about the coming change in the law, "is whether the newspapers will refer to me as 'the well-known homosexual'."

In the pubs I began to cut men who kept asking me when they were going to see me in another film or play. They clearly didn't understand why Daniel Henry couldn't find work, but I thought they began to enjoy embarrassing me. I much preferred the company of an educator who droned on endlessly about the book he was writing on ways to tap children's potential. I'd make all-purpose sounds of assent or empathy while I concentrated on the flux of the pub that had stopped surprising me a long time ago. Since he taught during the day and was out drinking every night I couldn't work out when he did his writing. He was talking himself into achievement, perhaps. I was being too fussy, perhaps, about what work I was willing to accept.

At night the solitary physical discipline of my days unravelled. Some nights I went out although I felt so sick of the bars I knew nothing good could come of my going there. One night when I was full of a head cold and queasy from the cold medicine I'd taken, I picked up a sweet puzzled-looking bodybuilder from Brighton.

I caught some kind of delay in his registering my instructions on how to drive to my flat.

He decided he might as well come clean before we got into our cars. 'I'm a bit slow,' he confessed ruefully.

I didn't mind: I was tired of people who had a quick response to everything.

The muscles rolled around under his shaved skin like ball bearings. As soon as I tried losing myself under his weight, drink and the medicine turned my stomach and I fled to the bathroom to throw up. He showed only a helpless concern

246

for me. I snuggled against him, turning my mouth away because it must smell foul. Just when I thought I could at least suck his cock I had to run to the bathroom again. I turned away from him, sinking weakly into sleep. I hardly heard him get up before dawn to drive back to Brighton.

Things had to be better or different someplace else. There was always the imperative to find new pubs or places: the East End, the dockside pubs on Saturday night, though the clientele and I were so suspicious of each other that the only man I ever picked up there lived in South Kensington and worked in P.R. It turned out that I knew his ex-lover, a music critic, about whom he still felt bitter.

"Does he still have a low stool and a cheesy cock?" the P.R. man inquired.

Even the *Champion* pub, as close as the Bayswater Road, was a change of pace, though the couple of miles difference demonstrably lowered the income and spirits of the customers. One desperate night I picked up a man who I chose to believe was safe. He bought me a bitter and I thought he had a kind of shine to him, though he seemed to have trouble talking. He lived in a room near the pub with just a cot and a couple of chairs and a single electric ring. As soon as he closed the door I knew I'd made a mistake. He was far drunker than I'd supposed, incoherent because all his strength was concentrated on staying conscious. When he pushed me towards the bed I thought of bolting, but he had a heavy determined glitter about him, and a tray with his cutlery on it, a couple of knives and forks and spoons and a kitchen knife, was a foot away from the bed.

He wanted to fuck me but he had no KY or even Vaseline. All he could find was a bar of margarine that he dug into with rough fingernails and smeared on his cock, which somehow stayed erect while the rest of him wavered. The moment he tried pushing into me, my arsehole started to burn. I wanted to open up and let him get it over with but I was too raw. Every time I relaxed his stabbing at me made me yell and tighten up again. I thought he was ready to hit me if I tried to stop him. For a relentless time he seemed to be still pushing to get inside me and I still couldn't help

247

resisting, but then I heard the unmistakable tense catch in his breath that told me he was about to come. I felt him squirting. I didn't realise how far inside me he'd got until my insides rolled agonisingly over his cock as he pulled out. He fell into an immediate dead sleep. I rested, then crawled out of bed and got out of that room.

I paid no attention to my arsehole until my first bowel movement the next day. Sharp pain made me gasp and want to run away from it, even though the movement of reacting to the pain bolted it deeper into my body. All I could do was wait in a cold sweat while the agonising waves subsided.

"Were you raped?" my doctor asked, cheerfully surveying the damage.

"No, of course not," I snapped, ashamed that anyone could think I'd let that happen to me.

He prescribed an ointment, painkilling pills and sitz baths, and, without mentioning it to me, a small glass dilator that I found in the bag the chemist handed me. When I got over the shock I realised that the doctor thought he was doing me a good turn.

Shortly afterwards the evening papers carried a front page photograph of stage and screen star Nicholas Sherwood, the three smudges of ink that made up his face still somehow recognisable as Nick, balancing precariously on an Earl's Court rooftop while a bobby urged him to get away from the edge and a crowd collected in the street. The story said he'd been admitted to St. Stephen's for observation, but he was home again when I phoned to commiserate with him.

"I don't remember a thing about it," he said rather jauntily. "I don't even remember going up there."

"Was it an LSD flashback?" I asked, hoping to find another reason to justify my separation from Patrick.

"No," Nick said. "That's been a tremendous help to me."

I tried to cheer him up by sharing gruesome details about the condition of my arsehole. "It's like having a baby every time I go to the lavatory."

Nick didn't sound particularly impressed, but he must

248

have registered every word.

"I hear you've been having health problems," Tom Finlay remarked roguishly the next time I ran into him in the King's Road. I looked blank until Tom told me Nick had passed on my news in the course of a phone call in which he tried to borrow £250.

"You know how Nick always exaggerates," I said airily, seething. "I had some slight pain for a couple of days."

Tom would have been my natural confidant, but I wanted to be the one to tell him. I was certain Nick had told him out of malice, which was further proof that actors and actresses weren't to be trusted as friends. When Maryann Macready still lived in London a journalist had published a book on the new generation of playwrights and actors. Maryann told me we were mentioned in it.

"What did he say about us?" I asked eagerly.

"Oh, he was rather dismissive. He said we were promising, but it depended on how we turned out."

One day I came across the book in Foyles. Maryann had reported accurately what the journalist said about her, but his remarks about me were glowing. Of course his powers of prediction weren't so hot: Maryann now had a career in Hollywood.

Three months later Nick Sherwood appeared on the front pages of the evening papers yet again. He'd married Cynthia Gardner, an actors' representative who was five years older.

✻ ✻ ✻ ✻ ✻

I still wouldn't leave London for more than a day or two at a time and never if it meant missing the Sunday run. Two years in a row I declined Tom Finlay's invitation to join him for a holiday in Greece. Part of me still thought to go abroad was an arduous and expensive undertaking. Part of me was afraid to leave London in case I chose the wrong moment and missed important developments in my life.

Then I discovered Amsterdam. As often as once a month – but never on a weekend, and only in winter: I only felt

happy abroad when I could bundle up against the cold – I'd
be sitting at home reading audition pages or a novel and it
would occur to me that by evening I could be drinking
Genever in a bar or club or having sex at the baths in
Amsterdam. Three hours later I'd be on a plane; five hours
later I'd be changing five pound notes for guilder.

I always stayed at the same modest hotel for queer
foreigners. I spent two Christmases in a row there when I
discovered that in Amsterdam it was possible to pretend
that Christmas Day was a day like any other. All I did was
walk the streets. The small bridges and cobbled streets
under an economical layer of snow, the air frosting the
lights inside sash-barred windows, had the compressed
magic of the first string of coloured lights I ever
remembered seeing. I'd found a safe extension of the few
streets in London where I spent most of my life. Everyone I
met spoke English – the bartenders in the bars where I first
heard Elvis sing *'In the ghetto'*, the blond expatriate from
San Diego I met at the open-air stand that sold fries with
mayonnaise, the men of all ages who relied on tourists for
sexual variety and the possibility of romance.

"Are you in love?" a Dutch businessman asked me
gloomily one morning over coffee in bed.

I found it easier to be honest when I woke up with a
hangover in a foreign city. "Yes," I said.

"Poor bastard!" he said, not needing to hear anything
further.

At the very latest, by lunchtime on the third day in
Amsterdam, and always in time to get back for the Sunday
run, and whether I was sexually sated or depressed because
I hadn't got what I wanted, I departed as abruptly as I'd
arrived, needing to find out how the circumstances of my
life had changed while I was away. After ten minutes back
in my flat I regretted coming back so soon.

In Amsterdam I started paying attention to a dream I
was having, about a play I'd appeared in a short while ago,
such a solid success that it put to rest any doubts about my
future as an actor. Part of the dream, or part of waking
from it, was a prolonged struggle to determine if I'd only

250

dreamed such a play.

'A face from the past.' I looked up, but saw no one I recognised amongst the closely-packed faces of the sun worshippers on the grass outside the Serpentine enclosure. I wondered if the speaker remembered a one night stand or was talking about my professional absence.

I began to wake up paralysed. Or maybe it was a recurring nightmare, or maybe that was what I told myself to make it tolerable. Certainly it was too terrible to bear thinking about. I'd wake up in the morning on my back unable to move any part of my body – I'd snap out of sleep my head already bursting with the effort to break through the steel coffin of my skin. I never really panicked, my condition was too dire to allow panic. I lay there forced to watch the ceiling, scared to strain any further in case the confirmation that I couldn't move drove me mad. Thoughts, the only unshackled part of me, darted like insects around my brain. Who knows how long it lasted? I was freed from an incarceration that seemed endless in an arbitrary instant, as if someone had flipped a switch. I jumped out of bed to make good my escape and set about forgetting what had happened. If it happened. If it wasn't a dream. I remember thinking that if the telephone rang while I was paralysed and I couldn't move to answer it, then it wasn't a dream. But the phone never rang at those times. Or perhaps it rang and I couldn't allow myself to hear it.

I met men who danced a daily jig of deception or despair that made my concerns over my uncertain prospects seem trivial. It was unusual to go to the *Coleherne* and not find George sitting on a stool facing the bar, a position which told you immediately that he'd curtailed his sexual ambitions, because it cut down on his mobility and view of the crowd. Or else he had unrealistic expectations of suitors picking him out and pushing through to be beside him.

At twenty-seven or twenty-eight he was hectically pedantically verbose – expatiate and eschew were favourite words of his – more intent on banishing colloquialisms from his conversation than on saving his own life. He'd got into the habit of attempting suicide.

251

The first time someone in the pub told me he was in the hospital I went to see him, and found him in a coma. I laid two fingers on his shoulder and his entire fleshy body shuddered, rattling the system of tubes and monitors he was hooked up to.

A doctor came in and asked me if there was anything I could tell him that might help. I pointed to the shelf, out of George's reach, with the half-full bottles of pills that the ambulance men had brought along with George's body.

"Is it a good idea to prescribe a ton of tranquilisers to a man who keeps attempting suicide?"

The doctor gave me an uncomfortable smile; either what other doctors did wasn't to be questioned, or he agreed with me and was afraid to say so.

Two nights later George was back on his stool at the *Coleherne*. Before I lost touch with him his skin and hair got dirtier, and sometimes he wore a vest spotted with blood from the pimples he scratched on his shoulders and back.

"We're alone in a cabin in the mountains," Richard grunted as I fucked him, "and all the passes are closed for the winter. We have nothing to do but fuck till the spring."

He was an American merchant banker who lived in a small expensive flat in Belgravia chosen solely for its address. On the dressing table near the cupboard in which he kept his lumberjackets and black leather was a framed photograph of his wife of eighteen months, a horsey upper-class girl who spent a great deal of time in the country. Richard's face was almost immobile, rigid from conforming to the social requirements of his job and the class he'd married into. I saw him relax a little only while I was fucking him or when he drove his sports car at great speed. Years later I came across his picture in a magazine ad for his bank. He got away with, or survived, his deception.

I rescued a few friendships from the bars. One or two of us took the time to realise we liked each other even though we weren't what we were looking for. Stephen was a film editor who shared all my interests except that he played squash and I was a runner. Our first and only trip to bed ended after five minutes when I made it clear that I would only settle for fucking him and he made it clear he would only settle for fucking me. My arsehole had stayed raw and itchy, a reminder of what it had been subjected to, and I wasn't ready to let a stranger make it any worse. But we could have found other ways to accommodate each other. We knew we weren't meant to be more than friends. We'd never have the power to hurt each other, though Stephen managed to anger me when he hopped into bed with a New Zealander I introduced him to.

"You could have waited," I complained. "What happened to loyalty between friends?"

"I thought it was over between you," Stephen shrugged, direct and heartless.

Clive was an interior designer, far tougher than his frail body suggested. Once a month we went to dinner or a play and ended up in bed, but unable not to hold back from each other. He could be sharp with me – he got impatient when I treated a winter cold as a major calamity, holing up for a week – and sentimental – he pretended that Peter Sarstedt's *Where Do You Go To?* was the story of my life. I dismissed such nonsense but was secretly flattered. I think he wanted, and would have returned, an offer of love from me.

We all wanted a boyfriend, lover, partner, saviour from our incomplete selves, except that I was a lover in disguise, unwilling to admit that I'd already met my lover and was waiting for him to come back. The passing of the Sexual Offences Act scarcely seemed to change our notion of ourselves: what we did in private might now be legal (though that didn't stop people talking), but our condition was regarded as no less shameful. We still had no guidebooks. Queer couples kept to themselves, maybe through fear of losing the other to a newcomer, maybe, bewildered as the rest of us, unwilling to admit they were together through luck.

Clive echoed the conventional wisdom: "Men and woman are luckier because society encourages them to bond."

"Nobody, normal or queer, knows how to live," I argued. "We're all lucky to get by in a class-ridden patriarchal society that uses every means to enforce its values." I heard another man's voice in my own. "Nothing changes in Great Britain. Plays of protest open and close in three weeks and are forgotten. Do you know what still passes for insight into human nature in Shaftesbury Avenue? Lines like 'You know how men always seem to have everything they need.' Or 'Life is full of disappointments. We have to learn to live with them.' That's as deep as it goes. Queers are lucky to have a stigma to fight, to stop us being passive recipients of the culture. If we're able to overcome what it does to us."

One night Clive invited me for drinks with two other friends – an American who ran a business shifting polystyrene around the world, and Jackie, a hairdresser who regularly did the town with Clive. Unlike me he believed it was important to keep a foot in the normal social world. We drank too much wine and grew suddenly ravenous on a little pot, and since nobody wanted to go out Clive scrambled eggs while the American confided to us that if he didn't leave his boyfriend he'd commit suicide. I'd met the boyfriend, who worked in the family business in the Midlands and drove to London at weekends, and I tended to agree: he'd told me quite seriously that the working class didn't deserve subsidies because they still kept coal in their bathtubs.

It seemed that tonight the American was going to take comfort from Clive. Jackie and I decided simultaneously that it was time to go. She hesitated before heading for her car, a little perplexed with me. I tried to treat her warmly but I couldn't help feeling that women were beside the point. Tonight I needed her.

"Would you like to come back for a drink?" I asked.

"I'd love to," she said happily, and followed me home in her clapped-out MGA.

On a whim I found myself in bed with a woman who was eager to be with me, and it worked, though I'd noticed no changes in my feelings about women or my physical responses to them. I didn't pretend she was a man. I enjoyed being a man fucking a woman, even if it was still a man I really wanted.

I liked our bodies' differences in size and strength. When I stretched out on top of Jackie my body extended beyond hers at every point. Her full breasts meant little to me: I examined and kissed them with perfunctory curiosity. I couldn't even think of going down on her because her sweet-sour smell came close to turning my stomach. But I enjoyed kissing her and liked burying my face in her fluffy blonde hair. She was so generous in showing pleasure and gratitude that I knew she wouldn't dismiss me the moment it was over, the way men dismissed each other. She comforted me and I used her.

Fucking her was easy. She wasn't as tight as most men's arseholes and the fucking aroused unfamiliar smells. She seemed to have a ridge, like a row of tiny teeth, that rubbed against the base of my cock, that made the act feel potentially hazardous. But I'd be lying if I didn't admit I felt finally admitted to the universal club of potential procreation, to what the majority did, though I'd never been able to imagine the English getting much pleasure from it. I'll even admit to toying with the notion that it felt somehow more authentic than the things men did together. But it wasn't my reality.

"You're a wonderful lover," Jackie whispered. I had reason to believe she was telling the truth, though I knew she was also reassuring me because she knew I was queer.

I turned my back on her to go to sleep. I wouldn't betray myself by giving her my body in sleep, in case I got used to her and forgot what I wanted, in case I told her my dreams.

Jackie told Clive how much she liked me and he passed it on to me, as she probably expected him to. I enjoyed disgusting my drinking cronies by telling them how Jackie had her period one night and left a stain on the sheets. I treated her badly. When the bars closed and I ended up alone, I'd phone her and she'd get into her car, because I was too drunk to drive, and head for Kensington. I saw the inside of her flat in Fulham once and worked to keep my expression neutral. She worked not to show that she was ashamed of her few sticks of furniture that might have been picked off the street. She'd been married and had obviously brought nothing out of it. I grew to admire her disregard for security. But maybe she thought she deserved nothing.

I finally groaned to her in bed that I was unhappy.

"You have friends," she offered, including herself, afraid to offer anything more.

She finally asserted herself. One night when I called her late she refused to come over.

"You never go out with me," she complained. "You never take me to dinner. If Alison had agreed you'd have gone to bed with both of us."

She had justice on her side. She was referring to a party at Clive's at which I'd urged a friend of Jackie's to come back with us.

"Thursday," I said. "Thursday I'll take you to dinner."

First we went to see a Maryann Macready film at the Columbia, based on a 'daring' American bestseller. Maryann played a bored Malibu housewife who seduced her auto mechanic and then got gang raped by his buddies. Maryann's American accent, and attempt at playing a bitch in heat, were diligent, but somehow lacking in conviction. Maybe the best parts of her performance were missing. The censor had hacked the film to pieces in order to grant even an X rating. In the rape scene Maryann kept appearing abruptly in different parts of the room halfway through a movement or line of dialog, while the male characters did a jagged dance around her.

Jackie was always an appreciative audience. Over dinner at *The Casserole* I told her the story of Maryann's night in the bushes.

"Maryann Macready has come a long way," she said. "It's funny how everything goes right for some people."

When she realised she might be skating on thin ice she switched to a story about how one of her girlfriends had been done in by a man. I'd noticed that certain Chelsea women seemed to invite betrayal, and afterwards exclaimed 'Bastard!' with great satisfaction.

We were sitting in the alcove behind the front door. If I bothered to, I could see the restaurant's traffic over Jackie's shoulder. Someone was leaving, then instead of opening the door he stopped where he was. When I realised he was staring down at me I looked up.

"Hello, Daniel," Ben said, looking worried.

First he moved to open the door again, and then he changed his mind again and moved his arm slightly to indicate the man behind him waiting to leave with him.

Rage and gratitude threatened to drown me.

I wanted to run away. I couldn't let the moment pass so quickly. I glared at Ben but at the same time I telegraphed the message: "Don't leave."

He heard me. "How are you?" he asked, and blinked more than was necessary.

"Well," I said.

He wore a blue suit and had put on weight that showed in his face and under his waistcoat. The man waiting for him might or might not have been queer: a tall man with wavy brown hair.

Jackie looked up at Ben.

"Ben, Jackie," I said, not taking my eyes off him. They shook hands.

Ben's eyes returned to mine. He hesitated, then some need to know overcame his fear of embarrassing me.

"I haven't heard much about you lately," he said, and I thought I saw bewildered concern in his face.

I said silently: "I told you how it would be."

"That's the way it goes sometimes," I said aloud, while I wondered what I could do to keep him there.

A small queue was building up behind Ben, urging him to move on or let it push past. He sensed the other people without letting go of my eyes, and finally he gave a helpless shrug.

"See you," he said, looking from me to Jackie and back to me.

I thought it was very hard for him to tear his eyes away, but he made a decision and opened the door for his friend and followed him outside. I tried to follow his back receding into the night but the busy pavement swallowed him up.

"Nice looking man," Jackie said, and then shut up when

257

she saw my thunderous face. We didn't speak for five, ten, minutes.

"I'm sorry," I managed to say at last. "I'm really sorry."

She nodded, her eyes filling.

"Do you mind if we get out of here?" I asked. "I need to be alone tonight."

✳ ✳ ✳ ✳ ✳

"See you," Ben had said. Only a fool would suppose he meant it or would do anything to bring it to pass.

I poured a strong Scotch and took it straight to bed, the same bed in which Ben had slept with me for years.

He'd looked a little flushed, a little more cynical, a little drunker than I was used to seeing him. But he didn't need me to comfort him, he'd chosen to take away my power to take away his pain.

I wondered what we could really say to each other if we sat down to a drink or a meal together.

Could I be stupid enough to believe he still wanted anything from me? After the years in which he never got in touch with me, had scrupulously avoided all the places we went together?

What would Ben say to me now? At best: "Those were the happiest times of my life."

But not to be returned to. Because if Ben had ever wanted me, in all the times he'd been unhappy or defeated since he left me, he'd known he only had to pick up the phone. He hadn't wanted me enough to try to talk to me, even if he wasn't certain how I'd receive him. And how could he be uncertain?

I thought of phoning him now. Each time a new directory arrived I checked to see that he was still listed at the same Canonbury address. But I was afraid to. If he was still with his wife I'd be intruding in a relationship where I could be discussed and put finally in my place. If he was alone again I'd still be where he'd left me, pleading for his love. It wasn't enough for him then. Why should it attract him now?

Hopeless. When I got up to pour another drink I fetched my supply of Valium and Seconal from the bathroom. Only as an option. I noticed how cold the room had become. I settled under the blanket, propped on one elbow so that I could retrieve my drink from the nightstand and watch the small plastic containers: man-made, with power to put men to rest.

A disinterested voice spoke in my ear, the kind that never questioned its power to judge: 'A very promising start, but he tried to reach too far above himself.'

Too true. I reached out, letting the blanket slip from my shoulders, and picked up the Valium container and twisted it open and emptied it into my palm. It was full enough to spill onto the sheets. I crammed the tablets into my mouth, licking up the ones that were left on my hand – bitter chalk – and washed them down with the Scotch. The Seconal was what would really finish me off. Fewer of them, ten or twelve, but more than enough. When they were in my mouth I took a swallow of the drink and crunched the sticky mixture with my teeth to get it over faster. Two more swallows of the drink almost got rid of the taste.

I lay back, wondering how long it would take. Almost immediately. Too soon. I was drowsy already, and suddenly as aware as drowsiness would let me be that this wasn't a good idea, though I didn't have time to formulate why not: perhaps curiosity unsatisfied, need unmet, a fight to try to win. I couldn't hurt Ben by doing this.

My movements were already slowed. The phone was by my bed, but after I picked up the receiver and dialled 999 my head toppled back against the headboard.

A man's voice answered before the second ring.

"I've taken an overdose," I said, full of trust in a stranger.

He sounded distinctly unimpressed. "What's your address?"

I gave it to him, and knew from the effort it took to produce a voice that I had only a few conscious moments left.

"Leave the front door open," he said. "Can you do that?"

"I'll try," I promised, and hung up at once so that I

259

wouldn't be distracted from the single action I had to perform. I swung my body in slow motion out of bed and flung it towards the front door.

I lost some time, as if I'd blinked and ceased to exist, before I came to hitting the wall three feet from the door. Pain was there, but dulled. So far so good. I reached out for the door handle and it was a hundred yards away, swimming away from me. My hand, a heavy weight, dropped towards the floor. I fell against the wall and dragged myself to the left. The door had gone away. The impossibility of finding it made me so tired that it was absolutely necessary to slide to the floor and get some sleep.

More time missing. I came to holding the door handle, but my own weight against the door was stopping me opening it. I turned the handle with both hands and fell back against the wall, pulling the door with me. My forehead bounced off one of the panels.

"I'll have a headache tomorrow," I told myself out loud through cotton wool, even laughing until I heard my gloomy weighted voice.

I sank to my knees, still holding the handle with both hands. It was time to go to sleep. If they didn't reach me I'd never know about it. But they weren't going to reach me, because the front door of the house was also locked. I was able to make a complex calculation, amazed at my ability to still do it. Unless they broke down the front door the ambulance men would have to rely on the middle-aged couple in the upstairs flat to let them into the house. What if the couple weren't home? Did the ambulance men have the authority to break down the door? What if the couple were home? Did I want them to see my half-naked body being carried out on a stretcher? If I could reach the front door and open it, mightn't they sleep through everything? Unless I created a sensation in Kensington High Street and joined the Nick Sherwood club for suicidal actors.

I woke up on my knees in the hallway. I knew I couldn't stay awake more than another second. My only chance was to repeat the movement that had got me to the front door of the flat. I raised my rear end and got ready to push off with my hands and propel myself forward. Nothing happened. It was like pushing through white syrup. I tried again. More time lost. My body, so heavy that it dragged me off my trajectory, was bouncing off walls and falling down. I started to crawl, getting very bad-tempered, swearing out loud at the effort I had to put into it, laughing at myself and sobbing.

I was on the rubber rug inside the heavy street door and the ridges hurt my knees. The door loomed above me like a barricade. To open it I had to reach the bolt at shoulder level. It occurred to me that it just wasn't worth any more effort. My body, so heavy that it was impossible to lift, was also turning into white bread and floating away from me. I couldn't keep my eyes open.

I pretended I was a high jumper gathering my strength for one last leap. Nothing happened when I leapt. I swore, then began to inch my body up the door, digging into the wood with my fingernails.

❋ ❋ ❋ ❋ ❋

Under bright lights a man in white forced my mouth against the rim of a large metal bowl.

"If you don't drink it we'll have to pump your stomach."

He was not to be argued with. I opened my mouth to let him tip warm salt water into my mouth and passed out again as I started to vomit.

I was talking out loud in bed in a large hospital ward.

"What was I just saying?" I asked a nurse who was busying herself by my bedside. My left arm hurt. The rest of me felt light, as if I'd lost weight.

"I wasn't listening," she said. "But you had plenty to say for yourself last night."

I didn't ask her what I'd said, afraid of what I might hear, as afraid of embarrassing her as she was afraid of embarrassing me. She kept avoiding my eyes and hesitated over how to say anything she had to say to me. The heart's misery was clearly outside the scope of hospital rules and training.

261

At first I thought the entire ward was embarrassed by me. I counted sixteen beds in two rows, most of them occupied, though the bed to my left was empty. The older man on my right studiously avoided looking in my direction, and the patient across the aisle might as well have been blind. Sitting up in bed directly across from me he still looked through me. Eventually I noticed that none of the patients talked to each other. In a place with almost no privacy there was a not unfriendly conspiracy to pretend that the other patients weren't there.

I dozed again after the nurse left me, and woke to the sounds of lunch coming round. For a time I was content to stare at the high ceiling, every nook and cranny of it immaculate in light so dazzling it might have been filtered through ice crystals on its way through the high windows. When my tray arrived I had to eat with one hand because the fingers of my left hand were simultaneously numb and painful, the inner arm below the elbow bruised and swollen. But my appetite had returned.

As soon as I'd eaten I got up and went to the bathroom. My legs were shaky and I had trouble walking straight, but I was starting to get the hang of it.

When a nurse saw me I caused a minor sensation.

"You're not supposed to get out of bed on your own," she cried.

"Nobody told me. I'm fine. Where are my clothes? I want to go home."

"You have to see a doctor first." She insisted on helping me back into bed. To tell the truth I was secretly grateful for the extra time in bed.

"So when can I see a doctor?" I persisted.

"I'll ask," she said. "In the meantime stay in bed."

I lay resting, less sleepy from lunch than I'd expected, thinking how comfortable my flat would feel when I got back to it. A scrawny matron began to make duty rounds, stopping to talk to each patient.

"Did you enjoy lunch?" she asked the patient on my right. Two bright pink spots burned on her scrubbed cheekbones. Only her conviction that it was the right thing to do saw her through the painful embarrassment of doing it. I could almost hear her counting the seconds before she could move on to more embarrassment without feeling she'd skipped any part of the ordeal.

"I hate frog spawn," the man next to me complained.

In her shyness matron blurted the truth. "I don't like it much either," she said, and blushed at her own daring.

I thought only the English would put such a fettered personality in charge of so many people. Of course I was fettered too, but I wasn't sure what my fetters were.

With me she was clearly even more at a loss. She paused at the bottom of my bed smiling a determined smile.

"If everybody hates sago pudding," I said relentlessly, "why do you have it on the hospital menu?"

She blushed further. "I don't know," she said brightly, and gave a startled little laugh at her own willingness to admit to ignorance. She moved on almost gaily. Both of us knew sago would remain on the menu.

I got my interview with a doctor at three o'clock in a small space partitioned off from the rest of the ward. I'd been allowed to put on the clothes the ambulance men had brought with me, so the outcome was a foregone conclusion.

The doctor told me my arm would heal in time. "You were very lucky. Do you remember hitting it against a sharp surface?"

I didn't. "Maybe the front door. Maybe the hall table."

"You came close to severing the nerves. As it is they'll heal by themselves. There's nothing we can do to hurry the process."

The next transition was a problem for him. He looked concerned, but at a loss.

"Would you like me to arrange an appointment with a psychiatrist?"

I shook my head and he opened his mouth to protest.

"I was seeing a psychiatrist," I said. "Look, it won't happen again. The moment I did it I realised it was a bad idea. I want to live."

He seemed relieved to believe me.

The hospital was St. Mary Abbots. When I stepped

263

outside I paused, delighted. Two inches of snow had fallen in the night and lay untrodden in the gardens. It was a charming gift, a reason to live.

I was still shaky, uneasily aware of an impetuous enemy within me. After only a moment's hesitation I headed for the pub across from the hospital. A little something to warm me up, to settle my insides, would do no harm. I felt too tender to drink spirits. The taste of the bitter was fresh, more complex than I'd noticed for a long time, but after a couple of mouthfuls I felt queasy. I left the rest of the beer in the glass and found a taxi to take me home.

I was beginning to wonder about consequences. No one at the hospital had mentioned my profession or given any indication that they recognised me. But even if I was only semi-famous, I was a lot more famous than Nick Sherwood, and he'd made the front pages. I knew nothing about the mechanism of how the papers got news of suicide attempts – were they tipped off by nurses or ambulance drivers or other patients?

When I got home the hallway showed no signs of disarray. I even checked the small table behind the street door for signs that I'd crashed into it. Nothing. The folded *Standard* was pushed halfway into the letterbox, but I wanted to be safely inside my own flat before I opened it.

I wasn't in that night's *Standard*, or the next night's. It seemed I'd escaped the world knowing I'd done what everyone always called 'something silly.' Once I knew I was safe I began to have unworthy thoughts. Who really told the papers about the suicide attempts of the stars? Their press agents?

✻ ✻ ✻ ✻ ✻

That evening, as I sat in front of the box gobbling cheese sandwiches and taking tentative sips of red wine that stung my insides, an old friend returned to talk to me.

"Work was never as joyous as I claimed," Oswald said. "My friends who were painters could talk up a storm about it over Sunday dinner, but the truth is we were talking away the dark. Usually I had to force myself out of bed in some chilly room in a country where I didn't belong and huddle over my work waiting for the light. Nearly all the time I had to work laboriously to create the warmth I didn't feel." He gave a shrug that looked indifferent. "I never felt my work was totally accepted, or that I was accepted. Everyone always seemed to have reservations."

"But you had friends," I said, taking it for granted that he knew how grateful I was for his presence.

"They didn't always stay," Oswald said. "Couples didn't always stay together. Couples I spent happy Sundays with sometimes separated by the middle of the week. More than once I was told I hadn't wanted to see their difficulties. I always felt alone, two steps ahead of a fearsome dark."

Yet he knew, and I smiled at him to acknowledge it, that there was comfort and companionship for me in his sombre message.

✳ ✳ ✳ ✳ ✳

By Sunday morning I was well enough to head for the Heath. If Ben felt he wanted to talk again after running into me in the restaurant, this would still be the logical place for him to come.

✳ ✳ ✳ ✳ ✳

Three months later Harold Brookman phoned me. "How are you, Danny?"

"I'm well," I said cautiously. We hadn't talked since we said goodbye at Heathrow after the Vienna fiasco.

"What are your plans for the autumn?"

It took me a second to realise he was talking about work. "I have none," I said cheerfully. I'd finally chosen to be honest.

"I have a play that might interest you," Harold said, sounding grim, which was how he sounded when he talked about professional matters. There was a silence. "Are you there, Danny?"

265

"Yes." I hadn't realised I was expected to respond. "I'd like to read it," I said dutifully.

"When can you come and pick it up?"

"Now."

"I have to go out in an hour," Harold said.

"I'll be there in twenty minutes," I said.

Harold squinted, looking me up and down when he opened his front door.

"You're far too thin, Danny," he said disapprovingly.

"You look well," I said. He did in fact look blooming, his cheeks rosy, his brow clear.

I wasn't invited any further into the house than the front hall. Harold left the door open while he picked up the script from the table where he usually dropped unimportant mail. "Let me know what you think of it as soon as possible," he said.

"I will," I said stoutly.

He turned back to the door, ushering me into the street again. "You are eating well, I suppose?"

"Like a horse," I said.

"Then you really ought to cut down on this ridiculous amount of running you do," he said, dismissing me.

I couldn't make up my mind about the play, except that I knew it wasn't first-rate. It was too messy and inflated. The title was *Quartet*, a terribly unimaginative name, and of course it had four characters, a middle-aged couple and their grown-up children. It was a drama about the murderous effects of middle-class family life and its members' inability to communicate their deepest feelings. The artistic mother and materialistic father live in a permanently hostile state; the mother's determination to thwart her daughter from turning into a younger more attractive version of herself has emotionally crippled the child; the father's determination to make his son succeed at all costs almost destroys both of them.

During a weekend visit the daughter reveals that she's aborted the child of her married lover. The son, a stock-broker, reveals that he is going to be prosecuted for his involvement in the shady dealings of a financier his father

266

pushed him into working with. The play culminates in the attempted suicide of the son.

I could manage only a knowing smile. I saw it coming from the end of the first act – the play needed some physical action to resolve its talky plot of multiple failures to communicate true feeling. The coincidence didn't make the play seem any more truthful to me. It felt somehow empty. Too much time was spent on the charades the family played in order not to face up to their problems. There were too many easy laughs at English sacred cows in the first act, and suddenly too much drama in the second. The play seemed to flatter rather than challenge the theatre audience by telling them that the mirror it held up to them also mirrored the state of England.

But my part, the son, was by far the largest. Philip was the only character who ever fully found his voice, in two long tirades about what the family had done to his heart and soul.

I phoned Harold the morning after I picked up the script.

"I love it," I said. "It's very striking."

"Do you think Philip is right for you, Danny?"

"I think I can find his truth," I said. "The question is, do you think I can play Philip?"

"I rather think you can," Harold said.

I hated the courtly la-di-da way Harold conducted business.

"I'd like you to meet the playwright. I think it's an extra-ordinarily good first effort."

The playwright, when I met him for drinks at Harold's two nights later, seemed in no condition to object to Harold casting me, he was so shy and impressed by his good luck. But he was also so determined to assert himself that he could well have thrown a spanner in the works. I deferred to him, pointing out all the things I thought he'd done so well, as if his unease was exactly suited to the circumstances. I wondered why we relied on the socially inept to analyse the condition of society. Perhaps writers wrote to prove, despite appearances, that they were experts on the human

267

condition. Perhaps actors acted for the same reason.

When I left Harold's house that evening, pretending another appointment and leaving the playwright alone with Harold, we'd shaken hands on my playing the part. Rehearsals were to begin in September with a one-week tryout in someplace like Manchester and a West End opening in October. I thought that if we were very lucky we'd run three months, but I kept that to myself. In bed that night I wondered if Harold hadn't concocted a complex revenge on me for not loving him, if after rehearsals started he'd suddenly find me unsuitable. I'd grown fatalistic. I'd enjoy myself until the worst happened.

Next morning I phoned Beryl, insisted on talking to her right away, and told her curtly to conclude the terms of the contract. My tone told Beryl that things had grown dismal when all she could do for me was draw up the contracts for work I'd got myself.

Having a job coming up took getting used to. For a few days I holed up with my news, running and eating and reading and sleeping a lot. One morning I woke up light-hearted, having somehow shed the weight of not being suitable for so long.

But now that I had work again I found I could afford to question it. How could I let my happiness and livelihood depend on somebody's whim, on the accident of what was available, on everything but my own talent, which was the only constant, which could only change by withering through lack of use? For the first time since I heard the 'I want to be an actor' programme on Children's Hour over twenty years ago I allowed myself to wonder if I'd chosen the wrong dream.

✤✤✤✤✤

I could now declare myself a bisexual, having passed the only test that mattered. But I think my main purpose in going to bed with women, apart from the novelty, was to experience more of what most men experienced, so that I could become more like them, and more attractive to the men I wanted. No woman, not the kindest, strongest, most loving, could hold a candle to a man who somehow caught my fancy, who matched the unfathomable criteria by which I looked for love.

One night in August, when everybody was tired of summer, and the pubs were as crowded as ever, I picked up an American woman at the *Markham Arms*. Few English-women except drunks or trollops would have walked into the *Markham* alone the way Anne did, ordered a half of cider and stood so unselfconsciously in the middle of the crowd, making herself so available to be included in what was going on around her. I'd once caught the novelist Iris Murdoch standing alone in the middle of the *Boltons* on a slow night, but she was obviously soaking up material for a scene in a book.

I caught Anne's eye and went over to her because she was clearly so open to me, not because of any strong attraction – I didn't know what attracted me to women. Anne wasn't very young, maybe two or three years older than I, and a walking dismissal of what remained of swinging London. Her features were blunt, her brown hair brushed straight back off her forehead and banded before falling halfway to her waist, her faded cotton dress touching her ankles. She made no attempt to camouflage hands that were bigger than mine. It turned out she was a sculptress, on her way home from a holiday in Italy. When I told her I was an actor she accepted me as a soul mate, though she'd never heard of me.

I glanced around at the crowd, indicating that it was interesting but not good enough for the likes of us – a ploy I'd perfected on what by now seemed like hundreds of men. "Would you like to come back to my flat and talk?"

"Sure," she said, then thought of a possible impediment. "I have a cold," she warned me, sounding as apologetic as she probably ever got.

"You're past the infectious stage," I said confidently.

I'd always heard that women had to be wooed, that they didn't hop into bed with you as men did, but I found a lot of men far harder to get into bed than the women I ended up with. Perhaps my information was five or ten years out of date; perhaps it didn't apply to certain emancipated women at that time; perhaps the women who slept with me might have refused men who yearned to be inextricably bound to a woman the way I yearned to be bound to a man.

The night Anne came home with me I supplied the Scotch and she supplied a little dope and after a short while it seemed only natural to go to bed. The only inconvenience her cold caused was that I didn't feel like kissing her much. But I did kiss her once on the mouth before burying my face against her cheek. Her body felt monumental, rougher and rawer than most men's bodies, maybe because I assumed it would be softer. The fucking was a simple ordinary act: I shoved it in and banged away assiduously, trying to tear past layers of tissue or emotional restraint, trying to make her feel the full force of me. I got to her fairly easily.

Next morning we lingered over the breakfast I made for us. I was grateful for another human presence in the flat, but I felt, felt her feel, a drained discontent. A night with not exactly the right person left us feeling no less alone in the light of day. I wondered if this was how Ben had felt the last few years. Or perhaps his sense of duty stopped him missing joy. Hard to imagine.

Anne was flying to New York that night, and straight on to Iowa, a place I knew nothing about.

"Why Iowa?" I asked. "Isn't that in the middle somewhere?" She'd sounded serious about her work. "Wouldn't it be easier to make contacts in New York or Los Angeles?"

She hesitated. "I don't want to expose my sons to New York just yet," she said. "They need some regular childhood first."

I made a comic guilty face. "Is there a husband waiting back in Iowa?"

She shook her head gravely. "I've never been married." Her voice, strong with the experience of space and weather I could only guess at, held no defensiveness.

"Is their father waiting back in Iowa?" I persisted.

"Their fathers have never been part of the picture,"

Anne said. "I wanted to have children."

I recognised that her expectations of the men who came her way, though she clearly appreciated them, did not include sobriety, fidelity or child support.

She wanted to say something else to me that morning but it never got said. I forgot her last name, though she'd told me the previous night.

❋ ❋ ❋ ❋ ❋

I took two Valium before I left home for the first day of the *Quartet* rehearsals, and another at lunchtime, just practicing caution. Maybe it was my slightly dulled senses that made the trappings of an empty theatre seem less potent than I remembered. It was good to be back in the cocoon, but once I confirmed that I belonged here, I could afford to wonder about other places I might go instead.

Harold was notorious for a hands-off approach to directing actors that sometimes devastated them when they were floundering. I soon felt safe working with him once I realised he wasn't still hankering after me – he was having an affair with the playwright. My confidence grew as I observed the way I handled myself. I knew Harold's silences didn't mean he was bewildered; he'd eventually tell me anything I needed to be told. I thought my performance would lack only one thing – a kind of instinctive passion that had come naturally when I played Oswald and William Wilson. That might be because I was no longer fresh, but it was also because I didn't trust the emotional line of the play. I believed my life had proved it was necessary to walk away from families like Philip's.

On the first night of the Manchester tryout, when I got my first whiff of the onstage air heavy with light and energy and smell, yet buoyant with the echoes and desires of real and imaginary people, I believed again that this was the only place for me to be.

When the play opened in London the critics had only praise for the play, the cast, and Harold's direction. We were a success.

271

✳ ✳ ✳ ✳ ✳

One afternoon three months into the run Harold phoned to ask if it would be convenient for him to drop by my dressing room after that night's performance.

"Of course," I said.

It would be good to hear his opinions firsthand. Harold's habit of writing us notes critiquing our performances drove the two older players wild.

"Cheers, Harold," I said, sinking gratefully into the chair in front of my mirror, safe amongst the tools of the trade. "How was it?"

"I thought it went rather well," he said, his head rearing as it always did when he expressed an opinion. Harold's 'rather well' was the equivalent of my 'extremely well.' He might once in a blue moon term an extraordinary magical performance 'divine,' but never if he'd been involved in it, and usually only when he was talking about some comedienne or singer.

I'd have to be satisfied with what I got. "I think it's going very well too," I said. "I'm starting to like it –" I caught myself. "– even better than ever."

"It's about time, Danny," Harold said slyly. "You never much liked the play or your role in it, did you?"

I stared at him. "That's a bit strong, Harold. No, actually it isn't. You knew all along?"

"Of course I did, Danny."

"Then I should be doubly grateful to you for giving me the part," I said, and meant it. I could afford to be honest this late in the day. "I always thought another actor might have brought more fire to it, but I wasn't about to tell you that."

Harold snorted. "You surely don't imagine that liking a role has anything to do with how well you play it?"

"Yes, Harold, I do rather imagine that, all other things being equal."

"Nonsense," he said. And left it at that.

I was too relaxed, still full of confidence and goodwill after the performance, to press the argument. "What did

272

you want to talk about?" I asked.

Harold took his time answering, sucking at his drink, then fitting a cigarette into his holder, perhaps trying to arouse my curiosity, perhaps genuinely shy about what he had to say. "I have a favour to ask of you, Danny."

In a rush of emotion that took me by surprise I recognised that I owed Harold a great many favours, and it would be good for me to start acknowledging them. I gazed at him candidly, apologetically. "What could I possibly do for *you*?"

His eyes narrowed. He was surprised and pleased. "You know how I loathe and despise what the press writes about me, Danny? *Theatre* magazine wants to do a cover profile of me." He pronounced it 'profeel.' "They aren't a sensational publication but they do make the most embarrassing mistakes. I wondered if you'd care to do the interview for them."

I stared at him. "You mean *write* the interview?"

Harold gave his snorting wheezing laugh. "Of course. What else could I mean?"

I felt the dawning of ambition. "Do you think I can do it?" I asked.

"Of course you can. Their format is a five hundred word introduction followed by a long question and answer section. As an actor you'll know the right questions to ask, far better than any stagestruck journalist."

Even as I opened my mouth to protest a little more my head began to buzz with possible beginnings: 'Harold Brookman one of the quintet of distinguished actors who defined the art of classical acting for the modern stage. So pre-eminent for the last twenty-five years that it's hard to believe his first attempts at acting met with qualified praise.'

"Why didn't you ask your playwright to do it?" I asked, suspicious that I might be Harold's second choice.

"I don't think that would be entirely suitable at the moment," Harold said primly. "Besides, he knows nothing about acting."

"Will the magazine go for my doing it?"

"They have to. I choose my interviewer or I don't give the interview."

273

"Then let's do it," I said, still not certain I could. "I'll use my tape recorder. Shall I come to you or shall you come to me?"

Harold took out his pocket diary. "Thursday afternoon at two at my house? Is that too early in the day for you?"

It wasn't.

Harold glanced at his watch and got up to go. "Are you walking out, Danny? Can I give you a lift?"

"I'm not leaving quite yet," I said. I'd grown fond of my dressing room. It was a safe place where the world could find me. Ben might knock on the door one night.

"Are you meeting someone?" Harold asked as he turned away.

I shook my head.

"Are you seeing anyone?" he asked.

"No one in particular," I said.

He turned back to me, rearing his head and squinting down at me disapprovingly. "Still holding onto your secrets, Danny? When will you learn to let go?"

"I like my secrets, Harold," I said.

I showed up on Thursday with my tape recorder – Daniel Henry, Cub Reporter. Once I got started my only worry turned out to be that I'd run out of tape. I asked Harold the questions I wanted to know the answers to: how he'd approached certain roles, how much directors had contributed, how he'd felt after his great successes, how he'd made the transition to directing. It seemed he'd known what he was doing when he asked me to interview him. I knew the details to dig for when a journalist might have been satisfied with a more general explanation. Of course I had to rely on Harold telling me only what he wanted to about working for the great Shakespearean companies. There our experience didn't overlap. I noted that Harold had made smooth transitions that would have seemed impossible leaps for me to make. When you went to Eton and Cambridge you assumed you were ready to try anything in the arts.

Harold got tired before I did. "That's enough for today, Danny," he said after two and a half hours when I was getting ready to launch into a new phase of his career.

He was impressed. "I've never seen you work with such concentration," he said, chortling over the discovery. "Except perhaps when you're tackling some problem with a role."

"Same time tomorrow?" I suggested.

The interview appeared three months after I turned it in, with a flattering brief biographical sketch of the author written by the magazine. Four or five months later, as *Quartet* neared the end of its run, a letter from a publisher was hand delivered to the theatre. We met for lunch, he made me an offer, and before we parted we'd shaken hands on a deal. This time I hadn't hesitated.

A fashion photographer, as a prestige project, had travelled round the country shooting portraits that were to be published in a coffee table book. No one had come up with a title, so I suggested *Islanders*. I was to do the interviews for the accompanying captions. For a pittance, compared to what I was paid to act, but I smelled fresh air outside the cocoon. Even less real writing was involved than in the profile of Harold. All I really had to do was turn on my tape recorder and ask questions; the text would be edited transcripts in the first person. I knew I was being hired for my novelty value. A thousand writers could have done a better job, could have used the work, and would be justifiably envious when the book appeared.

The photographer created problems for me from the start. He'd wanted the publisher to edit his own notes and use those as the text, so that the book would be a one-man project. The publisher, who'd initiated the book, refused. The photographer retaliated by refusing to show me contacts of the photographs. I retaliated by choosing to ignore his existence, pretending to myself that he'd taken photographs to illustrate my text.

Most of these 'islanders' lived in or near London, and almost none were Scots or Welsh or Irish. I did most of the London interviews while *Quartet* was finishing its run, then spent a month driving around England dipping into strangers' lives.

I met a twenty-four-year-old revolutionary Socialist who urged workers to take control of industry and students to seize the universities. He told me that people with respectable voices phoned him with death threats. "I don't want to die, not as yet," he said, "because it's not going to serve any useful purpose." He lived on £10 a week from the newspaper he edited.

I met a tycoon who'd worked his way up from driver's mate in a sanitation company to control of the company, then turned it into a £10 million waste disposal group. His wife met him by appointment through his personal assistant, who lived in their home. "Tycoonery is little more than opportunism," he told me. "Commercial flair is a poor substitute for real talent. I've worked hard and I get on with people, and that's all I've got."

I warned him that if I ever went through another bad time in my acting career I might come knocking on his door for a job.

I met a nun in an order dedicated to the service of the poor who in the 1930s had saved her pocket money and sold her second evening dress to pay for flying lessons. By the time she entered the convent she'd logged thirty hours' flying.

"It was a thrilling kind of thing," she said. She treated me with good humour, but seemed briskly unimpressed. "I enjoyed the daring and risk of it, but my heart wasn't in it. I'd wanted to enter the convent since I left school. I could tell you the date and the day and the hour of my vocation. I was in a nursing home for a tonsillectomy and I knew God wanted me and also that I was to be a Sister of Charity, because you don't give yourself in a vacuum, you give yourself to serve."

She insisted on seeing the transcript of the interview and returned it to me in due course covered with changes: sentences rearranged or transposed, sloppy phrases clarified.

I met the general president of a great trades union over lunch at the *Jardin* and he talked frankly about men in physically exhausting or mentally unsatisfying jobs who were against a shorter working week because they had no experience of living with so much leisure time. Four months later, while the book was at the printer, I read that he'd died of cancer at forty-eight.

I drove to a Northern town to meet the man who tended the last Bessemer converter still in use in the United Kingdom. The factory he worked in was one of the last left open in a town of crumbling jerry-built houses and shuttered shops. A pub owner agreed to rent me a room and grudgingly tore herself away from her regulars to find me a towel.

I drank a pint of bitter amongst men and women who were sallow and anxious and unforgiving. A night in the pub with cigarettes, I calculated, would cost them a tenth of the price of the clothes on their backs. Yesterday's necessity would turn to today's luxury when they counted their money in the morning. But they treated buying a drink for a friend as an act of moral generosity in a sparse world.

I interviewed an advertising executive who'd prepared three files for me by the time I went to see her: 'Miscellaneous Information;' 'Some Miscellaneous Thoughts that Might be of Interest to DH;' and 'Extra Quotes for DH.' These papers included information about the flat she lived in and the car she drove, noted that she read anything and everything she could lay her hands on, admired Queen Elizabeth, the Queen Mother and Sheila Scott, hated injustice of all kinds and was particularly appalled by cruelty to children and the present attitude and behaviour of many university students, was hopeless at anything mechanical and terrified of spiders, thought more than ever that people should be able to communicate with one another, thought serenity and poise were vital qualities, and had recently attended a conference where she was one of two women with five hundred men, and the first person to ask a question at the end of the speeches. Despite the flow of information I could never satisfactorily pin her down on exactly what she did at the agency she worked for.

She took me to a House of Commons dinner where Lord Goodman spoke to an ordinary and unappreciative crowd. I recognised again that I still thought like a provincial – I assumed such people and places were difficult to gain access to.

The publisher had arranged for me to use the library at a news agency to look up cuttings on public figures I was interviewing. The cuttings about the shadow Minister of Transport had been taken out and I had to do my interview with her blind. I waited on a landing in a warren of pieds-a-terre in Westminster until Margaret Thatcher laboured up the stairs, ten minutes late, hauling evening dresses in dry cleaner bags.

She was clearly glad to sit down. No offer of coffee or tea. The room, just big enough for us to sit at a comfortable distance, was clearly a way station: nothing extra, the furniture like rejects from other houses.

"What would you like to ask me?" Mrs. Thatcher inquired brightly.

I tried to put a brave face on my ignorance. "Tell me about your life," I said, "the things that are important to you."

I fumbled with the tape recorder and scribbled words on a scrap of paper to look professional: "pretty blonde – smallish bright red mouth."

Mrs. Thatcher paused, seemed to asses the situation rather scornfully, then launched into an account of her career. The daughter of a grocer who became an alderman and self-educated man, she'd gone from reading Chemistry at Somerville to a first career doing research into 'surface tensions' to another degree in Law. She was first chosen as a Conservative candidate in 1948, at the age of twenty-three, and eventually reached the Commons ten years later.

"Where did the *confidence* to do all this come from?" I interrupted, wondering how deliberately the grocer's daughter had modulated her accent into such bright entitled tones.

"At home I was never stinted, never flush," she said, "but every mortal thing I ever needed, educationally or culturally, I was given. There are times when I've been desperately unhappy and disappointed. I married at twenty-six. I knocked about a bit, as they say, and I was unhappy when my personal affairs didn't go right. But I was never without hope for the future or something to do. Looking back to the confidence one had, it was boundless."

"But where did the confidence come from?" I insisted. "Lots of people with a background similar to yours end up failing."

"In every sphere of life there are people who are less able and perhaps not so absorbed in their work as one is oneself," Mrs. Thatcher said. "These people now, planning, so utterly unaware of the limits of their own power and ability. You can't control incomes. You *can't*."

"And what about the future?" I asked lamely.

"Sometimes I wonder how I will react to a life without a future," Mrs. Thatcher said, "because it's something you have to realise, sooner or later you are cast aside politically. I look at some of my colleagues who have done top jobs and are now on the back bench. Perhaps the satisfaction of *having* done a job is enough."

I turned off the tape recorder. "Thank you very much," I said.

Mrs. Thatcher couldn't resist a parting shot before she got up to go back to the House: "Funny the different techniques different reporters have."

"I don't *have* a technique," I said apologetically. "This is all very new to me."

I realised this wasn't something I'd want to do after the novelty wore off: I didn't want to be a transcriber of other people's lives.

I found myself in a council house in Deptford, not far from the settlement house where Ben worked when I met him, interviewing a thirty-five-year-old housewife, her labourer husband, and the fourteen children who lived with them.

"The old woman who lived in a shoe," she said. "There's my lot," and she ticked off their names and ages, "and my sister's lot. We took them in when she died of a cerebral haemorrhage. Eventually we couldn't afford looking after them, and that's how we came to be fostering them officially, because it's the only way we could get money to keep them. I have £15 off my husband, and £17 from the

279

childcare people."

I wondered how she kept the peace.

"We are busy," she said. "You know where I took them?" She gestured towards a small crowd of younger children. "The open-air lido. Sixpence for the kids and two bob for me. I didn't care. We took sandwiches. Tell him how I go down the chute."

"Like a bomb!" the children chorused.

"Because I'm fat," she said cheerfully. "They reckon half the lido goes up when I go in."

My eyes had filled with tears, for which I was grateful, as if I'd been scared I'd forgotten how to cry. But I had a fairly bad hangover, and the after effects of too much drinking sometimes mimicked strong emotions.

✳ ✳ ✳ ✳ ✳

Work was no more plentiful after *Quartet* than before, but there was a possibility of a part in a large-scale World War Two film, and the *Quartet* playwright was working on a new play.

At a party I met an American, a sound engineer in London for a year to work for his recording company. He was dark-haired, with the same reticence about his inner life as Ben, and the sex was exactly as I'd grown to like it: this masculine man lifted his feet onto my shoulders, urging me to get inside him.

On the second night in a row that we were together, I took him to dinner at *Alexander's*, and we found ourselves at a table next to Nick Sherwood and the director of *The Careless Husband*, who'd since done better things in the theatre.

"What are we doing here?" I heard the director ask Nick cautiously.

Nick's ambition took precedence over privacy. "We're here because we're attracted to each other," he said.

I thought his performance lacked conviction.

The American had to take a break because of his commitments. He was coming to dinner on Thursday, and on

280

Wednesday morning it occurred to me that it would be sensible to talk to Ben before I finally committed myself to excluding him from my life.

I went to the phone and dialled his office number as casually as if he'd left the house an hour ago, though I wasn't even sure he still worked in the same job.

The same secretary answered.

"Mr. Talbot, please. My name is Henry."

I thought I heard a flicker of recognition in her hesitant murmur. "I'm afraid he's at a meeting. May he ring you back?"

I almost said: "He has the number," but decided to leave Ben no room for excuses.

I stayed close to home for two days while Ben didn't phone me. There seemed to be a moratorium on anyone phoning me, so that I didn't even get to feel my heart leap with the certainty that it was Ben each time the phone rang. For two days I was patient and fatalistic. I was, after all, embarking on a new life. It was time to find out where I stood.

Late on Thursday afternoon I finally went out to buy groceries. There was a note on the mat inside the front door when I got back. From the American, cancelling: afraid to phone me, afraid to have to explain himself to himself and to me.

That night I sat drinking to 'MacArthur Park,' the song soaring me to feelings of complex loss I'd shut off from myself. Emotions I could have uncovered in a role, but not in Daniel Henry as he went about the business of conducting his life. I wondered how Ben treated queers these days: was he tolerant, pretending, from a distance, to understand, or had he grown harsher? Or was he queer again?

I remembered one of the last things he'd said to me: "If you're ever in need, Daniel, all you have to do is ask, and I'll do anything I can."

The intent behind promises faded with the years.

That night it was the feeling in the song I drank to keep alive inside me: the raging loss, the matter-of-fact determination to survive.

I woke up in another American's bed to find him nudging a Bloody Mary into my hand. A hammer pulse beat inside my head, my throat was sick with hangover.

"I have to be out of here in fifteen minutes," he said.

I had no memory of ever seeing him before.

I gulped at the drink. "Do I have time for a bath?"

"A very quick shower," he said, looking drawn and shaky himself as he drank his coffee and puttered around in his light shiny suit doing things that didn't look absolutely necessary.

In the bathroom I used his toothbrush then cocked my head under the shower to let the water drain down my nostrils and into my throat to get rid of the sick.

He had coffee ready for me. "We've got to go," he said as he handed it to me.

My jeans and blue shirt and brown leather jacket were waiting folded on the bed he'd just made.

He led me down dark stairs into a street of tall terrace houses with railed basements. I guessed we were somewhere in North London. The American shook hands with me, clearly not wanting me to accompany him in the direction he was going. I was happy to wander off by myself, to clear my head and lecture myself that the drinking wasn't worth this kind of pain.

The streets I was walking in looked so unfamiliar that I began to wonder if I was in some provincial town. Then I saw clear sky behind the houses in front of me and realised I was probably somewhere near the river, Greenwich or Rotherhithe.

Something made me check my wallet. The moment I felt its weight I had a good idea what I'd find. It had been cleaned out. Nothing left: no bank card, no driving license, not even a stamp. I checked inside my other pockets as I turned the corner towards the open sky. Light blinded me so that I squinted down at what I'd pulled out of my jeans. I still had my keys, and crumpled around them a pound note. The other pocket had some small change. Enough to take a train or bus home. Or else I'd take a taxi to the bank.

When I looked up at the space and light in front of me I

was dazzled, then bewildered.

I was at one end of a long promenade above a wide stretch of water that flowed into a great harbour.

My body reacted before my mind: bile surged into the back of my throat, hovering while it decided if it wanted to push into my mouth.

Across the water, glinting metallically in sunlight, pierced by so many thousands of windows that it gave me vertigo to think of people reduced to living so precariously, were the unmistakable pitiless confident towers of Manhattan.

To be continued

Author's Note

Daniel Henry and the film, theatre and television productions in which he appears are imaginary.

The remarks attributed to Margaret Thatcher are taken verbatim from a profile of Mrs. Thatcher I wrote for the *Observer Magazine* in 1969. I used material from other articles I wrote for *The Observer* to document Daniel's brief experience as a journalist.

I am deeply indebted and grateful to Simon Laws, my London private eye and antique car dealer.

KM

Also Available

Packing It In
David Rees

This collection of essays, written and arranged to form a year long diary, opens with an all too brief visit to Australia, continues with a tour of New Zealand and a final visit to a much loved San Francisco, before returning to familiar Europe (Barcelona, Belgium Rome) and new perspectives on the recently liberated Eastern Bloc countries (highly individual observations of Moscow, St Petersburg, Odessa and Kiev). Written from the distinctive and idiosyncratic point of view of a singular gay man, this is a book filled with acute and sometimes acerbic views, written with a style that is at once easily conversational and utterly compelling.

'Rees achieves what should be the first aim of any travel writer, to make you regret you haven't seen what he has seen . . .'

Gay Times

ISBN 1-873741-07-3
£6.99

A Cat in the Tulips
David Evans

Both in the later flush of life, Ned Cresswell and Norman Rhodes, room-mates of pensionable age, set off on their annual weekend visit to enjoy a traditional spring break in a quiet Sussex village. Where angels would fear to tread, in rushes the feisty Ned – whilst the conciliatory Norman becomes more reluctantly involved. The village begins to hum, including various brushes with the law, an exciting cliff rescue, a hard-fought game of Scrabble, Agatha Christie in Eastbourne and a dreaded Sunday sherry party, the weekend lurches socially from near disaster to neocataclysm. Further complications ensue, despite Ned's forceful objections, when the currently catless Norman falls in love with an irresistible pussy looking for a new home. Comedy and thrills combine in this delightful and most British of novels.

'It's like Ovaltine with gin in it.'
Tony Warren, creator or Coronation Street

ISBN 1-873741-10-3
£7.50

Heroes Are Hard to Find
Sebastian Beaumont

A compelling, sometimes comic, sometimes almost unbearably moving novel about sexual infatuation, infidelity and deceit. It is also about disability, death and the joy of living.

'Highly recommended. . .'   *Brighton Evening Argus*

'I cheered, felt proud and cried aloud (yes, real tears not stifled sobs) as the plot and the people became real to me . . .'
                                             All Points North

ISBN 1-873741-08-1
£7.50

The Learning of Paul O'Neill
Graeme Woolaston

The Learning of Paul O'Neill follows the eponymous hero over nearly thirty years – from adolescence in Scotland in the mid-sixties to life in a South Coast seaside resort in the seventies and eighties and a return to a vibrant Glasgow in the early nineties. As the novel begins, fifteen-year-old Paul is learning fast about sexuality as his Scottish village childhood disintegrates around him. After many years in England, he returns to Scotland trying to come to terms with the sudden death of his lover. His return brings him face-to-face with the continuing effects of adolescent experiences he thought he had put behind him. And his involvement with an ambiguous, handsome married but bisexual man raises new questions about the shape of Paul's life as he arrives at the threshold of middle-age. This is an adult novel about gay experience and aspects of sexuality which some may find shocking but which are written about with an honesty that is as refreshing as it is frank.

ISBN 1-873741-12-X
£7.50

On the Edge
Sebastian Beaumont

An auspicious debut novel which combines elements of a thriller and passionate ambisextrous romance and provides an immensely readable narrative about late adolescence, sexuality and creativity.

'Mr Beaumont writes with assurance and perception. . .'   Tom Wakefield, Gay Times

ISBN 1-873741-00-6
£6.99

Ravens Brood
E F Benson

The latest in our highly successful series of reprints of novels by E F Benson dates from 1934 and was almost the last novel he wrote. After *Ravens Brood*, he published only two more novels, *Lucia's Progress* (1935) and *Trouble for Lucia* (1939). By 1940, this most quintessential of Edwardian writers was dead, leaving a legacy of at least one hundred books – destined for seeming oblivion. The 'rediscovery' in the 1960s of the 'Mapp and Lucia' novels was the slow beginning of a revival of interest in Benson's work – which has subsequently produced biographies and family studies and two societies dedicated to his memory.

But *Ravens Brood* is quite unique in the Benson canon, a novel utterly unlike anything he had written before or would ever write again. 'It bristles with sexuality from the moment we meet John Pentreath, farmer and religious bigot, at his Cornish farm near Penzance,' Geoffrey Palmer and Noel Lloyd wrote in their invaluable *E F Benson: As He Was*. 'In the first thirty pages there are references to fertility rituals phallic symbols, lustful boilings in the blood, trollops, shrews, whores and harlots, a cockney strumpet, witchcraft, lascivious leers, a menopausal false pregnancy, and all seasoned with a touch of blasphemy.' The book includes, too, the character of Willie Polhaven (the name is ripe with innuendo) – perhaps the most overtly homosexual of Benson's gallery of ambiguous young men. *Ravens Brood* is atmospheric and outrageous: a rollicking good read.

ISBN 1-873741-09-X
£7.50

Summer Set
David Evans

When pop singer Ludo Morgan's elderly bulldog pursues animal portraitist Victor Burke – wearing womens' underwear beneath his leathers – to late night Hampstead Heath a whole sequence of events is set in train. Rescued by the scantily clad and utterly delicious Nick Longingly, only son of his closest friend Kitty Llewellyn, Victor finds himself caught up in a web of emotional and physical intrigue which can only be resolved when the entire cast of this immensely diverting novel abandon London and head off for a weekend in Somerset.

'Quite simply the most delightful and appealing English gay work of fiction I've read all year. . .'   Scene Out
'A richly comic debut. . .'   Capital Gay
'Immensely entertaining. . .'   Patrick Gale, Gay Times

ISBN 1-873741-02-2
£7.50

Unreal City
Neil Powell

One week in a hot August, towards the end of the twentieth century, the lives of four men overlap and entangle, leaving three of them permanently uprooted and changed. *Unreal City* is their story, told at different times and from their various points of view. Set partly in a London nourished by its cultural past but oppressed by its political present, and partly in coastal East Anglia, it is also the story of two older men – an elderly, long silent novelist and his retired publisher – whose past friendship and subsequent bitterness cast unexpected shadows over the four main characters. *Unreal City* is about love and loyalty, paranoia and violence, the tension of urban gay life in the century's last decade but it is about much else too: the death of cities; the pubs of Suffolk; the streets of London, and the Underground – in more than one sense; Shakespeare's *Troilus and Cressida*; the consolation of music; the colour of tomatoes, and the North Sea. It is a richly allusive, intricately patterned, and at times very funny novel.

'*Unreal City* is brilliant, understated, but powerful and should
have a wide-appeal '   *Time Out*
'*Excellent. I suggest you buy it immediately.*'   *Gay Times*
'*An excellent, extremely satisfying novel.*'   *The Pink Paper*

ISBN 1-873741-04-9
£6.99

Vale of Tears: A problem shared
Peter Burton & Richard Smith

Culled from ten years of *Gay Times's* popular Vale of Tears
problem page, this book, arranged problem-by-problem in
an alphabetical sequence, is written in question and answer
format and covers a wide range of subjects.

Problems with a lover? Who does the dishes? Interested in
infantilism? Why is his sex drive lower than yours? Aids
fears? Meeting the family? How to survive Christmas?
Suffering from body odours? Piles? Crabs? Penis too small?
Foreskin too tight? Trying to get rid of a lover?

Vale of Tears has some of the answers – and many more.
Although highly entertaining and sometimes downright
humorous, this compilation is very much a practical
handbook which should find a place on the shelves of all
gay men.

'An indispensable guide to life's problems big or small . . .'
Capital Gay

ISBN 1-873741-05-7
£6.99

Millivres Books can be ordered from any bookshop in the UK and from specialist bookshops overseas. If you prefer to order by mail, please send the full retail price and 80p (UK) or £2 (overseas) per title for postage and packing to:

Dept MBKS
Millivres Floor
Ground Floor
Worldwide House
116-134 Bayham Street
London NW1 0BA

A comprehensive catalogue is available on request.